The
CHESTER A.
ARTHUR
CONSPIRACY

by William Wiegand

AT LAST MR. TOLLIVER
THE TREATMENT MAN
THE SCHOOL OF SOFT KNOCKS

Lincoln
1861–65

Johnson
1865–69

Grant
1869–77

Hayes
1877–81

Garfield
1881

Arthur
1881–85

Cleveland
1885–89

Harrison
1889–93

Cleveland
1893–97

The CHESTER A. ARTHUR CONSPIRACY

A Novel by

WILLIAM WIEGAND

The Dial Press
New York

John Wilkes Booth

Published by
THE DIAL PRESS
1 Dag Hammarskjold Plaza
New York, New York 10017

COPYRIGHT © 1983 BY WILLIAM WIEGAND

LIBRARY OF CONGRESS CATALOGING IN PUBLICATION DATA
Wiegand, William, 1928–
  The Chester A. Arthur conspiracy.
    1. Arthur, Chester Alan, 1829–1886—Fiction.
  2. Booth, John Wilkes, 1838–1865—Fiction. I. Title.
PS3573.I336C48 1983   813'.54   82–22183
ISBN 0-385-27874-8

For Cary

Preface

We now know that John Wilkes Booth was not the man killed in the tobacco barn eleven days after the assassination of President Lincoln. The account that follows—derived from fresh source material—traces the involvement of Booth with the family of another prominent public figure of the time—Chester Alan Arthur. Arthur's career is one of the most enigmatic in American politics. Throughout it, he exhibited some of the most corrupt as well as some of the most selfless behavior. The bafflement of historians on this point was compounded for decades by the virtual absence of any public or private papers of Arthur's. Even the fact that he suffered through his final years with Bright's disease was concealed until very recently.

A clue to Arthur's mysterious character lies in the divided loyalties in his household during the war between North and South, at the outset of which Booth and Arthur have not yet met.

Table of Contents

PART ONE
In
WARTIME

On a wet March morning in the early months of the War Between the States, General Chester Arthur, in charge of the defenses of the city, sets out down lower Broadway on urgent domestic business. The stable has been late in bringing up his horse, as it no doubt would be were the Confederates shelling Wall Street from the harbor. Up in the stirrups he sees he has about ten minutes to get to the damned ferry before it leaves the pier for the East River. With Nell, his damned copperhead wife, aboard.

Still, he tries to keep his mount moving at a moderate pace through the traffic, and he looks at people calmly so that none of the peddlers or the shopgirls—few of whom are paying much attention to him at that—will get the idea that it is an emergency and start a damned panic. A tall and slender man in his early thirties, who sits a horse well, he knows he has a reassuring air about him when he is in uniform. His dark eyes and dark, full moustache relieve the somewhat feminine cast of his face.

But imagine waking up in one's bed before it is fully light—with the wind blowing and squalls of rain hitting the windowpanes—and not finding your wife on the pillow beside you! Naturally he goes to check the damned crib, kept in the sitting room for the warmth there, and he sees that the baby looks all right. No sicker than usual. But instead of Nell in attendance, the hired girl—a nursemaid fresh off the boat from Donegal—is lolling in the broken rocker, half asleep, squinting at him in his nightshirt.

He soon gets out of the damned girl where her mistress has gone.

"T' the military prison, sir," she bawls. "She made me come early t' see after the child."

Ah, the military prison, where else? David's Island, way up in the damned Sound where the ferries seem either to get icebound or to have to put in at New Rochelle for three days getting repairs. What appalls him most is that he has promised to take her to the prison himself on Sunday if there is the slightest break in the weather. He promised this not more than fifteen minutes after they learned that her cousin Lieutenant Dabney Herndon of the Confederate cavalry, taken prisoner near Fredericksburg, was on the island. What more can a man do?

"But he may stahve to death by Sunday!" she cries, her hand over her heart.

Why, he is as fond of Dabney as she is, he tells her. She continues to rave angrily, fancying that Dabney is wounded, or—damned preposterous!—that they will torture him to obtain military secrets.

"I will not allow you to go alone," he tells her firmly. By Sunday he will have arranged for them to have a secluded conversation with Dabney, a decent conversation, just the three of them, away from the prying eyes of the guards.

To this well-meant plan she has paid no damned attention.

And on a day when the rain is getting worse and worse. The closer he gets to the piers, the denser the traffic is. Peddlers are coming off the ferries with their dray carts, and the ordinary laborers disembarking from Brooklyn, for the horsecars have already started to pile up, two and three deep.

"When the visibility is poor on the river," he has tried to explain to Nell, for in some ways she has been very sheltered, "all the passengers must gather in the front of the ferry, and try to call out to the pilot if they see he is about to run into something."

It is the damned truth, he tells her. Accidents happen in foul weather. Her own father, a naval captain, went down with his ship in a storm. Chester has no compunction about reminding her of these things. While she is an astonishing woman in some ways—beautiful, and sensitive to art and music—she is also stubborn and without practical sense.

He tries to weave webs whenever he feels he must convince her of something. She cannot go, alone and unprotected, to David's Island. The river birds, which she likes to watch as they curve and shuttle over the shore of the lower harbor, further up the river will be larger and shaped like albatrosses. Her cousin is held in a snow-covered fortress there.

Never having been above the Croton Reservoir on 42nd Street, to Nell the whole North is a vast snow-covered fortress, and he the damned emperor of it. Even his place of birth—north of the northernmost village in Vermont—has taken on a mystic significance for her.

He has grown tired of the whole business. Other men have wives from the South and do not seem to be troubled with all this mumbo jumbo. His fault in large part, he is willing to admit, for catering to it. She knows he does not care about the uniform he wears. Professional men must lend the army a hand during time of war. He takes off the damned blue as soon as he comes home at night. Does he not?

But as he tries to rein his horse around a phalanx of delivery wagons, he cannot help but picture the chaos if the military needed to use those piers during an emergency. Orders could not be heard: the groaning axles, wheels against cobblestones, chains on wagon tailgates being raised and lowered, and now the river noises, the tugboat croaks, squawking birds, cargo being unloaded. From a Jersey ferry a small herd of cattle comes thundering down a closed gangplank into a maze of boards for the steers to bump and tumble into.

At least, poor Dabney, out on the island, should have been given his breakfast by now, more than he could say for himself. How close the two of them once were: Dabney in medicine, and he reading law. Then one day Nell and her mother paid a visit to New York. Bringing that buck slave Leander with them to damned Union Square! But after Nell and Chester were engaged, they all went down to Fredericksburg, where he met the Herndon family: Nell's Uncle Brodie, and her dear aunt, and the other son, who was also captured when the fighting began. Chester adored the Herndons, every last one of them. He trembled when he learned of their griefs and always made use of his private connections to find out how they were faring and what he could do to help.

With relief, Chester sees that the ferry for the East River has not yet departed; in fact, it has not even pulled into the slip. He finds a place to tie up his horse, and dumping the water off the top of his garrison cap, he dismounts and strides to the ferry house. Right in front of the door stands a damned girl of about fourteen, the back of whose skirt is sopping wet. She must have fallen into a puddle, and she looks at him with annoyance as he tries to step past her. Most of the other people waiting inside give him equally unfriendly looks. Wrapped in their warm clothing and holding bundles in their laps, you would think they had nothing to look so angry about. Suppose most of them are copperheads going to visit men held on David's Island, that's damned all right with him! He is not here to take prisoners in the Battery. Even a general may have friends and loved ones.

The loved one he is trying to find does not, however, appear to him. Wet wool assaults his nostrils, along with the spiced sausages that some of the travelers are carrying for their meals. The bad weather has not discouraged these females, for most of the company are women. The paddlewheeler, meanwhile, is visible through the rain-smeared glass about to dock and load.

Good God, he sees Bridget, the family cook! Large, heavy-lidded eyes in her old wrinkled face seem abruptly to focus on him, and with subtle right-to-left motions of her head she signals to him in some fashion.

As he approaches her bench—the one closest to the gate—he sees what she is calling his attention to. Seated next to her is Nell, but in a guise that dumbfounds him. Her distinctive jet-black hair, always perfectly coiffed, is concealed under a bonnet so stained and unbecoming he could not imagine giving it to a servant. Her downcast eyes stare at a muff in her lap that is lumpy as a wet cat. She is wearing an ugly gray jacket that is too large for her, and a skirt that is so frayed and fading he cannot guess the fabric. Since the jacket looks like one the nursemaid wears, he assumes the whole outfit must come from the servants' slop chest.

It is too embarrassing for him even to speak. She knows he is there, for she can see his boots within the range of her lowered gaze. For a moment he feels the breath drained out of him, and can only sink to the bench next to Nell with an involuntary sigh.

Then, at last, under his breath, as the gateman noisily shoves open the metal gate, and attention shifts to the boarding platform, he says, "My dear Nell . . ."

At least she does not stand with all the other passengers when they begin to move toward the gate. Neither does Bridget.

"My dear Nell," he begins again, his voice level. He is tempted to ask her why, if she must go to David's Island, she dresses in such a fashion. But he knows the reason she would give him: to be seen visiting a Confederate might embarrass him in his position.

He crosses his gaitered legs. The idea that he might have brought her to this—traveling in rags—is unbearable to him. He swore when he married her that, although only a poor preacher's son himself, he would never allow her to be degraded in any way.

"My dear Nell," he finally murmurs when all are surging for the gate, and not even Bridget can hear, "you debase yourself when you appear like this. Do you not want to seem a rational person?"

For a moment he is not sure what she is going to do; the other passengers are spilling through the gate, and Bridget looks about anxiously as though waiting for a cue.

Of course Nell, for all her frozen posture, hears every word and knows that he has come to the ferry house to prevent her from leaving. The blast of the boat's whistle is heard.

For one more instant the three of them remain seated tensely side by side, then Nell stamps her foot and jumps up, grabbing the damask-covered basket that has been prepared, the one incongruous note in their damned costume party. She heads not for the gate to the ferry, but for the door to the street.

He follows her, with Bridget trailing.

Angrily, she wrests open the door before he can hold it for her, and stepping out into the rain, she cries back over her shoulder.

"You make me feel mortified! These ah mah people here, and I feel mortified because I cannot be one of them!"

2

WALLACK'S THEATER

A week later, at the theater, she sits down well to the back of the box. Though the men try to prevail on her to sit forward, she knows she does not want to be looked at by the Yankee women in the audience. In her mind she is composing a letter to her mother, who has been living in the south of France ("Dear Mamma, We have seen Dabney in the military prison in Long Island Sound. A cold journey it was, but some sunshine, and he appreciated the food and provisions I brought him....").

She looks straight ahead. Below her in the orchestra many of the women are wearing low-cut bodices that went out of fashion in Fredericksburg and Richmond at least a year before the war started. That much she has noticed before taking her seat. Some wear their stoles with such carelessness that one can count the freckles on their shoulders.

Nell wears a high-necked gown of a distinctive nut-brown color. Petite, with dark, lustrous eyes, she watches Chester chatting with Colonel Jones. Another occupant of the box is a doctor from the medical college in Philadelphia, on whom she smiles benignly as he catches her gaze. Neither the doctor nor the colonel has brought his wife, for which she is content ("Dear Mamma, I try to do my social duty to my husband, but . . ."). The truth is she cannot wrap bandages, can she, for the Yankee wounded? These ladies were all very well before the war, but what can she talk about with them now and yet keep her temper?

When the colonel begins clearing his throat and stiffening his back like a poker, her instinct tells her the play is about to start. Too bad she has never been fond of the theater, although she once enjoyed certain musical evenings well enough, even in this city.

As the flickering footlights grow brighter, the leading actor walks on, playing Richard of York. A Booth he is. Not Edwin. Rather "Booth the Lesser," a younger brother. He is talked about some—not much, but some—when she hears the men discuss such things. They say he is anxious to draw attention to himself because of his rivalry with his brother.

Mercy, one knows he would have to be a show-off. What Nell resents most is that he is supposed to have had his greatest successes in the South, for he travels freely across the lines, and of course they say that his "flamboyant" style appeals to the South. She is prepared to hate him.

"*Now* is the winter of our discontent . . ."

She is startled at first. The voice is not well trained, and he seems to force it. At the same time, he does not gesture too much. He wears a cape of dark velvet and a doublet, yet manages not to look a pussyfoot. He cuts a fine figure, she will grant. Still, she does not like him. Chester has brought her here, no doubt imagining she will be pleased by Booth's magnolia accent. Is it Maryland in his voice? Aye, mere Maryland.

There, he leaps onto the parapet as the soliloquy begins to soar. An acrobat he is. Still, not very tall for all his athletic airs. Personally, she thinks it is a disgrace that some Yankees would fancy that this actor's style is the style of the South. She feels the bile rise in her, thinking of the calm, masculine grace of Dabney Herndon, caged like an animal, yet an avatar of dignity as he moved across the prison compound to them, a gray scarf around his neck, the eerie hoot of foghorns in the sound. She was shivering so badly, Dab took off his coat and put it around her before uttering one word.

Chester glances back at her as though he knows her mind is wandering, as though he wants to tell her to attend to the play ("Dear Mamma, Don't we have enough of conflict and bloodshed without going to plays that only remind us of more?").

But she smiles at Chester, reassuring him that she will concentrate

("Dear Mamma, He says he will resign his commission soon, for it is causing me too much hurt. In the meantime, the influence he has may help get Dab exchanged and back home again").

In the meantime, Nell also reflects, all those profitable investments will continue to be made. Investments "in the cotton," she is told. As long as one is in a position of influence, one makes shrewd investments "in the cotton." Most of the time she believes that Wall Street runs the war for the North and does it to make killings "in the cotton."

When the play is ended, Booth stands center stage with feet wide apart, taking deep bows as the audience offers its little rivers of applause. Nell applauds with the others although the performance has not impressed her much. Booth stands there now, his face sooted with battle, his doublet disarranged. All that shouting for "a horse! a horse!" has quite done him in. Does he want Mother's sympathy for his anguish, no matter how much the villain he has proved? How forlorn he looks. His brother Edwin, a stouter fellow and more patrician, would never have played it so *pathétique*.

Chester, now standing beside her, asks in a hearty voice, "Nell, would you care to meet Mr. Booth? The colonel—"

"I have no interest in that," she says at once. Likely he thinks she will be distracted from her concerns about Dabney if she is presented to this facsimile cavalryman. A horse! A horse! Goodness me, she feels like laughing.

Looking disappointed, Chester mentions that a couple of the other officers "and their ladies" are going to join Mr. Booth, as though that might persuade her. The "ladies" mentioned are bold enough to eat her. Still, she wonders why all these Union officers are consorting with a copperhead like John Wilkes Booth.

"I am not going," she says with emphasis. Deliciously she wonders if Mr. John Wilkes Booth is but a false friend of the Confederacy and is actually in the pay of the Yankee Secret Service. She pulls her cape over her shoulders abruptly, just before Chester can do it for her. "But if you attend them, I would like to be seen home."

Her own duty, she now avers, is with her child: Baby William has a touch of the croup.

Chester smiles boyishly, offers his arm. Presently they are outdoors where the wind is brisk, waiting for a carriage. The wealthy are already ascending into their private landaus and victorias. Chester tarries in order to greet some political acquaintances. Tall and well muscled, Chester likes to clasp a friend to his bosom when he converses; he loves gentlemanly conversation. But he glances at her now and then, ever dutiful in that regard. A Virginia husband would probably ignore her.

The carriages for hire are lined up just beyond the penumbra of the gaslights around the theater entrance, extending into the mists of lower Broadway. She is impatient to get under way lest some politician or politician's wife be presented to her. An irresistible impulse strikes.

"A horse! A horse! Mah kingdom for a horse!" she calls out to no one in particular, and makes a moue of despair in the manner of John Wilkes Booth at Bosworth Field.

Surprised, Chester turns to look at her, but in reality she has not called loudly enough to cause any embarrassment. When he realizes that, he smiles and the two of them laugh together. Stirred to his proper business, he gestures for the carriage.

She allows herself to remember the day they met. Excited, she and her mother were going to visit her father's ship, lying to in Aspinwall. Before leaving, they hired a carriage in order to stop by Dabney's rooms in the Bancroft House. Leander, her mother's handsome Negro, sat beside the driver on the box of the cab, and when they arrived he handed them down onto the curb outside the Bancroft with such easy style as had never been seen on 14th Street. So they thought at the time ("Dearest Mamma, I am as cared for and protected as a woman could possibly be. Do not come back. For you it could be heartbreaking here").

3

THE ASTOR HOUSE

"If I were you, I would not tell him about it today," Dun advises, taking his cigar out of his mouth. Robert Dun, a short, earnest man with a spade beard, is Chester's oldest friend in New York.

"Ah, but I have to," Chester replies.

"I could prepare him if you like."

"Not at all."

Still, Chester fidgets. In full uniform as he is, the smoking room of the Astor is uncomfortably warm, and his stomach feels upset. With his infant son's illness he has had nothing but sleepless nights all week. The damned generals in the field endure much worse, he knows, and do not complain. And they face encounters with worse than Thurlow Weed.

Chester asks if Weed seems to be in a bad temper today.

Dun laughs. "Well, the news on the blockade has not cheered him up."

"The hell with him," Chester says, laughing too. The truth is that since Lincoln dried up the cotton passes, nobody knows where the weaknesses in the lines are anymore. A bad time to have sold short. But undeterred, when Weed comes down from Albany, where he has his newspaper and his legislature, he must gather his generals and his journalists around him for parley. Dun, one of the journalists, makes his living putting out a daily sheet of uncensored war news for the exclusive benefit of Wall Street.

"Dammit, do help me out if I need it, Robert," Chester implores.

A moustachioed waiter has come by, leaning down with the advice that Weed and "the gentlemen" have moved from Mr. Weed's suite on into the bar.

Dun winks at Chester, and they get to their feet. Having just resigned his commission, effective in a week, Chester is set to make his final report to Weed. He supposes he will have to forgo the market tips when the epaulets go. Well and good. He has begun to feel a traitor to the uniform, something he would not have expected. It would be easier for him to be out of it.

In the gentlemen's bar, Chester and Dun walk across the tiled sanctum to the gathering in the corner. Weed has never been concerned about privacy in his dealings. When things go badly—as they have this week with barrels and barrels of contraband pork being seized by Lincoln's troops before they could reach the lines—he makes himself as visible as ever, only more shameless.

"Whiskey for two more!" Weed calls to the waiter as he greets the newcomers. He is sitting under a filigreed chandelier in the corner with two others, neither of them the men Chester expected. Senator Conness, a Californian, is drinking brandy; the other, a dapper young stranger whom Chester does not recognize, sits quietly with his gold-topped cane held at a jaunty angle.

"Wilkes Booth, the actor," Weed says at once, presenting the young man. "Wilkes, are you acquainted with General Arthur, the smartest general in the North? Not sayin' much, is it?" His large mouth forms a smile. "And Robert Dun, who will sell you war news that even *you* may not know. He'll throw in a few market quotations gratis."

Dun grunts that he would sooner be selling candy apples. "But news is what's wanted."

While Weed banters with him, Chester glances at Booth, who seems uneasy. "We were fortunate to see you as Richard, Mr. Booth," Chester says. "A most affecting performance."

Booth flushes, apparently pleased, but says nothing, and since the others are paying no attention, Chester adds impulsively, "My wife is from Virginia. She was charmed throughout."

A damned odd thing to have said, Chester realizes, when Nell, in fact, reacted quite indifferently to the show. But Booth says, "I would be honored to meet her some time." Then he is on his feet, a lithe individual of medium height with dark, piercing gaze. Does he expect to meet her at once? Chester wonders.

But no, Booth tips his soft-crowned hat to Weed and Senator Conness, regrets that he has other engagements.

"One minute, please, Mr. Booth," Weed says, lifting his hand. "I would like to write a little note for you to take to your friend. If you don't mind?"

In the pocket of his gray coat Weed has found the stub of a pencil, and while Booth sits down again, smiling sharply, everyone around the table falls silent while Weed writes. Four young army officers have meanwhile come into the Astor bar; Chester recognizes them as Seventh Regiment, on leave after recent engagements under fire.

While Weed writes, Chester sees Booth catch the eye of some of the officers and then look away again. He wonders why the officers need gaze at Booth with such contempt.

Meanwhile, Weed folds the piece of notebook paper he has been writing on. "Thanks for waitin', Mr. Booth."

Without comment, Booth takes the message. As he leaves, he says again to Chester, "Your compliment was most kind, General."

Chester nods, wishing the man well. Although an actor, he seems more down-to-earth than his brother Edwin, who is a fellow member of Chester's club. Nothing down-to-earth about Edwin. A stuffed shirt at times, a drunk at others. Chester wishes that he might put Wilkes up for membership some time. Not now, of course, but after the war, when there will be no such thing as copperheads.

While the waiter sets the glasses and a bottle of Guinness scotch from Weed's private stock on the table before them, Weed rumbles, "It's gettin' so Richmond doesn't have any flexibility at all anymore."

"It's Washington that doesn't have the flexibility," Senator Conness remarks.

"Yeah. Well, it's Lincoln," Weed says gloomily, taking a cigar as Dun offers one from the large silver case he begins passing to each of them. "I hear you're gonna resign your commission, Chester."

Startled into candor by the hawklike gaze of Weed, Chester says, "Well, I'm here to tell you that. When I took it, you said—"

Weed interrupts him with a laugh. "Good idea to quit," he rumbles. "Idiot new governor, idiot old President. Why not quit? I think I'd quit myself if I had anything to quit from."

Senator Conness says that Lincoln won't be President forever, as though that might change Chester's mind.

"True, true," Weed agrees in an exaggeratedly mellifluous voice. "He might be gone before you know it."

Chester says that Lincoln does not make any difference to him one way or the other. Lighting the cigar that Dun has given him, he looks squarely at Weed, who, in spite of the white hair, has a lot of Lincoln in him. Rangy, and with the same kind of chin whiskers and sculptured-granite cheeks, he talks with the rural mannerisms, dropping his "g's" and other nonsense. Chester—who really *was* born in a one-room cabin—finds a lot of damned fakery in both of them.

Weed says, "Why, I believe, Senator, that it's Mrs. Arthur's situation that makes Chester resign. Isn't that about it, Chester?"

Chester shrugs.

"Your wife's cousin get back to Virginia all right?" Weed asks.

"Yes. Lieutenant Herndon was in the exchange."

"Good. Glad I could help on that," Weed says. Then, confidentially to Conness, with feeling: "Mrs. Arthur is a Virginian. That makes it hard for poor Chester at home."

Chester takes another drink of the scotch, which explodes in his touchy stomach. It would be a lot easier for him at home if he could get out of the family hotel where he and Nell and the baby are living and into a house of their own, where they could get heat in every room and not cause the baby to die of pneumonia.

What he does say to Weed, with sudden emphasis, is, "Well, they are going to fight this time. I am convinced of it. I hope you take it into account." He tries to explain to Weed why this time the Union offensive must take place.

"Oh, General," Weed says. "If I really believed that, I think I'd get out of the market and back into active newspaperin'." His glance catches the Seventh Regiment officers. "Does the new offensive start in the Astor bar?"

Enough smart talk, thinks Chester. He has himself visited the lines and would not scorn the brave men there, even if they should ever scorn him.

"Well, hell, we're with 'em," Weed declares abruptly. "Cotton passes or no, here's to Abe." Weed lifts his glass. The Senator and Dun eventually lift theirs too.

"Here's to Abe!" Weed says again. "Long may he waver!"

Chester takes a last torturing gulp of the scotch and gets to his feet. A plague on both their houses. Lincoln's offensive might be slow in getting started, but Weed's intrigues against Lincoln were going even slower.

"Robert, I'll see you tomorrow," Chester calls. Why, he wouldn't be surprised to see the damned war over, and they would still be fiddling around trying to get rid of Lincoln! Count him out of that business.

4

A FAMILY HOTEL
NEAR BROADWAY AND 22ND

Her mother is still in the south of France.

"Dearest Mamma," she writes, "Our kinsman, John Maury, long listed as missing in action, is now given up for dead. . . ."

And a few months later: "Dearest Mamma, I have not been able to write. Sad, sad news to tell you. We have lost our darling boy. They say from convulsions brought about by some affection of the brain. It came upon us so unexpectedly and suddenly . . ."

And then again: "Dearest Mamma, Brodie Junior was captured again in Maryland during heavy fighting. We do not know where he has been taken, but will try to find out. . . ."

She finds herself shouting at her husband more and more. Sometimes he shouts back: does she imagine that he still has access to War

Department telegraphs, that he can discover at a moment's notice where all her rampaging relatives are? . . . Does he not have relatives of his own in the fighting?

"Dearest Mamma, Chester's brother, a major in the Union army, has been wounded at Ream's Station, Virginia. He is hit in the face, the ball entering the right side of the cheek just above the upper lip, Chester says, passing straight through and coming out the back of his head. He suffers greatly from the matter running from the wound internally. . . ."

But you must believe, Chester tells her, that a normal life will be possible when the war is over. The war is coming to an end. She does not agree or disagree. He tells her, "We will have a home of our own. With adequate heating. I will have a room for my desk and my law books down the stairs."

"Dearest Mamma," she writes, "I am expecting a child. Would that you could be with me as you were when the other was born. . . ."

Then: "Dearest Mamma, I am sorry you have not been feeling well since Leander went off and left you. Just take care of yourself, I will try not to write any more bad news."

"It is a terrible snub if you do not call on Mrs. Roosevelt," says Chester, "after she has called on you."

And she replies, "But I am showing already."

Chester keeps poking at the fire in the stove, and says, "You aren't showing at all, Nell; Mrs. Roosevelt is a fine southern woman of excellent breeding, who might be your friend. Don't you want friends anymore?"

No, she says, she is showing. The only persons she wants to see are the Herndons when the war is over. Probably, she thinks, it is Chester who wants to make a political friend of Mr. Roosevelt, and that is why he wants her to pay a call on his wife.

But she writes, "Dearest Mamma, Everything is going in a normal way during my confinement. The weather is warm. Brodie Junior is still in the federal prison in Massachusetts, but seems all right."

Take the fans into the bedroom, she hears her husband saying in the other room. Here are the fans. One of the midwife's helpers is beating the air with a great cardboard fan. The windows are open and she can hear traffic in the street. Oh, oh, it's coming, the midwife says. Now, love, you been through it before. Oh! Oh! And from the other room, Are you fanning her? Are you reducing the strain on her heart? . . .

"Dearest Mamma, We are the parents of a boy. He is finely made with dark eyes and hair and at birth much larger than the other. His name is Chester Alan Arthur II. My husband seems pleased. We will call the baby Alan with the accent on the second syllable. . . ."

But losing servants is not your fault, Nell, he says to her. It is simply that they are paid more elsewhere. She does not look at him; you see, that is one of the advantages of slavery, she would like to say. But she continues to brush her hair before the mirror without speaking. She finds she does not care so much about the war since the birth of the baby, although she would like not to have to do all the servants' work. I suppose he is warm enough, Chester says, looking down at the child in the crib. Last night he kicked off the blanket, Nell says.

"Dearest Mamma, Thank you for your gift for Baby Alan. I hope you are feeling well. The baby is in excellent health, but we hear in New York that General Lee has surrendered to General Grant. If the news should prove true, we should not despair about it since it means an end to the fighting. In any case, my husband says it was inevitable. I have been trying not to write any more bad news, dear Mamma. . . ."

And a few days later, while she is in the bedroom looking over some of the old sheet music that she keeps in the cedar chest, she hears a commotion from the front of the apartment and wonders if the new hired girl can have dropped the baby on the floor.

For the first time in months Nell is wearing a new dress, a light-colored poplin, because today the baby would be crawling on the girl instead of herself. Hurrying out, she sees that the hubbub is caused by Chester, who left for the office half an hour before and now stands in the foyer, breathless and red-faced, blurting something to the hired girl, who holds Baby Alan on her hip.

Chester waves a newspaper, includes Nell in his excited report.

"The President has been shot and killed by John Wilkes Booth!"

"Dear me," Nell says.

The hired girl, an Irisher named Maureen, lets out a little scream. For a moment, Nell fears she is going to drop the baby. "Maureen!" she says sharply, and snatches the child away from the girl until she can compose herself. What nonsense! As though Maureen knew President Lincoln!

Chester, who seems to be having trouble drawing an easy breath, says, "I must get downtown." He throws down cane and homburg, takes off one coat and puts on another.

"The fighting is not ovah after all," Nell intones. She has been duped again.

Chester fixes a cold gaze on her.

"The war is over," he says quietly. "But stay at home today. Do not go out in the street."

"Why not?"

"Because I tell you."

Maureen begins to weep. "Kin I not go home to me mither, sir?"

"*You* can go home," Chester says. "There is nothing for the damned Irish to be afraid of!"

The child begins to cry in Nell's arms. As they watch Chester running up the street in the bright spring sunshine, Nell says to the child, "Pooh, stop it. . . . Stop it now. . . . Now, pooh, stop it. . . ."

She has almost forgotten who John Wilkes Booth is. When she remembers, she imagines the killing to have taken place on the stage of a theater. Caressing the quieted child, she begins to feel awe and wonderment.

5

12 WEST 12TH STREET

A dinner invitation arrives for the Arthurs from Miss Harriet Weed, Thurlow Weed's daughter and hostess (Weed has recently decided to make his chief residence in New York rather than Albany). Harriet encloses a dazzling little note: "Although it is not a season for parties, with the nation in mourning, quiet gatherings of friends help sustain us. . . ."

The Arthurs are not social acquaintances of the Weeds. Indeed, Nell has never met father or daughter, and does not want to be their friend. But she feels a strange appetite for the visit. Chester's tension over the invitation piques her curiosity.

His strange comings and goings in recent days she has been inclined to connect with the murder of the President. While she does not read the newspapers, she eavesdrops on conversations between Maureen and the cook in the kitchen when they talk about the flight of Booth through the Maryland and Virginia marshlands south of Washington. In her mind's eye, Nell sees Booth, still in cloak and doublet, leaping, leaping from shoal to shoal in the overgrown snake-infested swamps.

Then, shatteringly, Booth is captured and killed. (From the kitchen: "Did y' hear, Maureen? They got him." "Did they git him then?" "They got him, the soldiers got him. The telegraph man says they shot him dead.")

On the way over to the Weeds' in the carriage, Chester compliments her on her appearance.

"I try to dress well for people I have not met," Nell says.

"Well, Thurlow wouldn't want us to think of them as strangers."

"Oh, I won't," she replies dryly.

They are met at the door by two servants, and almost at once by Harriet, a rather rawboned woman with a friendly manner. In his new fawnskin coat, Chester looks most attractive as he presents her, first to Harriet and then to Mr. Weed. Both Weeds are rather plain-featured, although Harriet wears a magnificent solitaire in each ear.

Harriet says, "We hope to see you more in society, Mrs. Arthur, now that the difficult days seem to be over."

Thurlow Weed says, "Society be hanged! We hope that *we* may see you more often!"

In the Weed drawing room before dinner, conversation proceeds pleasantly, much as Nell remembers such conversations in bygone days. A mention of President Lincoln by their host alerts her, since she believes Lincoln somehow to be the reason they are there.

Presently they are all trailing Weed into his library.

"A letter from President Lincoln," he explains. "Written but a month before the . . . the tragedy. I hope you will excuse me, Mrs. Arthur, for wanting to show it to you both."

A tic douloureux of grief pinches Weed's craggy face. His white, bushy eyebrows are gravely knit, his eyes downcast. While he hunts up the letter, Nell surveys the sumptuous library, graced by two of the largest full-length portraits she has seen in a long time. One is of Archbishop Hughes, hung, she supposes, for the sake of the brilliant purple regalia that he wears. In the gilded frame opposite is Secretary Seward, stabbed, she believes she heard, by the Lincoln assassins on the fateful night.

"Ah, the letter! It is like holy writ to me already," Weed exclaims with a rueful smile. "My eyesight is growing so poor that I need a glass to read it. But—here!"

He hands the letter to Nell, who glances at it, without being sure what reaction she is supposed to be having.

Executive Mansion
Washington
March 15, 1865

Dear Mr. Weed:

Everyone likes a compliment. Thank you for yours on my little notification speech and on the recent inaugural address. I expect . . .

Weed interrupts to say with some passion, "He and I had no lasting political quarrel! He recognized the deep sincerity of my compliments."

"I surely see that," Nell murmurs. What does she care of his political quarrels with Lincoln?

"But I interrupt your reading," Weed says.

Her eyes drop to the signature—"Yours truly, A. Lincoln"—and she quickly passes the letter to Chester, who knows how to ponder a bread-and-butter letter with gravity.

When he reads it and looks up, Weed says, with sepulchral voice, "Ay, and once we harassed him for cotton passes."

Chester nods in sad confirmation.

Whereupon Weed turns to her yet again. "Selfish mercenary motives are universally attributed to me, Mrs. Arthur, whatever I do or say. But I believe I am as mindful of the public good as any man."

Should she say that, dear me, she has never even met Mr. Lincoln?

Chester says, "Then you must doubly appreciate this letter, Thurlow."

"Ah," Weed says, clutching Chester's arm as his eyes grow misty, "I, too, want to bind up the nation's wounds. I want what he wanted at the end. We are not a vindictive people—"

Harriet clears her throat. "I think dinner is served, Father." The butler stands in the doorway, ready to pass them through to the dining room. To Nell's relief, Thurlow Weed stops talking and takes her arm, but with Harriet and Chester following behind, he soon launches into a new vein.

"Y' know, when I was a boy, Mrs. Arthur, I used to stand barefoot in the taverns up the river listenin' to the tales of the fellows who fought in the Revolution. I never knew what a pair o' shoes felt like. . . ."

Two and a half hours later she and Chester are being driven back to their rooms by Thurlow Weed's driver. The air is crisp, and Chester has fallen unusually silent. His profile in the darkness beside her is like the silhouette of a Grecian bust. She expects him to tell her shortly what the comedy that was played at Weed's was all about.

In truth, during the later stages of the evening, she rather enjoyed herself. Following Harriet's rendering of some of her father's boyish adventures, Nell gave accounts of Chester's dangerous experiences in Bleeding Kansas when he was there for some months just before their marriage. By that juncture of the evening, Chester was not present to hear, having gone into the library with Mr. Weed for after-dinner cigars. When he emerged from the library, he seemed chastened. His manner was distracted and courtly, but no longer tense as it had been in the early part of the evening.

"I was pleased, Nell," he now says to her, taking hold of her hand in the carriage, "that you were willing to come out with me tonight."

"Why should I not?"

"You were quite adamant about—about Mrs. Roosevelt. I was beginning to wonder—"

"I do not *always* feel like calling on people."

Well, it didn't matter, Chester says. "Thurlow and I were talking about a serious concern of his. In fact, I am going south tomorrow, and you must not tell anyone of it, for it is a secret errand."

She waits for him to go on.

"There is a Confederate sympathizer," he says in a nearly tone-less voice, "in hiding not far outside of Fredericksburg. His leg is broken, and unless he can get medical attention, gangrene could set in. I am going down to help him."

"Yes?" she murmurs. Harriet Weed had remarked when they were alone that her husband seemed "a compassionate man"; it had never occurred to Nell before, one way or the other, that Chester was "compassionate."

"The doctors I will take this man to are Dabney Herndon and his father, so you must know of this." He grips her hand more tightly. "Thurlow did your family a favor in the past . . . as you recall, when Dab was in the exchange."

"Now Mistuh Weed wishes to be repaid?"

"Apparently." He turns all the way toward her, his voice huskier. "And since you must know sooner or later, the fugitive is Booth."

"Booth!"

"Hush!" he says sharply, so that the driver on the box outside will not hear. "The man killed in Garrett's barn was someone else. In the meantime Booth has sent out word to Weed and Weed's friends that he needs help before he can go on."

Bewildered, she asks him why Weed cares about the safety of John Wilkes Booth.

Chester hesitates a moment. Their carriage has been reined to a stop while two other carriages cross, going down 20th Street. Then he says, "During the middle of the war—and it is death, Nell, to reveal this—Weed and Booth were associated . . . in some political attempts . . . to replace Lincoln. There are some documents that say—uh—to kill Lincoln." Chester says that the documents seem to be in safe hands for now, but Booth must be kept safe, too, lest he be captured and speak of it.

"Are you supposed to dispatch Mistuh Booth?" she asks, feeling trepidation.

"Certainly not!" He turns his head. "Didn't I say we mean to save him?"

When the horses are presently brought to a halt outside their building, she lifts her gloves from her lap. Almost at once the tall young driver has sprung down onto the sidewalk. "Ma'am?" he calls, opening the door, handing her down onto the step. She feels herself trembling as she thanks him. When he turns away in his velvet livery, she notices he has a bent spine.

In the sitting room, when they are alone again, Chester, pouring himself a brandy, sits down on the edge of the settee, then leans back. "There should be little danger in this, Nell, for any of us. Booth is well disguised, I am told, and no one is looking for him anymore. He calls himself Captain Boyd, the man they shot, thinking it was Booth."

"The little popinjay!" she says suddenly. All she can really remember is "A horse! A horse!" That strained voice calling "A horse! A horse!"

"The one time I met him," Chester says, "he seemed a damned unassuming man—"

Very well, she says, without speaking it aloud.

"He may have killed an enemy in a dishonorable way," Chester muses, not looking at her, "but other men did it too. Dab himself came upon the tent of one of our colonels one night. . . . He told me this. . . ."

"I shouldn't care to hear," she murmurs. "I am weary." Sitting on the broken rocker, she starts to unhook the buttons on her shoes.

"In any case, Nell, you must believe that Mr. Weed had nothing to do with—nothing, that is, to do with—"

"I know. He loved Mistuh Lincoln. I realize that I was asked tonight in order to be instructed about that." She picks up her shoes, one in each hand, and walks across the carpet to him. "What do I care if he told Booth to kill Lincoln? I do not want to hear anything more about it till you get back." She allows her body to press gently against his shoulder.

"One other thing," he cannot resist adding with a sly smile, as he half turns to her. She wishes he would keep quiet, and let her think him a compassionate man. But he cannot resist.

"You know the brownstone we looked at on Lexington Avenue, the attorney general's home? Thurlow holds the mortgage on it, and he now insists that we take it off his hands."

She does not say anything. What better did she expect of Chester? He is taking a large risk. He has marshaled the Herndons for Mr. Weed, and should be recompensed.

"We will finally have a properly heated place," he says. "Enough room to raise a child properly." He reaches for her hand, which he cannot seem to grasp since she has shifted to his blind side. "A melodeon perhaps for you, so that you will be able to resume your music."

"I do not care a great deal about music anymore," she says, walking from the room.

6

FREDERICKSBURG

In the darkness of a windless night, on the road below the farmhouse, Booth lets the other two riders dismount first so that they can help him off his horse. He has his bandaged leg tied to the stirrup; and Henson, the first rider down, loosens it. To Booth's nostrils, Henson smells nearly as bad in the open air as he did in the river cave. But Henson, untroubled, is whistling. When he has it loose, Weed's man—the "Yankee"—walks over. Henson loves the word "Yankee," drawled slowly. The tall Yankee comes over and lifts Booth from his horse as though he were a sack of meal. The Yankee keeps his face muffled and speaks little.

The leg does not hurt bad. Henson has brought along the crutch that they put together in the cave, and Booth leans on it, indicating he does not need any help to walk on it. Since they are still close to town, and right on the main road, Henson ties the horses up under some trees along the lane leading up to the house.

To have to crutch up the path for thirty or forty yards will try him, but it is not the leg so much as it is his back that gives him pain when he leaves the saddle after the long ride. Even the ankle does not throb as it did. Perhaps that is a bad sign.

They do not hurry him along, Henson or the Yankee. But it is late, and there are no horsemen or carriages along the road. Booth trusts the Yankee; the Yankee has the polished complexion and trimmed whiskers of a city man, but he has sat the horse well on the long ride.

Ahead, there are two lanterns held by men who have raised them high as they come out of the door of the farmhouse. The landhold seems eight or nine acres at least, about the size of the place he was raised on in Maryland.

A dog starts barking and one of the two men quiets it with a sharp command. The dog seems to scuffle for footing and can be seen running around the corner of the house.

Then Booth's crutch catches momentarily in a rut, and he curses.

"Hold on to me," the Yankee says, and with his free arm Booth grasps the Yankee's shoulder and hops forward again, vaulting the crutch along the path. Henson, who has dropped back, begins whistling again, as though nervous.

But it is all right. The two men from the house, still holding their lanterns high, greet the Yankee with warm embraces. Three women have come out onto the porch to gaze at the party coming up from the road.

"This man," says the Yankee, "is Captain Boyd, that I wrote you about."

"It's pretty hard, Captain," one of them calls, "to walk all the way from the road on one leg, ain't it?"

"I think it's going to be worth it," Booth replies.

The faces he sees are kindly, almost without apprehension. The younger of the two men wears a buckram shirt and what appear to be the gray trousers of a Confederate officer's uniform.

"This way, Captain," the man says. "Ah you able to walk all right?"

"As you see," Booth says wryly, stumping along.

The young doctor smiles and touches him gently on the back. Pushing forward quickly, Booth casts a longing eye at the lighted farmhouse but proceeds to a small outbuilding. He recognizes it as a slave cabin. Dark and with door ajar, it is deserted.

Inside, there is crude furniture; the Herndons duck their heads on entering, as does the tall Yankee. Henson, still whistling, remains outside.

"We can examine your leg now if you like, Captain." The younger Herndon lifts his lantern toward one corner of the low room while the older one puts down the black leather bag he has brought with him from the house.

Booth leans his crutch against a table, and in the rush of relief there is a sudden dizziness in his head. He steadies himself against the table so as not to pass out.

In the next few minutes he is helped to the bed. His head is swimming. The tall Yankee, sent by Weed, has vanished by the time he is aware of it. The Herndons lean over him, their faces moving in and out of the lantern light. He is flat on his back. He feels their fingers loosening the grip of the splints.

"If you have to cut off my leg, I guess it's all right," he says with what he hopes is courage.

"I don't think we'll have to do that," he hears one of them say.

Tears form in Booth's eyes. He yields to the men. He puts himself in their hands. He is a child again. A long journey just to be a child.

Later, in a fog of half-consciousness, he hears two horses ride off into the night. A kerosene lamp has been left by the doctors burning on the table beside him.

Half asleep, half awake, he is back in the theater. . . . Giddy with drink he swings toward him the hinged partition leading into the occupied box, and he takes in the four shadowy figures, all of whom turn sharply to stare. He raises his derringer and fires it—crack!—at the bony man seated in the rocking chair. No, he does not look long at the face. The scene is throbbing before him.

"Sic semper tyrannis!" he remembers to cry.

There is a gasp, and then a groan. He starts back the way he came, only to be confronted by the surprised face of a young major.

"Out of my way!" he whispers harshly. He draws the knife.

". . . shot the President!" the woman is screaming. "Help us!"

The young major staggers, struck by the slash of the knife. But Booth cannot get past him. Real urgency. He turns, pushing aside the chair that Mrs. Lincoln has been sitting in. He climbs to the railing of the box, holding momentarily to the upright beam.

He sees the actor below. His feet start to slide as the slick-soled riding boots lose purchase on the draped bunting, soft. But he has made the leap before. The leap from the box. One actor below. Macbeth?

Something catches on the bunting as he falls. A terrible landing. The actor on stage stands there staring. Harry Hawk. A great murmur has risen from the audience. Then he feels the pain in his leg. His head is dizzy.

But he stands up, dragging his leg behind him. Is the leg broken? No, it couldn't be broken. He is walking on it. Another man behind the wings. He shoves that one out of the way. There is the stage door. Well, when he is on the horse, he will not feel the leg so much.

Outside now. He looks up the alley. Where is the horse? The horse!

PART TWO
The FRUITS
of PEACE

1

Aboard a railroad coach on the Richmond, Fredericksburg, and Potomac line, Chester Arthur sees water through the trees, and he checks his pocket watch to learn if the train is on time. The Rappahannock River, blue and somnolent, is shielded by stands of oak and maple, already in full leaf, and on the low bank, leaning willows brush the surface of the water.

The train is not late. In spite of the stories he has heard about the decline of service on the carpetbagger lines, he has found the trip satisfactory. How much better, in any case, than riding horseback through the damned center of Fredericksburg—protected barely by the cloak of night—with John Wilkes Booth on one of the other horses.

Chester closes the window beside his seat; he is puffier in the face than he was then, rounder in the gut. But he gets his window shut as easily as any of the other people in the car against the soot, which blows in suddenly as the tracks change direction.

Soon he will join Nell and his son, who have been staying with the Herndons going on four weeks. Nell pays these long visits for Alan's sake, she says. She thinks it is good for Alan's soul to spend more time on the land, to be away from New York.

"But he lives in damned New York," Chester tells her. "He is not going to be a plantation lord when he grows up."

"Shall I tell him he must be a city commissioner like his daddy?" she asks.

"Is Booth a better example?" he retorts, for Booth—in metamorphosis Captain Boyd—has not departed from the Herndons in the four years since he was brought here. Incredible and outrageous. Alan calls him Uncle Jim.

Yesterday a wire from Brodie reached Chester at his Wall Street office, advising that Alan had come down with a case of dysentery, not judged serious. Could Chester see to it that some of the new medicine, available, in New York, be got down to them? Chester could and would. He'd damned well bring the medicine himself.

At the stop, several Union regulars precede Chester down onto the platform. Seated on benches around the station, others are lounging idly, chewing tobacco, and holding their garrison caps on their crossed knees or wearing them at clumsy angles on their heads. Chester is attired in a duster coat, wears a dark-colored derby, and carries his own valise. He feels contempt for the troopers and is annoyed at their presence, barely consoled that they will finally be ending their occupation of the state next month on President Grant's order.

A porter, wearing half a uniform, shambles forward to take charge of his valise. Midmorning, there is the odor of jasmine on the air, and then he catches sight of Dabney, laughing and making a damned beeline for him from the far side of the station.

"Well, now, y' came yourself! Good chap!" Dabney exclaims. The two men embrace heartily, Chester feeling Dab's dark whiskers against his face. When Chester asks after Alan, Dabney nods. "Doin' fine. Started to cry just as Nell was goin' to come on the wagon. . . . So I brought Lucifer instead."

Lucifer, Dab's man, is standing at the wagon. He giggles a salute to Chester. "G'mawnin', Gin'ral."

"Good morning, Lucifer."

"Be dis all ob de gear, Major?" he asks Dabney, lifting the valise onto the bed of the wagon.

Chester nods. Dab still has the damned cavalryman's look. He is in riding boots with trousers tucked in at the tops, and he wears a calf-length coat, flecked here and there with mud.

"How's the family? Your little ones?" Chester asks.

"Fine," says Dabney. "Y'all looking prosperous, Chester."

Once they are away from the station, Chester surveys the landscape. There are a lot of people in town, but the litter of the war still stands everywhere. The broken masonry of buildings hit by Burnside's shelling in '62 still looks the same as it did when he first saw it two weeks after it happened. Had they moved one damned stone since then to clean up the place?

"Hear y'all a city commissioner now," Dabney drawls, leaning back.

"City commissioner means you're looking for a better appointment. If you can get it."

Dabney laughs easily. Lucifer has turned the wagon down the river road, where one can see the blasted brick pilings that supported the old bridge looming irregularly above the current. At the beginning of the war the Herndons lived in an elegant house in town until the

Union troops commandeered it during one of their occupations. None of the Herndons felt like going back to it afterward, and they sold the property to the bank.

"You prosperous too, Dab?"

"Heck, I'll say we are," Dabney says. "We got us a piano now, out of tune but full payment for a cure, and we sing and dance the whole night through."

"You still like to sing?" Chester has a fleeting recall of fellowship with Dabney at the Bancroft House twelve, thirteen years before, and Nell arriving with her mother one afternoon. A few nights later, at the piano in the parlor, Nell sang "Robin-a-Dair."

"And the captain?" Chester asks after a moment. "I hear he's still with you."

Dabney shrugs. "Yeah, he's out to be your Alan's hee-ro, showing off his ridin' and his shootin'. Or he sits by the side of the sickbed and tells Alan stories."

"Stories! What kind?"

Grinning, Dabney raises both hands. "Mistuh Shakespeare."

"It's time he was sent packing," Chester says disagreeably.

The sun has grown warm and he has taken off his derby and fans himself with it before setting it on his knee. Of course Dabney starts in with another damned account of all the services Booth has performed for the Herndons, the same sort of thing Chester has heard many times before from Nell. The hunting of the venison and the bear. The fishing in the streams. The catfish. The hard times.

"Soon as his leg was mended," Dabney drones on, "—he could hardly walk on it straight—he was out huntin'. He'd be gone for two, three days, and he'd be back with meat. I tell you somethin': I was nevah any good with a rifle. Here I was a high-rankin' military officer and I doubt if I could hit a bear at ten feet. Then this actor come along—where'd he learn how to do all that! Really do it! Y' 'spect him to be able to tell stories. But the rest?"

Chester takes out his kerchief and wipes the dampness off his forehead. The Herndons will have to learn to get along without Booth. That is part of the serious business of Chester's visit.

When the wagon reaches the Herndon farm, there is still no sign of Nell. Laura, one of Dabney's daughters, shouts to Chester and jumps into his arms. There is a new coat of paint on the house, he notices, and the few window shutters remaining—those not used for firewood during the war—have been painted a damned surprising navy blue. On the porch, asleep, are both a big Irish setter and, in the swing, a towheaded boy wearing faded overalls, Dabney Junior.

In the large bright kitchen Chester is greeted by Dabney's wife Susan, and by Dab's father, Dr. Brodie Herndon. How warmly they welcome him, full of gratitude for old favors, interest in his work and his opinions. But he keeps looking at the stairway uneasily, wondering why his wife does not appear when surely she can hear his voice.

"Nell's upstairs lookin' after the boy," Brodie Herndon tells him at last.

"Shall I run upstairs and tell her you're here?" Susan asks.

"No, no," Chester says quickly, and sets off for the stairs. He knows the way. As he reaches the top of the stairs, he experiences a sharp taste of bile in his throat and a sudden hot flash such as he used to get occasionally during the war.

The door to the bedroom is barely ajar, but through the opening he can see his son lying in the bed, eyes closed, his small hands resting on top of the counterpane. As Chester pushes open the door, he sees Nell, and by her side, the damned frontiersman looking down upon the sleeping boy as though the three of them are posed for a family portrait. Booth is wearing a small beard but looks altogether sturdier than he did the afternoon in the Astor bar, to say nothing of the night that Chester carried him bodily into the slave cabin.

Nell exclaims as she comes forward, "Why, Alan just fell asleep this minute!" As she goes past Booth, she carefully avoids brushing against his clothing.

Chester touches her hand and says to Booth, who stands stiff as a poker, "I'm sure you'll excuse us, sir. Perhaps we'll talk later."

Booth bows his head in deference. With his long, black hair down to his shoulders, he strides out of the room in a rigid way, shutting the door behind him.

Nell, fingering the buttons on her bosom, says, "I hope you brought the medicine."

There is a faintly unpleasant odor around the large four-poster. Alan has not stirred. "I brought it," he says coldly.

Her eyes peer up at him in a haunted way. "He is kind to Alan. I cain't keep him out of the bedroom." Suddenly she bursts into tears. Her whole body begins shaking. She sinks onto a chaise longue beside the bed, burying her fingers into a quilt lying there.

"Stop crying," he mutters. "Some respect is all I want. Can't you make it look as though you have a little respect for me in front of people?"

"But I do respect you!" Her lip quivers. "You care only how it looks, not what I do!"

Confused, he starts to reply, then realizes it is hopeless. Of course he cares what she does. If she does right, it will look right too. To do right is the easier way. It is much harder to do wrong and look right. Why is that so difficult to grasp?

Meanwhile, Alan has awakened and draws a plaintive sigh. He clenches his fists and calls out. He has a self-conscious and faintly demanding way of calling "Daddy," but his physical beauty, now paled by illness, lifts his father's heart. He has great dark eyebrows and deep brown eyes. Nell muffles her weeping.

Tremulously, Chester sits down on the edge of the bed and draws his son toward him. He feels great love for this boy; and as he perhaps did not with the one who died, he will try to placate this child. No one will outmaneuver him; no one will take his place.

After darkness falls over the Herndon farm, and when the others have retired for the night, Chester lights a lantern and walks the matted path back through the trees to the slave cabin that Booth still occupies.

Frogs are croaking, the night air is warm. A kerosene lamp can be seen burning inside the crude dwelling, and when Chester knocks, Booth calls for him to enter. The resident is seated on a low stool a few feet away from the light, applying saddle wax to his calfskin riding boots.

Booth gets to his feet momentarily. "Sit down, General, if you will."

Chester sits. The crude furniture is no different from what he remembers four years before. The layers of dust have been wiped away; there is a cookpot over the embers in the fireplace. But Booth lives even as the slaves must have. Or perhaps it is Booth's vanity to want to leave that impression.

Chester says, "We must talk about the world outside, Captain."

"I have somewhat lost interest in it," Booth says.

"That may be." Damned monk in a cell, Chester mutters to himself. "But since your safety here has depended on the pages of calumny that Secretary Stanton removed from the diary you left behind, and which he has been hoarding like gold ever since, you have to understand that these pages are about to change hands."

Booth hardly glances up. The lamplight plays over his coarsened features.

"For your own sake," Chester says, "you must leave the Herndon farm. Mr. Weed has negotiated to obtain the pages of your diary from Stanton. Once this record has been turned over, the only voice to accuse Weed and the others of collaboration with you will be the living voice of Wilkes Booth." He leans forward with his elbow on his knee. "These men may have treated you benignly so far, but once they have the diary pages, I warn you, Booth—"

A mock sigh. "So I am to believe you are now saving my skin for a second time?"

Booth's visitor gestures to be allowed to finish. ". . . At the first vacancy in the Supreme Court, the President will appoint Stanton, whereupon Stanton will hand over the diary pages to Weed. From the time of that appointment, you can look for trouble."

Booth puts down one of his boots on the table beside Chester and begins rubbing the other with the malodorous wax. Then, abruptly, he stands, and with a species of smile, says, "Come, General, I do not care to leave the Herndons." He fetches two glasses from a wooden shelf nailed up beside the fireplace and he brings out a jug from which he proceeds to pour an amber-colored liquid into the glasses. "Corn liquor," Booth pronounces. "Made here in the mountains. Don't you believe, as I do, that destiny looks out for me in these hills?"

When Booth takes a sip of the liquor, Chester samples a bit on his tongue too, barely able to swallow it. "Will destiny look out for the Herndons as well if hired executioners come down here searching for you?"

Booth sighs and glances about the cabin in a theatrical way; Chester clamps his jaws. He feels surprised at how badly he misjudged the character of the man at their first meeting.

"General," Booth challenges, "are you sure you are not simply annoyed with me because of the attentions I've paid to your son—and your wife . . . ?"

Chester keeps his gaze level, his voice steady; the man's damned cheek need not be pointed out. "Both my wife and my son have too sound a judgment to be long distracted by you. If I thought any differently, I would not permit them to stay here."

For a moment, there is an injured look in Booth's eyes; Chester rises to his feet.

"What the Herndons and I share," Booth now exclaims, "what they and I have given each other—why, it is something the soulless moneychangers of New York hate and fear."

"If you love the Herndons so much, stop talking and get your poisoned carcass out of here!"

Booth's face reddens. "The Old South—"

But Chester has retrieved the lantern he brought down with him from the house. "The Old South is decay and rot!" Chester cries. "Put it behind you!" And this time he turns on his heel and on his way out pushes shut the door of the slave cabin so hard that the report rattles every stick of furniture in Booth's humble abode.

Chester feels satisfied. He has known how to deal with egoists since his war service. And every word he told the man was roughly the damned truth. If he knows Weed, it is the damned truth.

2

Fredericksburg
December 29

Mr. Chester Arthur, Esquire
124 Lexington Avenue
New York, New York

My dear Chester,

We are overwhelmed by the generosity of the Christmas gifts that you and Nell sent. The children never saw anything like the dolls, the wagon, the wooden soldiers, all the rest.

As you foretold, our Captain has finally left us. He left behind a note of farewell on Christmas morning, and a quantity of gifts for the household. It will be strange not to see him riding off at dawn any more, or see him coming back at twilight with his gun across his saddle and his game bag full. But I know it is for the best. The children wept to hear he was gone for good, and even some of the neighbors, who laughed at him behind his back for his hifalutin tricks, said they would miss him. The farmer down the road said he guesses, "Waal, the Cap'n was one o' them hotbloods who didn' know when he was licked."

Susan is happy for Nell that she is expecting again, and would write to Nell soon, except you say that Nell does not want anybody to know. We hope this doesn't mean she's out of sorts about it.

You were right when you said you thought the Captain would leave as soon as he learned that Mr. Stanton had been appointed to the Court. When I told him I read of the appointment in the paper, he looked unhappy and said that it meant he had to make certain sacrifices for the sake of his friends.

Then a day after he left we read in the paper that Mr. Stanton had died of pneumonia in Washington. Chester, I don't know what that means. When the Captain finds that out, is he likely to want to come back to us? On balance, I think I would take the risk and let him in.

As the farmer says, "If he don't know he's licked, mebbe he ain't."

Faithfully,
Dabney

3

NEW YORK CITY

Weed's eyesight is now so bad that on the street he sticks his cane out in front of him as a blind man would. But he spends the day much as he likes, visiting familiar haunts and passing the time with old friends. Johnny-on-the-spot at the Stock Exchange when it opens, he inhales some of the familiar excitement there even though he can't make out the numbers anymore when the boys chalk them up on the board. Later, he stops past the customhouse where his old friend, General Arthur, has recently been appointed collector of the port. But the visit is too early in the day for Weed to run into the general, who scarcely ever gets to his office before noon, they say.

Eventually, Weed drops in at a prayer meeting in a converted stable off Bleecker Street. Attracted by the lusty singing of familiar hymns, he jumps at the chance to enter and to participate. So what if most of the singers are drunks and reprobates? The older he becomes, the more satisfaction he feels with the "old-time religion." "It's good enough for me!" he shouts out with the others when that particular hymn is offered. He feels no embarrassment that he prefers these services to those in the Episcopalian "cathedrals" uptown. He has always felt himself to be a man of the people, believed in hard work, and excused drinking. He defended the Catholics, and the right of the breadwinner not to have his wife marching around all the time in pursuit of the vote.

Although he is no longer active in public life, he is writing down his convictions daily in his memoirs, a chore that awaits him in his library when he returns home. He knows that people are still interested in his thoughts. How many greet him by name on his walks about the city! One day perhaps he will count the number and make a fitting remark in the memoirs about the wide acquaintanceship that a poor boy from upriver has been able to make in the great metropolis.

Panting a little, his white sideburns wet, Weed climbs the steps to his residence to hear his butler announce a "gentleman waiting in the middle parlor."

"Gentleman?" Weed grunts, faintly pleased at the news. Never mind hemorrhages in both eyes, an enlarged heart, and dropsy; he still has callers.

"It's some kind of headwaiter, sir," the butler adds.

Astonished, Weed goes in at once. The "gentleman," agile as a cat, leaps to his feet. He holds a narrowly cut black topcoat over his arm and wears black formal clothes with a vest and cravat. His moustache is fastidiously trimmed.

The man says:

"*Je suis honoré que vous m'acceptez.*"

"André?" Weed exclaims. The man looks like the wine steward at Delmonico's. "Are you André of Delmonico's? What are you doing here?"

"*Je me regrette que l'heure est avance,*" the man says.

Weed blinks. But of course it cannot be André, who would not go on babbling in French, who would never presume to call on him here. As he realizes this, he also realizes that the voice is faintly wrong. And the French is corrupted from a phrase book.

"What's goin' on here?" Weed asks, peering closely at the man through his watery vision. "Speak English, man. You're not André, are you?"

"Ah, to tell you the trut', *M'sieur*, I am André's brahther."

"Come, come, my man," Weed says. An arm-waving gesture, although very like André's when the quality of the wine is questioned, does not persuade him.

"*À qui est-ce que vous vous adressez?*" the visitor persists.

"Really, your accent is ridiculous!" Weed now declares, for surely the brother of a Frenchman should have as pure an accent as the original.

"Perhaps it needs more rehearsal," the man says in perfect English.

"As I thought." Weed snaps. But then, eyes widening, he takes two involuntary steps backward. Far from being in the presence of a wine steward, he realizes, he is in the presence of an actor. Quickly he pulls shut the drapes, darkening the window that overlooks 12th Street. His visitor laughs.

"Sit down . . . Mr. Booth," Weed says.

Running a finger between his thickened neck and his starched collar, Booth sits. "You seem to know your French, Mr. Weed," he says. "But then you and the bishop spent time in Paris on diplomatic missions, did you not?"

Still shaken, Weed disdains reply.

"My accent will improve," Booth says in the voice Weed remembers. "The reason I am rehearsing André is that it is his position I want now that I am settling in New York."

"What!" Weed cries. "Impossible!"

"But I hear that André is leaving Delmonico's and retiring to a patron's estate in Languedoc." With animation Booth leans forward and describes how he could be introduced to Delmonico's by Mr. Weed—if he were so kind—as André's brother.

"And you think that would fool André?" Weed asks, laying a nervous hand on the mantelpiece. A madman through and through. Only a madman would have tried to save the Confederacy after the Confederacy had already surrendered.

"I can be whatever kind of wine steward you prefer," Booth replies. His resources are unlimited. He has recovered his old theatrical trunk in Baltimore, and has spent time experimenting there. "I've developed techniques of impersonation—using makeup—that not even the gypsies know."

"You are mad to be in civilization."

"I propose a challenge, Mr. Weed," Booth declares, rubbing his hands. "Give me a glass of wine. I will identify it for you. I have been practicing to be an expert on wines."

To show he is determined about this, Booth jumps up and leads the way through an open door into the adjoining library. Numbly, Weed follows. Beams of filtered sunlight are at the moment bathing the portrait of Seward, sorely wounded by one of Booth's henchmen on an occasion Weed would like to forget. He watches Booth study the Seward visage calmly, like a visitor to an art gallery, then move on to the next object, a cut-glass Italian carafe on the library table. Booth pours out a thimbleful of wine into a glass.

"You must think I'm some kind of magician," Weed grumbles, "to imagine I can get you a position at an exclusive place like Delmonico's."

Booth is passing the glass of wine back and forth under his nose. "Delmonico's must import thousands of dollars' worth of goods through customs. Surely the influence of General Arthur—"

"Then ask General Arthur to do your dirty work!"

Booth has tasted the wine, smacking his lips elaborately. "This one's too easy. Chateau Lafite '68. Everybody has it."

Through rheumy eyes, Weed focuses on the forged iron poker standing beside the cold fireplace.

"I could be a German sommelier if you like," Booth says, filling his glass of wine to the top. "If my French is a little off, it could just as easily pass for a German accent, don't you think? I have a gift for languages."

Sic semper tyrannis is the language that Weed recalls.

"Get out of my sight!" Weed suddenly declares. "You have more to fear from me than I do from you. I will not sponsor you again!"

He sees that Booth is beginning to look actorish, showing his profile. It must be a scene at court that he is going to play, out of Webster or Bulwer Lytton.

"You mean," Booth asks slyly, "now that you have my diary pages that I am easier to threaten?"

Weed says nothing.

"Unless," Booth proclaims on a right-angle turn, "Mr. Stanton died so soon after his appointment that you did not get the pages from my diary and still don't know where they are. Booth's manifesto may still survive!"

"You wish the cursed thing did, I can see."

"A bargain, Mr. Weed," Booth says, sitting down before the knee-hole desk under the portrait of Archbishop Hughes. "I will here and now write you a letter on notepaper. I will date it—say—April 25, 1865, from the swamps of Virginia. And in this note I will say, 'Dear Mr. Weed, I cannot find my way to freedom and already regret my dastardly act. On my flight from Washington I have lost a diary in which I libeled you and others as conspirators with me. Should I be killed and that diary later come to light, the world must know how crazed and persecuted I felt at the moment I wrote it, for there is not a word of truth in it. Signed, John Wilkes Booth.' "

Weed scratches his chin thoughtfully as though considering the matter.

"Well, you have given the game away," Booth says sorrowfully. He is holding the quill pen in his hand, rolling it in his fingers. "If you had received the pages from Stanton before his death and destroyed them, you would not be thinking whether or not the letter I describe might be a good idea."

A discreet tap on the library door, and Weed quickly calls out, "I don't want to be disturbed, understand?" As footsteps move away from the door, Weed begins shutting the drapes on the library windows. "Good Lord, don't be an idiot, man, go abroad, go west. I know a virgin area of Oklahoma—"

"No. I am already banished from my Oklahoma—'twas in Fredericksburg," Booth says, a lulling harmony in his voice. "At the Herndons I had a function. But now I am out in public life again. You evicted me from my haven. Face up to it, Mr. Weed."

"Don't blame me for that. It was General Arthur did it, who truly does have more influence than I at Delmonico's."

With an air of sudden caution, Booth points to a chair so that Weed may seat himself.

"As to that," Booth says, "it is best that I confide in you. The general is not a man I can deal with, since my secret source of information in New York is none other than . . . his wife."

Having sat down, Weed rubs his eyes, astonished. "You are scandalous, sir."

Booth shrugs. "Without his knowledge, I have been in New York for some months now. I tell you this so you do not give my presence away to the general: Mrs. Arthur and I are lovers."

Weed's grasp tightens around the curved grip of his chair arm. "Unspeakable!"

While Booth bows his head as though chastened, there is another knock at the library door, and Weed bursts out, "What the hell do you want out there?"

A feminine voice calls, "It is I, Father. I've come home and just wanted to make sure you were all right."

"Of course I'm all right. Why wouldn't I be, you idiot?"

When the footsteps depart, Booth says in a measured tone, "Nell

is the love of my life, Mr. Weed. Her passionate belief in secession has alienated her from her husband, a marriage that might have been somewhat happier in less troubled times."

Weed's watery vision focuses again on the cast-iron fireplace poker.

Booth says, "I will cause no trouble to anyone if you write this simple letter to Delmonico's. Refer to me as Götz. When a boy I always wanted to play Götz von Berlichingen." Draining his glass, Booth paces. "Mention that I was formerly in the service of, possibly, the Count von Bismarck—"

"Go at once and I will write your cursed letter!" Weed bursts out. Still in his chair, he cannot believe what he has just heard. "Is she not aware she is mixed up with an assassin? . . . And an actor to boot!"

Not noticeably perturbed, Booth dons his light topcoat. For weeks he has been observing that most of the high-toned waiters and restaurant workers wear such coats, and his mind is already out on the street again. As a parting shot, he says, "You are not as much a man of the world as I once gave your credit for being, Mr. Weed."

4

ON THE HUDSON RIVER

Awakening suddenly in his stateroom, Chester rises so quickly from the overstuffed pillow on his bunk that he strikes his head a glancing blow on the wooden shelf above him. Silly damned place to put a shelf. He rubs his forehead. A sharp report—something like a shot—has echoed in the night, arousing him over the noisy wake of the paddle-wheel against the side of the boat.

He starts to speak out to his cabinmate, Roscoe Conkling, to ask him whether he, too, heard the shot, but then remembers that Roscoe is not in the other bunk this trip. Roscoe's new idea of dignity is that he must have a separate stateroom. Never mind that it is not the French line to Le Havre, only the Albany night boat.

Chester puts on trousers and shirt and runs his fingers through his hair. It is time for a turn on deck. In the dark he believes he can make it to the gentlemen's lavatory without his appearance disgracing him too much. His face feels warm to the touch and he wonders that he neglected to open the window vents before retiring. Since his extremities feel normal, he prefers to believe that the warmth in his face and at the back of his neck is related to the closed vents rather than to his kidney trouble, which the doctor in Albany has given him medicine for. He is saving the medicine for the damned convention in Utica next week, when he will probably need it.

Outside in the companionway, buttoning his coat, he asks a young room steward if the shot came from on board.

"Did ye hear a shot, sir?" the steward asks, puzzled.

"It must have come from the shore."

"Sure, on the port side we didn't hear nothin', sir."

Chester hopes to run into Roscoe in the lavatory, or even into damned French and Wheelhorse, the other two members of the steering committee returning to New York on the night boat. He wants to make sure he is not imagining shots in his sleep, as they say some battle-scarred veterans of the war continue to do in their dreams. His Philadelphia acquaintance, Dr. Weir Mitchell, has written on the subject.

But in the lavatory he finds no one at the sinks, and both compartments unoccupied. The mirror reflects a complexion ruddy but smooth. He hangs up his coat, washes the sleep from his eyes, then combs and fingers his pomaded hair, as well as his handsome graying sideburns.

On his way up to the deck—he has fetched his hat in case he should encounter a lady—he hears violin music, apparently from one of the aft saloons where the second-class passengers sit up all night. Music is allowed there: once he remembers an Italian playing the concertina half the night, and himself standing with the others beating time to the music and applauding the musician, leaving coins at the end.

The violinist is dishing up a Scottish air: "Comin' Thro' the Rye," or one of those. Chester has heard Robert Burns set to music before, but he believes the sentiments are too bitter and laconic to make good songs. Some lines come to mind.

> *We think na on the long Scots miles*
> *The mosses, waters, slaps, and styles,*
> *That lie between us and our hame*
> *Where sits our sulky sullen dame.*

His own sulky sullen dame he prefers not to think about. He looks forward rather to seeing his children—his restless, impossibly skinny Alan, his doll-baby Nellie. But how could one look forward to seeing Nell anymore?

From the rail, lanterns of smaller craft are visible here and there on the water. It is a clear night with a mild, fresh breeze. Not even the offer of a vacation in her beloved Fredericksburg delights her anymore. She says the baby is too young.

"Would you like to visit your mother in France, then?" Chester has asked, for Nell's mother has become too infirm to travel.

"If I cannot take Nellie to Virginia, how can I take her to France?"

The only hopeful sign is that she goes out more. The Mendelssohn Society to which she belongs has frequent meetings. Also, she goes on shopping trips, but rarely buys anything. In fact, he probably has become more damned extravagant than she is. Strange when one thinks that at his father's knee he was taught to want little in life. Compensation, Emerson would call it, one supposes.

The uninterrupted darkness of the eastern shore has begun to depress him; he wanders closer to the area where the violin music is coming from. A number of passengers are enjoying the music from benches and on deck chairs just outside the saloon. A man, his wife, and three small children are eating bread and sausage. Even in the open air the sausage smells strong, and he gives them a wide berth. Tipping his hat, he sits down next to a young woman, who seems youthful but whose form and figure are shrouded in the darkness.

"May I?" he asks.

"If you want," she says. It is an alto voice with just a touch of coarseness.

He keeps his hat on and does not say anything for several moments. He has glanced about the area to see if she appears to be accompanied by anyone; one is inclined to be doubtful about a woman alone on deck at so late an hour. Then as he moves a foot involuntarily, he hears a damned growl from under the bench.

Startled, he asks the woman, "Is that a dog?"

"Yes, mine," she says. "Please excuse him."

But he feels uneasy and peers downward, trying to get some idea of the size of the beast in case it should fasten itself onto his ankle. A large dog might suggest that she employed the beast for protection, while a more delicate breed—a poodle, say—could imply that her favors were for sale, or so he has heard. Men were enticed into conversation more easily by a woman with a dog, as long as the dog was not too damned threatening.

"If he makes you nervous," the woman says, "you can move on the other side."

"I think I'll do that," Chester says.

She seems to have an Old Country accent; perhaps that is what he has mistaken for coarseness. She is dressed conservatively enough, wearing a pert hat but with a spinsterish shawl draped over her shoulders.

"The music really seems to carry over open water, doesn't it?" he asks, sitting down on the other side of her.

"I think it woke up a farmer before," she laughs, "who fired his shotgun at us."

"Did you hear a shot too?"

"I did."

"I'm glad to know it!" Chester exclaims. "I thought maybe I imagined it. The steward didn't hear any noise."

"Maybe he just says he didn't," she replies.

Chester looks at her with curiosity.

She turns her face to him. "If the captain's drunk and is shooting off guns in the pilot house, the steward's not going to tell you that."

Chester laughs. "I suppose he isn't!" He steals a look down to the vicinity of her ankles to see if the dog's nose has emerged any further.

"The gentleman I saw you with earlier—" she asks, "was that Senator Conkling?"

"Yes," he concedes warily. It sometimes seems that Roscoe is recognized most quickly by women of a certain kind. He wonders if the whole sisterhood knows what a rake he is, knows that he keeps a mistress in Washington.

"He has a face like a triangle," she says. "Do you work for him?"

"No," he says. "Although I do work for the government."

"Not in the Tweed Ring, I hope," she says coolly.

He laughs, enjoying the wryness of her manner. "I work for the federal government. The customhouse, port of New York."

He half expects that she will make the proposition to him now; she will deduce that he has money. For the first time, he is not sure how he will react.

"Do you come from upstate?" she asks.

"I grew up there," he replies, startled into candor. "My sisters still live in Newtonville. And my pa is alive . . . although my mother died not long ago. . . . Do you . . . reside up there?"

The violin music has stopped. But the sweep of water from the locomotion of the paddlewheel cushions their conversation, giving it privacy from other passengers sitting or standing nearby.

"I work in New York," she says. "I was glad to get away from upstate."

He realizes he is nodding to himself; but he tries to restrain the responsiveness he feels.

Without rancor, she says, "There was so much narrow-mindedness. Maybe your folks were different."

"My pa didn't like anybody else's opinions. I think I'd call him single-minded. He was not courteous enough to let somebody else finish a sentence."

"Mine tried to take me out of school."

"No, mine believed in education, but . . ." He takes a sudden breath, realizing that his heart is beating fast, and that if she is a prostitute after all, he is nearly helpless. He does not want her to be a prostitute, he believes.

"What work do you do in New York, miss?"

"I'm . . . a writer," she says softly. "My name's Victoria."

"Well, mine is Chester," he says uneasily. With his hat in his lap, he takes out his kerchief and begins wiping perspiration from his forehead.

"I write for the *Herald*," Victoria says.

He feels cold water down his spine. A writer of three-volume romances, he had imagined. Or else a suffragette. Not a damned newspaper reporter!

Hoping she is lying, he says, "I did not know the *Herald*—or any other New York paper—employed female reporters."

"Well, they do."

"I see."

"If you ever have a story for me," she says, "or if Senator Conkling does, just get hold of Victoria Coventry through the *Herald*."

"We always cooperate with the press." His manner is cold. Corruption, he supposes, is what she is really looking for. Since the Tweed Ring, that is all any of them care about.

"I hope you think of me as someone special," Victoria says.

He is beginning to recapitulate. What has he said to her? "My name is Chester"! Good Lord, what if she puts that in the damned paper? Except, of course, the *Herald* supports Conkling. They would have no reason to ridicule Conkling, or Conkling's friends.

Nevertheless, feeling misled, he puts the words together that will smooth his escape. ". . . think I can promise you that I will never do anything newsworthy . . ."

"Ach!" she cries suddenly, jumping to her feet, for they have been hit by spray. "Is that the rain coming?"

Chester says he believes the boat changed course abruptly and that the moisture is wake from the wheel. He smiles at her popeyed expression in the moonlight, and the surprised way she said, "Ach!" He offers his handkerchief with which to wipe her face.

As she makes use of it, dabbing here and dabbing there, the animal comes out from beneath the bench and looks around casually. It is a medium-sized dog, a terrier. Of no particular significance.

She folds the handkerchief into neat sections before handing it back to him. But before he can take it, she reaches up and inserts it into his breast pocket.

"Thank you for your kindness . . . Chester."

He realizes, with reluctant pleasure, that she knows very well who he is, and has ever since he first sat down.

5

DELMONICO'S

Because of the sudden rainstorm, Edwin Booth has decided to dine nearer to his hotel than usual. At Delmonico's, while turning over his umbrella to the checkroom attendant, he surveys the sumptuous banquet area, where many early diners are already seated. Edwin, in good health, has the large, rugged-looking features of a trustworthy man, with none of the ferrety aspect that all the illustrated graphics once gave to his notorious brother.

The small string orchestra has begun playing from the parqueted dais at the far end of the restaurant. Tables are set with beautiful linen cloths, fine silver, and vases of fresh flowers. On some of the tables are engraved reservation cards.

The captain has approached him, a tall, pale man with ruffled shirt front and long tails. "What a pleasure, Mr. Booth! May I seat you?"

"Rapidly, if you please. A tedious job of makeup ahead, you know?" Edwin Booth smiles, flexes his wrists faintly, a mannerism of his. All New York knows he is doing Richard the Third these evenings.

"Of course."

In the mezzanine alcoves, toward which the captain now leads him, draperies can be drawn to give privacy to the diner. In the years immediately following the assassination, the brother of the assassin was occasionally reproached in restaurants and other public places by self-dramatizing patriots. Even though he bore himself nobly in these scenes—which have more or less terminated—tradition has required that Edwin Booth be partially sequestered.

But when he is seated tonight, he declines the captain's offer to draw the curtain. Smiling, he decides to see and be seen.

His gaze, in fact, falls on the table directly before his alcove, at which a youthful couple from the provinces are dining. The husband is plainly a glutton. Although Edwin can see little more of the man than his back, he would guess a clergyman from some place like Syracuse. The wife, on the other hand, is a vision; she seems much in awe when Edwin turns his profile this way and that.

The wine steward enters Edwin's alcove, passing between Edwin and the lovely young female. Since the new steward has hardly glanced in his direction (unlike André, who was always prompt in his greeting), Edwin ventures to beat time with his forefinger as the orchestra strikes up a mazurka. The music is so infectious, he would let the lady know, that he is unable to resist beating time.

However, the steward makes a loud, grinding noise as he rotates the wine back and forth in the ice bucket. Edwin clears his throat. The steward—an agile-looking man in his thirties, wearing a thin beard—half turns and stares at Edwin for a moment. An expression of naked surprise registers on the man's face, whereupon he shows his back.

Stunned, Edwin stares. His veins have frozen. He does not need to see the steward's face again. Something in the way the thin shoulders move from side to side, and the way the feet are planted, speak to him with shattering eloquence.

If only it is a joke! But would someone be so cruel as to impersonate the luckless Johnny in this public place?

Edwin's throat feels dry. With the eyes of the clergyman's wife still on him, he picks up the tumbler of water. The steward turns with a sudden flaring smile.

Edwin gasps, "What vile frivolity—"

"Nay," the steward whispers at his shoulder. "Control yourself,

Ted. While it is a small part I play, have respect for the illusion."

Edwin Booth drops the glass, splashing water on the padded tablecloth. Immediately, the wine steward pulls shut the long, maroon-colored drape that closes off the alcove from the rest of the dining room.

The clergyman's wife toys with her bisque in hopes that the drama she has seen is not over, but rather at intermission. Without remarking a word to her husband—who has objected to her remarking about too much that she has seen today—she keeps her eyes on the maroon curtain. When the orchestra stops playing briefly, she believes she hears excited conversation from the alcove.

Then, from the kitchen, a tuxedoed waiter appears, pushing a wheeled cart directly into the curtained sanctum. At once the wine steward emerges, walking very rapidly in the direction of the kitchen. He and the waiter appear angry with each other, as is evident when the waiter reopens the alcove by pushing back the drapes with several forceful jerks.

The clergyman's wife now sees the rugged-featured patron still seated in the same stunned attitude as when he dropped the tumbler of water. The diner's elbows remain flat on the table, and his gaze rigidly forward.

"Sir?" she sees the waiter say, offering a silver tureen with serving ladle. "Sir?"

Slowly, the diner turns and begins to serve himself.

The lady ponders the meaning of what she has seen. Once—in a theater in Schenectady, attended before her marriage and without her father's knowledge—she saw such a scene when the curtain opened for the second act of a play being presented. Revealed on stage, a middle-aged man, full of cares, was seated at a table with a decanter of wine before him. Like the man in the restaurant, he was long motionless, the burdens of the world on his shoulders, before another actor entered and the play resumed.

Here there is no resolution. Although she looks for him, the wine steward does not reappear, and eventually the patron finishes his meal and, with heavy tread, departs from the restaurant.

6

SPRINGTIME SOCIAL NOTES

Among those booking passage for Le Havre aboard the *Cimbria* is Mrs. General Chester A. Arthur, wife of the Collector. She is accompanied by her personal maid and by her young daughter, Ellen, Jr., known as Nellie. Mrs. General Arthur is to visit her mother, Mrs. Captain William Lewis Herndon in Hyères, France. Mrs. Herndon, formerly of Culpeper County, Virginia, has been maintaining residence in Europe for much of the period since the heroic death of her husband, Captain Herndon, at the helm of the *Central America*, which sank in 1857 with loss of life. Friends of the Arthurs hope to hear of an improvement in Mrs. Herndon's health.

CONSTERNATION IN PARTY RANKS

The Senate of the United States, rallied by Senator Roscoe Conkling (R., N. Y.), once again refused to confirm any of the new appointments submitted by newly inaugurated President Rutherford B. Hayes for the Customhouse in New York. The Senate action leaves General Arthur continuing as Collector at the Port. The Secretary of the Treasury, William Sherman, has alleged that irregularities in assessment have been complained of at the Port, amounting to at least $42,000. Also, that Collector Arthur has taken no action against the Customs officers responsible; instead, he has recently promoted one of them.

Last week private claims were filed against Customs personnel who levied penalties on importers for alleged undervaluation. In their briefs, the importers assert that the "undervaluations" are never demonstrated. General Arthur is said to be investigating.

OTHER SOCIAL NOTES

Also Le Havre-bound on the *Cimbria* is Mr. Götz Dörfer, sommelier at Delmonico's. He will be assessing the new vintage throughout the Provençal region, which bodes well for keeping Delmonico's the best-stocked cellar in New York.

7

THE MANHATTAN CLUB

"Well, Dun, if my eyes don't deceive me," says Thurlow Weed, gazing across the table at his luncheon guest, "you are lookin' most prosperous."

Dun smiles patiently. Of the several clubs Weed belongs to, Dun is a little surprised to have been invited to this one, and can only suppose that the business is excessively confidential: a club where the preponderance of members are Democrats will be the least curious about the conversation of two Republicans.

"I am just about the opposite of prosperous," Dun says, "as you are well aware." Already Weed is nodding in frank delight, knowing, as he does, that Dun has been having reverses lately, trying to compete with market journals that printed on both sides of the page.

"Tut, tut," Weed says. "At least you must have brought for me one of those perfect Havana *claros* I adore."

"Sorry, out of them."

"What, has your runner been arrested?"

"Not that. But his racing skiff, as he is pleased to call it, is forever going aground."

As Weed is clucking his tongue, the waiter comes in. A private room has been provided for the two men, and when the order has been given and the waiter withdraws, Weed says, "Dun, a viper is in our midst."

Dun strokes his shovel-shaped beard.

"John Wilkes Booth is alive," Weed declares. "Moreover, he is actually employed in this city."

Removing his spectacles, Dun wipes them. "We've had three rumors of that," he says, "the last about two years ago. Only the first one set the market back at all."

"Dammit, Dun, this is the gospel truth!"

"Did you see him, then?"

"Saw him. Talked to him . . . and"—here Weed laughs wryly—"helped him get his job. He pours wine at Demonico's."

Raising his eyebrows, Dun says, "Well, well."

Over the soup course—once the waiter has again retired—Weed

is emboldened to continue. He explains the mistake at Garrett's barn and why Stanton covered it up. He mentions the pages of Booth's diary that contain the names of the supposed conspirators, like Jay Cooke and Chaffey and—yes, dammit—Thurlow Weed. Then he tells of the aggravating failure to get the diary pages when Stanton dropped dead. "Frustration at every turn," Weed says, pausing to take a spoonful of the clear soup. "We hoped to get the diary and somehow be rid of Booth. Instead, we have Booth and not the diary."

Having finished his soup, Dun leans back. "I still can't see how it would have any effect on the market at this late date. Cooke is bankrupt, as you know. Union Pacific's too big. Chaffey's small potatoes . . ."

"Forget the market, will you!" Weed exclaims. But must interrupt himself as the wine steward comes in to decant. Both diners eye the steward with narrow gaze although the latter is a diminutive man with bulging eyes and small fingers. Nothing like Booth.

When the steward has left, Weed says, "This son of a bitch Stanton put the diary pages in a file called the Fredericksburg File. He threw anything in there that might discredit us. There were letters of marque from Richmond certifyin' that Booth was a bona fide Confederate agent. Other documents about us. I don't know what all was in there."

"You've tried to find the file?"

"Of course we've tried to find it. We've gone after the heirs—discreetly—and searched the War Department archives. No luck. So the hell with it."

After the whitefish is served, Weed gets to the crux of the matter. "And if it ain't bad enough that Booth is workin' in the center of town, now it turns out that he's wormed himself in and is Nell Arthur's lover besides."

"Her lover?" Dun echoes, a forkful of whitefish halfway to his mouth. "Impossible."

Sadly, Weed nods. He mentions the period Booth spent with Nell's Fredericksburg relatives and the subsequent events. "If you need any more proof, both of them are sailin' right now on the *Cimbria* for France. Ain't that a delight!"

Dun pushes back his plate. "Are they coming back, do you think?"

"How should I know?" Weed asks. His tone is pettish, disgusted. "But if they do, I think it's high time somebody got rid of Mr. Punchinello without any more ceremony. . . . Don't you?"

The waiter comes in, goes out, comes in again. Breast of veal, boiled potatoes, and creamed carrots compose the entrée today. Dun looks at the food without appetite.

Weed says, "I don't like to think of the fuss Chester would make if he finds out about this. Can he keep the lid on it? You're Chester's friend. Will he keep his mouth shut? Will any of them?"

"Chester's been busy with his work on the Party Committee . . ."

"Chester's been busy keeping his ass covered, I know that much," says Weed, carving up his breast of veal. "I'd like to do him a favor, do us all a favor. . . . I thought you might know some rascals who—"

"Not really," says Dun, although he is trying to feel indignation at Booth's behavior. His loss of appetite is something like indignation.

"God almighty, I'm no moralist," Weed says at last. "Haven't I defended the Fisks and the Goulds, whose sharp practice is notorious? I've said, live and let live. But you've got to draw the line someplace. With Booth, we're talkin' about personal moral violations—murder, now adultery!—that rip up the fabric of the society. . . . I told you I protected him for a long time. No more. . . . Am I bein' too unceremonious about this, Dun?"

Fidgeting, Dun says, "Maybe they won't come back from France." He does know a few rascals, of course. Some would be better killers than they are smugglers. They are so erratic as smugglers that Dun doubts he would have retained them had he not been able to count in an emergency on his friend Chester as the highest official in customs.

During the dessert course, Weed says, "You know that eight-cylinder Hoe press that I brought down from the *Journal*? You can have it. I've decided that I'm liquidatin'."

Dun turns the plate around that contains his slab of lemon meringue pie. "But . . . can I afford it?"

"No charge. You need it. I don't," Weed says. "You need it to compete."

"Well . . . I . . . appreciate that immensely." With a newspaper printed on both sides of the page, one could have articles again, opinion, perhaps cartoons. Not just market quotations.

And he could hope that the lovers wouldn't come back from France.

8

"*Adieu*, Mamma," says Nellie, charming in her new white dress with the low sash and the bow in back. She holds on to her nursemaid's hand.

"Give Mamma a kiss," Nell says.

It is a Sunday in May a few days before they are to return to America, and Nell and Booth are managing a day in the country by themselves away from the child and other burdensome business of their weeks in France.

The hotel where he is staying is some distance away from the Ritz, where she has taken a suite for the week, but she finishes with her dressing as soon as Nellie and the maid are out the door. He has asked for a serious talk with her on the outing, and for the first time since setting foot in the country she is wearing something other than black: an expensive, deep-pleated skirt of claret faille, a gray foulard jacket with claret trim, and a Tuscan straw hat. The man at Worth's assured her that the suit was very conservative, and she feels sure that her poor, dear mother would forgive her this one afternoon out of mourning.

The odor of violets fills the room. Paris is so much pleasanter than Nice, where they have spent the last several weeks under a sun that grew hotter and hotter. Booth thought they should remain there until her mother's affairs were completely settled. Her mother died without pain, the local doctor said. But still, such a shock! To be informed of the death even as they were disembarking at Le Havre. Of course she broke down weeping. Booth would have liked her mother in a way that Chester never did. Booth would have flirted with her in that southern way he had.

The only consoling news, when they reached Hyères, was to discover that the family holdings had not been invested in Confederate bonds, as Nell had anticipated. On the contrary, left behind in a will so lucid that not even the grasping French lawyers could find anything wrong with it was a cornucopia of solid European securities, all bequeathed to Nell.

Nell says wickedly to Booth that she will not tell Chester of her mother's gilt-edged investments. "It would spoil his picture of mah vain old mother throwin' it all away on the Confederacy."

"You sound vindictive," he tells her, laughing.

"Do you think I'm sinful for not telling Chester of this?" she asks.

"What do I know about sin, my darling?"

They lie in each other's arms in the poisonously warm Riviera nights, falling asleep just before the morning light, he before she. It pleases her that he seems indifferent to her inheritance. She has heard that he once made twenty thousand a year on the stage, and walked away from it.

"*Enfin*, we must get to Paris," he says to her one night. He is restless. He has done his work in Languedoc, and has had enough of the provincials. The "legal eagles," as he calls them, will see that her securities are safe; fine, the interest will accumulate for whenever she wants it.

"I thought you wanted to show me the wine country," she says.

"I will show you the *Comédie* instead."

In Paris, he revives. But they have little time left. After the weeks and weeks in the South, there is already pressure on her to return to New York. Chester cables that he misses his daughter, that Alan is asking after them. He also writes letters containing political news, chiefly how basely he is being hounded by the administration in Washington.

Even Jenny, the nursemaid, wants to get home to New York. She is tired of poor-Pierrot shows in the Parc. She is even tired of Nellie, no matter how good the child is. And as a strict Catholic girl, she more and more casts a suspicious eye on Uncle Götz.

On the train to St. Germain, Nell watches Booth carefully. From time to time he gazes across at her and absently smiles. When he looks out the window again, she wonders how she will respond if he tells her today that the two of them must not return to America after all, that she must send Nellie home with the nursemaid and make her life with him in France.

Ah, he will not say it. Soberly, she watches the scenery. Along the railroad there are tall trees and odd little houses built in complex ways. Crossing the Chatou bridge over the Seine, she sees long boats flash by beneath them, propelled by oarsmen looking intense and joyful. At stations where they stop briefly, men and women sit at outdoor cafés within sight of the tracks. Glasses of wine or steins of bock are placed, as if for paintings, on the small tables.

After the railway carriage passes through a tunnel, they are suddenly at St. Germain. The train comes to a full stop, and Booth holds the door for Nell to step down onto the arrival platform. She raises her parasol and smiles at him, feeling rather young. Her figure, shown to advantage in the new suit, is still slender and compact. They are no more than a few months apart in age, but over the years he has disguised himself to look older than he is. No one would guess that she is the older of the two.

On the terrace they stroll to the wrought-iron balustrade that fronts the great panorama of the plains below. She can see roads and villages, green and distant. The white roads run through clumped forests. Carts moving like ants crawl along the roads. A light mist hangs over peaks with names like Argenteuil and Sannois.

The river completes the landscape; its grace and beauty thrill her, and she exclaims, "Oh, Wilkes, can we stay here forever?"

Booth is leaning backward against his cane, smiling faintly.

Touching the sleeve of his coat, she says, "Sometimes I wish I could be dead like you." Her voice has a low and toneless quality. Then she laughs. "Shall we send anothuh cable to New York saying that Nell Herndon Arthur has followed her deah mother to eternal rest?"

Behind them, Parisians promenade back and forth, stopping to take the view. Children hold on to the hands of their mothers. Most of the men look like shopkeepers.

When Booth says nothing, Nell twirls her parasol and with her tongue in her cheek says, "We'd have to tell Nellie that I'm not really dead. And then I'd want to bring Alan over, too, although he's almost a man and surely doesn't need me."

"Don't you think Chester would want to come over as well," Booth says laughing, "and check on such details as a motherless child?"

She says that Chester worries about his politics and his tailor more than he does about his children. "Besides, if I died it wouldn't embarrass him near as much as if I left him."

She realizes she is being unfair to Chester. In his younger days he was not like that. He was no dandy when he came back from Kansas. Her mother indeed thought him unkempt, too careless of his appearance. Now he is forever trimming his whiskers, calling his valet. She shudders, guessing it to be partly her own fault.

"But why should I take my mamma's money and give—" she begins and then drops it. What she intended to ask was why she should take the money to Chester, who would use it to replenish his wardrobe and to give horrid dinners lasting until two in the morning for this and that horrid man in the customhouse. She couldn't look Mamma in the face if and when she got to heaven.

Later, when Nell and Booth are lunching at the Pavilion Henri IV nearby, she wants to tell him that what she has learned from him is that with courage anything is possible, that no social convention need stand in the way. But he looks so distressed that she has no choice but to listen when he begins to speak.

"I have been wanting to tell you what happened," he begins tensely, "why I did not go in disguise . . ."

"If you ah going to talk about *that night*," she says promptly, gently, "I do not need to hear about it."

But his eyes have left her.

"If I meant simply to fire and flee, do—do you not suppose that I would have been able to conceal my identity and escape without being recognized? Then if my flight were successful, as it turned out to be, one day I could return to the stage as—as John Wilkes Booth!"

He speaks his name with such a defiant raising of his voice, that she glances around to see if any of the Frenchmen at adjoining tables take notice. But nearest them, a fat man chews at a chicken leg, and another man, across the table, fills a glass with seltzer water. Both men have napkins tucked under their chins.

Nell wonders if the story of Dabney's slipping in on the Yankee colonel in his tent will head off the story by showing how philosophical she is about what was done in the war. "It's so much like—" she begins.

"I *wanted* them to know," he declares, "wanted them to know I was Booth, for as Booth I had letters of marque from Judah P. Benjamin, Secretary of State to the Confederacy. I was a soldier, Nell, not an assassin, and when I stepped into that box, I said clearly to Lincoln, 'Sir, I arrest you in the name of the Confederate States of America. You must come with me as my prisoner of war!' "

She owes it to him to seem interested. "What did he say?"

Booth pushes aside his plate with a rueful air. "He was just about to speak. Then that fool Rathbone—" Booth allows himself a grimace of disgust, and draws himself together again. "You see, the same thing happened to me in that box as happened to my brave lieutenant,

Payne, at Secretary Seward's residence. We were interfered with, we were not permitted to complete our capture!"

"Did you show him your letters—" Nell begins.

"That fool, Colonel Rathbone," Booth drives on, "came at me from behind. You understand the box was not large, and his sudden attack could only have the effect of endangering the ladies, Mrs. Lincoln and Miss Harris. They still had their bonnets on, the two of them; the evening had been cool. . . ."

Again Booth pauses, either for dramatic effect or to ascertain whether there are eavesdroppers. But the two diners near them are in a loud conversation that is quickly turning into a dispute.

Booth says, "As Colonel Rathbone struck my arm, the pistol went off. I had supposed, my dear Nell, that the bullet had struck the wall of the box, but even as I started grappling with Rathbone, I saw a look of astonishment form on his face. He had observed, of course, that the accidentally discharged bullet had struck Lincoln. Except for this moment of hesitation I might never have had the opportunity to escape. But as he recoiled, I was able to drop the derringer and draw a knife with which to forestall his renewed assault. Needless to say, a general hue and cry had been raised by this time both on the stage and from the women in the box.

"My only possible recourse was to fling myself over the balustrade onto the stage below. . . . I see in your eyes a look of disbelief. But, no, I had many times made a leap from such a height while playing Macbeth. This time, however, as ill luck would have it, my spur caught on the bunting, or on the framed portrait attached to the box—and I fell headlong."

"You made the leap in *Richard* too!" Nell exclaims.

"My heart was pounding, as you can imagine," Booth goes on, "and when I landed on my knees, although I felt a searing pain in them at once, I did not realize at first that I had injured my ankle seriously. It was fractured—"

"Mah poor Wilkes," Nell murmurs. She has realized that this is what he means to talk about today, not their future together.

"I must make this short," he says, clearing his throat. "I promise never to speak of it again, since it upsets you—"

"I must hear it," she says, knowing her duty. "You served, Wilkes, you served."

Booth flicks his hand. "Ah, my dear, we served, but we also bungled. We did." He lowers his voice in harsh self-contempt. "A carriage was to have been waiting beyond the stage door, in which the

President was to be held. You realize we intended to hold him and the Vice-President and Secretary Seward to ransom our own brave prisoners and as a means to get civilized terms for the Confederacy.

"But no carriage was there! I hobbled frantically to the stage door, threw it open—" For a moment it seems as though he might rise and show her the way he hobbled frantically. Instead, he lets his shoulders sink. "No carriage," he repeats, *tremolo*. "My comrades-in-arms had failed me, Nell. I hurled myself on the first horse I saw, my ankle afire, and whipped the poor beast into the night—"

"Many failed, John Wilkes," Nell whispers. "Not you alone. The army failed. The government at Richmond fell."

Her point is conceded. Booth stops a waiter to order a cognac.

"Yet you found the Herndons at last," Nell concludes with a sigh.

"I performed Christian service there," he suddenly asserts. "I found perfect fraternity at last. Then I was thrust out like Lucifer."

"Well, you should have gone back."

Booth shakes his head. "No, it was too late. When I was a boy, I sometimes tried to be Christian. But my sister told lies about me. My brothers tortured me. You see we were all bastards. Never truly good. My father didn't marry my mother until we were all half grown."

Nell looks around the pavilion uneasily. Afternoon shadows have fallen. The dispute between the Frenchmen seems to have subsided.

"One way I know I tried to be Christian at the Herndons," Booth declares, "is that I was celibate. What better way to test oneself! For four years I was celibate."

She feels a blush come to her face. "I should think so—"

"You should think so!" he retorts harshly, mocking her. "Recall I am an actor, not a divinity student."

Her heart gives way for a moment. Some things she can recall too well. "Is it true," she cannot resist asking, her chin steady, "that you and that senatuh's daughter—I can't remember her name—that you became engaged to her?"

In truth she remembers the name well—Lucy Hale—and it was said that Wilkes took her daddy's tickets to the inauguration, and accompanied by his men stood close enough to the platform to have kidnapped Lincoln even while he was taking the oath of office. For some reason, they didn't.

Booth gives her a withering look. "Is that what they discuss at the customhouse?"

She decides to drop the subject.

*

Later, they return to Paris in the dusk. He has behaved pleasantly in spite of her remark about Lucy Hale. It is a cool evening and Nell helps the nursemaid put Nellie to bed. How complaisant the child is. She is like an enormous china doll, her cheeks rosy, her chin rounded, her eyelashes long.

When Nell and Wilkes go in to supper, he tells her that they must return to New York for the present, but when he can arrange it, they will return to the Continent for good.

Emerging from the long narrow dining room of the hotel are two elderly nuns carrying their rosaries as though they have just attended last rites. Nell half turns away from them; she is wearing black again herself. Her wrap is bordered with the thinnest strip of velvet.

Passing along behind the headwaiter, she looks without appetite at the food the other guests are eating: oxtails served in sherry, stewed mushrooms, Jerusalem artichokes, celery and horse radish, truffles, curried lobsters.

"Am I to get a divorce then?" she asks her escort when they are seated and alone. She knows that somehow it is impossible, that it will ruin Chester and cause her children to blame her for that ruin.

Wilkes's gaze is calm and steady. For the first time all day his smoldering eyes seem to turn directly toward her. "You wanted to die, as I have," he replies to her. "Do you have the courage to die?"

Her lips part delicately. If we can be together always, she is about to say. Lovers, after their deaths, are together always. But to achieve that transcendence without actually dying is the miracle he has in mind. She cannot speak. Would God's special providence protect her as it has protected him? He could hardly have survived all these years if God had found him wanting in any important way.

9

THE FIFTH AVENUE HOTEL

"Is it a touch of the gout you got there, General?" Ulysses Grant asks him, chuckling rat-tat-tat.

Chester denies it jovially. The pain is still shooting through his leg, but he is smiling as he shakes Grant's hand. It is the tail end of a damned jolly evening. Grant has invited a number of them up to his suite after the finish of the banquet, and he and the general have fallen into reminiscence about the war. As the clock in the suite strikes one (truly one A.M., and not eleven thirty), Chester realizes that Roscoe and the others have left some time ago. He eases onto his feet from the comfortable cut-velvet upholstery of the sofa when he feels the coursing pain which makes him stagger.

"When your wife gets back from Europe, she must give you a . . . rubdown," Grant says slyly, rising to his feet.

"Oh, she's back," Chester says. "Her ship docked the day before yesterday." Perhaps he should not have mentioned it, seeing that he is the last to leave. Across the room a couple of the general's aides are looking at Chester, none too sympathetically.

"Is there anything I can do for you, my friend?" Grant asks at the door, clapping him on the back. "You are all right?"

"I should say I am," Chester replies. They may have pushed him out of the damned customhouse this year, but if Grant should head the ticket next, who knows what might happen?

"Splendid, splendid," Grant says. "Once more into the breach, eh?" This time Chester hears a hint of weariness in the rat-tat-tat chuckle. Well might the great man be weary, having arrived from Philadelphia at dawn (it was the ex-President's "triumphal return" to America after a long stay abroad). Servants meanwhile have begun buzzing around the damned suite, picking up ashtrays and glasses. The aides and a young male relative of Mrs. Grant are the only others still around, conversing quietly in a corner.

"I will see you again tomorrow, General," Chester says. The aide-de-camp holds the door open between the suite and the corridor, stony-faced.

"Yes, yes," Grant muses, smiling, waving his cigar. "Marvelous hospitality. Marvelous reception."

On the carpeted staircase down to the main lobby, Chester stops for a time until the pain is truly gone. He is worried about it, but did not mention it to Nell. Judging by her mood, hopeful tidings were about all she seemed to want. He tried to oblige. She was not to fret about the loss of the customhouse for he had a definite, absolute promise of Roscoe's support for the damned job of junior senator from New York as soon as Kernan's term expired. What did she think of that? Senator? She could be in Washington—the South! She could be near her friends and relatives in Virginia.

What she thought was that the voyage home had wearied her too much to enable her to think.

In the lobby a nodding checkroom attendant is bestirred to fetch Chester's overcoat. The hotel seems damned quiet to him. When he has the coat and is outdoors, he cannot find the doorman, who is supposed to call up a cab.

Sighing, he starts to lift his own hand to signal to a carriage standing just outside the lighted area of the porte cochere, and is relieved when it moves forward at once.

"You are a savior!" he calls. It is a driver he knows, who climbs down at once to hold the carriage door open for him.

"Home, Gin'ral?" the man asks.

"Yes, home, Frank."

Frank's face emits a ruddy glow; he is an old-timer. As the carriage starts forward, Chester reaches down beside him on the seat. Frank always keeps a lap robe there. It is a bit threadbare, but good for an extra tip.

Chester realizes he is not tired himself. The banquet and reception went damned well. It has been good to rub shoulders with real Republicans again. Being hounded by the Hayes crowd over these months has been an ugly experience. The damned irony of it is that he helped save the disputed election for Hayes in '76, when he hied himself all the way to Tallahassee, Florida, in order to get the proper votes counted. His reward is to be fired and to be charged with sharp practice.

"How be the young'uns, Gin'ral?" Frank calls down from the box. He has reined the horses to a stop before turning onto Broadway.

"Doing fine, Frank." In truth, Alan has become a disgusting rogue with nothing on his mind but riding, and the stablemaster says he is cruel to the animals besides. "And how is your eldest, Frank?"

"Ah, at Bellevue," Frank calls back. "Back on the ward."

"I'm sorry to hear that, Frank." The boy is fifteen, Chester remembers, hardly older than Alan. His lungs are weak.

Misty coronas of illumination give Broadway an eerily vacant look, compared with how it was when the crowds gathered here in the afternoon for the review that greeted General Grant. The Boys in Blue paraded a large detachment of men in uniform past the reviewing stand set up in Madison Square. Chester sat in the back row, where he could keep his foot discreetly propped up on a block of wood. The band played all the favorite songs.

In the cab now, Chester beats time to the clattering hoofbeats as he sings one of the songs: "Goodness, how delicious! Eatin' goober peas! Goodness how delicious! Eatin' goober peas! . . . Peas! Peas! Peas! Peas! . . ."

You did not hear that one very often. It was a good camp song, probably a reb song to begin with.

The carriage stops just before turning onto Lexington Avenue. "Lot o' your customhouse men out o' work now, Gin'ral," Frank calls. "I see 'em ev'ry day."

"That's right, Frank," Chester says ruefully. Some of these men were wondering where their family's next meal was coming from. What could they do but go over to Tammany when they saw that the party wouldn't support them no matter how well they had supported the party?

"The new men don' know me," Frank says.

Chester is about to offer something hopeful about General Grant and the election to come, but the carriage is rolling again and does not stop until it reaches the front of his brownstone. He is somewhat surprised to see a lamp burning in a second-floor window.

He pays Frank hurriedly and hobbles up the steps. Letting himself in with his latchkey, he does not stop to remove his overcoat but struggles up the staircase, gripping the banister with one hand, holding his derby hat with the other.

The lighted room is Nell's sewing room, where she has again been sleeping since her return from Europe. He raps on the door softly. It is opened at first a crack, then all the way. In her haggard face he has the brief unsettling hint that she might have been hoping it was someone besides himself.

She is wearing a white silk dressing gown that is new to his eyes although it appears to have been worn frequently while she was away. It is low-cut, barely covering her full bosom. The mandarin sleeves reveal her bare forearms in the lamplight. Her dark, lustrous hair hangs negligently over her bare shoulders and halfway down her back.

"I thought one of the children might be ill," he says.

"No," she says tonelessly. Although she steps away from the door, she does not invite him inside.

"I do not like to disturb you," he murmurs.

"It's all right." She has folded her arms at the waist, gazing at him neutrally. "Did you enjoy the banquet?"

"You know how those things go," he says.

"I have a headache, that's all," she remarks. "That's why I am awake."

"Bridget still keeps the powders in the pantry." He is fiddling with a loose thread on the button on his coat.

For a while she watches him, then takes up a pair of shears from her sewing basket, comes over to him, and snips it. There is the faint odor of lavender sachet in his nostrils; in the next moment, she is back across the room.

"Do you think Washington will be any better for us," he asks suddenly, "—if we get there?"

"I simply have a headache, that's all," she says, her back against a pier table where three dolls with staring eyes lean their china heads back against the wallpaper, their small hands afloat on layers of skirts and petticoats. "The crossing was very tiring. There were fogbanks . . ."

He takes a step forward. "Don't you think—"

"No, I don't," she says, the voice toneless again, half hollow as though it is coming from beyond the grave.

Disgusted, he turns sharply away. In the corridor he closes the door behind him with a bang. No one could believe this damned woman. No one could find it credible that such bitterness could develop in a sweet and talented young lady for no reason whatever but some primitive attachment to a place and a group of people, and that that damned bitterness should survive time and change and every other person's growing out of it long ago. Her father's death was no doubt a shock, and her mother's abandonment of the country must have been terrible for her too. But did she not have a husband who cherished her, and children, and caring relatives from back home as well?

He wonders again if one of the new nerve doctors might have help for Nell. How his father, the elder, would scoff at such an idea. So much the better. It was a new age. His father read much, but believed nothing. He was a stubbornly primitive man, in the last damned analysis.

Chester flings his overcoat onto the neatly-turned-down quilt of his cold bed.

10

14TH STREET

As Booth strides up Delmonico's service ramp after work, he buttons up his light topcoat. It is late at night and there is a chill in the air. He will walk, as is his custom, the few blocks back to his rooms.

Rows of empty wheat flour barrels have been left near the building to be picked up by the carters at first light. As he steps off the curbstone, he notices a parked carriage suddenly start up from out of a darkened area down the street. He squints; fast-moving clouds filter the light of a gibbous moon. No one else is on the street. He hurries his crossing as he realizes that the carriage is picking up speed. He hears the crack of a whip.

Startled, he recognizes he will never make it to the opposite curb, for the driver has reined his horses in that very direction. Not Hercules himself could stop them! Feeling helpless but primed for action, Booth feints a move toward the far curb, then with desperate energy reverses his field to try to get back to the spot where he stepped off. Halfway there, his foot slips on a wet paving stone. He stumbles and starts to reel, his cane clattering away from him. Simultaneously comes the hurtling streak of the team of horses and the screaming carriage behind. A glancing impact from the traces . . . he expels a grunt of shock and dismay! But spins and lands just wide of the lethal wheels in a clump against the steep curb.

Gasping for breath, he hears the carriage careen past him in full flight toward Fifth Avenue. His left shoulder has borne the brunt of his fall. Sitting in the gutter, he leans his right elbow on the curbstone, watching the driver veer the team sharply onto Fifth Avenue. In another few seconds they are out of sight, although he can still hear the echo of the hoofbeats.

Pain now floods his left kneecap, and he has sudden sharp memories of lying in the cold reeking swamps of southern Maryland, bearing that same pain. For dizzying seconds he fantasizes that he is waiting for daybreak, or waiting for nightfall, whichever is needful at the moment, in order to resume the agonizing journey south.

He hears voices. Two men are hurrying up the street toward him. They are dressed like gentlemen and seem solicitous. He realizes they are probably coming from one of the bawdy houses in the neighborhood, and are not policemen, who might conceivably cause him trouble.

"I say, were you struck?" the one calls.

"Were you struck?" echoes the other.

Comic-opera Britishers, they stare at him, faces swimming in and out of his vision. He does not want to be the center of an uproar.

"No harm done," he says abruptly. They help him struggle to his feet; his shoulder seems all right. Tweedledum hands him his cane, Tweedledee his hat. He thanks them. Two more gentlemen have been alerted and are crossing the street. Booth spots a lone man on horseback, probably of the constabulary, heading toward them from Fifth.

"That bloody jehu should be hanged as a homicidal maniac!" one of the Britishers declares. By that time Booth has staggered down the dark ramp and has let himself back into Delmonico's cellar. None of his rescuers seem to know how he has disappeared so quickly.

Thirty minutes later he opens the door from the cellar and listens at the crack to see if his rescuers have dispersed. The street seems silent although he can hear the rumble of traffic from a block away. He emerges, dressed as a laborer, wearing a narrow-billed cap, a gray ribbed jersey, and heavy wool trousers, the bottoms of which are tucked into a pair of scuffed boots. He has put lifts into each of the boots to make himself look taller. Although he limps from the pain in his knee, his head has cleared, and he believes he can get back safely to his rooms in the new garb.

But as he pauses on the sidewalk he again sees a parked carriage not far from where he saw the other one. His nostrils catch the aroma of fresh horse droppings. Then footsteps. Almost before he can draw a breath, a lowering driver—well over six feet tall and holding one hand tautly in the right pocket of his coat—comes rapidly toward him on foot.

Instinctively he grabs for one of the empty wheat flour barrels, as though to use it as a shield. But the driver stops, as though in puzzlement; he is looking toward the gutter. And Booth, remembering that he is a laborer, picks up the barrel and loudly rolls it down the ramp toward Delmonico's cellar as though it is the most natural work in the world to be doing at three o'clock in the morning. In nonchalant rhythm he heaves a second barrel down after the first. The noise might serve him, if the performance does not.

"Hey!" the driver demands of him. "Did y' see the accident?" His right arm quivers nervously.

Booth has no doubt there is a concealed weapon in the man's pocket. He pauses and wipes his forehead on the sleeve of his jersey. "Aye," he says. He looks the driver right in the eye.

"Was the man all right then?" the driver asks.

"The police wagon come and took him to the morgue," says Booth crisply.

The driver lets out a low whistle. "Was he dead then?"

"That's for them to say at the morgue, ain't it now?" Booth hurls one more barrel down the ramp, causing the driver a little uneasiness. The man looks anxiously up and down the street. A private carriage is passing, pulled by two matched bays.

"Did they see who hit him?" the driver cannot help asking.

"Some jehu, I guess," says Booth.

It is enough. Hurrying back to his rig, the man leaps up onto the box with the agility of an athlete. Booth stands stock-still and examines the rig in the moonlight as it rolls past him. One of the horses is a paint.

He waits until the carriage is out of sight, then undertakes, with great caution, to limp home.

The next morning, before he is to pay his visit to the morgue, he decides to write a letter. Picking his way through the heavy pieces of mahogany furniture that crowd bedroom and sitting room, he sits down in his underwear and pens a short letter to his brother, Edwin, now on tour in Cincinnati.

He has concluded that either Edwin, or Chester Arthur, or Thurlow Weed is responsible for the attempt on his life. To take care of the first of these possibilities, he snaps open the leaden lid of the inkwell on his dressing table, and without date or salutation begins writing:

Personal and Confidential—

I warn you—call off your agents; if there is any further attempt on my person, I will present myself at once to Mother and to Rose, and accuse you of assaulting me. You can well imagine the shock of my sudden reappearance to them as well as the news of how you are bearing yourself toward me.

He signs the note with a flourish, "Richmond," which was the first role he took as an actor and the first city in which he won success. He addresses the missive in care of the stage manager at the theater in which Edwin is to open the following night in Cincinnati.

That done, he pulls his makeup box toward him and begins the daily routine of becoming Götz Dörfer. Watching his face in the mirror, he grays his temples with a preparation he has devised, then inserts cork rolls inside his cheeks to make his profile rounder and more rubicund. He finally fills out his eyebrows with delicately preserved natural hair that matches his own. Most of the time he adds nothing more. But this morning he applies a nearly invisible compound, also self-created, in order to cover the bruises he suffered the night before.

When he finishes, he tries on the boots again, just for a look-see, to discover how many inches in height his cunning lift devices give him. He has been playing with the idea of making himself an exact twin to a certain Austrian nobleman—distant cousin to the Hapsburgs—who has recently dined at Delmonico's. While decanting wine, Booth has overheard the young count von Kaufnicht's plan to try to flush game in both South America and (incredibly) Australia over the next two years. He sees himself during this period escorting Nell—in the role perhaps of the bachelor count's new bride (Duchess Elinora of York?)—to some of the better watering places on the Continent. Given their ample means, such a progress would be more civilized than if they traveled as arriviste Americans; besides, he could keep his Dörfer accent as the count. He has become fond of it.

Dressed for the street, he takes the precaution of leaving his rooming house by the back entrance, in the process barely eluding his landlady, who is dumping out the water collected overnight in a chipped dishpan under the icebox.

On the horsecar he hands the conductor his nickel fare, experiencing the first twinge of the day in his knee as he mounts the step. Since all the seats are occupied, he holds on to a pole with one hand and props himself with the point of his umbrella against the floor. Across the aisle sits an actress he once knew, and judging by her plain cotton frock and straw hat he guesses that she is now working as a domestic. But then she was never a good actress, incorrigibly insensitive to what was really happening on the stage.

In New York he often sees people he knows. They look right through him. The other night at Delmonico's, General Arthur looked through him. Booth does not favor the general as the one responsible for the previous night's attack. But he is meeting Nell later and will question her closely.

Getting off the streetcar on 26th Street, he has to push his way through a gang of urchins who are begging for pennies in a rude and mocking way. They have thick Irish brogues.

"Sir, ye give alms and Our Lady'll bless ye."

He eludes them, whistling a tune. The river carries a sharp smell from the docks. The wind is blowing directly toward him. Ahead is the huge, gray stone building that is the city's chief hospital. On the lowest door in front is a single word in gilt letters: MORGUE.

He has stopped here before and knows the routine, but he does not feel depressed about it this morning. He has a sense of quest again, of purpose. The toot of the tugboats in the river seems musical to him, and the gathering rumble of cart traffic that is common near the docks offers counterpoint.

Inside the reception area of the morgue, just opened for the day, Booth pauses to survey the crowd. Among the visitors emerging from the Dead Room are a neatly dressed middle-aged woman and a boy about ten, who holds his mother's hand because he keeps his eyes tightly closed. She now commands him to open his eyes; by the relieved expression on her face Booth concludes she has found no one of her acquaintance within.

"My friend is missing," Booth says to the man on duty. "May I step inside and look for him?"

The attendant waves him on, then lowers his spectacles to return to the newspaper he is reading. Two idlers are talking and smoking cigars over a spittoon next to the partition that leads into the Dead Room. Booth tries to decide if they are as natural as they seem, for surely some agent of whatever devil it was who set the horses on him must turn up here this morning to make sure the job was done.

Inside the Dead Room the odor of formaldehyde is overpowering. A young morgue worker, hardly more than nineteen or twenty, is hanging up the clothing that has been removed from the cadaver nearest to the entrance. The mottled torso, that of a middle-aged male, is exposed to just below the navel, up to which point a sheet has been carelessly tossed to keep the genital area covered. The young attendant, a short lad with dark hair and deep-set blue eyes, gives Booth a pleasant, open smile, like a salesman in a haberdashery.

Booth considers the corpse. A thin shower of water plays on the deceased's freckled forehead and then trickles down through his sparse hair into a trough that runs the length of the wall. In this manner the features are kept recognizable for a decent time.

On a slab against the opposite wall is the cadaver of a young woman covered by a sheet to her chin. Her blond head, under the shower, has been tilted backward very sharply for some reason. By and by, Booth calculates, his Nell will need such a corpse, preferably one with darker complexion and hair than this one.

Drowning has been the fate of the present victim, judging by the stretched and water-soaked garments hanging on the hook behind her. Probably the body was recovered promptly, since the flesh visible to him is not bloated.

He speaks to the attendant.

"I am looking for my brother . . . missing since last night. He looks very much like me."

"None but these two since midnight, sir," the lad replies at once.

The frank eyes face him so candidly that Booth is impressed. The lad wears a starched smock that reaches nearly to his ankles. He does not appear to possess that undernourished dullness of mind so common in the less fortunate classes.

Booth says, "Some other kin may have been in here looking for him too. Would you perhaps—"

"Does your brother also wear greasepaint on his face, sir?" the attendant asks.

"I beg your pardon?"

"Since your brother resembles you, I wondered if he also wore greasepaint on his face, as does yourself. Like an actor does?"

"No. No greasepaint," Booth says, disconcerted. He is astonished that anyone should notice cosmetics on his face.

"No offense, sir," the young man says quickly. He comments that many of the victims of sudden death expire while wearing heavy greasepaint.

"Indeed?" Booth says. "I'm not an actor."

"No, sir."

"But I don't take offense." Quickly Booth smiles. "Perhaps you can do me a service. I'll give you a dollar if you keep an eye out for anyone who comes here seeking a dead man who looks like me. If you are able to find out who these people are and where they live, I will give you two dollars more. I am anxious to get in touch with . . . with these relatives." He produces a silver dollar from his watch pocket and gives it to the boy. "Your name would be?"

"Raymond, sir." He takes the silver dollar impassively. "Thank'ee, sir."

"You understand?"

Raymond nods. He leads Booth to a narrow table under a skylight, on which lie some squarish cardboard tags, some wax crayons, and a torn-covered copy of Horatio Alger's *Ragged Dick,* which the boy has evidently been reading.

"If you give me your address, sir," Raymond says, holding one of the crayons, "I'll inform you of the—"

"No, I'll call on you," Booth says. "I see you read and write. Bravo. I'll call here in a day or two to see if you've learned anything. In the meantime you must not let them know I am looking for them. Ask them how they can be reached, tell them you've heard that such a person was found dead near—well, near Delmonico's—and that the cadaver has been delayed, but that it is 'on the way.' Say you will notify them when it appears."

The frank eyes register no surprise. "I'll do it, sir." In Horatio Alger's world, such things happened.

Booth claps the young man on the shoulder and walks out quickly —an exit he has seen his brother do in *Caesar*.

Outside in the anteroom he makes the same proposition to the older attendant, the one reading the newspaper. But here he surrenders the silver dollar reluctantly: the man is as stupid as the boy is clever.

A third person has meanwhile joined the two derby-hatted loafers at the spittoon. Booth sizes them up either as City Hall or as good-for-nothings supported by wives working at the nearby shirtwaist factory. Seeing three of them for some reason makes him less suspicious.

Even Nell's mood does not undermine him. He can read the stiff anger in her back as he arrives just a little tardy for their rendezvous. Today it is in the fabrics and upholstery department of Lord and Taylor. Normally on these occasions he pretends an accidental encounter with her: while tipping his hat, he whispers in her ear to tell her where he will bring up the cab.

With the floorwalker some distance away and the clerk waiting on someone else, he sidles up directly to her as she stares blindly at fabric samples. "Is your husband on to us?" he asks half playfully, in a voice of normal volume.

Startled, her eyes register apprehension, then distrust and anger, and then barely concealed pleasure that he is there at last. Anger surges again at the end. "You ah late," she hisses.

"Come, give me a smile," he says lightly.

She scowls, furious that he should be playing with her in so compromising a location. Two red spots appear in her cheeks. Since the floorwalker is now looking in their direction, Booth whispers, "The Broadway entrance in ten minutes," and moves away at once. When a woman of obvious means shows annoyance, the man involved can be seized as a masher within seconds. Sometimes before questions are asked.

Back on the street he finds a deluxe cab and waits inside it for her to emerge. "The lady in the sable-trimmed jacket," he says to the driver. He has already shut the cloth curtains, and as soon as the horses have pulled up and she is safely inside, he locks her in an embrace designed to dispel all her doubts. She returns his passionate kiss as the carriage leaps forward; then she pulls away.

"This won't do anymore," she declares suddenly. Her face is pale. "I can't abide it."

"I hoped you'd like it."

She keeps her face turned from him. "Chester talks of Washington all the time. How can I go on pretending? I'm not goin' to Washington with him . . . am I?"

"You know you're not."

She heaves a sigh. "Then why can't we go abroad at once?"

Booth drums his finger on his knee. His voice, however, is calm and rational. "We are making these preparations for the sake of your husband's career as much as for your own happiness. We are proceeding with . . . with proper caution. You are continuing to be cautious, are you not?"

"What do you see there?" she asks him, disturbed to observe his fingers parting the curtains in order to peer out at the Broadway traffic.

"You are sure that he has not had you followed, that he still suspects nothing?" Booth asks.

"He would say if he suspected!" she cries. "What is the trouble?"

As the carriage stops, preparatory to turning north on Fifth—the route he has asked the driver to take—he continues to hold her hand, considering whether he should hold his tongue, too, and say nothing. Or must she face up to it that she has no ordinary lover?

When the wheels begin moving again, he says, "Someone was hired to try to run me down with a carriage last night as I left Delmonico's. Only by the merest fortune was I able to save myself. I was rolled into the gutter, and it took further guile when the driver came back to see if he had done the job properly."

She has drawn her hand away from his, and looks at him with a kind of disbelief.

"Never mind it," he says. "I doubt that your husband is involved, and they will not find me so easy to surprise again."

Suddenly, her body shivers in a large, racking spasm. She begins sobbing as violently as though she were gripped by nausea. He is shaken for a moment as he watches her bend forward from the stomach, clutching and unclutching her hands.

"Why are you weeping?"

"I am frightened. . . . I love you."

She has a strange way of crying. "Boo-hoo-hoo-hoo! Boo-hoo-hoo-hoo!" is the sound torn from her throat. He listens to its unvaried rhythm. "Boo-hoo-hoo-hoo! Boo-hoo-hoo-hoo! Boo-hoo-hoo-hoo!"

He cannot help it. He bursts out laughing. In Boston once, an ingenue they were rehearsing was supposed to cry poignantly when her lover abandoned her. All the girl could manage, shrill and tearless, was "Boo-hoo-hoo-hoo! Boo-hoo-hoo-hoo!" The entire company, one after the other, dissolved in helpless laughter, and the poor girl began to cry in earnest.

Not Nell. The sobs catch in her throat. Hearing his laughter, seeing it, from somewhere she finds control. Her knuckles go white. She gives him a murderous look.

"I'll never cry over you again, Wilkes Booth!"

"I advise you not to," he says, still laughing. "Iron is what is needed, not tears."

He also hopes that she will not too often shout his name to the world. But if she does, so be it. He turns his palms up to see if she will accept the gesture as apology.

11

The Hoffman House

The passage of forty-eight hours finds Booth no closer to his quarry, and more than a little discouraged. Having hoped to be spending his time seeking the swiftest means of translating himself and his lady to the land where they would be beyond fear, his cunning must instead be employed in learning who is out to kill him.

To lift up his spirits he has taken refuge in the elegant bar of the Hoffman House. He drinks with one foot up on the brass rail, unabashedly Götz Dörfer in his dress and appearance. Although for reasons of strategy and prudence he has not gone in to work at Delmonico's since the night of the attempt on his life, he knows that sooner or later he will be recognized as Dörfer, perhaps in this very bar. The word will reach his would-be murderers that they have not killed him after all.

Drinking rum straight—not good for him—he ponders the ignominy of having failed as a secret operative. It reminds him of the fumble-fumble of so much of what he and his brave cadre attempted during the war. Divinity may shroud his own person, and destiny still have its special role for him to play; but he cannot ignore the fact that his disciples have seldom been as lucky as he.

This morning it has been particularly disconcerting to have returned to the morgue and to find that the lad Raymond no longer worked there. In terms of faith, he has invested much more than a dollar in the young man; he has seen unlimited promise in Raymond.

The aged Charon to whom Booth gave the other dollar was still manning the outside desk, but he reported nothing that would help Booth. He turned sly when asked about Raymond.

"Quit," the old man says, baring his teeth in a grin. "They jes' tol' me he quit."

"You don't know where he lives?" Booth asks. "Or perhaps his surname?"

The man shakes his head. "A little half-pint like that; what's he need two names for?" The hideous smile flashes again.

Booth turns away, worried that Raymond might have been done in by the very detective work that Booth assigned him. He should not like to think of Raymond lying on one of the stone slabs in his own morgue after being fished from the river, a thought nearly as shattering as having his own naked remains spread on a table with his face the target of a stream of water from above, the way a hayseed gets it in a rude farce.

Leaving the morgue in some distress, he notes that the spittoon around which the City Hall loafers gathered is no longer there. A heavy walnut piece of furniture with a mirror and high hooks has been installed in its place. Even that troubles him.

On his third rum at the Hoffman House, still savoring loneliness and despondency, he suddenly hears in the rumble of conversations around him the word "Booth."

The interlocutor, Booth presently notices, is a gentleman engaged in conversation with two other men—probably all are stockbrokers—

near *The Three Graces,* a large spttlighted study of nude figures recently acquired from France. The gentleman holding forth can next be heard to say "Edwin Booth." Dramatically he points his finger and intones in a resonant voice, "Arrest that man!"

Startled, the eavesdropper perceives that the stockbroker is passing on a newspaper account of an event that seems to have taken place "in Chicago." Booth plunks down his glass, tosses some coins after it, and rushes out to find a late edition of the *Herald.*

Halfway across Broadway he locates a newsboy, who sells him one. Presently, standing in an arched colonnade, he locates the story: Edwin Booth has been shot at while performing in *Richard II* at Mc-Vicker's Theater in Chicago. The two shots missed only because Edwin by chance altered his usual procedure in the dungeon scene and thus, by good fortune, avoided the line of fire.

Breathing hard, Wilkes Booth reads that "the bullets sang past him," but "the quick-thinking actor, foremost American thespian of his time," moved to the apron of the stage, and while pointing to the miscreant in the audience, cried out, "Arrest that man!" The suspect was overpowered before he could escape, being a young man from St. Louis with the name of Gray, who then gave the police several garbled reasons for his attempt on the actor's life. One of them was that Edwin Booth spoke the young man's Christian name—Mark—sneeringly in a certain speech in the play: "Mark where she stands."

With anguish, Wilkes realizes that in spite of the apparently demented character of the assailant, Edwin might well fear that the man was hired. He will think I am behind it! Wilkes exclaims, recalling the perfervid threats contained in the letter that he sent to Edwin in Cincinnati. He looks about anxiously, trying to remember where the nearest Western Union office is. He hurries in the direction of Union Square.

The low-angling sun, along with the rum he has ingested, makes him faintly hysterical. He can no longer believe that his dear brother could have had anything to do with the attempt on his own life. How could he have been so stupid as to have written that accusing letter? If Edwin had died on the stage, what would have been left of the Booth honor? Edwin ennobled the family escutcheon.

At the telegraph office the only message that seems possible is "I am innocent," signed Richmond. Scrawling it on one of the blanks provided, he rushes to stand in a line that has formed in front of the receiving clerk. He has time to look at the newspaper story again. "A kind of second sight," they write, appears to have saved Edwin Booth.

They have recognized it, then: divine protection! Of course they make it seem like a gift from the devil when they remind their readers of the "legends" of "the mad Booths of Maryland!" On page two they print again the poisonous illustrated graphic of "The Crime of the Century, the Martyrdom of Lincoln"—the five-person panoply in the high box and the single startled actor, with head lifted and arms thrown back, on the boards below.

Wilkes crushes the newspaper in his grip. Never would it change! Never would that deed be recorded as an act of war—the Union commander struck down by a Confederate privateer. *In time of war,* by God: Joe Johnston was fighting on!

Someday, he senses, he is going to have to locate the missing pages of his diary himself. Edwin, we are not mad!

"Is this your message, Mr. Richmond?" the clerk asks as Booth reaches the head of the line. "Ten words come at the same rate as three." Behind him vibrate the chirping telegraph keys.

"Yes, yes." Booth grabs back the blank. The trained fool! "Very well, ten words it shall be." *Edwin, we are not mad,* he adds. *Tell me.* He flings a silver dollar down on the varnished counter and does not wait for change.

Taking up his duties at Delmonico's again, Booth pours the wine with a new diffidence. When the patrons he is serving watch him with any special attention, he stares back with stoical defiance as though they are vermin. Meanwhile, he declines to converse with his fellow employees, and spends extended interludes in the special wine closet to which he has the only key. In most ways his behavior gains him new respect as a sommelier.

But at last a letter arrives from Chicago, written on hotel stationery, which he anxiously reads in a corner of the kitchen where glowing coals radiate the heat that braises half a dozen fat game hens.

Chicago
April 24

I hardly know any longer whether the greeting in this letter should be "my friend" or "my enemy." Shall I hurl thunderbolts at your head in reprisal for those you flung at me so recently? Shall we behave like the coxcombs in The Roses?

My heart tells me no, that I should believe your telegram, no matter how characteristic the Mark Gray attack on me is of your own "use."

of the theater. I know too well how you mesmerized other poor wretches into your delusions and how they wound up on the scaffold as a result. Mark Gray seems a pure lunatic, but I also know your ability to captivate.

As to what you imagine that I have been responsible for against your person, I cannot guess, I made no attempt on your life, either by myself, or through agents. I have acted the roles of murderers on the stage, my brother, but I know the difference between make-believe in the theater and the real thing.

Just the same, the ironic result of your paranoiac letter to me was that I was acutely alerted to possible danger to myself. I cannot otherwise explain the intuitive action I took on the stage at the crucial moment, which turned out to have saved my life.

But I feel no gratitude toward you for the tension I have been under, and will remain under, day after day. My advice to you is to go abroad at once. Our sister Asia is living in England and will help you there.

In the meantime, as you "warned" me, so must I warn you. If I learn of any new violent act, committed by you or your agents on anyone, I shall expose you, accuse you, and array the rest of our family to join me in the indictment. No matter what it costs us, we will see to it that you are stopped by being brought to justice.

I pledge to continue this vigilance to my dying day.

For both our sakes, burn this letter.

Ecstatic, Wilkes shoves Edwin's letter into the burning coals of the roasting pit. He has saved his brother's life; he now understands destiny's purpose in sending that carriage hurtling down upon him. Except for that, he would never have written the letter that enabled Edwin to protect himself. Providence watched out for the Booths.

"*Zut!*" says the French chef angrily, seeing the flag of dark smoke rise from the burning letter to pollute his pretty guinea hens.

Just for spite, Booth tosses the envelope in too. "*Scheisskopf,*" he murmurs under his breath.

Walking off, he wishes he could tell Nell about this excellent omen. She does not believe that divinity hedges him. She imagines that since love and transcendence seem to be theirs for the taking, they must move at once, or suffer the consequences.

Nay, time but seasoned love. He must try to get across to her that the leap which the actor takes on the stage is nothing to the leap of faith which the member of the audience must take. That *she* must take. Without that leap, love and transcendence dissolve into air.

Sometime later, after Delmonico's last patrons have departed for the night, Booth makes his way down the steps to his private alcove to prepare himself for his return to his rooms. One of the waiters calls "Good night" to him.

"Sleep well," Booth says. It is the waiter who once called him Montresor, as a joke, after the main character in Poe's story "The Cask of Amontillado." "What do you do down there in the dark, Montresor?" the waiter jibed. "Wall up your enemies?"

They laugh. The story—about revenge on a tyrant—has always been one of Booth's favorites. As a boy he was once presented to Poe by his father Junius in a Baltimore saloon. Much later—with Poe deceased—he trimmed his moustache like Poe's and carried a cane very like the author's. People remarked on the resemblance.

This night he finds his way by means of the flickering jets of gas-lights through the damp aisles of the cellar, flanked on either side by squatting casks raised well off the level of the floor. Unlocking the closet door, he lights a kerosene lamp and hangs it on a hook before closing the door and locking it behind him.

Surveying the several sets of formal clothes hanging there—all from his old wardrobe trunk—along with the pairs of boots, each with different-size risers inside, he is half tempted to eschew it all and dare the streets as plain Götz Dörfer once again, naked to his enemies. As things stand, in spite of his many disguises, he is only putting off the crisis anyway. If Weed's men—and he is beginning to feel it must be Weed—are out there waiting, sooner or later they must penetrate his mask.

Still, he cannot deny himself the pleasure of going home at least one night as Count Karl von Kaufnicht. He has brushed up his finest tweeds for the occasion. Moreover, the count wears riding boots—containing concealed risers that add four whole inches to their wearer's height—quite the most that Booth has attempted, although he knows from practice that he will appear to move with ease.

He hurries into the tweeds, set off by a Tyrolean hat and a Burberry hunting cape. Theoretically, he can imagine the count in opera-wear with a full-length formal cape. When dressing at home in the family Schloss in Bavaria, the count will have developed a technique with the right drape of the cape so as to keep it clear of the mud common to the roads there in early springtime. *So much rain this season, my princess,* he will say. And swish the cape.

Extinguishing the kerosene lamp and relocking the wine closet, Booth decides on the 14th Street exit, the same one he employed on the night he was struck by the carriage and had to undergo the epilogue as sidewalk stevedore, hurling barrels about like a lunatic. Recalling the latter part of that episode with some glee, he actually now feels less at ease on the street as a nobleman than as a laborer. But the presence of well-dressed gentlemen such as himself in the after-midnight hours is not at all unusual here: witness the attendance on him of the two Englishmen the other night.

Waiting on the curb, he sees nothing remarkable. Two carriages pass while he is standing there, but neither of them is threatening. Much further up 14th, very near Fifth Avenue, he sees a group of three, one of whom is apparently a woman. On the opposite side of the street, strolling rather slowly, is a young lad, short of stature. He is dressed neatly in rather tight-fitting clothes.

Booth hesitates, then decides to cross the street and go along in the same direction the young lad is walking. He reaches the opposite curb without incident and moves easily through the shadows at his unaccustomed height. The lad looks familiar, and Booth quickens his step in order to catch up with him.

12

A. T. STEWART AND COMPANY

In the meantime, however, Nell has reached the end of her tether. While Booth is changing costumes in the blind vaults of the wine cellar, she is staring sleeplessly at the figured wallpaper of her sewing room. She cannot continue leading the double life; she knows it now. Before her trip to France with Wilkes, Chester seemed barely interested in the life she led during the daytime. Now that she is back, he is less tolerant of her headaches and her indifference. While the move to Washington may belong to the future, a move to Cooperstown for the summer—with first a medical visit to Philadelphia—is to take place at once. On this family vacation, the "damned situation," as Chester calls it, will be looked into. Without the customhouse to occupy him anymore, Chester is concerned with questions about his marriage and household. He is soul-searching.

She has decided she must give Wilkes up. To be painfully accurate, he has perhaps given *her* up. By refusing to resolve the situation, he has made her life impossible. She wonders that she could have believed the tale of dying and being reborn again abroad. How could she be dead to the rest of society and yet alive to her own children? Because he worked on her sympathies, he could make her believe almost anything he told her.

Their rendezvous in the Ladies' Gloves department of A. T. Stewart and Company she has determined will be their final one. Wilkes will not be surprised at her decision, she believes; he has had warnings. Her one endeavor will be to try to persuade him to be gone from New York by the end of the summer, when she and Chester and Alan and Nellie return, so that she will never have to see him again.

On this warm afternoon, however, chosen by her for their last meeting, she is momentarily taken aback to find that he has arrived in the store ahead of her. While she moves into Ladies' Gloves, he is standing three aisles away, his back to her, in Yankee Notions. Moreover, he is in large expostulation, while pointing his cane in the direction of the displayed goods.

"The bootjack? The doorstop?" the saleswoman is asking while Booth continues to wave his stick insolently.

"These ah too heavy," Nell says to the clerk waiting on her.

"More sheer, madam?"

"Of course. For the season."

Nell spreads her fan and stirs the air under her chin while the salesman retires to the stockroom. She has always disliked Stewart's. The little bells keep ringing like a barnful of trolley cars and the floorwalkers behave with near rudeness, unlike the way she is treated at Lord and Taylor's or McCreery's.

Wilkes is truly exasperating her. The saleswoman is wrapping up a package for him. With all the playacting he does, she wonders sometimes if he really did shoot Lincoln. Lincoln seemed to be dead all right; everyone said so. But in a playhouse, with a man like Wilkes around, who could say for sure what really happened?

On an impulse she sweeps to her feet. The salesman has just reappeared with another gross of white gloves, but she shakes him off impatiently. Every step she takes down the aisle toward Booth, she fans herself.

As she passes him, even as he is turning around, she gives no sign of recognition although he tips his hat gallantly. He has no trouble keeping in step with her as she forges toward the stairway.

"Are you in a hurry today?" he asks.

"We ah off to Cooperstown for the summer," she says without looking at him. "We ah staying with mah husband's relatives there."

"Leaving this afternoon?" Booth asks, matching her stride for stride.

"We are calling in Philadelphia first," Nell says icily. "Mah husband requires that I see Dr. Mitchell, the nerve specialist there."

"Is something wrong with your nerve?"

She has stopped at the head of the staircase that leads down three flights to the main floor; her large eyes narrow as she focuses on him. "I will talk to you for the last time, eithuh here or in the carriage. Which shall it be?"

"Your nerve is indeed bad today."

Annoyed, she turns from him and starts down the steps. "I can't stand this playacting anymore." With one hand, she elevates the hem of her skirt as she descends gingerly. A gentleman on his way up tips his hat; most of the lady customers use the lift.

Booth follows her down, a few steps behind. She feels conspicuous on the staircase. When they reach the main floor, she starts to bolt toward the Broadway entrance when her arm is gripped from behind. They are in the middle of everything, observed by floorwalkers, clerks, other customers.

"Nell," he whispers. "This way."

"No." She tries shaking off his arm, barely able to maintain her dignity, compose her expression.

Now he thrusts the package toward her. "Take this." It is the package from Yankee Notions. Dimly, she senses that to accept the package is to make their discourse seem more normal. She is not sure why that should be so.

"I have a carriage, Nell," he says. "This way."

Confused, clutching the brown-paper package along with her fan, she lets him guide her by the arm to the Fourth Street entrance. How vulgar it must seem to people watching: arguing in public, touching, now about to enter a carriage together! Only the awkward package that she carries—bootjack? doorstop?—gives her any vestige of being about the proper business of the establishment.

Outside, he has her wait beside the entrance while he hails a cab. With red spots burning in her cheeks, she hopes only that he will find one quickly before her embarrassment becomes intolerable.

In the next minute, however, her embarrassment turns to shock and terror. Booth is in trouble. As he moves to hail the carriage that has been standing alone in the parking area provided nearby—with a constant stream of pedestrians flowing between her and him—she notices that the carriage, as it has started up and stopped again beside him, is occupied. In fact, what grabs at her heart is a sudden movement of the curtains in the cab window just as Booth jumps onto the step, preparatory to opening the door and going inside. She sees the shadow of a face.

As her lover innocently reaches for the door handle and opens it, Nell screams.

At once, in events that elapse in seconds, arms reach from inside the carriage and clutch at Booth as though to drag him roughly off his feet and make him a prisoner to be abducted. But simultaneously, alerted either by Nell's scream or by his own sharp instincts, he thrashes at the villains with his cane, and in the same amazing movement, Nell sees the flash of a blade spring from the tip of his cane in some magical way. Dragged toward the carriage by a viselike grip on his left arm, Booth yet resists by slashing the assailant with the cane held in his right.

At this point the driver suddenly whips the horses forward, and as the carriage springs to life, Nell screams again and now hears other people shouting too. As Booth tumbles backward onto the paving stones, spun by the momentum of the moving carriage, she lifts the hem of her skirt and hurries toward him, still carrying her package. The carriage wheels have barely missed crushing him.

She is the first to reach him. The carriage noise, the angry hooves, still frighten her, but even with her heart pounding rapidly, she knows she must not cry out his name. To her shock, the cane, from which the concealed blade emerged, lies by his side, its tip agleam on the paving stones. Sensing at once that she must hide this weapon from onlookers lest it identify him as no ordinary man, she stoops down next to him so that her skirt covers the cane from the sight of those who are hurrying toward them.

"Have no . . . fear," he gasps to her bravely. She sees a horribly discolored mark on his forehead. "Have no fear."

She is touching his arms and running her hand over his brow. "Oh, don't speak. . . . I will take care of you!"

Running up from the direction of Broadway, the man on the beat calls to them, his nightstick in his hand. "Here now!" His whistle is held in his other hand, but as others surround Nell and Booth, Booth rises quickly to a sitting position.

"Ruffians in the carriage tried to rob this man!" a woman in the street declares to the policeman, who pushes his way through the crowd.

"I seen 'em," a newsboy says. "There 'uz two or three o' them in the carriage."

Nell has spent the time forcing the point of the blade back into the shaft of the sword-cane by pressing it against an irregular paving block. She is surprised at the clever way she accomplishes this under the drape of her skirt while everyone is looking at Wilkes or the man on the beat.

"Who seen the carriage?" the latter asks. "Which way did it go?"

"That way! That way!" the people call, pointing.

Booth has started to get to his feet. "No, I think it went that way," he says, misdirecting the pursuit. "But don't trouble yourself please, since I am not injured and have an appointment."

"Will you tell me what they done to you, sir?" the man on the beat repeats. He is a handsome redheaded Irishman who still has his whistle at the ready.

"Really," Booth shrugs. "Perhaps it was a mistake."

"Oh, they woulda tried to rob ye, sir," the woman assures him. "They'da drug you inside, and before you'da knowed it, throwed you out stripped of your money and valuables . . . all in broad daylight."

"I have the gentleman's cane," Nell declares suddenly. She is surprised to have restored it to its normal appearance, but now wants to help Booth get away.

"Why, it's Mrs. General Arthur. Be ye not?" the man on the beat says in delight and astonishment.

"I just wished to be sure the gentleman was all right."

"It's Mrs. General Arthur," the man on the beat now declares to the crowd, who show no signs of dispersing. She is not surprised to be recognized. After Chester's dismissal, many of his old customhouse faithful had to creep off to Tammany, where some wound up in the city police department.

"Allow me," Booth now says, picking up Nell's package and her fan. "May I find a cab for the lady? I've interrupted your business too long, ma'am."

In some confusion, Nell thanks him. Certain bystanders assist Booth in finding a cab for the lady; after all, the malefactors are out of sight.

But even as the new carriage is hailed up—and its interior examined lest it contain a fresh gang of robbers—a woman ventures a loud question to Nell.

"Be your husband back at the customhouse now, Mrs. Arthur?"

"No, no," others in the crowd murmur at the woman who has had the bad grace to ask.

Booth holds the door of the carriage open and bows Nell inside. Still holding her package, she finds herself suddenly disconsolate that he is not able to join her, and looks longingly at him for a sign that he will arrange a new meeting between them before she must leave for Philadelphia and Cooperstown. Instead he simply waves his cane at her, and the others in the crowd wave their hands as though she were some kind of royalty. Her heart is breaking at the thought of the constant danger he is in, and the disagreeable way she has expressed her doubts of him.

Following the scene outside Stewart's, Booth returns immediately to his rooms, having advised the young policeman that men of affairs, such as himself, did not have time to press charges in cases where life or limb was not forfeit. "A queer *modus operandi* nonetheless," the policeman remarks, taking the rare opportunity to use his seminary Latin.

Booth does not mind the bruises he has taken in the fall. Delighted with himself that he has not lost his old acrobatic skills, he ascends the steps of his rooming house, swinging his cane in a complete arc. In the upper hallway he nods pleasantly to a fellow roomer, who is returning from the toilet. His own rooms are at the front of the house, where the ventilation and the lighting are the best.

As he enters his own room, he is not surprised to see his new acquaintance, Raymond, sprawled out on the rug in a patch of sunlight, reading a book belonging to Booth.

Raymond looks up at once. "Now, sir," he asks with exuberance in his voice, "was the lady impressed?"

"Indeed she was," Booth says, tossing down the cane and pulling off his gloves. "Your timing was exemplary. I trust you paid the driver enough: he was well cast."

"I give him what you told me, sir."

"One says 'gave,' not 'give,' there, Raymond—if one would seem educated." But he smiles benevolently at the lad; in truth, he would prefer Raymond sit on the furniture while reading instead of lying on the floor like a seven-year-old.

"But your technique is marvelous!" Booth continues. "I swear it looked as though half a dozen arms were coming out of the carriage, all pulling at me—"

"You fell very nice, sir," Raymond says, and laughs to recall it, a rather harsh laugh, which he cuts off as though it might be another faux pas on his part. He assumes an earnest, well-meaning expression.

"Dammit, Raymond, sit down in a chair," Booth says. "Join me in a glass of wine."

An uncertain look crosses Raymond's face. But he seats himself in the mohair chair. Booth brings out a Chantilly of good vintage; he never plunders Delmonico's top stock, but he has come off with a bottle better than the likes of Raymond would ever encounter.

While pouring, he notices Raymond's expression. "Don't you like wine, Raymond? Is Ragged Dick—I hope not—a temperance man?"

"It's not Ragged Dick," says Raymond. "Many a man I've seen with drink his downfall."

"Well, you're right about that," Booth says, filling two glasses. "But this isn't drink, it's ambrosia. A gentleman must develop a palate for good wine."

Raymond compromises by getting Booth to pour half of what was in the glass back into the bottle.

"Will the lady now speak for you as you wanted?" he asks Booth. He has taken just enough taste of the wine to wet his upper lip, and now he licks it as though he may be indelibly stained.

"I think she will," Booth says. "But her faith was weakening, and we restored it today." He sees that Raymond's eyes have drifted toward the trick cane, which has been set in an umbrella stand near to the door. "Go ahead and try it, Raymond," he urges, laughing.

"I would sure like to." Raymond fetches the cane and grabs it gingerly by its strangely crafted handle.

"The release is just where you're resting your thumb."

The blade pops out before Booth has finished his sentence. Both of them laugh in surprise. Raymond's eyes glitter with delight. "In the carriage I was skeered that I'd be skewered."

"Feel it," Booth says. "Feel the blade. It's very thin, and not sharp at all. I got it from some stage people. It would be no worse than skewering you with cardboard."

Raymond feels the blade and shakes his head in awe. "For a fact, it looks real."

"That's what counts," Booth tells him.

A few minutes later Booth goes to his bedroom and returns with a stack of five silver dollars, which he sets on the table in front of Raymond. "How'd you like your payoff?" he asks.

But Raymond is still hypnotically playing with the spring lever on the cane.

"Is that not the sort of payoff you're used to?" Booth asks after a moment.

Raymond keeps his eyes on the tip of the cane. "Thought y' was gonna give me salary, not a payoff."

"Sure. Call it a salary," Booth says.

"Thought I was to be your apprentice."

"Well, you are!" Booth says with some warmth in his voice. "Didn't I say that was what you would be?"

Slowly, Raymond's face brightens. "Thank ye, sir. I 'preciate it."

Booth nods, satisfied. He takes another sip of wine, studying the lad again. The milk-white complexion could make one believe the lad was only thirteen or so. But he says he is nineteen. And he has hair all over his body.

Booth shudders at that recollection. A most paradoxical occasion, the meeting of theirs on the darkened early-morning streets and the temporary misunderstanding that resulted. But perhaps there was destiny even in that distressing misunderstanding, which it has become here appropriate to relate.

13

14TH STREET

The figure of the lad walking down 14th Street that night has compelled Booth's attention, not because he originally recognizes the lad as the one he met in the morgue, but because the youngster is wearing knickerbockers, usually a mark of an upper-class boy and one not older than thirteen or so. At two or three A.M. one does not see such boys on the streets. Indigent boys are seen, but they are most often dressed in the baggy, cut-down trousers of their elders.

As Booth draws nearer, he senses that this youth is more than thirteen. The way he wears his cap reminds Booth for a moment of poor, brave Davie Herold, rebel and martyr. But when he looks closer, he sees that it is Raymond from the morgue. A great feeling of relief envelops him. Raymond is no victim after all. It is almost as though providence sent Davie Herold back to him without his neck stretched.

Quickening his pace, he overtakes the young walker, who gives him an unsurprised glance even though Booth thinks it not likely that Raymond could remember him from the morgue, given his Count Kaufnicht tweeds and the inches he has added to his height.

"Good evening," Booth says, drawing abreast.

"Good evening, sir," Raymond says easily. "A bit of a chill in the air."

Against such remarkable poise Booth can only assent. While he is eager to find out from Raymond whether there have been inquiries at the morgue, he finds it difficult to explain himself when his physical appearance has been changed so greatly.

"A late spring," Raymond offers. "Much rain."

In a voice modulating more toward his natural one, Booth says, "I believe you are familiar to me."

"Yes, sir?"

Considerably puzzled by the ambiguous manner of the lad as well as by the knickerbockers, Booth says, "May I invite you to my rooms nearby for wine and a talk? I assure you I would make it worth your while."

"That would be kind of you," Raymond replies.

They pass the rest of their stroll to Booth's rooms in amicable conversation about the weather, but also about literature and politics. Raymond is an inveterate newspaper reader and appears to be a supporter of General Grant for a third term as President. Booth, of course, declines to remark that Grant would long be moldering in the grave if he had but accepted Lincoln's invitation to the theater that famous evening.

At the rooming house Booth and Raymond tread the squeaky stairs carefully so as not to disturb the widow Van Duysen or any of her roomers. In Booth's sitting room, with the lights up a little, Booth detects Raymond's disappointment; perhaps he expected grander living quarters from a gentleman so elegantly dressed.

"Let me excuse myself a minute," Booth says. "I'd like to change into more comfortable garb. . . . My title is, by the way, Count."

"You go ahead, Count," Raymond replies, his blue eyes appraising Booth readily.

"Please put yourself at ease too," Booth says with an effort at joviality. He nods toward the mohair couch where half a decanter of wine and some glasses stand on a table.

"As you please, sir," Raymond says.

Booth retires to the bedroom. With some dispatch, since he does not wish the lad to drowse off over the wine, he quickly shucks the garments he is wearing, including the false-bottomed boots. Then he smears cream on his face in front of the mirror in order to remove the rubicund flush he applied at Delmonico's. He wipes the makeup off with the cream and combs his hair back the way Raymond saw it that day at the morgue. From the closet he pulls out the same suit he wore that day.

As he works, he experiences a pleasure very like that of the theater, where in certain roles one could look forward to the responses of an audience to a character who undergoes a dramatic change of fortune in the play and becomes nearly unrecognizable when he reappears in the last act. Booth can imagine that poor Raymond will be startled at a transformation from nobleman to democratic idealist, but also deeply interested in the explanations Booth will be able to offer. I hardly know where to begin, such characters often say. Booth expects Raymond to be an excellent audience.

Although a thin curtain hangs in two sections between bedroom and sitting room, Booth does not simply walk through it when he is ready to appear. Instead, dramatically, he separates the curtain with outflung arms so that the metal rings collide along the curtain rod.

But it is not Raymond who experiences the greater surprise. Instead, it is Booth. Raymond lies, lewdly, on the coarse mohair sofa, stark naked.

Booth flushes deeply, first embarrassed, then angry. "What— what—"

"Sir?" Raymond says tremulously. Sensing his mistake, he sits upright in confusion, putting his hands over his private parts.

"Indeed!" Booth exclaims.

"The other gentleman—" Raymond begins, pointing in the direction of the bedroom.

"I am the other gentleman!" Booth declares. "The only gentle-- man present!" At once he turns his back on his guest.

"Criminy!" he hears Raymond say, and there is a scrambling of clothes to cover himself. The shocking hairiness of the boy's body makes Booth doubly enraged. It gives the lie to knickerbockers. "You swine, you're not a child at all!" is all that he can think of to say. Children sometimes pulled off their clothing unexpectedly; it was disgusting for a man to do it. "You can't behave like a child anymore! You're a man!"

Booth averts his eyes in contempt until he is completely certain Raymond is dressed once more.

The dawn's early light has begun gently to creep into the sitting room before Raymond quite finishes his account of what has happened to him since leaving his position at the morgue. He is distressed at having misinterpreted Booth's invitation to the rooms, which was to have been made "worth" Raymond's "while."

"I b'lieved," Raymond says, "that where you seen me before was my . . . new place of employment."

Raymond has had to confess that he presently works in a house of assignation not far from Delmonico's. Sometimes he meets on the streets the men who know him from the house. Now and then he is able to make independent financial arrangements with them.

"The house don't say nothing about it," Raymond goes on. "I'm the only boy there. They're strict with the girls, sure enough."

Booth scowls. "You mean they promote this vice and find sufficient gentlemen to make it profitable? I cannot—"

"What vice, sir?"

"Why, why, sodomy! What else?"

Raymond blinks. "There are gentlemen enough for it," he admits. "They say the—the di-version is fashionable in England."

"But don't they find you hairy!" Booth glares.

"It's a matter of taste," Raymond says forthrightly. "I keep in my knickerbockers to give a youthful look."

Booth has begun to recover a little from the shock to his nervous system. He inquires if the lad does not have parents or guardian to give him guidance.

"My pa's at sea," Raymond says. "My dear mother's passed on. I go to see my aunt in Bellevue sometimes. In the contagious ward."

Booth sighs. "And when does your father reach port again?"

This is not known. "When the Chief comes in, well, he drinks a night or two at the Flowing Sea Inn, then goes out to look for me."

With sudden resolve, Booth says, "In your father's absence I could take it upon myself to lead you away from this life of vice. You are too promising a young man to waste your good spirit in this manner."

In the past, Booth adds, he has engaged loyal apprentices who like to function boldly, whether for reasons of honor or other reward.

Raymond's eyes glitter at that. "Indeed I have some information for ye, sir," he says. He has been sitting quietly on the mohair sofa with his thumbs hooked in the waistband of his knickerbockers, and he now leans forward and regards Booth with his candid blue eyes.

"Yes?" Booth says eagerly.

"A man come lookin' for your dead body, sure enough," Raymond says. "He was about six-foot-six. A roughneck!"

"As I thought," says Booth. "Did you get his name?"

"Well, I ast for it," Raymond says regretfully. But the man thought he was too nosy, and said he might cut off Raymond's nose for asking too many questions.

"And he didn't come back?" Booth asks.

"Should I let him cut off my nose? I quit the job."

"In order to become a . . . a catamite instead?" Booth is unable to restrain his distaste. "How in the name of Our Lord did you come to this disorderly house anyway?"

"Must I say?"

"Tell me!"

Raymond sighs. "Oh, this missus, she was at the morgue a few weeks back about a girl of hers that was drownded." He heaves another sigh and looks away. "Said to me she was seldom taken by a lad more. . . . I was to look her up if I ever needed room and board."

"An offer that tempted you more than the two silver dollars I offered you for but a single name."

"As to that," Raymond says sulkily, "won't be hard to find the roughneck's name out. I seen him on Water Street at the dog pits a couple of times. He lives down there. People'd know him."

"Indeed!" Booth exclaims. In the light of this disclosure, he offers Raymond a sincere apology. For it appears, he tells the lad, that perhaps he "jumped to conclusions" quite as foolishly as Raymond himself earlier had. . . .

On Water Street, over the next two days, Booth and Raymond search for their quarry. "Mercenary" is the way Booth thinks of this man, this hireling, this Hessian, who will stop at nothing in the service of the soulless barons of commerce. It is like the war, the agents of Mammon out to kill you. You had to find who they were, identify their chain of command, or they would nip your plans in the bud.

"I'll ask a friend of my pa's who this man is," Raymond says the first morning they are on Water Street.

"Let us not be in too much of a hurry," Booth says, "to expose our mission. We shall use our eyes and ears to find the man."

Booth has dressed himself as a merchant seaman with trousers tucked into boots, a navy blue coat, and a woolen cap. Raymond he casts "against type," as he terms it. The lad wears a brown double-breasted coat, edged with dark braid, then a dark puff tie and patent leather shoes. Errand boys for ward politicians are often dressed this way, even on Water Street, and no one bothers them for fear of the powerful men who might be behind them.

Still, on the second day, having prowled the docks up and down, among drays and ice wagons, carriages and pushcarts, both singly and in company with each other, their "eyes and ears" have not been adequate to find the murderous mercenary. Weary, the two of them enter the Jolly Tar, a saloon where workingmen drink, and where a few of them, Raymond avows, have even been shanghaied late of a Saturday evening onto ships bound round the Horn.

Booth makes Raymond order beer, and Raymond sits there staring at his overflowing glass. Then some stevedores carrying buckets come in through the swinging doors; a large, pockmarked man leads the others to the bartender, who begins filling their buckets with foam from the cask on the bar.

"That's McHenry," Raymond declares. "He's a cousin to my pa, the Chief. I'll ask him about our man."

"You know what to say?"

"I'll ask McHenry where he is, and if McHenry knows who pays him. Is that right?"

Booth agrees. He is pleased to see Raymond carry his drinking vessel over to the bar with him so as to seem more natural. The lad is promising, no doubt about it, and there is probably little harm he can do with McHenry. The pockmarked man greets the youth with warmth, Booth sees. Soon the two of them are engaged in conversation of an earnest nature. Raymond's clothing now seems wrong to Booth; it would have been better to have dressed Raymond as a lad of the streets, a bootblack perhaps. He would have had a more poignant effect in a situation such as this one.

"Was McHenry of any help?" Booth asks when Raymond has returned to the table.

"Some," Raymond says, sitting down. "The bum is named Meyer, a German. This time o' the season he goes out on his smugglin'. He's got a crew that goes to Cuba in a boat."

"Then he's gone?" Booth laments.

"Well, that's where Meyer is," Raymond says. "And the one he works for is the gentleman at the Mercantile. Meyer brings in special seegars for him from Cuba."

"Dun?" Booth gasps.

"That's him, Mr. Robert Dun. . . . Do I still have to drink my beer now, Count?"

Fiercely, Booth shakes his head. Dun trying to kill him! To Raymond, he says, "I may not be a count today, my lad, but you will yet be in the service of one if you keep faith with me."

"I don't mind callin' you Count," Raymond replies.

The next morning, with the bells of Trinity Church sounding out over the avenue—a society wedding perhaps—Booth, dressed for the street in frock coat and tall hat, proceeds alone by carriage from his rooming house to the Arthur residence on Lexington Avenue. He knows that General Arthur keeps late hours and does not leave his home until close to noon. Booth anticipates a long and serious conversation with the general, but he has dropped into his pocket, just in case, a small derringer with which he is prepared to protect himself.

In the beautiful sunshine with the church bells ringing, it seems a shame to think in such terms. But he has never been one to let things drift and simply hope for the best. It is a disappointment to him, first of all, that the attempt on his life has now quite apparently been motivated by his love for the general's wife. He has hoped that Weed was the instigator; that was the terrain on which he wanted to fight, where the old intrigues between him and that avaricious band of Yankees would be alive again.

Instead, with Dun the general's best friend, Booth can only conclude that the general is not as ignorant as Nell thinks of the affair, and that he has asked Dun to help him eliminate his rival in love. A poor excuse for a general! Could one imagine a Beauregard or a Jubal Early humbly asking another man to find a hireling to do away with the rival who had won his wife's love!

Only the Yankees, like modern Borgias, hired others to do their dirty work for them.

Growing more and more incensed at the enormity of the outrage, Booth has all to do, as he stands off the carriage in Gramercy Park, to control himself. He knows that the door off the street-level entrance to the Arthur home leads down to the office that the general maintains. The impulse he fights is to burst through that door and, if he is lucky enough to find the treacherous general there, to give him his comeuppance without warning, to pay him in kind.

But he reminds himself that it is premature to think in such terms. He is no hothead, after all. Bargains could be struck with men like the general; the only difficulty was in getting them to keep their word.

Accordingly, he rings at the front door. When a maid appears, he says to her, "Good morning. I am here to see the general. Would he be in his office?"

She smiles pertly. "The general's not at home, sir. Would ye care to leave your card?"

Booth looks at her disbelievingly. "It's most urgent that I see him."

Behind her in the hallway he sees a mélange of steamer trunks, parasols, butterfly nets. Plainly, the household is packing for the summer holiday. No doubt the one in Cooperstown that Nell mentioned.

"The general won't be home till evening, sir," she repeats. "If you state your bissness, p'raps—"

He hears a familiar voice from the stairs. "Minnie? Who is at the door?"

"Never mind," Booth says to the maid and starts to go.

"A gentleman to see the general," the maid calls to Nell, leaving the door.

For a moment Booth hesitates. He hears Nell's steps, descending. Then, with determination, he turns away.

Too late.

"Sir, sir," Nell is calling plaintively to him. "Do wait a minute."

In the next moment she is beside him on the lower steps, having pulled shut the front door behind her. "What on earth ah you doing here?" she demands in a husky whisper.

He glances at her. She has a loose ribbon in her hair and perspiration on her forehead. "I call on your husband."

"For what reason?" She draws him into the stairwell that leads down to Chester's office just as the postman passes. "What do you want of him?"

"Is he away?" Booth asks her.

"In Albany. But you must tell me why you wish to see him."

Has she not wanted a resolution to their mutual problem?

"No, no," she cries, grasping his arm. "You cannot believe it is he who is trying to kill you!"

"And if it is, should I not try to stop him?"

"But you are wrong!"

She clutches him as he tries to draw away from her.

"This is no place—"

"Wilkes, I love you!" she cries. "Remembuh the plans we made in Paris."

"I remember, and we can't talk here," he says, wrenching himself away. "Tomorrow at two in Stewart's . . . if you must."

"Don't be cruel! I must be clear before I leave for the summer."

"We will be clear." He is halfway up the steps.

"And you will do nothing before I see you—"

"My dear Nell."

A sober elderly couple, arm in arm, are passing even as he reaches the level of the street. Dammit, Nell should know it is no place for an interlude. Clapping his hat on his head and flicking his walking stick out in front of him, he hastens down the avenue, not looking back. All the trees are in leaf.

At the Stock Exchange, not long afterward, Booth has begun to feel in a better mood. A piece of good fortune it was to have not found Chester Arthur at home. He cannot imagine what went through his head to have taken a pistol with him to the house. Does he want to wind up but another name in the weary annals of adultery? A fine comment on Booth honor!

On the ground floor of the marble edifice that he now enters, a loud din arises from an irregular bazaar where the lesser folk—curbstone brokers, they are called—buy and sell their wares. Booth does not doubt that Christ must have found the moneychangers on the steps of the temple behaving in much the same manner as these—the sing-song voices, the prancing gestures—a foretaste of their eternal damnation in hell.

Robert Dun, he has been told, might be found on the second floor, and Booth ascends the grand staircase along the echoing main hall toward the visitors' gallery. The certified brokers whom he sees en route look no better to him than the hoi polloi below. Some are haggard. Some have the appearance of apoplectics—red-faced and with puffy jowls—although not many of them are of an age greater than Booth's own. He recognizes it as an occupation with high mortality.

Indeed, now that he thinks of it, how many of the Yankee bankers with whom the noble Judah Benjamin and the Montreal Confederates did their business during the war have not gone either to their Maker or long since to the bankruptcy courts!

Booth has to push his way to the front of the visitors' gallery, nudging onlookers lined three deep. He scans the sea of men on the exchange floor below for some sign of Dun. What a temple Mammon has provided: a vaulted, sky-blue ceiling, lofty bronze pilasters, thick draperies on the windows! In the pit below, youthful runners write and erase numbers along a great blackboard as they scurry about clutching ribbons of tape retrieved from the ceaseless telegraph tickers.

Booth wishes to catch Dun by surprise. Men who could cope day after day with the tension and hysteria of the exchange have nerves of steel and an unscrupulousness to match. Dun is the anointed scribe to this infernal congress.

Moving down the corridor from the gallery, Booth stops outside a large room where he can hear the chants of the damned: "I'll give one fifteen, fifteen for a thousand, fifteen for a thousand . . ."

From another: "I'll give fourteen for a thousand, fourteen! . . ."

On the dais and among the seated bidders there is laughter. The presiding officer pounds his hammer. "Fine Jennings fifty cents!"

"Fourteen for a thousand!" the member repeats.

"Fine him again!"

Canes are pounded on the floor, and some of the men rap on their benches with the energy of fractious schoolboys. The handful of on-lookers watching the auction have begun laughing too. Among the men grouped just inside the door, not far away from Booth, the man with the spade beard, smiling wryly, is Robert Dun.

Their eyes lock. Dun, who has been carrying his hat in one hand and a lighted cigar in the other, drops the hat. His smile has vanished. With a quick gesture, he picks up the hat and pretends to watch the bidding again. Booth keeps his gaze coldly on the man. The dropped hat is a chink in the armor.

When Dun presently starts to move toward the exit, Booth is there standing athwart the doorway. He tilts his chin upward, his face mere inches from Dun's.

"Do you know me?" he asks defiantly.

With the softest contempt in his voice, Dun says, "I know you for a scoundrel."

"I insist that you withdraw that remark!"

Dun laughs. "You are not only a blackmailer and an adulterer, but you cuckold the man who saved your life. How long do you think you can go on without his finding out about it?"

Suddenly Booth draws a pair of white gloves from beneath a sleeve of his coat, and giving no warning, he lashes Dun across the face with the gloves. "My seconds will call on you this evening!" Booth declares.

Under his thin Vandyke beard, Dun's chin trembles indignantly. Gentlemen pass them in the marbled hall, but either they have not noticed Booth's assault, so rapidly was it delivered, or else they are accustomed to passion at the exchange.

Dun pulls himself together and scornfully says, "You swine."

But Booth has turned on his heel and walks off in triumph. Dun has told him what he wants to know: Chester Arthur remains ignorant, and the true author of the mischief directed against him can be none other than Thurlow Weed!

The barons of commerce and corruption still feared him, then. They wanted to exterminate every vestige of the bargains they had made with the Confederacy. As if murdering him and destroying his diaries were enough! There were others who knew the truth. There was Nell, for instance. Did they think she would keep silent about them if her lover was killed? Oh, they regarded her with contempt. They would not let her secede from her marriage; in that way, they were Yankee to the core. But he would show them. No union was indissoluble. None!

A great scenario begins to suggest itself to his mind.

As he passes the Long Room of the exchange on the way out, the sounds that issue forth are like the baying of animals following a scent. Atavistic memories ensue. He has felt like quarry too often.

But no more, gentlemen, no more.

14

CENTRAL PARK

Two carriages are bound for a rendezvous at the dairy end of the marble arch in the central park. It is a cloudy day, with drizzle having begun, but Booth has hired for the occasion a fancy closed brougham that seats four. The dark, musty upholstery, done in patterns of fleur-de-lis, is said by the hostler to be the same as that used in the Astors' carriages. Booth does not want Dun and Weed, who are arriving in the other carriage, to continue to think of him as some species of waiter. Too often they have forgotten that he is a member of a distinguished American family of the theater, as well as a patriot in his own right. They are the arrivistes, he the true aristocrat.

On the ride out, he keeps his hand on Nell's. It is the last time they will see each other for a while.

"Do you find this a difficult undertaking, my darling?" he asks her.

"I know they are tryin' to murduh you," she says tautly. "I do not look forward to seeing them." She holds the handle of her dark parasol up close to her veiled face. On her head, tilted forward, is a green hat shaped like the ones Scottish pipers wear.

"When the summer is over and you are back in New York," he declares, "nothing will stand between us and the Continent!"

She is silent; Booth is gratified by the severity of her demeanor. No seconds have been sent to Dun. Instead, after two days, Booth has penned a crisp note to Thurlow Weed's residence, requesting that Mr. Dun and Mr. Weed meet him for a discussion of their mutual situation. During the interim Nell finds a ruse to postpone for a week the family's departure on vacation. She will stand with her lover in the scene that must save his life.

"You know I love and cherish you, Nell," he says to her with deep feeling. "But I cannot run craven from these shores while they who have used me go on multiplying their profits."

She understands, she tells him haltingly. She is relieved that Chester is not involved, and will not be involved in any way. She has rallied her patience and her strength.

In the park, the bridle paths are crowded with riders in spite of the misting rain. When Booth's carriage reaches the dairy end of the arch, another carriage is already parked there. A door opens, and Dun steps down and comes over to request that the party should continue in Weed's carriage, since the old man has become enfeebled. Dun holds his hand on the brim of his hat while he talks, as though he is afraid the wind might blow it away.

"Mr. Weed will be quite comfortable here," Booth says to Dun. He has read in the papers that Weed has been seen gadding around the city to revivalist meetings and such. Usually on foot.

"Very well," Dun says after a moment.

A footman descends from Weed's carriage, then the driver too.

Both assist Weed across to the other carriage, an umbrella held over his head to protect the white thatch from the rain.

Silently, Weed settles into the seat opposite Nell. He takes off his hat and holds it in his lap.

"Mrs. Arthur," he says solemnly when Dun is settled in too.

Dun and Nell have barely nodded to each other, the door is closed, and immediately the covered brougham leaps forward as the matched bays fall into their pace. While Dun is still glaring at Booth, Weed says, "I hear you two bloods have met at the exchange."

He glances at Nell, who casts a downward look. Dun keeps his hat on his knee; he is a short, wiry man who sits at an odd angle. Weed relaxes with patrician ease.

Booth says, "In the last few days, gentlemen, I've written fresh accounts of meetings I attended and duties I was assigned during the war. Since it appears that pages of my diary which contain the same information may be lost forever—or have been deliberately destroyed —I have taken this less satisfactory way of documenting what occurred."

Now Booth reaches beneath the seat and from a leather case extracts sheets of foolscap that contain the longhand account he has described to them. He now hands copies—there are two—to Weed and to Dun, and he waits while they peruse them.

"Now," Booth continues, "if it should prove that any kind of accident befalls me in the forthcoming months I have arranged with Mrs. Arthur that these documents be forwarded both to the free press and to proper federal authorities. Mrs. Arthur has, in the meantime, made similar arrangements for making sure these documents reach authorities in case something happens to her. . . . Although I am presently recorded as deceased, I have every reason to believe that documents in my own handwriting may have some important effect in persuading people that the facts here alleged are true."

As he collects the documents back from Weed and Dun, Dun says, "What you claim here about the death of Lincoln is part exaggeration and part pure fantasy." He looks levelly at Nell. "You should be aware of that, Mrs. Arthur."

"If it is fantasy," Booth retorts, "why do you meet me here, why do you fear me enough to try to kill me!"

Nell says, "You hate Mistuh Booth because he was an actor."

Weed politely objects.

"He is a great artist," Nell adds. "And cannot follow his art because of his service in the war."

"We do not stop him from acting, Nell," Dun says.

"I'll say not!" Weed affirms. "He keeps actin' day and night."

"Judas!" Nell hisses. "*He* killed out of his duty during the war; you kill out of greed and cowuhdice!"

"One day I will be vindicated," Booth declares, patting her hand.

After a moment, Weed sighs. The horses' hooves have settled into an agreeable rhythm, and Weed says, "Well, what the hell do you want, Booth? Lay it out. Speaking for myself, I'm old, but would just as soon my daughters, after I'm gone, not have to defend our name against charges that I was in some kind of conspiracy against Lincoln. . . . Robert, what do you think about all this? If what he wants is a promise we won't try to do away with him, that's an easy promise to keep, isn't it?"

Dun grunts, and Booth says at once, "Mr. Dun naturally doesn't believe that news of the conspiracy would go down well at the Stock Exchange."

"The market would recover soon enough," Dun sniffs. "Your presumption is what I find disgusting." Here he casts a glance at Nell.

But Booth, unruffled, is now prepared to name the rest of his price.

"What we want, gentlemen, is very much what you want. Our secession. I am suggesting that this time you join in a new conspiracy with me—this time a benign conspiracy, more appropriate to the times. Let Mrs. Arthur and me reach the Continent safely and live there under a new name, unbothered by any vestige of the past, either my past or Mrs. Arthur's past. That suits your interests, doesn't it? If you help us 'dispose of' Mrs. Arthur the way I have been disposed of, she and I need no longer fear when we reach our haven abroad that we will be disturbed by any claims from the past."

"Why should we stop your going," Dun asks, "if that is what Mrs. Arthur wants? There will be scandal certainly, and Chester will suffer from that, but—"

Booth raises his finger.

"But there will be no scandal! Mrs. Arthur will be *disposed of*. *Deceased*. General Arthur's career will thus not be harmed, and we hope it will motivate him, when he finds out, to accept her act of secession in good grace. It will allow him, for that matter, to marry again. The children will have to be confided in sooner or later, but, knowing them, Mrs. Arthur and I believe that that can easily be brought about."

"What!" Dun exclaims.

Nell has assumed a transcendent expression, eyes thoughtful. "Chester will be deceived, but for his own good," she murmurs. "The children will be educated quietly in France."

"Absurd," Dun scoffs.

Booth smiles. "The two of us have agreed on a date for the demise—a little after Christmas, when the general will be out of town with his committees." Grasping Nell's hand in his, he gazes amicably at Weed. "You will find the Arthur conspiracy far more benign than the one involving Lincoln."

A hopeless glance is exchanged between the two men who sit opposite them. The rain has become so insistent on the carriage roof in the last few minutes that even the sound of the horses has become altered. Dun starts to speak, then seems to think better of it. He pushes back the window curtains with the head of his cane and looks out. The old state arsenal building stands dim in the rain; for a time during the war it was a central heavy-equipment warehouse managed by General Arthur and the Quartermaster Corps.

Booth says, "No way of life, no set of great principles, is ever dead, gentleman, when a strong man and a strong woman come together to preserve what they believe in."

"The dead phoenix rises from the ashes; godspeed, Mr. Booth," Weed says with a note of finality. "Your plans are always challengin'. . . . But can we go home now, sir? Dun, you want to go home, too, don't you?"

Dun looks around him as though he is in Bedlam, and offers no objection.

Booth, opening a window, and leaning out into the stinging rain, calls heartily to the driver to take them back to the starting point.

15

GRAND CENTRAL STATION

So the summer passes, and most of the autumn.

In the gentleman's retiring room of the great railroad depot, Roscoe Conkling, Senator and orator, is splashing water onto his face and making a great hubbub of spitting and snorting in the process. For a man-about-town he is a damned cacophony of throat and digestive noises, Chester reflects as he comes up beside Roscoe at the lavabo.

"Extend my Christmas greetings to Julia," Chester remarks, adjusting the tap water. Roscoe, who does not reply, is making one of his journeys home to Utica, a ritual of his before Christmas and before state party conventions.

Roscoe waits for the Negro attendant to hand him his towel. Without looking at Chester he says, "You must get some rest, my friend. Be ready for work after the holidays."

"I'm fine," says Chester. But the truth is he has spent many exhausting weeks on party business, stopping in Syracuse and Auburn and Rochester; Cooperstown merely served as his jumping-off place during the summer.

"What do you think, boy?" Roscoe now demands of the lavatory attendant. "Does the gentleman look as though he needs a rest?"

"Yassuh, he a li'l tahrd," the attendant agrees patiently.

"I am not tired," Chester says sharply. Roscoe's habit of involving men in the street in their private conversations annoys him; but Roscoe believes it proves he has the common touch.

As Chester takes the towel handed him, Roscoe trims his beard in front of the large mirror with something that looks like a pocket cigar clipper. "Obesity is thought by some physicians," Roscoe goes on, "to be unhealthful."

"I would not call it obesity," Chester says. Besides, he privately knows that obesity is not the problem. Bright's disease is. Or so the doctor in Albany has advised him. Chester trusts that this infirmity is a secret from Roscoe, who would otherwise talk about it as freely as though Chester were a washerwoman, no matter that it would kill Chester's hopes for the Senate. And perhaps his marriage as well.

"Take several days off completely," Roscoe advises while being helped into his coat. Even though they are both looking at their reflections in the mirror, Roscoe's eyes never drift from the contemplation of his own triangular visage. When the days of rest are over, it is understood Chester will throw himself into his duties as state chairman once again; the Utica convention is but two months away and they are fighting tooth-and-nail for every delegate they can get for Grant.

Chester leaves a large coin on the lavatory attendant's tray.

"The open letter in the *Herald* hit the right note," Roscoe says as the two men pass through the swinging doors into the public waiting room. "That sort of thing is excellent—"

In the open letter Roscoe speaks of, Chairman Arthur has been urged to clear the Republican rolls of all the names of the dead who might inadvertently still appear on it. "A Party Regular" has signed the letter, thereby giving notice to Tammany and the Democrats that at least one of the two parties will enter the canvass with a conscience.

"What day do we see George in Albany?" Roscoe asks.

"The second."

Roscoe is leading the way through the throng toward the gates to the upstate trains where Phillips, his secretary, is holding the luggage. On the way, his hat is tipped to numerous gentlemen, and, most gallantly, to a lady, who seems perhaps to recognize him. Roscoe is avoiding, Chester notices, the vicinity where a boys' choir is setting up to sing carols near the large Christmas tree at the far end of the public waiting room. It looks like a Tammany project.

As they get closer, however, they see that it is a Protestant group, and Roscoe begins beaming. One of the boys in the choir, a friendly lad, son of the banker Fielding, waves to Chester. He is from the Arthur's own church; Nell participates in the ladies' choir when she feels up to it.

"Happy Christmas!" Roscoe calls, returning the boy's wave. He is convinced that he and he alone is famous in the state, even if all are not willing to admit it.

Near the gates to the upstate trains, moving at a tangent to their own path, is a lone young woman, pulling a tan wolfhound on a leash. She looks familiar to Chester, but he cannot exactly place her. She wears a chic felt hat, but the coat is dyed rabbit fur, not expensive. Her eyebrows are plucked, her facial bones prominent. She has an exotic look.

When she passes very near them, Roscoe's interest flickers briefly, but the nod she gives them, along with an enigmatic smile, is directed at Chester.

He is damned annoyed at not being able to place her.

"Did Nell and the children enjoy my gifts to them?" Roscoe now asks. They have come to a stop in the area where Phillips is checking Roscoe's luggage with a porter. The muffled thunder of an arriving train is heard.

"You're always very generous, Roscoe."

"I try to be." The Senator looks at his pocket watch. "Nell is . . . feeling better again?"

Chester says that she is. During the months in Cooperstown she behaved compliantly. Earlier, in Philadelphia when they consulted

Weir Mitchell, the nerve specialist, she was so bland and charming that Mitchell gave Chester an herb tonic for himself and told Nell that *she* was fine—indeed, splendid.

"Splendid" put it too strongly for Chester's taste. But he and his wife did sleep in the same bed at his sister's farm in Cooperstown. Or they did when he wasn't traveling for the party. On nights when he had hot flashes, Nell brought compresses soaked in cool well water. Occasionally she asked him how it had gone in Auburn, or whom he met in Batavia. She seldom seemed to listen for the answers. But she watched Alan and him play ball one afternoon, laughing with pleasure a couple of times, and she crocheted Nellie a pretty little cap. He has hopes things will be better if they get to Washington.

"Are you ready to board now, Senator?" Fred Phillips asks. The porter has carried some of Roscoe's luggage off toward his drawing room, and the conductor begins admitting the stream of passengers at the gate. Behind them, the carolers have started singing, a cappella, "O Come All Ye Faithful!"

A quick handshake with Chester as the current moves the departing passenger along. "Happy Christmas, Chester!"

"Same to you, Roscoe. . . . Happy Christmas, Fred!"

Chester takes a deep breath as they disappear into the stream and the darkness. He enjoys seeing friends off. Perhaps things are not so bad. He seems to feel cltse to his family during the Cchistmas season.

But as he starts to leave the station he is astonished to find the woman with the wolfhound directly in his path. She so plainly wants to talk to him that he tips his hat and stops in front of her.

"Excuse me," he says, with a frank smile. "You are not a feat of my imagination, are you? We have met before, I think."

"It was in the dark," she confides to him, still with a trace of Old Country accent. Her manner is natural and unaffected, belying the exotic makeup and the conspicuous dog.

"I have it! On the riverboat from Albany! You have a new dog."

"Goodness, now you will remember I am a reporter and you will run away."

He smiles at her playfulness. The truth is that after meeting her he did some checking and found that none of the New York papers employed a female reporter. "For what paper are you working now?" he asks slyly.

"Oh, I am free-lance."

"I see," he says. "Do any of the papers buy your material?"

"Occasionally," she replies. "But they do not give me a by-line, for who would credit what a woman claims?"

He studies her with amusement, still not certain that she is telling the truth. She does not ask questions the way a reporter would. Besides, she affects him too personally; she materializes improbably and they converse as though they have known each other all their lives.

The dog starts to rise, but she touches him softly on the head and he immediately sits. Perhaps he is reacting to the sound of a train or the gathering volume of the boys' choir, lustily singing.

"I was working on a story the night you saw me on the ferryboat," she says to Chester.

"I hoped you were not writing about me, or the Senator."

"About acts of prostitution," she says, and then adds, "the kind women perform."

He blushes; he has never heard a woman utter the word before. "I did not see . . . such a story in the papers."

"No, they declined to print it," the woman says, her manner more remote. "But they said I did a good investigation. On the ferryboat."

Chester looks around him uneasily; he starts to take out his pocket watch, then realizes he is content to hear the woman out.

"I don't mean to shock you," she says. "But I think you, too, thought I was a prostitute that night on the boat. . . . Many men did." Suddenly she laughs.

He smiles too, wishing he had the nerve to ask how far her investigation took her. "Well, when you are ready to do a political story, you must look me up some time." He is surprised to hear himself say that.

"Don't you think I might be doing a political story at this very moment?"

"You mean," he laughs, "while walking a wolfhound around Grand Central Station?"

"While talking to you."

Again he is surprised, this time by the twinge of pleasure that he feels. Her eyes falter from the openness of his gaze. "Why don't we meet for a real interview sometime after the holidays, Victoria. . . . Is that not your name? Victoria?"

"Yes. Victoria Coventry."

"I'll be in Albany for the organization of the legislature, and then in Utica for the state convention."

"I do not always do things . . . in the conventional way," she remarks after a moment.

He hears himself say that that is all right, that he feels she is on his side

"Yes, I feel that too," Victoria Coventry replies, frowning. "We will talk in Utica."

16

123 LEXINGTON AVENUE

In packing for the long sea voyage ahead Nell hardly knows what to take and what to leave behind. What did one take to "the other world"? The old Egyptian pharaohs, she once read in school, tried to fill their tombs with gold and playthings from their earthly existence, but in the end the graverobbers got it. It is the lesson of too much materialism. Nevertheless, she hopes that some of the objects she must leave behind will fall to the children while she and Wilkes are realizing the more eternal values on the distant shore.

She has felt progress toward that shore in the last few weeks: first, Wilkes has helped her select a casket and a tasteful design for a tombstone bearing her name. Also, a proper cadaver has been located and will be adequately preserved for the funeral services. Finally, the steamship tickets have been handed to Nell, first-class stateroom reservations for herself and her personal maid (under the names Mrs. Madeline Usher and Miss Lettie Franklin). Wilkes would follow on a later ship, when all the details were over with, bringing Nellie and her new governess with him. He would have broken the news of their "secession" to Chester in the meantime.

She cannot imagine Chester's resisting the force of Wilkes's plan. A fait accompli it would be. Chester would learn that she was not in Virginia, as she would have told him, but abroad for good, and that he must undergo a funeral service for her besides. Of course he would be out of patience at first, but eventually persuaded by Wilkes's logic, his natural discretion would prevail. After a brief period of mourning, he would bounce himself right back into his politics—live all the time in Albany, if he liked, or Washington—eat and drink with his cigar-smoking friends, do his work. Marry again, for that matter. . . . She had given him little enough as a wife.

Gradually emptying the top drawer of her armoire, she has permitted herself to take along the fragile and filmy things—the white summer gloves, the thin stockings, the dainty fans—objects that are to travel with her to the warm and distant shore. How pleasant the weather will be there. Here, outside the window a new fall of snow is covering the drab slush, already gray and trampled under the impact of horse and carriage. The children will be all right, she continues to tell herself. Alan, for all his willfulness, can be counted on for discretion in family matters. Nellie would soon be with her in France, and right after New Year's all the household servants would be given a long, long vacation.

On an impulse, Nell visits the nursery, where her daughter is playing with some of the toys she received for Christmas. The door to Chester's room is closed; right after church he went in to lie down, complaining of a touch of indigestion. She wonders if he senses something going on, but she thinks not. She has not mentioned separation or divorce, except for one time just before he dragged her off to that fool Mitchell in Philadelphia. "Stupid," he called her then. "We are well off, perfectly compatible, and have growing children. Enough of that." Very well, then, it would have to be done Wilkes's way.

The nursery door is ajar. When her daughter turns from her play on the rug before the fire, Nell's heart catches for a moment. The expression is impassive, almost bovine. Yet the girl is bright enough. Nell wishes the girl looked more like her. Instead, with the curly light brown hair and the large, perfectly round face, she looks like the Arthurs.

"When you get to your aunt's and uncle's," Nell says to the girl, "remembuh to be as good as you always have in the past." Nellie is to spend a short time upstate during the "death" and the funeral.

"Oui, maman," Nellie says obligingly. She has been asked by her mother to practice her French by speaking it exclusively for a day. Nell wants to be sure Nellie is wholly comfortable with the language by the time she joins her mother in Nice.

"Remembuh to be patient with your cousin Jessie, who is only seven and not as old as you." A surge of tears comes into Nell's eyes, but she turns aside and regains control. "I will be thinking of you."

Nellie does not change her position. Perhaps she is a little embarrassed. *"Oui, maman,"* she pipes again.

Nell shifts her feet. "You needn't speak French today, dear. Do it after today when Mam'selle is here." On the floor near the fire is the book of little French stories about princes and princesses that Nell gave Nellie for Christmas.

Nellie does not say *"Oui, maman"* this time. She says nothing.

"While you are at your cousins'," Nell says tremulously, "I am going on a long trip. Whatevuh anyone says, you must tell them your mamma is on a long trip, and one day soon you will join her."

"Are you going on a long trip?" Nellie asks, her face turning away.

"Yes, isn't that what I've just told you?" When Nellie doesn't reply, Nell says, "Can you say it now? My mamma is just on a long trip."

"My mamma is just on a long trip," Nellie replies without much enthusiasm.

"Can you say it in French too?" Nell asks. She tries for a lighter tone, suggesting that it is possibly a game they are playing. Adults enjoyed games too.

"Is Mam'selle going to ask me that?" Nellie inquires, her large eyes patient and unamused.

"I am asking you."

"Uhh—*Ma mère—fait un voyage prolongé?*"

"You must say it like a spell," Nell says with sudden urgency, "so that nothing can go wrong."

17

FROM *The New York Inquirer*

SECRETARY STANTON'S SECRET

SCHENECTADY — When Mr. Silas P. Grandwitt, 80, succumbed here at his son's farm Thursday, he revealed to his son, Edgar Grandwitt, and other witnesses, that he believes former Sec'y of War Edwin M. Stanton, under whom the elder Grandwitt served as personal secretary, suppressed certain documents relating to the assassination of President Lincoln.

Among the documents were the missing pages of the diary of John Wilkes Booth, the assassin of the President. The file, at that time under lock and key in the War Department, later vanished, according to Mr. Grandwitt, who said he saw enough of the file to know its general contents without knowing specific details. Secretary Stanton died in 1869.

Booth has read and reread the item.

By a quirk of fate, it has appeared in the papers on the very day that Booth escorts a heavily veiled Nell to her stateroom on the *Gallia*. The weather is gray and cloudy, threatening snow, and Nell herself is far too nervous for him to be able to mention the article to her. But he interprets the story as a true omen: somewhere in Washington, he believes, lies the evidence that can redeem him. Stanton is dead, Stanton's son and heir is dead; but the documents still exist. He would like to be able to say to her, "Nell, one day in a more enlightened time we will return to this country in triumph."

Instead, at the door to the stateroom he fairly thrusts her into the arms of the new maid, another pockmarked Irish girl, who keeps hold of her, while Booth, backstepping, breathes reassurances: "We shall follow soon. We'll be on the way as soon as it's over."

For some reason Nell looks especially beautiful as she lifts her veil to give him a last look. He stands away to return her look. Even in the maelstrom of arriving passengers, ship stewards, and gurneyed steamer trunks filling the passageway, he can but admire how the tragic bearing in her mien enhances her.

"Don't ye worry now, Miz Usher," the Irish girl comforts her, drawing her back into the cabin as Booth wrenches himself away and hurries to the gangplank lest he lose his nerve and sail with her after all.

18

THE NEW DELAVAN HOUSE
ALBANY

Breakfasting in his suite on a Sunday morning affords Chester one of the purer pleasures of his political week. He can eat with the people he likes rather than trying to make hay with boomers from Buffalo. His guest on this cold, bright morning is the newly elected speaker of the Assembly, the Honorable George Sharpe, a friend from New York City, who shared an office with him at the customhouse for a time.

A dignified man, Sharpe knows the usefulness of silence. Sooner or later the two of them will seriously discuss which of the Blaine men and which of the Curtis men need to be named to which committee posts (easier to do when the volatile Roscoe is not present). But in the meantime they partake of the golden pancakes, the sausages and eggs, the pulled bread and freshly churned butter, the coffee seasoned with rich cream.

A knock on the door admits Tom Platt. Still in his overcoat and heavy fur mittens, he larks in, laughing and glowing rosily from the cold. "You don't believe I been to church, do you?" he chortles, tossing down his hat and unbuttoning his overcoat.

"I don't believe it," says Sharpe.

"Would you like some breakfast?" Chester asks, knowing the peace has been shattered whether he sits down or not.

"Naw," Platt says. "I'm ready for lunch." He is tall and thin with a hatchet face and the soul of a salesman. His actual occupation is druggist. "Say, I saw that girl reporter you was talking about. She was lookin' for you, Chet."

Chester has made the mistake of mentioning that he has promised a certain female reporter an interview, and should any of the others be approached, he doesn't feel it would be sporting to send her packing. Inasmuch as he gave his damned promise.

"Where did you see her?"

"In the lobby downstairs," Platt declares. "Heh-heh-heh. She was beggin' me to find out what your room number was. I says to her you was a hard man to see, very exclusive, not like me. I love to give out interviews . . . although sometimes a hard man myself. Heh-heh-heh."

Chester feels his face redden. No wonder that newspaper reporting could never be a safe job for decent women when politicans like Tom Platt were around! "Just leave her alone if she shows up here."

"Too late, too late," Platt cries, settling down on one of the chairs before the blazing fire. He holds up his hands against the warmth. "To tell the God's truth, I already been interviewed by her."

"Oh, shut your trap, Tom," Sharpe says. Platt laughs.

Maybe she did show up, Chester reflects, and then turned around and went right back to New York once she got a whiff of the druggist and his kind.

At another knock on the door, Platt cries, "See, Chet, she's tracked you down after all. George and I'll clear out . . . unless you could use a few quick pointers—"

In case it is she, Chester answers the door himself, dabbing his linen napkin carefully over his mouth and whiskers.

But it is a bellboy with a telegram for him. Blank-faced, he reads:

PLEASE RETURN TO NEW YORK AT ONCE STOP YOUR WIFE HAS FALLEN ILL WITH PNEUMONIA STOP SHE IS UNDER MEDICAL CARE AT YOUR HOME STOP ADVISE NO DELAY

PETER CLAYTON MD

"My dear man!" George Sharpe cries almost as soon as Chester finishes reading.

For Chester has grown so pale and drops so suddenly onto a settee near the door that Sharpe and Platt both see that he is close to swooning. He clutches the upholstered cushion on the settee and awkwardly sinks back to a recumbent position.

Only slowly, with the help of the other two present, is he able to restore himself and take the actions necessary for departure.

In the following hours, he sits shivering in the caboose of the milk train, which slowly plies its way between Albany and New York. While no new snow has fallen, stretches of the track along the route are being dug out of the windblown drifts and there are many delays. Spectators from the farms and small towns along the Hudson have stopped their horse-drawn sleighs to watch the workers clear the tracks and to admire the mighty locomotive close up. Chester gazes from the grimy window of the caboose, where he has been invited to sit by the Albany stationmaster, who is aggrieved that they have no faster train on that day to help the general meet the emergency in his family.

(Was that Victoria he saw disembarking onto the station platform in Albany? Strange. Even as he was climbing up the steps at the rear end of the train, he happened to glance forward, and there was a tall woman in a dyed-rabbit coat and a fur hat, who seemed to be gazing at him with a kind of lonely melancholy. She was not that far away from him, but he could not go back to her, not with the stationmaster so pleased to be ushering him to a seat near the stove in the car, carrying for him his hastily packed alligator valise to be set down beside the seat. Would he ever see Victoria again?)

The caboose turns out not to be comfortable after all. Every time the trainmen get in and get out, they leave the damned doors open so that the icy drafts whistle through the car. The stove works poorly. Chester feels familiar pain in the area of his kidneys, and has a giddy feeling in his head. To make matters worse, he has not had time to fill the new prescription from his doctor in Albany. He fears he will make a bad showing at his wife's bedside.

Drowsing on and off whenever the train begins crawling again between the frequent stops, he has odd dreams. Some of them involve Victoria Coventry beckoning to him; he does not recognize any desire to follow her. But he thinks about it, for the latest advanced thinking finds significance in dreams: they are to be interpreted, just as Pharaoh's dreams were interpreted in the Bible. Chester would like to read more about this from some responsible professional. He has long since rejected his father's literal readings of the more primitive parts of the Scriptures. But it is interesting to think that something like interpretation of dreams could come back into fashion again.

The windows are too high to see out of when seated. He finds himself contemplating objects like the stove lid, the pieces of old wood stacked in a pen in the corner of the car, and then, as dusk, and darkness, fall, the bilious glow of kerosene lanterns.

Around midnight, he climbs down off the caboose onto slippery right-of-way in upper Manhattan, well north of the station. The train conductor has suggested that a carriage would make more rapid progress through the streets of New York than would the slow-moving train, which drops off many cans of milk at every stop. A carriage has been wired for from Yonkers, and Chester, with valise, is assisted through the bitter cold to where the rig is waiting.

Now the horses gallop through the winter streets. People on foot along the sidewalks retard their pace momentarily, recognizing the urgency of the ride. The snow has been cleared on the avenues, and the hooves catch sparks against the paving stones. Along Fifth, in the careening interior of the carriage, Chester keeps tight hold on the doorstrap in order to maintain his seat.

As they are forced to slow down in the narrower reaches of the city he begins stamping his feet against the boards to get his blood circulating again. He pushes back the curtains when they reach Lexington, and finally looks out onto his own block.

At once he experiences a start, for a carriage is parked directly in front of his house. Surely it is the doctor, and not the death wagon! In the misty gaslight, he strains his eyes, trying to make an identification.

Not the death wagon at least. But who was Dr. Clayton, who sent the damned telegram? Some kind of specialist? In the next moment he is shocked to recognize two men emerging from the front door of his house, both of them newspaper reporters, one from the *Tribune,* the other from the *Standard*.

"Once more around the block, man!" he calls quickly to his driver. He cannot bear to hear the news from reporters, if news it is they have to give him. Now he fears the worst; reporters would not be on hand in the middle of the night if the news were tranquil.

As the driver shouts the horses up again, Chester sinks backward in the seat and feels himself wracked by tremors. He feels indignant that, exhausted as he is, he should be deterred from entering his own home by these interlopers.

The snow has begun to fall again. By the second time around the block, the carriage containing the reporters has drawn quickly away from the house; as soon as it is out of sight, Chester cries "Stop!" He flings open the door and jumps to the ground. Still not entirely relieved of his shaking, he runs up the steps of the brownstone to the front door.

It appears that he is expected. The door is opened for him as he is reaching for the knob. From inside, the light diffuses outward, and a young man, short of stature and a complete stranger to him, says in a hushed voice. "Good evening, sir."

For a moment Chester fears he has the wrong house. Then he remembers that Nell has sent the regular staff away for a holiday, apparently a longer holiday than he supposed.

The youngster at the door—who is dressed like a footman—says, "I'll help the driver with your valise, sir." The fellow stares at him with candid blue eyes and goes past him out of doors.

Seeing no one else about, Chester has started up the stairs to the second floor when the parlor door opens, and a voice calls out to him: "Chester, would you come in here, please?"

Chester is astonished to recognize Dun, who rarely calls at his home.

"For God's sake, Robert," he demands, "how is she?"

"She is in no danger," Dun says quietly. He reaches forth his arms when he sees the distress his friend is in. "Come into the parlor, please."

"But I must see her!"

He has started for the stairs again when Dun says, "But she is not here."

"Where then? The hospital?"

"No."

"Tell me where she is!"

Dun pauses a moment. "She sailed yesterday for Europe."

Behind Chester, at the street door, the cab driver and young footman are heaving his valise about. "But if she's ill," Chester says to Dun, following him to the parlor, "how could she—how could she go abroad?"

"She's not ill," Dun repeats. "Rest your mind. We have a fire going in here. Come in and get warm." He takes Chester's arm and starts to help him remove his coat.

Inside the parlor another unexpected figure greets Chester. He is a bent and feeble-looking man, occupying a chair near the fire—Thurlow Weed.

"Good evening. Now the charades can begin," the old man says. His voice is resonant, but he does not move in the chair, nor do his eyes focus well.

"What is going on here?" Chester cries in alarm. A paneled screen has been moved to an unfamiliar position in the room, and he has a sense that someone is behind it. He feels for a bizarre moment that he has entered a stage set designed to look like his own parlor.

"Sit down, Chester," Thurlow Weed says. "We have some disagreeable news to submit to you. But if it is any consolation, it is probably not as bad as you feared when you left Albany. The mother of your children is not at death's door. She has simply left you. That's all."

"Do sit down," Dun says. "Let me pour you a whiskey."

Chester looks from one to the other of them. Soon he is handed a glass of whiskey and holds it without drinking. The blinds on the parlor windows are tightly drawn, and Dun has closed the hall door behind them.

"Nell has left you a letter, which I'll presently give you," Dun says as Chester sits heavily on the settee opposite the fireplace. "The reason Thurlow and I are involved in this—what can I say?—Nell wants it to look, not as if she's left the country, but as if she has died. The attending physician has already informed the newspapers that she has passed away, and in a few hours—"

"Passed away! Are you all mad?" Chester cries.

"She is thinking of *you*, in part—" Dun begins.

"Indeed it works out that way," Weed echoes.

Chester exclaims, "I am dreaming! This is a farce!"

Dun attempts the fuller explanation. A funeral is to be held, at which the body of a derelict woman, recently drowned, will be in Nell's place. "Since the resemblance to Nell is at best approximate," Dun says softly, "no viewing of the body will be any part of the service."

Chester looks from one to the other with eyes widening. "And what does she want me to tell our children of this!" he exclaims.

Dun murmurs, "She expects Nellie to be allowed to follow her to France. They have done a job preparing Alan, I think—"

"*They!*" Chester rises to his feet and moves, red-faced, toward Dun. "*They,* you say! Now, my false friend, who is the man involved with her?"

Weed, rigid in his chair, says, "Who do you think it is, blind man? Who but one person could be Machiavel here?"

"We have little choice, Chester," Dun urges. "Think of the future, and it may seem like a fair gamble—"

For a moment, a crazed look crosses Chester's countenance. He seems unable to absorb what they are saying to him, and in a last effort, struggles back toward the door to the hallway.

"I must see this physician, this Dr. Clayton," he breathes.

Weed begins to laugh harshly. "Dr. Clayton is here," he calls. "He's in the room with us!"

As Chester turns back, he hears a stir behind the paneled screen. The screen is now moved, and from behind it, where he has been sitting on a cushioned chair, listening to what has transpired, a figure now emerges. He is dressed in fashion, carrying the kind of spotless gloves that doctors of a certain station often wear, and he sports a dignified beard. He paces two steps toward Chester. Then, with feet strongly planted, he raises his chin, his eyes fixed like a bird of prey's.

For a moment the unfortunate Chester really imagines that this is the mysterious Dr. Clayton, the specialist, and for yet another moment he cherishes the hope that the original telegram was true. The anguish of what he has been experiencing since entering his home is unbearable compared to the nearly manageable fears he has been undergoing all morning, all afternoon, all night.

"You call yourself a doctor—" he begins, but the word "doctor" turns to ashes.

The man—the slender man—stands not like a doctor but—arrogantly—like an actor.

"Booth! You!" he screams.

The great pain which earlier he felt in his shoulder and arm floods in again, and this time there is no stopping it. Like a damned express train it collides with him. His knees give, he topples, all six-feet-two of him. He notices, eyeballs rolling, the startled anxious movement of Dun as though to come to his aid, believes he even sees Weed react in the chair by the fireplace. And then the last thing, Booth's own surprised stare widening.

Then Booth, who could do nothing for him even if he wanted to, recedes back into infinity, and with the pain comes blinding darkness.

PART THREE
The LIFE
After DEATH

FROM *The New York Times*
JANUARY 16, 1880

MRS. ARTHUR'S FUNERAL
THE SERVICES AT THE CHURCH OF THE HEAVENLY REST AND IN ALBANY

The impressive burial service of the Protestant Episcopal Church was held yesterday morning in the Church of the Heavenly Rest over the body of Ellen Lewis Herndon Arthur, the wife of General Chester A. Arthur. It was attended by a congregation which included many prominent persons, among them being ex-Governor Morgan and his wife, Gen. Lloyd Aspinwall, Salem H. Wells, Dist. Atty. Phelps, Thomas C. Acton, ex-Senator Thomas Murphy, Col. George Bliss and wife, Judge Noah Davis, *et cetera, et cetera.*

The casket containing the body of Mrs. Arthur was covered with black cloth and ornamented with silver handles and a plate bearing the customary inscription. A crown of immortelles was the only floral tribute. The cortege reached the church at 9 a.m., when it was escorted through the central aisle by the officiating clergyman, the Rev. Dr. Robert S. Howland, rector of the church, and the Rev. Mr. Maurey. Following the clergymen were the pallbearers—Gen. George H. Sharpe, H. C. Hepburn, Robert G. Dun, Loomis L. White, Horace B. Frym, Charles E. Miller, Dr. D. B. St. John Roosa, and Charles Freichall.

During the services the Mendelssohn Glee Club gave a grand rendering of the hymn beginning, "There is a blessed home beyond this life of woe." After the usual prayers and scriptural lessons had been recited, the Rev. Dr. Howland pronounced the benediction. The body was taken to Albany for interment.

2

THE RURAL CEMETERY
ALBANY

On a snow-covered knoll too far away to hear the pronouncements
being spoken around the grave, Raymond stamps his feet to keep
warm. He has come over from the area where the drivers and footmen
are waiting with the horses and sleighs so that he can take a piss
behind a yew bush. Wearing leather boots, a belted coat, and a high
silk hat, he is a footman himself for the day. The stillness awes him.
He can hardly believe the vast expanse of countryside, down which the
wind currents are tossing the powdery snow.

He is too excited to feel truly cold. Under the flapping canopy
reared over the grave he can enumerate some of the cast of distinguished characters: the dauntless Senator Conkling, the suavely elegant
Governor Cornell, the preacher in his shabby black coat. All of them
would be getting ears cold enough to fall off if the service went on
much longer.

Mr. Dun spoke the eulogy. He was a bold one: he knew what was
in the coffin. All the way up on the train from New York he stayed at
the right hand of "the General," who, of course, never stepped out of
the private car, never showed his face. They were bold all right. Raymond was not sure any longer how many people were in on the deception. Sometimes he thought pretty near all of them were. Alan, the son,
knew what was going on. He put a sickly expression on his face, not
a very convincing one. But he stayed close to his aunts, his Aunt
Regina and his Aunt Mary. Raymond isn't sure how many of them
know which bodies are in the coffin, and who it is playing the grieving
husband with his coat over his chin.

Even now, as Raymond sees that the rites are finally over, he
wonders how the husband is going to keep that collar up so that
nobody quite gets a good look into his face when they are shaking
hands with him and he is making to embrace them one by one with
his arms around them and his head over their shoulder. Senator Conkling is the first one off; he is in a great hurry to get out of the cold. The
governor is more dignified; Mr. Dun and he exchange quiet words.

Raymond has heard that when you are in service to wealthy
people, you learn many of their secrets; he never expected to learn

them so fast. Even when he worked in "the house" doing the things his new employer thinks so disgusting, he did not learn secrets that seemed to him worth knowing. Now, for the first time, on the night of the unexpected heart attack of General Arthur, did he see how bold men of affairs could really be. He had heard of men who were bold in the market, men like Jay Gould or Jim Fisk, who could win a million by some bold risk they took. But this was a whole different order of risk; he is intoxicated that the tales have proven true.

As the sleighs begin to leave the cemetery one by one, Raymond starts to walk back to the line of them parked along the rutted lane leading through the gate. Some of the sleighs have lengths of black crepe tied to the door handles. On the general's carriage, black plumes are fixed to the horses' harness; the horses themselves are beautiful blacks. When the sleighs reach the lowest part of the river road, they will cross the river on the ice.

Raymond sees Alan slinking toward one of the sleighs, accompanied by two of his aunts and one of his uncles. Alan is so tall that Raymond hates him for reasons of his height as well as for the false expression on his face. At sixteen, Alan wears a coat cut for a grown man, which is both too short for his six-foot-four inches and too wide for him in the shoulders. It is a black coat with a brown fur collar. Raymond would like to knock him down and scrub his face in the snow. Perhaps he would like to tie Alan's hands behind him so that Alan would have to cry for mercy.

He has felt no resentment toward any other member of the Arthur family. Indeed, when the general died like that because of his grief that his wife left him, Raymond felt real sympathy. Toward Alan's sister, of whom Raymond has seen too little (she was kept away from the funeral), Raymond experiences an emotion like fascination. To be sure, she is a child, but she has such soft, large eyes that he senses both pure serenity and implacable depths.

A light snow has begun falling. Across the way only the undertaker remains with the last two mourners: Mr. Dun and "the General." Raymond believes he sees some heavy-coated men with spades lurking in the deepening shadows behind the canopy: gravediggers who will be ready to shovel the frozen dirt onto the lowered casket. The casket is safely sealed: they were told that much on the train up from New York. No one will trouble anymore to notice that its weight is far greater than the single body of a woman would amount to. Yes, they have added the general in a false bottom, buried forever in the same box with the bought corpse that looked something like his wife.

No question there is boldness in it: one gentleman taking over the household of another. Raymond feels sensual stirrings just thinking about it. Boldness stirs him nearly as much as the idea of purity does.

By the time the last two mourners have wended their way up the path to where the closed sleigh is waiting with the driver on the box, Raymond stations himself, touching the back of his hand to his cold, dripping nose. He opens the door, not daring to look into either of the two weary faces. Mr. Dun gets in first.

In a husky voice, with his collar held up by his hand, the other one says, "Will you be all right on the box for the ride back, Raymond?"

"Aye, General," he says cheerfully.

Riding on the box is still part of his station in life. If fortune fails his master, he can begin again with another master. For the time being, pulling the lap robe over the gentlemen, shutting them in, and climbing up top, he is well satisfied with his week's work.

Inside the sleigh, as the horses start forward, both men remove their hats, since the high crowns do not comfortably clear the low ceiling. Dun lifts his feet in order to place the soles of his shoes against one of the hot bricks that was earlier placed on the floor of the sleigh. Booth does not bother to follow Dun's example, since the lifts in his boots are too thick to gain any advantage from the heat still left in the bricks.

Neither of the men speaks for some time. Dun, who has been breathing rather heavily, either from the physical exertion of walking up the hill at the end, or from a deeper nervousness, at last locates his silver cigar case inside his coat. He offers the case to Booth, looking again into the carefully made-up face: the rolled sideburns, the rounded cheeks touched with red, the thickened lips, and prominent chin.

"Well, are you at last a believer?" Booth asks, leaning forward with the cigar to the light that Dun offers.

"But I never believed for a minute," Dun says. "You were . . . impossible."

Silently, Booth balances his hat on his knee and blows smoke out his lips.

"The ceremony," Dun goes on, "made it difficult for anyone to challenge you. You were helpless and . . . voiceless. No one had the nerve."

"But they will never have the nerve, Dun. As long as they are not inconvenienced by my existence, why should they? In the theater, you know, no one ever cries out to the actor, 'You are not Hamlet; you are really Booth, or Irving, or whoever it may be.' It is obscene to shatter the illusion."

Dun grunts. "You will not be able to pretend you have lost your voice indefinitely."

"By the time I come out of seculsion," Booth says, "I will have practiced the voice to have it down well enough. Some will already have forgotten the exact quality of the general's voice in the intervening weeks. My version from then on will become the definitive one."

"Come, come."

"Say a friend who has habitually worn a derby hat suddenly appears in a fedora. At first this demands a certain adjustment, but presently we expect the fedora. It even identifies the man. It is right for him. The derby would be confusing."

"But there is such a thing as character," Dun objects. "You offered tears and embraces at the cemetery. Chester was a more reserved person."

As the sleigh bumps down a declination toward the frozen surface of the Hudson River, Booth puts his hand to the window curtain to look out at the vast twilight canyon flecked by snowflakes. Other sleighs are visible, at greater or lesser distances, moving toward the western shore.

"In time of grief, a man may act out of character," Booth says. "And indeed they may eventually like me better in the new mode. If they do, they will find the changes natural and enhancing."

Dun continues to look skeptical.

Booth says, "Consider this: *you* have responded favorably to me, have you not? You are sitting here, sharing my sleigh, smoking cigars with me, quite as though we were best friends. In a way, I have persuaded you of this by my performance."

Dun says, a bit too quickly, "You know I had no choice. We had announced to the papers the death of Mrs. Arthur; then, suddenly, the death of her husband was presented to us. We had to accept a solution such as the one you offered."

"Ah, then our course was fated!"

"Not so. There is a difference between the will of fate and the will of Booth."

Dun falls silent; Booth, too, appears to lose interest in the disputation. A faintly mottled pattern, like a rash, has declared itself in his face. The black sleigh, pulled by the two black horses, has meanwhile reached the western shore a little ahead of most of the sleighs that left the cemetery before it.

3

THE NEW DELAVAN HOUSE

If one inadvertently startles a man to death, that is reason enough to want to take his place, Booth supposes. It is like a primitive form of compensation, to father the fatherless children.

Perhaps he should have said something like that to Dun. Alone in his suite with Raymond at the end of the day, he nibbles at the bone of a lamb chop, part of the special supper brought up for the guest by the captain of the waiters himself. The coffee provided revives Booth; he has forced himself, in conscience, to consume the heavy meal in its entirety with a view toward getting his weight up over the next few weeks to a point where he can dispense with pillows and padding. God knows that to have fled to Europe and lived the easy life with Nell would have been far more comfortable than to have entered this bloated world of public affairs, where the pursuit of honor has become a near anachronism. He could not imagine that Nell would understand the choice he has made, but he can no longer put off telling her something of it. The Herndons, weatherbound in Virginia, would also have to be told.

"Notice at your work there, lad," Booth remarks to Raymond, who is shifting clothes about in the mahogany wardrobe, "that the former general disdained the frock coat, often favored by men in politics. Instead, he chose the Prince Albert. Such coats were more becoming for a man of his size."

"Be these the Prince Alberts?" Raymond asks.

Booth affirms it. He wipes his fingers on a linen napkin and walks over to the fireplace, where a blaze is roaring in the grate. Examining Chester Arthur's wardrobe is a good way to come to know him; the Delavan House has reinstated them in the very suite that Chester left when he hastened to New York in response to the telegram sent him.

Except for the few articles he took along in his valise, the full panoply of wearing apparel remains where he left it.

"Do you know who Prince Albert was?" Booth asks.

"The Queen of England's husband," says Raymond.

"Indeed he was!" Booth declares. "If I am elected to the Senate, you will do well in Washington. I intend to grapple you to my soul with hoops of steel."

A little flustered, Raymond shifts his feet. He goes on brushing the coats in the wardrobe. For a moment, Booth studies the lad; he has not directed Raymond to brush the coats. In fact, he expected that when the door to the suite was closed Raymond would stop acting like a footman; instead, almost as though he were a professional trouper, he stays in character.

As Raymond's hands move presently to the umbrella stand where Booth's sword-cane reposes, Booth smiles. He has brought it along with him in case some impromptu melodrama should be called for like that staged by the two of them outside A. T. Stewart's.

"Yes," Booth murmurs, as if speaking to some secret part of the lad. "Yes."

A bit uncertainly, Raymond lifts the cane, first by its shaft, then, with a smile of his own, by its handle.

"Now release the blade," Booth directs.

Raymond presses the lever in his grip, and his eyes shine again as the blade springs forth from the tip of the cane. He takes the stance of a swordsman. While Booth watches, he feints, thrusts, and parries, dancing easily back and forth across the carpet.

"Where have you seen that done?" Booth asks.

"At the Bowery Theater."

"All right. . . . But hold the weapon higher. Try thrusting downward with it instead of up."

Raymond practices the actions, thrusts again, ripostes imaginary attacks from opponents, and says at last, "Should it not be armed with a real blade?"

Booth, who has turned to the vanity mirror in the room and has begun to remove his makeup, looks at Raymond's reflection behind him. "Would you have a cause that needs such defending?" he asks.

"I have my honor," Raymond replies lightly.

"Can you imagine running a man through with a blade?"

"Can you?"

Booth replies promptly that he has done such a thing once in defense of his cause and of himself.

"Was it in the war?" Raymond asks, his voice hushed.

"Yes, of course. I wounded an officer in the line of duty. A colonel. I had no choice." When Raymond says nothing, Booth goes on solemnly. "What if I gave you this sword-cane as a gift? Would you like that?"

Raymond's eyes grow large. "What would you have me do for it?"

"Nothing." Booth beckons to the lad. "Come over here." He has taken an object about six inches long out of his makeup case. Quickly, he unsheathes it, a straight razor. With calmness he nicks the forefinger of his left hand so that blood is drawn.

"Give me your hand," Booth directs.

Mesmerized, but with a look of fear on his face, Raymond rigidly extends his left arm. Booth must lean forward to grasp the hand, and then to cut the finger he pulls apart the fist, laying open the flesh with a neat flick of the blade.

Raymond grunts involuntarily and starts to yank the hand back to his mouth. But Booth retains his grip.

"No," Booth commands. "Now open your eyes!"

Unhappily, Raymond does so. A few drops of blood are on his finger. He watches Booth press his own bleeding finger to Raymond's wound. Then Booth lets Raymond go.

"Now we are in a *Blutbrüderschaft*," Booth says sonorously. Raymond has put his finger into his mouth, his eyes now aglow. "We pledge our lives, our fortunes, and our sacred honor," Booth tells him. "I give you this weapon as a mark of my faith that you will not employ it ignobly. I would not give a mere servant such a thing, only a person capable of living up to the high ideals that I live up to."

Looking stunned, Raymond retreats a step or two. Booth supposes that he may be embarrassed, for he presses the blade back into the shaft of the cane and turns his eyes to the floor.

When Booth finishes removing his makeup and begins looking for hotel stationery in the kneehole desk by the fireplace, he asks, "Is it clear to you the kind of faith we have placed in each other, Raymond?"

"Yes, sir," Raymond says with seriousness. He sits on the edge of a settee, waggling his cane vaguely, as though keeping livestock away from his feet.

After Raymond has gone to bed, Booth, in dressing gown, takes pen in hand in order to write Nell the letter that will supply her with as much information as she will need when she reaches Nice.

Mrs. Madeline Usher
Nice, France

My dearest,

How I have suffered thinking of you on your lonely journey over the winter seas! No love can be stronger than that which you bear me— and need I say it again?—that which I bear you. When has a woman ever shown greater faith in a man?

All has gone well. I send along the evening newspaper account of the funeral of "Mrs. General Arthur." You may judge for yourself the course of our endeavor. Let me simply say that I am fine, your children are well, and except for the prospect of a possible delay in our being reunited, the barriers between us have been substantially cleared.

The reaction of your husband to our enterprise was, I have to say, somewhat unexpected. Soon I will have more specific news for you in that regard. But at the moment, and you must trust me in this, beloved, I prefer not to go into detail. My feeling is that in the long run the situation will develop in a way that will be even better than anticipated.

In the meantime you must go ahead and establish your new identity. With your mother's securities, you should have no trouble even if I am delayed a bit longer than was my original expectation.

Until we rejoin each other my life will be a Sahara. Still, I am assisting your children as I am able. They value me, I think, each in his or her fashion. Nellie was kept at her aunt's through the day's ordeals. Alan bore himself well. I had a long talk with him yesterday.

I will write to you at every possible opportunity, and you must do the same, exactly as we arranged. No distance can be too great when the tenderness which exists between my soul and thine creeps yet again into your awareness, dear one.

Fear nothing. Burn this letter.

Booth folds and seals the letter. Although Raymond is snoring in his sleep on the trundle bed in the dressing room, Booth does not feel like retiring. The counterpane is turned down on the great canopied bed in the other room, but he does not yet feel ready to lay his head where Chester Arthur has laid his. Instead, he opens a packet of personal and political papers that he has brought along from the general's study and bedroom in New York. Alan, a practical child, has shown him where to look.

The first test of his impersonation will come, Booth knows, at the state party convention in Utica next month, where he presides. Roscoe

Conkling, Governor Cornell, and the rest will see him under more varied circumstances than they have today.

The task is to prepare himself, as he has always prepared himself for every part he has ever played. Tonight, as he reads the routine phrases of the general's note to a tailor, or a letter sent out to custom-house employees requesting contributions to the party—all of it forming indelible impressions in Booth's memory—he grows more and more confident of his mastery of the role.

He reads late into the night, until there is no more wood for the fire and his eyes smart from strain in the bad light.

4

UTICA

For Roscoe, the problems of the state convention begin on his own front porch. When he should have nothing on his mind but "Grant," "Grant," "Grant," and how he can get more committed delegates for that good man, his wife refuses to let him in the door of his own residence.

The entrance is locked and bolted, and she declares herself through the opaque lace curtains blowing in a window adjacent to the porch. When Roscoe, using hand gestures, declares himself in turn, the stalemate is complete.

"I have nothing more to say," he tells her after long silence.

"Well, I have nothing more to say," she replies.

"Then there is nothing more to be said."

Most embarrassing it is, since his secretary and a junior aide are with him on the front porch to hear it all. Of course they all repair at once to Bagg's Hotel, where Roscoe keeps a suite. The yellow press is to blame for his wife Julia's obstinacy. An account of the fisticuffs he had in Washington with Kate Sprague's husband has appeared in the metropolitan papers, and evidently in Utica as well. He finds it demoralizing that Julia cannot accept that he intervened in a quarrel between Sprague and Kate's music teacher. The Utica papers must have suppressed his side of the story; in any case, their only legitimate concern is whether or not he is the best steward of the public trust.

At Bagg's, Tom Platt comes up in the lobby and begins complaining again about poor Chester, who has shown signs of fumbling his chores. It is no light matter, for the state must be solid for Grant if they are to succeed in Chicago.

"He acts like he's got a hinge loose," Platt grouses.

"Make allowances," Roscoe says. "Others do. He's still in a state of grief."

Platt explains that poor Chester "is calling people he don't know well by their first names and old pals by their last names."

"Ridiculous!" the Senator sneers. He is accustomed to winning arguments by sneering. Besides, Platt's ill-fitting false teeth and bad breath distract one from what he is saying.

"You remember that girlie?" Platt persists. "The one he was looking for in Albany who said she was a reporter? She turned up here and he didn't recognize her."

"So what?"

"I think she's wonderin' if he lost his mind. . . . Even his voice is peculiar, more hoarse than I ever heard it."

"He has polyps on his vocal cords, Tom!" Roscoe shouts. "He wrote us about that. Can't you be a little charitable to the bereaved?"

"That's fine," Platt says blandly, "but he's not doin' us much good with the delegates, either, that I can see."

"Well, I'll talk to him," Roscoe says. It would not do if they lost delegates.

But by the time he heads off to the convention hall the following afternoon, Roscoe has still not had his talk with Chester. Confidently, he has assessed Tom Platt's backbiting as a typical symptom of ambition. That Tom would like to go to Washington ahead of poor Chester is common knowledge; besides, Chester has already done some grand things for the convention. How could anyone, for example, find fault with the grand welcome to Utica that Chester staged at the railroad station when Roscoe arrived yesterday on the six forty? How could one lose faith in a man who knew how to line the tracks with perfect little torpedoes so that when the train wheels passed over them they detonated one by one like a great artillery attack? It was an impeccable greeting for a favorite son, and when Roscoe climbed down the steps, there was Chester to great him warmly. Then Chester stepped aside to address the press, who had to be told that the mock artillery sound was to remind people of the battlefield lineage of General Grant, the man America needed.

As Roscoe climbs out of his carriage, now in front of the convention hall, the crowd in the street begins applauding. He waves his cane to the left and his hat to the right.

There are shouts. "Hurrah for the Senator!"

Groups of well-dressed gentlemen have formed outside the entrance with even a few ladies included. He sees Mrs. Gilhooley and Carrie Bender.

"Welcome home, Senator!" cries Mrs. Gilhooley and some of the others.

"Three cheers for General Grant!" someone has the presence of mind to shout.

A welcoming committee, including Speaker Sharpe and General Woodford, emerges to escort him to the inner door for his grand entrance. It is ten minutes past noon, and Chester has already called the convention to order. Mr. Pierrepont, ex-minister to the court of St. James's, whispers something to the Senator at the very threshold.

Roscoe nods. Nervously, he preens himself, wets a finger, and runs it over his eyebrows. Another of the welcoming committee reveals that General Arthur has begun the session precisely on time. As Roscoe passes through the swinging door, he is surprised to notice a woman occupying a chair at the press tables. She seems young. Is this the creature Platt was in an uproar about?

Now with a great sweep, the Senator is prodded forward, and the entire cadre surges through the doors, which bang backward so violently that an aged doorman is knocked off his feet. The Senator is the tallest of the group, and as soon as the convention spots him leading the contingent of his eminent supporters they burst into wild shouts of joy. All voices in the hall seem to join in the grand tumult.

Roscoe beams, glows. He strides across the back of the house, then down the center aisle. The posse around him keeps step. When he extends his arm, they extend theirs too.

A few, Roscoe can now see, are applauding out of mere politeness. Their faces, although benign, register no particular enthusiasm, and here and there Roscoe notices delegates—or could they be alternates?—who simply stand and stare. At least they are on their feet. Still he finds time to sneer at one of them before he resumes his progress toward the platform.

The gavel then begins slowly to echo through the hall—a minute too soon, in Roscoe's opinion. On the other hand, in saluting the platform where his friend Chester Arthur now presides, he has few qualms about what he sees. While Chester seems to have lost a little weight and almost—it is difficult to admit—appears to have shrunk in size in the last month or so, his platform manner is brisk and poised. He stands at a becoming angle, and when he speaks, although his voice is somewhat hoarse, he says the right words.

"The chair and the convention welcome the senior Senator from our great state—Utica's own Roscoe Conkling!"

A new round of cheers. The Senator begins bowing again. Clearly, Chester's voice is affected. But as Roscoe's escort settles around him, Chester allows the roll call to continue—"with the Senator's permission?" "With the Senator's permission" Roscoe thinks an ill-advised phrase, implying too much control of the convention.

Other than that, however, Chester is handling things all right. When a raucous delegate named Forster offers a motion which they have been tipped off about, Chester has a substitute motion ready. Eventually—after five or ten minutes of hornswoggle—Forster will withdraw his motion.

In this slough Roscoe feels the gaze of the girl reporter on him. She is a piece all right, large eyes and a slender body, but who on earth could have given her credentials? Roscoe stares back at her, wondering what she is up to. He has lately had his fill of dealing with women. His problem with Julia would be alleviated if he could get through to her that he is really finished with Kate Sprague. Kate is getting to be a terrible nuisance now that the newspapers are printing anything under the sun.

"The point is well taken!" Chester is saying from the platform, and Roscoe applauds automatically, whatever the point was, or who made it.

About a year ago the *Sun* was going to smear the whole story about his relationship with Kate over the front page. He had got wind of it just before press time; the thing was already in galleys.

He went foaming to the editor, of course. The most defaming and scurrilous libel he had ever seen in his life!

"I promise I will sue if you print one word of this!" he raged.

"Go ahead and sue," the editor said. A pipsqueak he was. But he was trying to be hard.

So Roscoe said in a dead quiet voice, "If you print it, I will kill you."

With that he left the office. The story was never printed.

Chester is pounding his gavel again. A vote has been taken—a voice vote—on the substitute motion, and Chester announces that the motion has carried. Immediate raucous protest from the back rows. Roscoe and others rise to stare disdainfully at their disruptive brethren. While Chester pounds the gavel, the Senator sneers at some of them, particularly the delegate from Westchester, a Blaine man for whom he has contempt. The Senator plans to chide him later, from the floor, for his presumption in identifying himself as a New York City delegate rather than one from Westchester.

Chester meanwhile is truly presiding.

"If the delegates do not preserve order, we shall be prepared to eject them!"

Roscoe nods his full approval. Bravo, Chester. If there is anything wrong with that, the Senator would like to know what it is. No amnesia there. In fact, the Senator is prepared to sneer at Tom Platt too, except that Platt's back happens to be turned. Roscoe is much disappointed in Platt that he should try to undermine an old trouper like Chester. While Chester was in his country's uniform rallying the Boys in Blue, Tom was still trying to learn how to fill prescriptions in the pharmacy.

Roscoe knows merit when he sees it. Hurrah for Chester. Hurrah for Grant. Enough of jealous mediocrity!

5

MADISON SQUARE

"As I live and breathe. General Arthur, is it not?"

She is walking her dog, a large poodle. He is on his way over to Thurlow Weed's. It is just past two o'clock in the afternoon a few weeks following the state convention. At first surprised to be accosted by a strange woman, he then recognizes her as the so-called reporter who pursued him in Utica.

"Miss Victoria Coventry, is it not?" he says, tipping his hat, in a way mocking the fashion in which she addressed him.

"I'm astonished that you remember," she says dryly.

With an effort he pulls himself into character. They have stopped on the sidewalk immediately in front of the park where Liberty's arm —intended to be part of a colossal statue for the harbor—is displayed. His gaze he permits to focus on its copper staircase which, for the price of a ticket, people are allowed to climb for a view from the balcony that girds the burnished torch above.

"You were much talked about at the convention," Booth says pleasantly. Each day his command of Chester's voice is improving. Still, this woman makes him feel uncomfortable by the way she scrutinizes him.

"I suppose I am notorious," she replies. "Was that why you didn't want to see me?"

"I was in mourning, as I told you in the note I wrote."

She continues to watch him with a noncommittal air. Beneath her sacque coat she is wearing a handsome woolen dress of a dark color; her soft auburn hair is coiled on her head and set off with a small, chic hat.

"I am not ready to be interviewed during the mourning period," he says. In the past, it would have been prudent to try to make love to a woman such as this, who could cause him trouble. But cushioned and puttied as he is, he dislikes to take the risk.

"Not even one question, General," she asks him, "out of consideration for the promises made?"

She makes him feel uncertain; it is difficult to guess the extent of her intimacy with the general.

"Why not ask it of Senator Conkling, or if that is impossible, Mr. French, or Mr. Wheelhorse—"

"I really do not mean to upset you," she now says. "I realize you are not yourself."

He focuses on her steadily, judging the weight of the remark she has just made. Her manner is insouciant, but probably harmless. She does not dress as a serious woman, rather more like a courtesan.

"Are you of the opinion," she suddenly asks, "that the state will, or will not, send a united delegation to Chicago?"

"We covered that with the male reporters," he says, tipping his hat to her. "Good day, Miss Coventry."

Briskly he walks on. Victoria Coventry is a vile name. He suspects she has tried others. Young actresses always picked names like that one. And was he after all not accustomed to dealing with "independent" women?

In Thurlow Weed's library, Booth studies a rogue's gallery of studio photographs of prominent Republican politicians from around the country. Weed has preserved them from his days at the *Journal*, when young reporters used them as an aid in recognizing important men.

"One of these days," Weed says jauntily, "they'll find a cheap process of reproduction. Then your front page'll be full of pictures. Every day of the week." A rum and water has been poured for the old man; he sits in the leather-covered chair near the window with the sun streaming over his shoulder.

Booth rehearses names and faces on the portraits. Whenever he looks up at his host, Weed is gazing back at him curiously. There is no sense of constraint in Weed's cooperation. It is as it was during the war. Weed is grayer and blinder, but just as pleased at his own resourcefulness.

"Were any of these men close to the general?" Booth asks. The assortment of faces reminds Booth of an assortment of Pinkertons whose faces he learned from photographs during the war.

"Dennison of Ohio was," Weed says. "For some reason Chester liked him, although Conkling thinks Dennison is senile and of no consequence. . . . But then Conkling thinks Grant can be nominated."

"And that is not likely?"

"Dammit, Booth, how should I know? I'm not active in the party anymore. . . . What do you think?"

Booth says that his interest is limited to becoming a Senator and endeavoring to recover his lost honor.

"You'll probably make a better Senator than Grant was a President," Weed allows, "even with the half-cocked notions you have. . . . Satisfied with my assistance, are you, by the way?"

Booth extracts a cigar case from the inside pocket of his coat. "In point of fact, I may need some assistance with a certain female reporter who has pursued me both at the convention in Utica and now again on Madison Square. She's unsettling."

"La femme?" Weed booms. "What in hell paper has hired a *femme* as a reporter?"

"None, but she gets credentials somehow." Booth lights his cigar. "Why not see if you can't get somebody to put her on their regular staff . . . and confine her to assignments that are more worthy of her?"

"Worthy?"

Booth says that any sort of feature assignment will do, so long as she is kept away from politics, which can only "bring her to grief."

He has spoken with such deliberate implication that Weed sets down his glass, acting displeased. "I don't like you to talk like that, Booth. . . . However, tell me her name."

"Victoria Coventry."

Weed sniffs. "She sounds like bad luck. Women in a newsroom are bad luck."

"She's nubile. She'll make somebody a good uptown mistress."

"Then let us not talk of bringing her to grief."

Seeing that he has won Weed's consent, Booth changes the subject back to Dennison of Ohio.

6

123 LEXINGTON AVENUE

Harder for Booth to control during this period than the undulations of public affairs is the restless sea of his domestic life. Over the springtime months his perfect immersion in the files of Chester Arthur (in order to prepare himself for the presidential nominating convention) is regularly disturbed by squabbling among the servants and by tiresome conversations with Alan, whose appetite for money compares with that of his late father—one who was, good Lord, no amateur at chicanery, judging by the copies of his customhouse correspondence.

One night, unseasonably warm enough for him to have left the window open, Booth munches croissants in the ground-floor office while writing letters to some of the county chairmen, using a model he has found in the files. As state chairman and future Senator he must stimulate the faithful to enrich the party coffers as much as they are able during the present prosperity.

A knock at the door around midnight is followed by the entrance of Alan. Blasé in a riding habit—even at such an hour—he ducks his head in order to come in. At sixteen, he towers at a height Booth is relieved that his father never reached.

"The gentlemen you ride with do not dress for dinner, I gather," Booth remarks. He has reached for the ledger containing blank bank drafts.

Ignoring the comment, Alan pushes aside a tray of stale bakery goods and drops into a chair. "I'm not sure at all that I like your young valet's manner." He has developed a faint drawl, probably an affectation common among his friends. His moustache has come on in recent weeks to add maturity to his baby face.

Booth starts writing a "pay to bearer" draft. "The last I heard, you were going to visit Princeton tomorrow with some of your friends. Is that still in your plans?"

"Yesss. . . . Your valet has moved into Mother's sewing room."

"Why shouldn't he?" Booth says. "He is running the house. Under my auspices." Alan is aware that the original staff has had to be let go except for Bridget, given permission to visit her dying brother in Ireland. Since Nell treasured Bridget, Booth has paid Bridget's passage abroad, hoping thereby to win her discretion when she returns.

"You allow a child to run the house?" Alan asks.

Booth replies that the child is older than Alan is.

"I am not speaking so much of chronological age," Alan sighs. "But he is infantile in every way." Has it been noticed, for example, Alan asks, that Raymond keeps a candle burning beneath the portrait of Nellie that he has taken into his room? "Since he met her, he behaves as though she were Bernadette of Lourdes."

"He values her as an obedient child," Booth says uneasily. When Nellie, who has continued to live in Newtonville with her cousins, paid them a visit one noon recently, Raymond kept bowing to her. Booth hoped it might have been the presence of the governess that was responsible for the awe in Raymond's face.

"He is demented," Alan says. "Nellie is eight years old."

Booth signs the draft as he has practiced: "Chester A. Arthur." "She looks older than that, you must admit."

Yawning hopelessly, Alan starts to reach for the draft as soon as Booth has torn it away from its perforations. But he does not get it. Booth waves the signed draft in the air, as though he is helping the ink to dry.

"You know, Alan," Booth says, "as long as I am writing your bank drafts—*in loco parentis,* so to speak—there is no harm in calling me sir, is there?"

"Not at all . . . sir," Alan says looking more alert.

"No legal executor of your father's estate is likely to have been as generous to you—a minor—as I have been. Would you not say that was the case?"

"I've known you since I was five years old, sir, and you've always been fair," says Alan, sitting forward in his chair. Booth respects that about the boy: he has an instinct about how far he can go, as children from moneyed families often do.

"Few young men are able to continue to behave irresponsibly after their father's death. Consider that, Alan."

"I do . . . sir," Alan says. His eyes are still on the draft, which Booth has not yet handed him.

"Then, unless you wish to huddle with relatives in the country, as your sister is doing, you must follow the line that I draw. You must show some respect to Raymond, my aide. And you must be ever discreet . . . if you want this arrangement to continue."

"Yes, sir," Alan says, more promptly. He shifts one lanky knee over the other. He clears his throat. "About Mother. You must tell me when I should write to Mother."

"You haven't heard from her?"

"No, sir."

"Neither have I, strange to say. But I will tell you when the time comes to write. In the meantime she will be most content if you remain a temperate and discreet young man, as your father always wished."

Alan, accepting the bank draft at last, scrutinizes the signature with sincere approbation. "I'll call you Father . . . if you want me to," he says after a moment.

"As you like," Booth says briskly. He does not wish to press for a relationship involving sentiment. He thinks, in fact, a measure of fear on Alan's part will be useful for future harmony.

"Good night, Alan."

"Good night, sir."

But Alan is no more than up the stairs when Booth hears loud noises from the foyer, and something that sounds like a scuffle. The voices are Raymond's and Alan's. A crash against the wall of the stairway resounds, and impatiently Booth gets up, opens the door, and calls up the stairs.

"Stop that! Both of you! Raymond, come down here."

In the shadow of the passageway above, the two figures manage to separate themselves. Raymond, looking smirky and disheveled, starts smoothing his hair and twisting his apron around so that it is positioned in front of his waist again.

"He shoved me into the banustrade!" Raymond says, descending. "I was comin' to get your dishes and he pushed me!"

"Keep away from him, then."

"He called me flyshit," Raymond declares. "He said when the

lady came back, I'd get pitched out o' the house. . . . But the lady's not comin' back, is she?"

Booth says, "Raymond, if you can't get along with the children in this family, you won't be of much use to me."

"I get along with Miss Nellie!" Raymond protests. He starts to give a long-winded account of what happened at lunch the day Nellie and the mademoiselle came to pick up Nellie's things. The mademoiselle was telling an "interesting story" about her life in France when Alan, who was also present, just got up and walked away. "He never even said 'Excuse me.' "

Booth sighs and says that this is tittle-tattle, not worthy of him. Raymond should start thinking about Chicago, where he is going to attend the national political convention. Doubtless there will be new adventure and challenge for Raymond in the service of the general, and he should stop prattling like scullery does.

"I respect and venerate Miss Nellie," Raymond reiterates, picking up the dirty dishes.

Booth turns away. Sometimes it seems that not even a lad of the streets could develop in a healthy normal way anymore. Candles in front of the portraits of eight-year-olds. Other exotic vices. Who knew what to expect?

With his feeling of depression growing along with his waistline, Booth risks a visit to the theater one evening. Since he is supposed to be in mourning, he considers a new disguise for the occasion, but decides it is too much trouble.

Sitting conspicuously in the back of the orchestra (where the only tickets are available), he is gripped with fresh anguish while watching his brother play Hamlet. Perhaps the feeling arises because the supporting cast is bad, and yet his brother muddles through. Perhaps it is because the theater bears the name "Booth's," but has slipped out of the family's control. Or perhaps it is simply that he yearns to be in touch again with his "Ted."

The closet scene he literally cannot bear to watch. The network of family relationships in the play opens old wounds. Vindication is the subject of the drama, and he must face it that he has always felt the need for vindication in his own life. All the years his father Junius lived out of wedlock with their mother embittered Wilkes, and even though they finally married, he knew the ceremony made him no less a bastard.

The tears that form in his eyes certify that his name, of all the

Booths, will be the hardest to vindicate. He hopes some day to accomplish it. One day in old age he would like to call on Edwin and Edwin's wife at their home on Madison Square—and be received. He probably will never see his mother again. Although she and his sister Rose have moved back from New Jersey, she will doubtless die in her rooms at the Grand Central Hotel, never to know that her son Johnny survived her.

During the intermission before the last act, standing in the crowded lobby near one of the smoking rooms, he notices the Rosencrantz and Guildenstern of the Senator's party: Messrs. French and Wheelhorse. The shorter one—Booth cannot remember which is which —seems to be watching him. But there is no smile of recognition. Has Platt put them on his trail? Surely they do not seem natural theatergoers.

He turns aside. The great lobby chandelier at Booth's is illuminated by electricity. As the lights inside the theater dim, so, too, does the large chandelier. Booth decides to forgo the last act and its heartbreak. Drawing his cape over his shoulders, he hurries out to Sixth Avenue to hail a carriage to drive him home.

In his haste he has overlooked the other personage in the lobby who has been watching him curiously. Victoria Coventry and her male escort are in conversation near a stand where a young woman sells beautiful intricate boutonnieres, all arranged on a large display board. Someone near them is talking about Lillian Russell.

Victoria falls silent in the middle of a sentence. After Booth has left the theater, she says to the young man (who sells bonds on Wall Street): "Excuse my staring off. But that gentleman who just walked out is a great puzzle to me."

"And how does he manage that?" her escort asks, turning around too late to have seen the man.

Victoria wears a long powder-blue gown with a fitted cape. "Why, by not being the man he claims to be." She cannot forbear laughing at herself. "He is what I think they call an impostor."

"Perhaps from Elsinore?" the escort offers.

"No, I think he's a genuine impostor!" she exclaims, but has begun to doubt her judgment. If an impostor were accepted by his colleagues, by his children, by his servants—all of which Victoria has found out through her queries—perhaps he ceased to be an impostor. *That* was a daring idea!

She takes her escort's arm as the lights go down so that she can follow him back into the theater. She would not trouble herself further with General Arthur, who was not a particularly important man. Monday she was to begin proper investigative reporting, the only kind of newspaper job she was willing to take when Mr. Bennett called her into his office at the *Herald*. Not society chatter, as he first suggested. Instead she would work undercover at Latham's, the hoopskirt factory, and write about the terrible conditions in which those girls labored. It would be like her series about the life of a prostitute, but this time the revelations could be printed in a family newspaper.

"Very well," Mr. Bennett had said. "But you must concentrate your energy exclusively on this project."

"Of course," Victoria replied, surprised. "And in return, you must tell no one what I will be doing."

"You have real grit for a woman," said Bennett.

How else could she get hired, Victoria would like to say to him, but by taking her life into her hands? How else, that is, if she wanted to be a true reporter and not just a society parasite? She has even had to tell the rather handsome man she is with at Booth's that she is going to be out of town for several weeks in order for a time to deflect his growing interest in her. . . .

7

CHICAGO

"Hurrah!" says Raymond as they arrive. "It do have a smell."

"Are you ready for it?" Booth asks him.

"As ready as you."

Ah, Booth is ready for it. No one is better rehearsed for the convention. He has spent the months of mourning in such conscientious study that when he at last arrives with Raymond at Union Station on the muddy river, he exudes an air of recovered confidence in his destiny as a future Senator. He has practiced a more dignified way of tipping his hat, his conversational pauses have become gentle and natural rather than overdramatic. Most important, he feels now that he can recognize all the important people; the unimportant should not be recognized anyway.

In the crowded corridors of the Great Pacific Hotel, where they have their private suite, he makes an immediate impression merely by being elevated a few inches in height above the surface of the restless sea of boys and bearded men. So great is the competition for attention that waves of partisans keep beating back and forth against each other. Booth and Raymond tread the currents, their senses alive. Signs are nailed everywhere. A four-piece band plays "Oh, Dem Golden Slippers" over and over. Firecrackers explode. From the first floor balcony where the Grant people have set up a colossal portrait of the general to block off an entire staircase, Booth watches Raymond and the others throw "Grant torpedoes" out the window near where the people are passing on the street below.

"Look at 'em run!" Raymond yowls. "How'd you find such noisy ones!"

Booth winks: he orders from the big theatrical wholesaler in Baltimore: "Gibbs—Best Tricks and Props in the U.S.A.!"

Within the bedlam of the Great Pacific, which is further swelled by office seekers of all shapes and sizes, half-frightened hotel employees, and farmers come to stare, Booth catches an early glimpse of Roscoe Conkling arriving, but does not see him soon again. Roscoe is keyed up to a perilous pitch; he feels too high-strung to come out of his suite. While Chandler of New Hampshire, who is Blaine's manager, and General Garfield of Ohio, who is Sherman's manager, circulate in the corridors and meeting rooms, amiably inspiring goodwill, Roscoe leaves the handshaking for Grant to others. He works on his nominating speech. Platt is twice called to the Senator's suite, while General Logan, a Grant man from Illinois, goes in once. General Arthur is not summoned.

But Booth feels no foreboding. He enjoys walking about in the elevating shoes, being already so graceful in them that he seems in constant *pas de deux* with the various gentlemen whom he encounters. His preparation has been excellent. When, however, he feels like getting away for a time from, say, French and Wheelhorse, who are usually loitering, he takes a stroll through the heart of the city with Raymond. While he cannot show the lad where the Great Fire started (or any charred corpses from the conflagration), it is diverting to point out some of the locations he is familiar with, anticipating Raymond's reactions. On the whole, Raymond is less impressed with Chicago than he was with Albany, perhaps because he sees it in some kind of competition with New York. But he thinks Lake Michigan, green and somnolent, worth looking at. The two of them smell the stockyards and wonder if there is anything in New York quite so foul.

Without comment Booth leads Raymond past some of the theaters in the area. McVicker's Theater, where Edwin was nearly shot, is closed but advertises a forthcoming opening of *Romeo and Juliet*. A playhouse where Wilkes once starred is closed and dilapidated. He recalls with a blush that the posters proclaimed in his behalf: "I Am Myself Alone!" That was before he had made a reputation in his own right.

When Raymond and he meet gentlemen in the street who are connected with the convention, Booth tips his hat to them austerely, and some of them nod and tip their hats, saying "Good morning, General Arthur" or "Pleasant day for this time of year, General." He has heard that midwesterners are garrulous, but he finds, on the contrary, that they appreciate your staying within conversational formulas and would not regard you as a gentleman if you deviated.

Raymond notices this, too, and expresses his suspicion of the type, imagining them all to be Blaine or Sherman delegates. He has become so fierce a partisan for Grant that Booth expects he will suffer a real disappointment if the nomination is not attained. On the first night of their arrival at the hotel, Raymond has led the way in hanging the great banner that says "New York Solid for Grant" outside their hotel room windows on the second floor cornice. He sincerely believes that they will yet be called upon to do something daring and devilish to help Grant.

"We shouldn't take any chances that they beat us, Gen'ral," he advises with a sly look.

Meanwhile Booth goes to committee meetings: Rules Committee, Credentials Committee, Permanent Organization Committee. All know that if the "unit rule" be but established for the convention, Grant will have a walkover. The opposition fears that Cameron, the temporary chairman of the convention, will force the rule through by the fiat of a voice vote. But if they can depose Cameron first—

Roscoe passes down the word: Cameron must not be deposed! At all costs, "Chester" must prevent it. Some hours later, the compromise is found: Cameron will be retained, but the unit rule decided on by a roll call, not a voice vote.

Head aching, Booth retires for the night, but not before explaining to a sleepyheaded Raymond that the other fellow's point of view deserves as much respect as one's own.

The next morning, Roscoe, emerging from his funk, invites the assembled lieutenants for breakfast in his suite.

"The temporary chairman can do anything he pleases!" Roscoe declares, with Adam's apple shaking. "No matter what was agreed upon, Cameron can call for a voice vote whenever he wants."

Booth lifts his chin. When gentlemen on opposing sides made preliminary arrangements on disputed points, such arrangements had to be respected. Even men who were blood enemies made such arrangements during the war.

"It is not honorable," Booth says stiffly, "to go back on negotiated agreements."

Roscoe's color rises. "Do you presume to instruct me on what is honorable, sir?"

For a moment, the forgathered start looking up from their breakfasts, one by one. Governor Cornell, soft of chin, has looked up sharply from his heaping dish of sausage and scrambled eggs, and he casts a meaningful glance at Tom Platt. But French and Wheelhorse happen into the suite just then. The shorter one—French?—irrepressibly begins a vulgar anecdote about Congressman Chandler, which makes the breakfasters, Roscoe included, dissolve into cackling laughter, and the previous issue is forgotten.

When French taps his derby against his thigh, there is laughter around the table all over again, although Booth has no idea why. Good God, he wonders what he is doing among such scum of the earth, promoting ignoramuses like Grant to the highest office in the land!

French and Wheelhorse have been invited by Roscoe to sit down, and by the time they have passed three or four more boisterous remarks while looking at the room service menu, Roscoe's mood is greatly improved. Jocular reference is made to General Arthur's having lunched with Dennison of Ohio the previous day. Dennison is still widely thought to be feebleminded.

"Indeed he *is* feebleminded," Booth says spiritedly, "but that is valuable information."

"Chester," Roscoe says in a patronizing tone, "is our spy in the enemy camp." There is an effort at laughter again. Toward the end of the breakfast, when the attention of all the others is distracted in various ways, Roscoe leans over and adds, "Perhaps nothing after all can be done about the unit rule, Chester." Surreptitiously he licks his finger and applies it to his eyebrows. "I know you meant well on the committee. I know it has been a trying year for you. But do keep your wits about you until you are . . . up to snuff again, my friend."

8

THE WINDSOR HOTEL

Three days later, on a Sunday—with the convention about to take its first ballot for the nomination the following day—Booth lunches for the second time with Dennison of Ohio. On this occasion they meet in the dining room of a more out-of-the-way hotel, where Booth trusts that the encounter will go unreported. He has been made nervous by several events in his own camp, the most recent of which has had French and Wheelhorse putting questions to Raymond as to how long Raymond has worked for General Arthur, and under what circumstances he came into the general's employ.

Although Raymond answered them cheekily enough, Booth senses that a tide has begun to rise that will either sweep him forward again or engulf his little craft. A letter from Nell in Nice, forwarded to the hotel, has added to his uneasiness: it is so piteously full of puzzled inquiries about his delay in reaching her that it nearly makes him want to trim his sail at once for Monte Carlo.

In this testing hour, he chooses for the Sunday luncheon a place on Monroe Street that he knows from his theater days. Most of the delegates have been exhausted by the nominating speeches, and with the convention in recess, many, including Roscoe, are not likely to emerge from their suites until later in the day. As far as the sprightly Dennison is concerned, he is like the early bird who has caught a worm. Once the wartime governor of his state, he is now, in assumed dotage, the "honorary" chairman of the Ohio delegation.

"Yassuh?" the colored waiter says politely.

They order steak with mushrooms à la General Grant, hash brown potatoes à la Blaine, asparagus Sherman, stuffed tomatoes à la Conkling, and coffee Washburne.

"Well now, this is a relaxing, homelike place, isn't it, General?"

Dennison says. He looks around with a bright gaze that at moments seems unfocussed. But he does not sham senility with Booth as he does with politicians he does not like.

Dennison says, "For a fact, that was some speech your Senator gave last night." They talk for a few minutes about some of the nominating speeches of the previous evening. Roscoe's, delivered grandly after he clambered onto a press table in order to second Grant, included the little quatrain made popular just after the war:

> *When asked what state he hails from*
> *Our sole reply shall be*
> *He hails from Appomattox,*
> *And its famous apple tree!*

After that, Roscoe elaborated for an hour. The name "Ulysses S. Grant" was the "most illustrious borne by living man." Grant had seen "not only the highborn and titled, but the poor and lowly in the uttermost ends of the earth, rise and uncover before him." The election ahead would be "the Austerlitz of American politics."

And for twenty minutes after the speech was over, Exposition Hall vibrated with shouts of "Grant! Grant! Grant!" Had the balloting been taken right then, Roscoe might have swept Grant in by a landslide.

"Except," Governor Dennison observes, after remarking on the drama of the speech, "oratory is not always wisdom. You're professional enough, I bet, General, to admit that criticizing the other fellow's candidate—easy though it may be—is not wisdom."

"You have more experience than I do, Governor," Booth says, "at these shindigs."

Lacking chin whiskers, Dennison's smile is open and gentle. As their meal arrives, he lets himself talk of Thurlow Weed and the old days—the Whig conventions—when they rallied for such men as Zach Taylor, and—truth to tell—abolition was the issue. Issues were issues then, opines Governor Dennison. Warmly, Booth agrees. He is ingesting his stuffed tomato à la Conkling.

"Of course," Dennison says, as though it were the moral of his account, "if you Grant men can't make it, be assured that when you bring your three hundred votes to Ohio's candidate, you will have ample consideration. Secretary Sherman is for all factions of the party."

Booth, sipping his coffee Washburne, listens as Dennison lays on the soap: although Secretary Sherman was technically responsible for removing "yourself, dear General, from the customhouse," there was nothing personal in it. On the contrary, it was only because the "reformers" had gotten the ear of President Hayes.

"Privately, I am no reformer," Dennison confides, "and truly believe that neither Senator Conkling, nor any of you, would have much to fear from a new—uhh—Ohio (!) administration." With eyes wickedly alight, he picks up his coffee cup and looks for Booth's reaction.

Booth says that some have thought that it is Garfield, and not Sherman, who is Ohio's true candidate. "A man with more inspirational qualities, perhaps," Booth says guardedly.

"Ah, well!" Dennison says with the broadest of smiles. He surveys the menu for the second time and decides on apple pie Edmunds for dessert. Edmunds is Senator Hoar's candidate, and perhaps that of twenty-five other delegates.

"It may come to pass," Dennison says, "that New York will be thinking about who will have second place on the ticket. You know?"

"You mean if Grant fails?"

"Yes, if Grant fails."

Booth starts to respond, then a sixth sense tells him that it will be better to smile and shrug. A divinity shaped one's ends. Chairman Dennison exudes an air of knowingness. As the two men dive into their desserts, Dennison into his apple pie and Booth into his bread pudding Windom, Booth feels that he better understands the process that he explained to Raymond the other night.

On the stroll back to the Great Pacific Hotel, Dennison walks with halting steps, but the two men continue their amiable conversation. Dennison explains how the achieved defeat of the unit rule will lead to Ohio's choosing the entire ticket. Booth now believes it too. He is not fearful of being seen with the governor.

On the carpeted central stairs and from one frescoed wall to the other, the Great Pacific lobby swarms with life. Men boost themselves to seats along the registration desk, shoulder through the potted palms, try to keep from stepping into the brass spittoons. Out of the noise and smoke, Governor Dennison has one more parting word for his luncheon companion.

"Watch Wisconsin," he says.

Booth nods with respect. Having schooled himself to watch Ohio, it could be a relief to watch Wisconsin for a while.

9

EXPOSITION HALL

"Do you know who I saw walking down Jackson Street this morning?" shouts Cornell, a minstrel-show Mr. Bones.

Booth, who has been standing in the aisle near the New York standard, gazes silently off toward the speakers' platform. The first ballot has just been hurried through so that all the states can get a count on the candidates' strengths. Once they have it—Grant 304, Blaine 284, Sherman 93, others 74—a dauntingly aggressive impulse seems to animate certain of the camps.

"Bunny Licks!" Cornell declares, staring right at him.

"Not Bunny Licks?" Booth echoes too quickly. In the next moment he senses that he has been tricked: there is no Bunny Licks. He tries to change the subject.

Malicious, Tom Platt calls over the din, "How's about one-eyed Mama Benson that you and Dorsey took the Illinois boys to in Cincinnati four years ago? That's a famous story."

"Go fall on yourself, Tom," Booth says. Quickly he drifts away from them, drifts up the aisle into the orbit of a tall male reporter, who greets him heartily.

"They call you the best-dressed delegate at the convention, General. What d'you say to that?"

Answer with a smile.

"All of us who wear Grant badges are naturally the best-dressed!"

Booth, working hard, also perspiring now, notes from a distance that Roscoe has suddenly rejoined the New York delegation for the second ballot. He sees a sneer on Roscoe's face, directed, he believes, at himself. Then Roscoe puts his head together with Platt's and Cornell's, and looks up to sneer again.

Booth, lingering in the crowded aisle, hears the chairman call out the vote totals as the state names are read.

When New York is called, Roscoe steps forward and cries out, "Mr. Chairman, I stand so all may know that New York harbors faithless men."

Suddenly there is an eruption of hisses and a long pounding of the gavel. In the present mood, Booth has the panicky thought that Roscoe will point him out under the very bust of Lincoln. Here stands Booth, Roscoe will declare, a viper in their bosom! Only Grant can save America from the outrageous insolence of escaped assassins!

But Roscoe proceeds apace.

"Faithless men, faithless to their common duty."

He merely wants the delegation polled, a purification rite, in order that " the world" may know which of their number are faithless to the pledges they made for Grant in Utica.

Very well.

"Arthur!" the clerk intones.

"Er—Grant," Booth calls from the aisle, and everyone laughs because he has been so slow.

"Birdsall!"

Birdsall, a balding and elderly man, mumbles "Blaine" and then reddens fiercely.

"How's that?" the clerk calls from the dais.

"The delegate says 'Blaine,' I believe," Roscoe jeers. "He seems without enthusiasm, but the delegate's vote—Mr. Birdsall's vote—is apparently for Blaine, B-L-A-I-N-E. Blaine as in Maine, Maine as in Blaine."

"All right, Senator," the chairman says from the dais.

Only one of the delegates—Judge Robertson—calls out Blaine's name loud and clear, and Booth's admiration goes out to him. Others in the hall cheer Robertson loudly, and Booth feels anger at Roscoe's tyrannical mockery. He does not mean to be treated by the Senator as Birdsall has been.

When the results of the ballot are announced, there are cries for recess, but the chairman orders a third ballot to begin at once.

"Recess, recess!" someone cries again.

"Conkling for President!" someone else calls out, and there is laughter. Roscoe rises and bows, smirking.

"Grant for President!" he calls back. Catching sight of the massive figure of General Logan moving up the aisle toward them, Roscoe says, "Chester, perhaps you wouldn't mind rounding up Don Cameron for us? I believe we could use an exchange of information right now."

Booth looks at Roscoe, then at Tom Platt and Cornell, who are giving him blind stares. He has contempt for them all. "Conkling for court fool," he sneers under his breath, and heads up the aisle in the direction of the Pennsylvania delegation.

*

When he has left, Platt says to Roscoe, "It's not Chester."

Cornell says, "I've felt it right along. The man is an impostor."

"He don't say 'damned' all the time, like Chester did," Platt adds, his false teeth clicking.

Roscoe touches his moustache delicately. "Whatever you see," he whispers, "say nothing to Logan. We would be the laughingstock of the convention."

"Then you do see it?" Cornell presses.

There is the faintest of hesitations in Roscoe, who says, "If it is not Chester, then surely it must be his brother William, the one who was said to be stationed in San Antonio, Texas."

"You mean because of the resemblance?"

"Obviously," Roscoe replies. "Said to have studied for the cloth. Like their father. It could be no one but somebody raised in the family."

Tom Platt throws up his arms. "Then what in hell has happened to Chester?"

"Deranged from grief, I should think, because of his wife's death. In a madhouse, perhaps."

Platt and Cornell gaze at each other in disbelief.

Roscoe says, "If Blaine is behind it, we will learn this Judas goat's motives best by watching him. Say nothing."

The three of them have their heads so closely together that Logan, arriving in their midst, has to take two of them by the shoulders and fairly pry them apart.

"Gentlemen!" Logan declares. He wants to know what their present judgment is on how the count will go on the next ballot. All Illinois wants to know the same thing.

Roscoe's head pops up. "Watch Massachusetts," he says.

For Raymond, seated high in the public gallery overlooking Exposition Hall, the excitement grows as each new ballot is taken. At first, the thousands of spectators piled in on the benches give easy applause and try to analyze what is going on below, but as the day goes forward, and one ballot follows another, they grow more restless.

Still no candidate with a majority.

On the second day of balloting the bottles of "medicine" that were hidden earlier are seen more openly, and as the weather becomes more humid, the spectators strip off their coats and open their collars and wipe their foreheads with large handkerchiefs. Cardboard fans furnished by local establishments, who print their advertising on both sides, stir the dead air, and all the speeches which last for more than a minute are booed in the gallery's greedy appetite for new numbers. Some keep a written score of the count on each ballot, and when there is any change in a state's vote, a fever of excitement runs through the crowd.

The members of the press, seated below in vests or shirt-sleeves directly in front of the rostrum, forsake their places at these times and go out among the delegates, who gesture in all directions when they are interviewed: toward the vaulted ceiling, the balcony railings swathed in red, white, and blue bunting, and the plaster busts of famous statesmen recessed in niches along the wainscoting.

Raymond cheers heartily whenever the Grant states announce their votes. He beats his hands together and raises his arms. Most of all, he cherishes Senator Conkling's style: "Two delegates are said to be for Sherman, seventeen are said to be for Blaine, and fifty-one *are* for Grant."

Arrogance like that tickles Raymond to the soles of his feet. Raymond savors the humiliation of men like Birdsall, who have broken the sacred pledge taken to Grant at Utica.

On one of the later ballots it is exciting in a different way to see his own general—once "the Count"—give the New York vote when Senator Conkling has stepped out for a moment.

"New York casts two for Sherman, seventeen for Blaine, fifty-one for Grant," his general says.

And everyone cheers that, too, because the general has given the count as though it were somehow comical. People hear a note of levity in the general's voice, and they seem to appreciate it. Raymond is aware that the general is popular even with those who do not care so much for Grant or Senator Conkling.

Vain of his connection, he takes the risk finally of speaking to a young man of his own age, who sits on the corner of the bench across the aisle. The young man has a "Blaine" badge, but when earlier they said hello to each other, it was good-natured enough. Raymond thinks the young man could be the son of one of the delegates. He is well-dressed, has a midwestern accent, and is built very strongly, like an athlete.

"I work for General Arthur! That's General Arthur," Raymond exclaims. "I work for him."

The young man has freckles and curly red hair. He glances at Raymond mockingly. "Looks like an asshole to me," he says, and he guffaws.

Raymond is stunned into silence. He is caught so by surprise that he feels his jaw hanging. Never has he expected to hear such language outside a saloon.

Then the red-haired boy says, "Well, he's probably not as big an asshole as Grant!"

Then he laughs again and claps Raymond on the back companionably. Raymond almost falls off the bench. His blood runs cold. It was not enough for a midwestern hick to call the New York state chairman an asshole, but to say the same thing of the greatest living American, perhaps the greatest man in the world! Raymond feels his hands trembling so hard that he has to clench his fists to keep from exploding. He would have fought him right there if the foulmouth hadn't been six inches taller and sixty pounds heavier than Raymond was.

By the end of the ballot the red-haired boy, noticing nothing of what Raymond has experienced, behaves jovially and with friendship. "Well, you picked up three votes on that ballot, and we stayed the same. P'raps you'll win yet, New York."

"We'll win," Raymond says coolly. "You'll see."

A supper-hour adjournment of the convention has finally been called for and seconded. As the red-haired boy leans over the rail to watch the vote on the motion, Raymond thinks, I ought to push the scoundrel over the railing onto his head. But with a head as hard as his, he probably wouldn't even feel it.

"Are you walkin' back up to the hotels?" Raymond asks. "Why don't you come past the Great Pacific? I'll show you somethin' from New York that I'll bet you never saw before."

"Okay," the boy agrees. "My name's Harmon." He sticks out his hand. When Raymond shakes it and gives his name, Harmon says, "Raymond what?"

"Raymond's good enough."

"Gee whiz," Harmon mocks. "Like some magician on the stage, eh?" But Raymond lets it pass. They push their way through the crush of people pressing toward the exits. Outside on the street the crowd is even worse. But Harmon slaps his cap upon his head and with his broad shoulders bulldozes a path for them through the throng, smiling winningly all the while. Chicago people look larger to Raymond than New York people. Also, there are more blonds—Swedes and Polacks, he supposes. The lake smells different from the East River, and the wind is strong in spite of the heat.

As the two young men dodge the stream of traffic blocking Monroe, Harmon motions toward an alley where they will be able to take a short cut. Raymond sees that Harmon's hands look soft; the overgrown oaf probably never had to work a day in his life.

Once through the alley, back in normal midafternoon traffic, Harmon begins talking to Raymond about politics: why there should be no third term for anyone, even Grant. Then he starts talking about civil service reform, and how the "big city bosses" simply used Presidents like Grant to "pad the federal payroll" and to "rob the public coffers."

Raymond sniffs to himself at Harmon's explanations. The "big city bosses" were Tammany Hall, everybody knew that. They were the Democrats, who got men drunk before they voted, and even voted dead men, pretending they were still alive. "Civil service reform" was for the readers of ladies' magazines. Raymond knows that much. He has heard Conkling say it. "Civil service reform" was like Pharisees pretending they were holier than Jesus.

At the Great Pacific Hotel a band is playing under the huge banner "New York Solid for Grant," still flapping in the wind against the elegant cornice of the building. From the direction of the nearby Palmer House a new procession is marching—another demonstration for Grant.

But the two young men do not wait for it: they have seen enough parades. Raymond picks up the room key at the Great Pacific desk and they worm their way down the crowded corridor. Outside General Garfield's door three or four men, wearing derbies and smoking cigars, are standing and talking.

With an air of nonchalance, Raymond ushers his new acquaintance into the Arthur suite. Although heavy drapes are drawn against the sunlight, the potted palms that have lined the hallways outside can be seen in silhouette to continue inside the suite, an elaboration of a "Sultan" motif. The marble-topped tables are covered with Cherridary scarves from India. Large ceramic elephants stand next to the fireplace holding tongs and pokers extending from holes in the elephants' backs.

Absorbing all this in the half-darkness has taken Harmon a moment or two. He has noticeably hesitated, as though a false panel might suddenly fall open and something strange spring out.

Indeed his intuitions are not far wrong.

"Stay there," Raymond is saying, "for what I have to show you."

Before Harmon's eyes have acclimated themselves, Raymond is back, carrying a gold-knobbed walking stick. As Harmon blinks, Raymond immediately raises the walking stick parallel to the floor and points it at Harmon's midsection.

In the same moment something flashes out of the bottom of the walking stick so rapidly that Harmon jumps.

"How d'ya like that?" Raymond snarls. "I *am* a magician."

Harmon tries a hollow laugh, but the pointed blade meets the fabric of his shirt and presses like an ice pick against the soft skin below his breastbone.

"What the hell—"

"And what d'ye think of Grant now?"

Harmon says nothing. His eyes widen. He dares not move, pinned as he is to the wall. A trickle of perspiration runs down his cheek.

"I said, what d'ye think of Grant now!" Raymond repeats. The rush of sensation he experiences is even more exhilarating than he expected.

"Hurrah for Grant," Harmon whispers, ashen-faced.

"You insulted America's greatest living man," Raymond advises him. His voice has grown quieter, more matter-of-fact, and he can see that this increases Harmon's sense of alarm.

"I'm sorry." Harmon murmurs.

"You're not worthy to be in the company of decent men, y'know that?" Raymond says. He holds the blade so delicately against Harmon's epidermis that his hand trembles for a moment. "You're a cur, and your man eats shit. Do you agree?"

When Harmon says nothing, Raymond presses the blade a little. Harmon cries out, and Raymond warns that if he does that again, he will be run through like the cur he is.

"Lemme go," Harmon bawls. "Please."

"I will let you go when ye show me what a cur you are. Get down on your knees and lick my shoes, you cur!"

"Will you let me go then?"

"If you do like I say."

Harmon is already squatting, and then kneeling. He has started to shake and falls prone at Raymond's feet. For a moment he does nothing but groan. Raymond places the blade warningly on the back of Harmon's neck, and slowly Harmon begins licking the top of Raymond's shoe. Raymond lifts his sole so that Harmon can lick that too.

"Lick, you cur! . . . Now tell me—Blaine eats shit. Let me hear you say it."

Harmon groans.

"Say it, you foulmouthed cur!" Raymond commands.

"Blaine eats shit."

Transported by his success, Raymond presses the blade. "Say civil service reform eats shit! Say it!"

"Civil service reform eats shit."

Without warning, Raymond is felled from behind by an enormous blow next to his ear. He goes flying against the kneehole desk, the sword-cane clattering out of his hand. Stabs of light startle his eyes, and as he caroms to the floor, he half imagines that Harmon has achieved the impossible and risen like a ghost to hit him from behind.

But it is Booth's voice that he hears.

"*You, you* are the cur! How dare you treat another man so ignominiously! You are barbarous, you are—"

Harmon has looked up from the floor in disbelief at his savior—General Arthur, a much firmer man than he would have imagined. But he does not mean to test the moment further. In one motion he grabs his cap, and half crawling, half running, he takes off for the door with a speed such as Booth has never seen.

"Wait, young man, wait!" Booth calls. But it is too late. Harmon has slammed the door behind him, and not even the crowds in the corridors are likely to detain him long.

Raymond, still on his back, watches Booth retrieve the cane, test the tip with his finger, and then retract the blade into its hollow retaining tube.

"I ought to thrash you with this," Booth says to him, glowering. "But I take no pleasure in inflicting pain."

"He called Grant an asshole," Raymond says. He does not want to whine or snivel; if he is to be thrashed, then that is what it would be.

"I'm not interested in the reasons!" Booth turns away from him.

"He called *you* an asshole."

"Get up!" Booth says. "You have behaved impossibly."

Raymond's lip quivers.

"Do ye wish me to leave your service?"

"I wish you to learn how a man should behave." Booth strikes the fleshy part of his own thigh aggravatedly with the stick. "I reclaim my sword-cane! I cannot tell you how much I regret letting you have it and . . . then remodel it when it has turned you into such a bully. Don't you understand the purpose of such a weapon—that it is a defensive weapon only to be used against fearful odds?"

"He was bigger than me," Raymond says, getting to his feet.

When Booth says nothing, Raymond looks disconsolately at the floor, half expecting another blow.

"When a man feels grievously insulted," Booth says tightly, "he advises the other man he will send him his seconds."

Raymond's expression is skeptical.

Booth begins pacing. "You may say to me, 'Well, I have no seconds.' That doesn't make any difference! You must challenge him to a duel, that's all you can do. If the offense is serious enough."

"It was serious."

"Pah, what do you know of General Grant? Booth scoffs. "Or of civil service reform? I heard what you said to him, and here assert that I don't believe you even know what civil service reform means—which you take so seriously!"

"It means—" Raymond begins, and as he pauses, Booth's stare withers him.

"It means," Booth says severely, "to reform present practices in the civil service, which currently provides no tenure of office no matter how well a man does his job. Each year workers have to donate a larger and larger proportion of their salary to the party in power in order to keep their jobs; much of the money goes to line the pockets of the party bosses. Then the workers have to spend their leisure time at meetings and rallies, cheering for whatever rogue is turned up by the powers that be. It is degrading, inefficient, and graft-ridden."

Booth paces in time with his own words. Holding up to youth the highest of values has always been his aim.

"This system," Booth declares, "is a national disgrace, which General Arthur helped perpetuate as much as any other man in the country, and which his colleagues will go on perpetuating, provided only that the great General Grant returns again to the high calling that only a man of his reputation can possibly perform. . . . Is that clear?"

"Yes, sir." None of it was clear to Raymond. But he was moved by the rhetoric.

"In penance for your unmanly act," Booth says briskly, "you will stay in these rooms tonight without any supper, you will not attend the evening session of the convention, and if I learn that you have ever touched my sword-cane again, I will give you such a thrashing that you will walk on all fours the rest of your living days. . . . Am I understood?"

"Yes, sir," Raymond says, his eyes shining in pride at the man.

"I do not tolerate," Booth concludes, "bullying, nor tyranny, no matter where I find it."

10

EXPOSITION HALL

As old Dennison has predicted, it is Wisconsin that turns the tide toward Garfield.

Booth watches with anticipation. He has an insight, as each candidate's fortune ebbs and flows, that destiny's true concern, her only concern, is for Booth and his vindication. First of all, Grant climbs to 312 votes, and Roscoe begins running back and forth to Pennsylvania, to Illinois, to Missouri, and (could such things be?) Virginia, exhorting them to hold the line. Blaine is cracking fast, and the hope is that the anti-Grant forces cannot find a candidate to unite on.

Sherman's total rises for a ballot or two when his manager Garfield wins over the Edmunds votes. But Sherman fails to hold, and Washburne is tried. Once Grant's friend, Washburne has since become Grant's enemy. But Washburne, it turns out, is liked by no one very much.

When Wisconsin's sixteen votes fall at last to Garfield on the thirty-fourth ballot, alarm does not immediately strike the Stalwarts. Roscoe rallies the troops.

"Keep steady, boys! Grant is going to win on this ballot."

But on the roll call that follows, Garfield's total shoots up to fifty when part of Maryland and almost all of Indiana goes to him. Roscoe sneers as Garfield ventures to protest to the delegates that he is not a candidate.

"I knew it all the time," Roscoe hoots at him. Then he glares at Booth as though he is the source of the perfidy.

The atmosphere becomes tense and exhausted for the thirty-sixth ballot, which it soon becomes obvious could be the final one. As the galleries cheer, Connecticut switches to Garfield, then Iowa, Kansas, and Blaine's own state of Maine.

"Stall!" Roscoe shouts to his lieutenants. "Call for a poll in every delegation!"

So Maryland is polled, then Minnesota. No one can think what else to do once Mississippi and Nevada are ordered polled too. Senator Jones of Nevada, a Grant man, comes hurrying down the aisle. With the din of the galleries growing more and more intense, he stands before Roscoe, shouting "You must throw New York's votes to Blaine!"

Roscoe stares at him. "Don't be ridiculous."

"If you shift," Jones cries, "the Blaine votes below us on the roll will hold for Blaine. It's the only way!"

Roscoe glances at Platt and Cornell, then at Booth, who sits nearest him. How humiliating it would be for Roscoe to cast the entire vote of the New York delegation for Blaine! Still, if he could do it, Grant might yet be saved.

"Yes!" says Platt. "We must try it!"

Roscoe says that he hasn't time to consult the delegates.

"Announce the vote for Blaine!" Jones insists. "*Then* let the delegation be polled!"

"Jones . . . Senator Jones," the clerk polling Nevada is calling.

In some confusion, Senator Jones looks behind him toward the Nevada delegation as though he might still be found there. People begin laughing.

At last Jones shrieks, "Blaine!"

The laughter increases.

Roscoe scowls. He can imagine himself, no doubt, butt of the same derision if he should call out "Blaine" as his own vote.

"New York!" the clerk calls.

There is a momentary hush as the great man rises. The great man is not ruffled.

"Two delegates are said to be for Sherman, seventeen are said to be for Blaine, and fifty-one *are* for Grant!"

A smattering of enthusiastic applause follows and a few shouts: "That's pluck, Senator." "Hurrah for General Grant!" someone in the gallery cries.

But almost everyone else knows that Roscoe has just sealed Grant's doom.

"Well," Roscoe says to them as he sits down again, "suppose Blaine won on our votes? What fools we would be!"

You are to be given power, Booth says to himself, because your purpose is noble. You see the truth and know that others must see it too.

He watches Governor Dennison make his halting way through the crowded aisles to the New York standard. Five minutes earlier, the cheering galleries and wildly emotional delegates have finished the final demonstration for the chosen nominee, James A. Garfield of Ohio. Roscoe has already stamped off in disgust, but others of the New York delegation remain slouched on their folding chairs still on the floor. Although Tom Platt has departed with Roscoe, Cornell is smoking a cigar and gathering his papers. Booth is standing with his hands in his coat pockets, his eyes cast neutrally in the direction from which Dennison is approaching with his little steps.

"General Arthur!" Dennison calls.

"Ah!" Booth says, feigning surprise.

"May I talk to you?"

"But first, my congratulations!" Booth exclaims, shaking hands warmly. "On another native son of Ohio winning the nomination. And your skill as a prophet too!"

"You're a good sport, sir," Dennison replies. "Your team is to be complimented on keeping three hundred six votes to the very end. . . . Now what do you think of the Vice-Presidency?"

Governor Cornell, a few feet away, has perked up his ears and risen to his feet.

Booth says to Dennison, "How do you mean that, Governor?"

"In the interests of a united party, we want New York on the ticket." Then, leaning closer to Booth, Dennison whispers, "I would like you personally to consider it, General. I think you have special qualities."

As Cornell begins moving in on the conversation, he gives a hand signal to French and Wheelhorse, who are drinking from a flask in the back row.

"Senator Conkling will want—" Cornell begins.

"Of course, of course," Dennison says. "But you must give the matter your immediate consideration. We are back in session within an hour."

Cornell shakes his head at French and Wheelhorse, then looks fishily at Booth. Across the way, the rest of the Ohio delegation have all vanished, most of them having formed a human shield around Garfield in order to transport him out to the carriages away from the howling mobs.

As Dennison starts to leave, he grasps Booth's hand one more time. "What a pleasure renewing acquaintance with you, General! One of the real high points of my stay!"

"Mine as well!" Booth affirms. His eyes meet Dennison's watery ones. Dennison squints curiously, then begins hobbling away.

An excited voice from the rostrum: Conkling has been seen nearby. Eyewitnesses have seen him in the gentlemen's retiring room, but someone else declares he has gone to the telegraph desk to compose a lengthy wire to Grant. Another tells Booth that he is in the press room excoriating Garfield to the reporters.

When they find him, he is in a small chamber off the main platform, passionately holding forth. A few other New York delegates are standing by, but as he paces, it is as though he is orating to himself rather than to them. Still, no one interrupts. Nearby a band has begun playing "The Battle Cry of Freedom" with such fervor that he is nearly inaudible anyway.

In the hubbub, standing to one side, French growls to Wheelhorse, "Watch him sling the leavings back in Ohio's face!"

Booth waits patiently with the others. At the very moment that the band strikes its triumphant final note, Platt comes up in a rush of excitement: "Garfield himself has sent a man to Levi Morton offering him second place on the ticket." Morton is a Wall Street lawyer, close to Roscoe and financially well-connected.

"I don't think Morton will do," Booth says loudly.

He has stepped forward, the tallest of the lot. His manner is unperturbed.

They all look at him now, and Booth says, "Dennison asked us to choose, and I don't feel Morton will do."

At this temerity, Roscoe Conkling stops talking, and with deep-set eyes smoldering like a beast's, strides toward them.

"Well, Senator," Booth begins. The lion is bearded. "We have been looking everywhere for you."

"Sir?"

"Ohio has offered us the Vice-Presidency," Booth says, "and I am glad to say I would accept the honor if the New York caucus agrees."

"You!" Roscoe exclaims, and then adds harshly under his breath: "You trickster! You and the trickster from Mentor would make a fine pair!"

"I covet your support, Senator," Booth says candidly. But for the first time he recognizes with certainty that Roscoe, Platt, and Cornell all regard him as an impostor.

"Support!" Roscoe hisses back. "I will drop you like a hot shoe from the forge!"

Although Roscoe's physiognomy has never appeared so sharply triangular, Booth says, in a very low voice, "Please reconsider, Senator, I beg you." In the same low voice he mentions Roscoe's correspondence in the Smyth case and in the Phelps-Dodge case, samples of which have turned up in the Arthur files. "Your letters, too, Governor Cornell." Here Booth glances at the governor of New York, who has taken a pose so judicial, he could have been a park monument. "It would seem poor judgment for discord to be permitted among us."

An eastern newspaperman named Hudson—they all have their eyes on him—has sidled over within earshot; immediately, Roscoe turns grimly on his heel and walks out of the room.

In a second the others follow, glaring back over their shoulders at Booth, the infecting agent. But they do not move so fast that Booth is not able to catch up with them. In the interests of harmony, all seem to sense, accommodations will have to be made.

Gathered in the dining room of the Windsor, where Booth and Governor Dennison have lunched but two days before, no one says anything until after the waiter has passed out the menus. Roscoe takes one look at the bill of fare and tosses it down in disgust.

"Simply ask Morton to decline Garfield's offer, that's all," Booth says to him. He has taken off his hat and slouches in his chair in a way that is not characteristic of Chester Arthur. It is his way of striking a more ominous note. Platt and Cornell have already recovered from their initial shock: they have begun to realize that with the impostor nominated as Vice-President, Tom Platt will have a clear field to the Senate.

Only Roscoe continues to vent his outrage.

"Invading the privacy of General Arthur's papers, as you have, would constitute a felony in some states. . . . I should think impersonating him was a serious felony in all!"

"Senator, you know the records I have," Booth says. In the Phelps-Dodge case, the most flagrant one, the importer Dodge was fined half a million for underevaluation when the actual liability would have amounted to no more than a couple of thousand.

"Oh, you can have the cursed spot if you want it so badly," Roscoe grunts, glancing at the others. "Huh! Studies for the clergy and aspires to be the Vice-President of the nation! Who put you up to this anyway?"

Booth says that the Senator has nothing to fear from him.

"No, I'll bet not," Roscoe sneers. "And what has become of your poor brother Chester? You fool no one."

"Hush, the waiter," Cornell warns them.

Booth looks down at the menu. Apparently they have concluded he is Chester Arthur's brother, by all accounts a military officer, hence superbly qualified for high political office.

Platt says, "If you want to be Chester, you have got to say 'damned' more of the time." He has offered the advice in a tone of goodwill. As the waiter appears, wiping his hand on the soiled white napkin hanging over his wrist, Platt orders quickly.

"I'll have the stewed chicken à la Garfield."

"Ev'ythin's à la Garfield dis aft'noon, gen'lmen," the waiter says cheerfully.

"Shitfire, this is where I want to be," Roscoe Conkling says, sinking into self-irony for one of the rare times in his public career.

11

THE HOME FOR WORKING WOMEN
NEW YORK

A few days later, in her dormitory room on Elizabeth Street, Victoria Coventry spends the summer night as she usually does—transcribing her notes. She is exhausted from the heat and needs to sleep in order to be back at the hoopskirt factory at six A.M., but a squall of rain brings a brief spell of coolness, and she decides to stay up a little later and read the newspaper.

General Chester A. Arthur, she learns, is the surprise selection for second place on the party's national ticket. His name, put into nomination by a member of the New York delegation and seconded by Governor Dennison of Ohio, has won the nearly unanimous support of these two delegations, and he easily holds off the challengers. "A man of impeccable dignity," the toadying *Times* calls him. "A man of notable service to the state in the war." It is rumored that Garfield might have preferred Mr. Levi Morton, the New York financier, for second place on the ticket, but that he deferred to the "broad sentiment" for General Arthur.

Victoria puts down the newspaper with a sense of excitement. The paradox that has struck her previously—that there could be no apparent motive for impersonating a man of General Arthur's small importance—now no longer seems insoluble.

She would give her left arm to get back onto that story. She is impatient to be through with the horror of the hoopskirt factory, where in the incessant din of machinery she stands upon weary feet all day long for fifty cents. She suffers degrading familiarities from the male straw bosses, who are still not as bad as the immigrant forewoman, who tyrannizes the workers with blows and kicks when their work is slack. Also, Latham's cheats them regularly on their wages. She cannot abide much more of it, although of course it is good material for the articles. She thinks now and then of the young man whom she has not seen since the night he took her to Booth's Theater.

In shirtwaist and pantaloons, sitting at the one table in her room, she notes on the inside page of the *Times* that at tomorrow evening's homecoming celebration for the general—still in mourning for his wife —son Alan and daughter Nellie will be among those greeting the successful candidate.

Victoria makes her plans. What if she were to reconnoiter Nellie Arthur and the governess when they arrive from Newtonville? There are some new questions she would like to ask the little girl. While such tactics are not considered sporting by Victoria's male colleagues, who believe that families of public men are not fair game, she has never been raised to be a sportsman, has she? Something is going on, and she does not mean to let others get the beat on her own story.

Thus decided, Victoria reclines on the metal-framed double bed that the Home for Working Women provides in each room. She does not have a roommate at the moment, for which she is grateful. She misses a little her "friends" at the kennel, each of those boarding dogs, marvelous and funny, that her brother-in-law would let her take for two or three days at a time. How miserable they seemed when she took them back to the kennel and they had to go on serving their term until Mrs. Vanderbilt or Mrs. Astor got back from Europe, or wherever it was!

Dogs belong on farms, Victoria reflects drowsily. Perhaps she does too. How far along, she wonders, are the fruit trees in her father's orchard up the Hudson a hundred miles north?

12

Nice
May 20

Mr. Götz Dörfer
General Delivery
New York, New York

Dearest—

Your letters become stranger and stranger. What am I to think when you do not give me any reasons for your delay? You assure me that you are doing well, that the children are doing well. But I feel that that cannot be so, or you would be here with me already.

What is going on with my Nellie? You pledged that you would see to it that the children wrote letters and that you would address them to me. Have they forgotten their mother? I am struck with the fear that they believe me dead. If so, what shocks may result to their nervous system when I resume my contact with them at last!

I do not regret leaving my husband. I never wanted that life of notoriety. I wanted privacy, and I wanted love. I thought you promised me both when we made our decision.

You must end my anxiety, or I do not know what I will do.

Forgive me if in this letter I do not add details of life on the Riviera. It has no interest for me. The name you gave me for my incognito has even become an embarrassment. Now that I have finally read the Edgar Allan Poe story from which you chose the appellation, I feel that you think of me as some kind of curse.

Tell me all!

In wavering faith
your own,

N.

✤   ✤   ✤

New York
June 7

Mrs. Madeline Usher
Nice, France

My faithful one—

Do you not know that I realize I have asked more from you than has ever been required of living woman before? Have I not asked you for your name, your children, your property? Moreover, I asked these things in blind faith. That is the kind of man I am—headstrong, implacable, ready to risk everything including my life.

Fifteen years ago I rallied a group of young men to a cause— The Cause! I asked the same dedication from them, and more. Not a day goes by that I do not look back on what they gave me with a kind of incredulity. Whatever mistakes were made by them, by me, there were no mistakes of the heart. Their loyalty was complete, even to the gallows.

When I tell you yet again that what we were concerned with was honor, the honor of Southern manhood, and of Southern womanhood, you will say, oh, I have heard that so often, now I want love and privacy. Can you not feel how deeply I share your yearning? But what holds me here is nothing more than honor again. A poor thing. Hardly more than a word. But men I trained—to say nothing of a tragically persecuted woman (Mrs. Surratt)—died for that honor. And when I now see a glimmering—and perhaps final—opportunity to snatch the battered diadem from the dust, why should I not make further unreasonable demands?

I say that there is no such thing as real and lasting privacy for one who bears the burden of his honor as do I. Nevertheless I mean to pursue privacy with all my heart and soul as soon as it becomes possible for us again. As for love, my dearest one, how can you doubt but that it is ours already? That we need not pursue for we already have it. We have had it ever since Fredericksburg when we clasped hands over the pain-wracked body of your little son, now sturdy, handsome, flourishing, as is the enduring affection we bear toward each other.

What fortitude you have shown so far, my own! Is it possible that you will find the strength to bear up a little longer? If you write the children, you risk the integrity of the entire enterprise we planned. You risk the political career of Chester Arthur if your letters fall into the wrong hands. You risk disgrace for your children as parties, however innocent, to the deception.

I can assure you of their peace and comfort. Alan, at Columbia Grammar, is as active as ever. Nellie's new social opportunities in New-tonville are similarly beneficial for she sees so much more of her cousins (on her father's side) than before. Mademoiselle is extremely attentive to her. But your own contribution is to have made both your children truly independent individuals. You have created character for them that they will never lose. (I will see to it that they write you letters: perhaps those they have already written are delayed en route, *or went down when that Atlantic steamer sank off Hoboken the other day—no hands lost, fortunately.)*

Your nom de guerre *should not trouble you, my love. It was selected with profound belief that your having risen live from the tomb can only end when we rejoin each other to cling together until the true finish of our lives, mutually experienced. When we fall, we fall to-gether. But let us stand tall until then, reaching, as we now must across the seas, until our final permanent embrace when flesh will engage flesh forever.*

Yours in faith,

W.

13

· 123 LEXINGTON AVENUE

The liveried boy-valet with the blue eyes, a figure all too reminiscent for Dun of the unhappy night when Chester breathed his last, answers the door to Dun's ring, and while the boy is obligingly taking Dun's hat and stick, a middle-aged woman accompanied by Arthur's daughter Nellie emerges from the back parlor, dressed for the street.

The woman greets him expansively.

"Oh, Mr. Dun, you don't remember me, I bet. I'm Mrs. Caw from upstate, the general's sister. We met once before."

"Of course," Dun says, having no memory of it. Still, the cheer-fulness of the woman surprises him, given the fact that the master of the house is no longer her brother at all but merely performs in that role.

"Good gracious, Nellie, you're getting to be a big girl," Dun says to the child. Nellie gives him a quick curtsy and passes forward with her aunt under the scrutiny of the young valet, who seems to watch the girl with an unnatural interest.

When they have left the house, Dun says brusquely to Raymond, "I think I am expected downstairs." Aware of the boy's background, Dun wiggles his nose, imagining, as he is led to the office below, that he can still smell the formaldehyde from the morgue.

"Mr. Dun is here," Raymond calls at the office door.

"Show him in."

Admitted, Dun watches Booth rise from a couch where he has been relaxing, and come forward, smiling, with his hand extended. "I'm damned glad you could make it, Dun."

Dun shakes the hand, immediately impressed with the more natural look of the flesh on Booth's face. The folds and shading are nearly perfect; by lucky coincidence, the pigmentation of the eyes was always correct.

"Sit down, sit down," Booth says warmly—a more open and expansive warmth than Chester's, but none the worse for that, perhaps.

"I congratulate you," Dun says, pulling off his gloves, "on your nomination. I presume you preferred it to the Senate."

With self-delight, Booth laughs. "Did you know they laid seventeen torpedoes on the tracks for me when our train rolled in last night? . . . All right for Grant, but for me I thought it was a damned infantry attack!"

Dun sits down, accepting the glass of wine that is offered. Booth's vowels seem to be coming around at last—more lengthened and nasal, as Chester's were.

"I ran into Mrs. Caw on the way in," Dun remarks. "Most interesting."

"Yes, the entire Arthur clan has been remarkable." Booth observes that while they appeared stunned at the funeral, they have since perceptibly melted toward him.

"Remarkable," Dun echoes.

"When I returned from Chicago with the honor of this nomination, they appeared both confused and flattered. Flattered when they saw me being interviewed." Booth, who seated himself briefly, now gets to his feet again, and speaks with animation. "As I entered this house, they were waiting. Then, suddenly, Regina—that is to say, Mrs.

Caw—embraced me. And she burst at once into tears. They were tears, not of pleasure, but of deep grief. Almost at once the other sisters began crying as well. Even the husbands had tears in their eyes, and as I am an emotional man, I wept too. It was quite unusual. We were all, you see, grieving for Chester Arthur, who they clearly knew had passed away.

"But when the grieving was over, they seemed to look on me with admiration. After all, I had taken up the burdens. The children were decently managed. If Nell was indeed on a long, long trip, as Nellie claimed, then think of the chaos here if I had not been present. Think of the damned problems with estate settlement. But because of my stepping in, the household remained intact, the breadwinner's career continues, and the reflected glory which he shed actually increases."

"Yes. Quite remarkable," Dun says.

"However, I will send Nellie and her governess as soon as possible to Nell in France. In this, I consider the emotional needs of both mother and daughter."

Dun forbears asking what account Nellie will carry to her mother. It was anybody's guess what Nellie believed, or for that matter, how much the governess knew.

"In the meantime—ha!" Booth says, rubbing his hands. "We have an election to win. Right? And our ticket is Wall Street's ticket, is it not, Dun?"

"Well, well, who can tell if the party will heal its wounds?"

"Ah, that is exactly why you must tell me," Booth says, producing a photograph from the papers on the desk, "what occasion this represents."

Dun is handed a small cardboard-framed print in which three fishermen are admiring a day's catch. The three are recognizably Dun, Roscoe Conkling, and Chester Arthur.

"It was taken on the Restigouche in New Brunswick. Our club owns a lodge there," Dun says.

"Will Roscoe be fishing this summer? If so, I would like to join you, for I am as aware as you that we must persuade our prima donna to do labor for the ticket."

In spite of himself, Dun laughs. Then he settles back into his chair, balancing his cane across his knees. "Should I ask what kind of fisherman you are?"

"The best," Booth declares, bringing other papers forward. "And please do not desert me, for I need your professional favor too. The *Century Magazine* requires statements from each of the four major candidates. Could you do me a paragraph or two on bimetallism, or hard money—something not too reactionary?"

Dun huffs an objection deep in his throat. "This is for press secretaries to do who will consult the party platform—"

"Tush, we can do it," Booth says, earnestly handing Dun a page that he has written himself. "These, for example, are my somewhat progressive views on civil service reform."

Dun reads the statement, then laughs again. "Not Senator Conkling's views, you are aware."

"Have I framed it too strongly?" Booth asks. "Do you think he could put it down to campaign rhetoric?"

For a moment Dun looks to the skies for relief. "And what, I'd better ask, are your hopes for the South? To restore slavery there?"

Booth says he realizes that that hope is no longer practicable.

"Practicable! Why, for you, all things may be practicable."

It is true, Booth reflects. Destiny finds a way. If, after a single stroke of the pen, Lincoln could set them all free . . .

One final question Booth asks of Dun as the latter is at the door.

"Does that female reporter, do you know, still work for the *Herald*?"

"Preparing a series of articles," Dun says lightly, "on the fate of the shopgirl. Or so I have heard."

"Then why does she pursue my daughter Nellie with questions at the railroad station?"

Dun says he has no idea. "She is undercover at Latham's, the hoopskirt factory. Bennett let it slip."

"I thought Bennett could control her."

"Ah, well," Dun murmurs, implying the need for tolerance.

"But something must be done about her," Booth says in a strangely euphoric tone. "What would Chester Arthur do? Pay her off? . . . Pay her off in what manner?"

14

ON THE BANKS OF THE RESTIGOUCHE

Under the midday sun Booth and Raymond sit on canvas chairs next to the tent that has been pitched for them high on the crest over the leaf-dappled river. Both of them are reading books—Booth a history of the Era of Good Feeling and Raymond a novel by Horatio Alger called *Julius the Store Boy*. Raymond makes sure to keep his legs doubled up on the seat of the chair, not having conquered his fear of snakes. Booth suspects that the snakes have long since vacated the area, inasmuch as the banks of the river are as crowded as a punting weekend at a British university.

Right below them, in denser shade, Cascapedia Club members Roscoe Conkling and Robert Dun are resting near their own tent, listening to the lap-lap of the river. They have caught over a hundred pounds of salmon during the morning, but will go out again toward nightfall.

Booth can see Roscoe fanning mosquitoes away from his nose with the flat of his hand. So far Roscoe remains unreconciled to the ticket. For three days he has continued to sneer silently in the direction of the tent on the upper bank.

An hour ago a typical exchange occurred with Dun calling up the bank to Booth, "How was your catch today?"

"Not bad. How was yours?"

"Fine! Come down and have a look."

But Roscoe disputed the invitation.

"Stay up there, you trickster!"

A disturbance in the undergrowth along the water's edge now attracts the attention of both camps. From the upstream direction of the river, a dark young man and young woman, both of the indigenous population, come jostling awkwardly through the bankside brush, occasionally casting their eyes on the river behind them. They are loaded with equipment. The woman—a tall, well-proportioned female with two braids of jet-black hair—wears a dress of a flimsy fabric and carries a camera and tripod. The moustachioed young man with her, wearing dirty boots, shoulders a smaller burden, chiefly a leather case that appears to contain photographic plates.

These two, Booth has been told, are natives sufficiently domesticated by the Cascapedia Club to be able during the season to make photographs of men holding fish. Booth watches as the dark man now sets up camera and tripod on a sun-drenched spot on the riverbank in readiness for a canoe that is even now turning the bend pointed in their direction. "Candid" photographs—much prized—require an air of spontaneity.

The timing at first seems perfect. There are three people in the canoe—in the front, two tweed-jacketed middle-aged men holding lines of fish, and in the rear, a guide with a paddle. The guide, however, has plainly misjudged the momentum of the current, and the photographer angrily commands him to stop the canoe at once. The craft veers sharply into the bank, jolting the two distinguished-looking men, one of whom has already started to rise with his string of fish held high.

"Non, mais non!" cries the photographer.

Both men have been jarred backward onto their buttocks. The older of them calls out, "It's all right, René. We'll try it again."

On the bank thirty yards away Dun tells Roscoe—and Booth, who despite Roscoe's enjoinder has come down to join them—that the new arrivals are Weir Mitchell, the Philadelphia nerve specialist, and his brother-in-law Cadwalader.

"Jesus," sneers Roscoe, who disapproves of vanity in others. "Weir Mitchell is the vainest man alive."

In time, Mitchell and his company are arranged into a new tableau. While Booth tries to recall how closely Mitchell was acquainted with the Arthurs, the irascible photographer sticks his head under the black cloth that covers the viewfinder on the camera. *"Attendez!"* he calls in a tenor voice.

Unluckily, the bristle-cheeked guide in the back of the canoe decides to rise at that moment with a string of fish of his own, causing the craft to wobble and nearly topple the two principals, each of whom stands, eyes glazed, with two strings each of fat gill-strung fish.

"Ah, *non!*" the young woman cries.

"Sit down!" Mitchell says peevishly to the guide, who sits down. As all parties wait for the tremor of the canoe to cease, Booth can hear Raymond's laughter from the high bank.

"Attendez," René reiterates from deeper in his throat. With wincing tension, he counts off the seconds of exposure while squeezing the bulb that opens the shutter. *"Un . . . deux . . . trois . . . quatre . . ."* Dr. Mitchell's expression has begun to cloud over dangerously.

As soon as René reaches *"Huit! Bon!"* Mitchell shouts, "René, do you remember my telling you something before?"

"Res' you' arm-uhs," René is saying. "You res' you' arm-uhs now."

Mitchell says, "Do you remember my saying that those are dry plates you have in the camera, René? They don't require eight seconds' exposure. A half-second is all it needs."

"Sans doute, sans doute," René says, preoccupied with moving the tripod for a second shot.

Noticing now who has been watching from the bank, Mitchell calls to Booth, "Is that you, General Arthur? I say, I have never been laughed at by so distinguished an audience. Should Cadwalader and I go on the stage, do you think?"

"I wasn't laughing at you, Doctor," Booth calls back. "I apologize for that rogue on the hill, whom I shall discharge at your pleasure."

"Well, in the meantime, come over here, for I want a photograph taken of you and me for my memory book."

Booth hesitates; during his stay in the woods he has been careless with his makeup. But the possibility of getting a closer look at the Frenchwoman, who is peering sullenly at him from the group at the water's edge, tempts him to advance toward the canoe. Mitchell reaches for him. A flurry of handshakes is followed by Booth's being helped into the craft for the purposes of the picture. It takes him a few minutes to get his feet properly planted; in the meantime, Mitchell is offering effusive condolences on the death of Mrs. Arthur. He makes a rapid reference to details of the visit that the general and his wife paid the doctor in Philadelphia last summer.

"Indeed, indeed," Booth murmurs. Although Nell's account is beginning to come back to him, he sees a suddenly anxious Roscoe glaring at them as though the imposture is sure to be penetrated by Mitchell in the next few seconds. Roscoe barks at the photographer, "Get on with it, man! Let the woman hold the portfolio!"

"Gracious, René, get on with it," Mitchell echoes. He has grasped Booth in an armlock, which he progressively tightens as he leers at Booth curiously. *"You* were the one who looked ill to me last summer. Yellow complexion, I can always tell. Bright's disease usually. You look better now. Or is it just the face powder you're using to cover it up? Mustn't cover up the symptoms, you know."

Mitchell takes his knuckle and rubs it across a spot on Booth's face, most fascinated by the result he is getting. "Strange stuff," he murmurs, while Booth writhes in his grasp. "Bad for the pores too. You know, you hardly look the same man."

The woman screams.

And in his viewfinder the startled René sees both of his standing subjects suddenly tip over backward like cardboard targets in a shooting gallery. The capsized canoe takes not only Mitchell and the vice-presidential candidate into the river but also the guide and Mitchell's brother-in-law, who have been foolish enough to remain seated in the back of the craft.

"Help!" cries Cadwalader, following his hat into the water.

Weir Mitchell utters a like cry.

The other two victims drop without comment into the water, the guide pillowed afloat by the heavy weight of his clothes. The strings of fish slither past him and start to sink.

"My error! My error!" Roscoe Conkling calls out to them. "Gentlemen, I beg your pardon! I thought I was stepping onto a rock in the reeds."

For Roscoe has thrust his weight onto the gunwale of the canoe at a crucial moment in Weir Mitchell's monologue, and with the proper angle of leverage has done just enough to tip the entire party into the Restigouche, salmon included.

Raymond is the first rescuer into the stream, splashing and scrambling with great energy toward the floundering Booth. The guide meanwhile has righted himself and sidestrokes toward Mitchell and Cadwalader. All are presently helped ashore by extended hands from Roscoe and Dun.

"Oh! Oh! The water is cold!" Mitchell cries. His little white beard has matted against his chicken neck. Cadwalader has begun shivering. He has lost his spectacles in the stream.

"My humble apologies, gentlemen!" Roscoe is exclaiming again. But as he assists Chester Arthur's duplicitous brother out of the water, his lips have turned downward in a suppressed sneer. The woman meanwhile has plunged back into the river to try to retrieve the strings of fish.

"Never mind the fish, Antoinette!" Mitchell shouts to her, sensing that his own welfare is taking second place to a salmon.

Up to her shoulders in the water, Antoinette has grasped all but one of the strings of fish, which floats lazily off beyond her reach.

"Hélas, les poissons!" she cries in disappointment, then asks him, *"Voulez-vous les poissons?"*

"You keep *les poissons!*" Mitchell cries, now swathed in a blanket. "Come out of there! We need gar-ments, *vêtements.* René, don't stand there! Senator, you are a careless man!"

"My sincere apologies, Doctor!" Roscoe booms again. Behind the doctor's back, he winks broadly at Dun.

It is presently arranged that René and the guide will help the distraught Mitchell and his brother-in-law back to their campsite a little upstream, where they have dry clothes.

"You 'av shainzh of clo-thing too?" Antoinette asks Booth. "I cooed geev you zum."

Holding the string of fish that is her gift from the other gentlemen, she looks marvelously attractive in the clinging wet cotton that she is wearing.

"It would be very kind of you," Booth replies. René and the others have just disappeared upstream. "We have no other clothing." When Raymond seems about to correct Booth's impression, Booth quickly adds, "Besides, I think we should see you home, since your husband is not able to."

Antoinette shrugs. She leads them off toward a pair of splay-footed horses, which she untethers from a tree, and mounting the one with her string of fish in hand, she waits for Booth and Raymond to mount the other.

"René, *c'est mon frère,*" she says abruptly to Booth. Sidesaddle, she prods her horse forward at a brisk pace.

The woods turn presently into meadow. The terrain is full of crocuses, and birds are everywhere. Booth has pulled his mount up beside Antoinette's. Because Roscoe has remarked that the smallest of the salmon will be good for her cat, Booth asks, *"Tenez-vous un chat, mademoiselle?"*

Antoinette glances at him. *"Parlez-vous français?"*

"Mais oui."

"Vous êtes allemand?" she asks him.

"Non, américain." He is puzzled, having supposed that all the years at Delmonico's would have diminished his German accent. *"Parlez-vous anglais, mademoiselle?"*

"Oui," she says sharply, winding the line holding the fish one more time around the saddle pommel.

"*C'est bon.*"

Nodding at Raymond, she now asks, "*Votre fils?*"

"*Mais non!*" he cries, pretending indignation.

"Ho-kay," Antoinette says.

Later, as Raymond and Booth have undressed in the pantry area of the stone house, and while Antoinette is hunting elsewhere for dry clothing for them, Raymond says to Booth, "She is a very agreeable woman, I think."

Raymond is standing in his underwear, half hiding behind the cupboard, as though embarrassed by the overlarge flour-sack drawers that he is wearing.

"Do you fancy her?" Booth asks. Much wetter than Raymond, he has stripped off all his clothes and is waiting in a large blanket that has been given him. It feels good to be totally unencumbered with lifts and pads, to be nearly without identity in this place.

"I don't fancy her," Raymond says hesitantly. "She is close to thirty, do ye not believe?"

"Oh, more like twenty-five, I would say. Her eyelashes are very fine."

Raymond says nothing for a moment. Then, in a very uneasy voice, he asks, "Do ye consider me a man o' the world?"

"Yes, I do," Booth says promptly and seriously.

Satisfied, Raymond has no further comment to make. When Antoinette brings the dry clothes, which respectively fit each of them well—rude though the garments are—Raymond takes it upon himself to decline Antoinette's invitation to a cup of coffee in order to wait discreetly outside the house while the general and Antoinette continue their conversation in French. Raymond can tell that Antoinette, although reserved in her manner, is drawn to the general. Antoinette's cat soon joins Raymond outdoors, having been evicted for making too much fuss over the string of salmon. Raymond attempts to play with the cat for a moment, but the animal, unfriendly, runs off into the woods.

It is, on the whole, a successful week.

By the time Booth's vacation on the Restigouche is over, he has obtained Roscoe's consent to lend his aid to the campaign. Never has Roscoe seen two greater tricksters on a ticket than Garfield and Chester Arthur's brother, but, alas, Hancock, the Democratic candidate, is a Tammany puppet. What choice does a man have? In any event, he wants them to know that he did not tip Weir Mitchell into the Restigouche River as a sign that he will be an automatic accessory to all their fraud. Some misfeasances he will not countenance, no matter how high the stakes.

Booth, in his borrowed tunic and heavy woolen trousers, manages to evade Weir Mitchell for the rest of his sojourn in the wilds. Regularly he calls on Antoinette, usually when René is away, to see if she needs the garments back, but each time she says, *"Mais non. Demain."* They therefore spend many hours in conversation and intimacies, and he realizes he has not enjoyed so irresponsible an idyll with a woman since the time he visited Lizzie, the mountain girl who was orphaned in the war. When he was staying with the Herndons and foraging the land, Lizzie lived a good day's ride from Fredericksburg. He forgot about Lizzie when he told Nell he had been celibate in those years.

Never mind. Nell has given him his most profound and enduring experience of woman. She alone possessed the true breeding of a lady, and also believed in transcending the ephemeral. No man of any worth could be without a sense of the eternal values. He knows that Nell symbolizes all the things that he believes in—birth, training, idealism. It is a shame he has had to deceive her now and then in order not to be deflected from their course toward the higher obligations. Perhaps the present arrival of her daughter in France will help make it up. He has taken a risk in sending Nellie to her, of course, but he has been more afraid not to.

On the afternoon that they are breaking camp and preparing to leave New Brunswick, Dun, lolling by a tree, watching Raymond do the work, says to Booth, "I have meant to ask you. Since young Nellie has sailed for the Continent, did you still find it necessary to pay off the lady reporter who was annoying her?"

Absorbed in sorting his fishing lures, Booth does not look up. "I am informed," he says, "that Victoria Coventry accepted the gift I sent her and sensibly returned to the provinces from which she came."

"Indeed?" Dun says. The wind has quickened, and he needs to use his hat as a shield in order to get his cigar lighted. The cigar is not his usual stock, his runner having been taken into custody in Florida and the whole shipment confiscated. "Indeed." He puffs thoughtfully.

15

NEW YORK CITY

By the first week of August, Booth has still received no letter from Nell to let him know of the safe arrival of Nellie in Nice. He has Raymond check not only at General Delivery but at Delmonico's as well, where the abrupt departure of Götz Dörfer, without notice, has left the management stonily unresponsive to requests for Dörfer's mail.

The candidate's own time is amply filled with disagreeable chores. As state chairman—a job he has not been able to get rid of—he must continue to write letters asking for contributions to the national campaign. Garfield, telegraphing daily from his home in Ohio, wants bankrolls of money sent on to Indiana, where the Presidency is being voted on a month earlier than anywhere else, and where shameless Democrats have already begun purchasing votes.

The man who must be applied to for funds in this crisis is Mr. Levi Morton of Wall Street, who resents Chester Arthur for having cheated him out of his rightful place on the ticket. Roscoe meanwhile is entering the campaign very sluggishly, having resolved not to participate until Garfield comes to New York. He mentions he has no intention of meeting Garfield face to face on this visit: that would be too demeaning. On the other hand, Garfield must be elaborately received at the Fifth Avenue Hotel.

"He will be offended when I am not present," says Roscoe, "but when you say, 'Yes, the Senator has his pride, one hardly knows what will induce him to participate in this campaign,' he will notice how the table is spread and will in turn say—are you listening to me?"

"Of course," Booth says, nearly dozing off.

The scenario is described while the two of them are sitting in great overstuffed chairs in the hospitality suite at the hotel. It is a warm afternoon. Party workers file in and out at will, helping themselves from a bowl of weak punch and a spread of canapés served on the hotel's best crockery. Since Garfield is expected on the morrow, Booth hopes for the recovery of Tom Platt so that Platt can shepherd the top of the ticket around. Platt has felt bilious from eating the hotel caviar and has retired to his rooms.

"Who's that dirty, ill-dressed man with the sandy beard?" Roscoe suddenly asks.

He is looking across the banquet table at a man of medium height, wearing a suit that looks too large for him. Although the man's back is toward them as he fills a plate with food from the table, Booth has no trouble recognizing the creature, since the latter has unnerved him several times lately.

"He claims to practice law in Chicago," Booth replies. "He's printed up a damned speech called 'Garfield Versus Hancock,' which he proposes to deliver publicly."

"God spare us," Roscoe groans.

The man in question has moved away from the banquet table; then, remembering something he has forgotten, he looks around in all directions before darting furtively back for a dill pickle.

Booth says, "I keep sending him to Marshall Jewell, and Jewell keeps sending him back to me."

"Shitfire, he's coming over here," Roscoe hisses. "Are we not expected elsewhere?"

The ill-dressed man has moved with great suddenness once he has made up his mind; now he stands directly in front of them, scraggly-bearded, holding his plate with its slices of ham and half-eaten pickle.

"Gen'ral Arthur," the man declares, "d' chairman, Mista Jewell, has designated me to be one of d' speakers at d' Twenty-fourth Street rally when Gen'ral Garfield is here."

"That's excellent," Booth says. Although he has heard the man's name only once, he has no trouble remembering it. "Senator Conkling, I would like you to meet Mr. Ghetto. Is that correct—'Ghetto'?"

"Dat is correct," Mr. Ghetto says. He shakes Roscoe's hand. "A great honor to meet you, Senata. I am a Stalwart."

"That's excellent, Mr. Ghetto," Roscoe says.

"Foreign affairs are my special interest," says Mr. Ghetto. "I seek the embassy in Vienna."

"Oh?" says Roscoe. "Have you spoken to General Garfield?"

Mr. Ghetto says that he has not yet met the general.

"And we, too, cannot tarry long, I fear," Roscoe says abruptly. He has gotten to his feet, and so Booth does too.

"Wait, wait," Mr. Ghetto cries most earnestly. As he turns his face from Roscoe to Booth, Booth sees that the left and the right sides of his face are shaped in strikingly different ways. Roscoe takes out his pocket watch, and Mr. Ghetto says, "To be a Stalwart is to have d' best credential, is't not so, Senatar?"

"Ah, I suppose," Roscoe says lightly, "that it depends on whether the party wins the canvass."

"Most certainly!"

As they start to move away, Booth says, "Good fortune on your speech, Mr. Ghetto."

"You will be dere, I presume. I speak on Garfield Versus Hancock."

"If we can," Booth replies.

"A pithy theme that fellow has," Roscoe observes later in the corridor when they have escaped Ghetto's clutches. Then he bursts into laughter. Booth laughs too. But less heartily, perhaps, than Roscoe, who has clapped him on the shoulder like a schoolfellow.

Booth has uncanny intimations about Ghetto.

16

MADISON SQUARE

The following evening, under torchlight, Booth sits on the platform, waiting his turn to speak. Thunderhead clouds have passed just to the north of the rally at dusk, and heat lightning punctuates the atmosphere in the distance over Central Park. Early speeches from the minor luminaries on the dais last until full darkness; then the parade begins. A little uneasily, Booth joins the others at the balustrade while the long procession of veterans, in tattered blue, marches past with torches high. He cannot explain his strange sense of apprehension.

The air is moist and unsettled. Over Garfield's shoulders a light summer overcoat is draped, which slips off on one side or the other as he raises his arm. He could have been trained in the theater, the way the slipping coat commands attention. Also, he is wearing a slouched hat that gives a rakish, friendly air, designed to lend appeal for the sophisticated.

He is not a guileless man, Booth has seen. Earlier in the day, in the private suite, he has shown them how puss in the corner is played. Initially, his manner has been humble, grateful, breathless. He is so overcome at meeting the dollars-and-cents man, Levi Morton, that

Roscoe's absence is beneath his notice. He says at once that, of course, the Senator and "his friends" will be consulted about patronage in the state. But when the question arises how exclusively consulted, the puss in the corner begins. Later, Platt claims they have won "total concession," "a great victory." Roscoe like to hear good news. A Cabinet post? Of course. Not the Treasury perhaps, but then again perhaps the Treasury after all.

On the whole, Booth has not been taken with the candidate. While the man has passion and stage presence—obviously admirable qualities—he seems too eager to please and is lacking in firmness. Garfield is the kind of man who will say yes to the last person he talks to. Booth was once acquainted with field officers of just such character.

Garfield's address is scheduled immediately before his own, and in the continuing mood of foreboding he scans the vast crowd while Garfield is introduced, trying to make out separate faces. While the voices around him sound happy, the horns impudent, and the drums vigorous, the illuminated faces he sees seem to belong to hundreds of Mr. Ghettos on every side. The veterans, the laboring men, the drivers of carriages all have the same unholy look.

With the crowd finally stilled, Garfield begins. "Comrades of the Boys in Blue and fellow citizens of New York, I cannot look upon this great assemblage and these old veterans that have marched past us and listen to the welcome from our comrades who have just spoken without remembering how great a thing it is to live in the Union, and be a part of it."

Booth has noticed a woman standing in the crowd. She looks, not like Mr. Ghetto, but like Nell.

"This is New York," continues Garfield, "and yonder toward the Battery more than a hundred years ago a young student of Columbia College was arguing the idea of the American Revolution."

The woman, dressed in black, is standing with a younger woman near a carter's wagon that has been drawn up close to the terrace. The younger woman—short and stout—is strange to him, and he cannot be sure in the uneven light that the first one is Nell. But the resemblance is so close that his jaw drops.

"By and by," Garfield goes on, "he went into the patriot army and was placed on the staff of Washington to fight the battles of his country."

Yet it could not be Nell, he tells himself. She would not stand there so stiffly without the least impulse to conceal her face, or to wear some disguise. Many of the people on the balcony were capable of recognizing her; some would have been to her funeral.

"Before he was twenty-one years old, upon a drumhead he wrote a letter that contained every germ of the Constitution of the United States."

But if it is she, my God, what does she think? That it is her Chester up here? The thought makes him unhappy. When he finally gets up to speak, will she recognize the imposture and raise a hideous cry? "Risen From the Dead!" the *New York Sun* would declare. "Woman Exposes Fraud on Republican Ticket!" "Most Shameful Ignominy Since Tweed Ring!" "Is False Candidate Really Notorious Assassin?"

"That student, soldier, statesman, and great leader of thought," says Garfield, "Alexander Hamilton of New York, made the Republic glorious by his thinking."

No, Booth cannot accept it. Surely Nell would have written him of her return. Has he not shown his goodwill by sending her Nellie and the mademoiselle? Whatever their garbled reports to her might have been, she would not have taken the risk of appearing in the middle of Manhattan only blocks away from where her obsequies have recently been performed. It is unthinkable.

He attends to Garfield, who at last has reached the inevitable topic—the war—the one the crowd always likes to hear about.

"Soon after the Great Struggle began we looked behind the army of white rebels, and saw four million black people condemned to toil as slaves for our enemies."

Booth tries not to listen. If they love black people so much, why don't they go down south and live with them? See how they like it. A mere twenty thousand blacks (and the best educated ones) live in New York, a city of a million and a half. What a pitiful sample on which to judge a race!

"And now that we have made them free," Garfield exclaims, "so long as we live, we will stand by these black allies!"

Black allies! Booth shudders. It is enough to distract him from what is going on down near the carter's wagon.

Garfield raises his fist.

"We will stand by them until the sun of liberty, fixed in the firmament of our Constitution, shall shine with equal ray upon every man, black or white, throughout the Union!"

*

The wind picks up. Garfield, having finished, waves his arms to his cheering audience. Booth struggles to regulate himself. Looking down at the wagon, he sees the woman there only as a shadow. He swallows and licks his lips.

People have come onto the terrace during the tumult of the moment just to touch Garfield. Young boys and middle-aged men run up to shake hands, or if that fails, just to lay a hand on him. One man begins a conversation with the candidate. It has been like that the whole day: well-wishers, and Mr. Ghettos begging for posts in Vienna.

When Garfield has fought his way through them, he raises his hands. "And now," he shouts, "your own General Arthur!"

The applause is very warm. Booth, feeling unexpectedly shaky on his boot lifts, rises, keeping one eye peeled in the direction of the carter's wagon. It crosses his mind what happened to his brother on the stage of McVicker's Theater in Chicago. Was Nell maintaining her concealment preparatory to drawing a revolver and firing? No, he cannot believe that his Nell—no matter what she has learned of the masquerade—would execute poetic revenge on him as he spoke. Still, he has decided to make his remarks briefer than planned.

"You all know," he says to them, hoarse-voiced, when the applause has stopped, "that I am not here to make a speech."

Some clapping here. He has remained as far back from the terrace railing as possible in order to be standing in the weakest light.

"I am here to unite with you as Republicans of New York in paying our respects and in doing honor to the distinguished statesman and soldier whom you have just heard and whom you are going to make President."

Many shouts here. Still no movement from the direction of the carter's wagon. "You are right, we are!" someone shouts. Booth has nearly forgotten what he has just said; the words, in any case, are like cotton in his mouth.

He clears his throat. "As a New Yorker I can hardly describe to you my gratification at seeing so noble and splendid an assemblage here to pay the tribute which we all owe."

Applause from the veterans. The words say themselves. But he can already afford to draw a halt.

"I will not make a speech because there are distinguished Republicans and statesmen from abroad whom you will be glad to hear and delighted to honor. I will ask General Logan to speak to you."

Cheers for General Logan, who rises like a weightlifting

champion, throwing both arms in the air. Of a sudden, he embraces Booth. Booth is prodded and carried to the very front of the terrace where this giant of a man lifts him off his feet in the burnish of refracting torches.

Logan encourages applause.

Booth gasps, "I thank you for your warm reception and leave you all my good wishes." He struggles to free himself from the embrace. "You will see enough of me in New York"—the woman steps out from behind the carter's wagon—"but you—you do not see General Logan very often."

Logan is laughing gleefully. . . . Then the loud report of a firearm. . . . As Logan releases him, Booth reaches for his chest, forgiving Nell —if the worst has happened—truly forgiving her. . . . But another shot is fired. And another. . . . It is a rifle being fired upward into the darkness. A few yells follow and great laughter and cheering. Booth takes his hand from his chest. The Boys in Blue acting up, that was all.

"Fellow citizens, good night, thank you." Booth pants, retreating, while General Logan grins like a mule. Booth bows toward Garfield.

But presently, just before he reseats himself, someone touches him, grabs for his arm, and he jumps.

It is the inevitable Mr. Ghetto, shaking his hand, his eyes alight.

"I chust arrived!" Mr. Ghetto exclaims. "An address dat was inspiring, Gen'ral!"

Another look in those eyes tells Booth that Mr. Ghetto is certainly mad.

The rain has begun to fall.

"Perhaps it was not the lady after all," Raymond says to Booth.

Having no luck in the vicinity of the carter's wagon, they have searched the streets following the rally and finally stop in the doorway of a closed haberdashery shop on Twenty-fifth to wait out the rain.

"You would not recognize her as I would," Booth says. "You only saw her once."

"Ah, I would, sir," Raymond insists. "There be the portrait in your office, and besides, she bears resemblance to her daughter."

Booth spots a carriage, but the driver, clutching the brim of his hat in the rain, signals that it is occupied. Probably Raymond is right: the apparition could have been created by someone with mischief on his mind. Or—dare he admit it?—like Banquo's ghost, the specter could have been the shadow of a guilty conscience.

"Let us try it on foot," says Booth. His makeup has begun to run.

Also, a small squad of ragtag veterans, staggering down the street, seems about to take shelter beside them.

Raymond laments for the third time having mislaid the general's umbrella. But when the two of them begin walking, first briskly, then breaking into a run as they reach Lexington Avenue, they are inspirited by the effort into childlike competition, laughing as they skid on the paving stones. Booth, on his lifts, nearly falls. They wind up breathless, and wringing out their hats, under the shelter over the fanlight, waiting for a tardy servant to let them into the house. Like children, they have forgotten their latchkeys.

While Raymond, teeth chattering, is sent at once to bed, Booth changes into dry clothes and, pouring himself a brandy, goes downstairs to his office, where he settles in next to a lighted lamp, smoking a cigar. He leaves the window open in order to listen to the rain; when it stops, he hears people walking back and forth in the street and the familiar rattle of carriages. For a time, band music is audible in the distance.

Eventually, he hears noises on the stair. They are footsteps, and he feels his heart beating faster, half in hope, half in fear. What does he anticipate? That the visitor could be Madeline Usher in some transmuted form? It is almost as though his dear Nell has become something beyond the grave for him, and not a living woman at all.

But when the knock on the door comes, it is very heavy. He is not altogether surprised, when he unbolts the door, to find Alan waiting there.

Alan looks wise and smirky at the same time. Booth can see at once that he knows about the woman in black.

He clenches his fist. "What have you to tell me?"

Alan is still wearing his hat. It has become the fashion for smart young men to sit down indoors with their hats on. Tonight Alan looks about seven feet tall.

"You noticed Mother at the rally tonight, I think," Alan drawls. "She wants me to tell you not to look for her, that she feels betrayed and wants me to see to it that the rest of her clothes are packed and sent on."

"Sent on to where?" Booth asks furiously.

Alan rolls his walking stick between his hands and says that he would appreciate it if Booth not give difficulty.

"Of course I will give you difficulty!" Booth thunders. "I love her! She is back from France without my knowledge, but apparently with yours. Is Nellie with her?"

"Yes," Alan says, more briskly. "Mother thinks it very common of you to have sent Nellie along without admitting what was going on. I had to write Mother and tell her that Father had passed away, and that you had decided to take his place."

Booth begins pacing. "Common of me, is it?" he hurls.

"So Mother believes," Alan says, holding his ground.

"You did not think me common when I taught you how to ride one summer in Fredericksburg. You knew then that I came from one of the Confederacy's oldest families, that my work in the war forced me to—"

"Yes, forced you to become a waiter, I know," Alan drawls.

"You are a snob!" Booth shouts.

"I have nothing against waiters. Nor does Mother. It is politicians that she cannot abide."

Booth is indignantly aware that Alan is finding the conversation between the two of them amusing! No more than that. "Does she know," he asks, trying to calm himself, "that there is a place for her in this house, that we will work out the comings and goings?"

"Rather too much like a scullery maid, I think she said, having to disappear every time anyone came to the door."

"Absurd!"

Alan says that in any case his mother has lost her faith and only wants the clothing she left behind.

Booth shakes his fist. "I order you to tell me where she is! I must talk to her!"

Alan's dark eyes blink neutrally. "Would you take a bit of advice, sir?" he asks in a more measured tone. "Mother may come around yet. She was understandably pained by your performance tonight, but after a few weeks with no one but Nellie to keep her company—the mademoiselle, you know, remained in France—she may have second thoughts. She isn't, after all, upsetting the applecart."

Booth makes a last effort with his most sepulchral tone. "Alan, Alan," he laments, "do you not realize how much better things would be if your mother and I reached a meeting of the minds now, at once? Not just for us, whom you love. But for you, too, whom we in turn love."

Alan merely smirks.

The smirk enrages Booth. "Do as you like then!" he thunders. "Both of you. Only leave me in peace!"

Alan gets to his feet with alacrity.

"Good night, Father."

"Don't 'father' me, you ingrate!"
Alan takes flight.

Brooding, Booth paces the floor to ponder the meaning of what has occurred. He can appreciate Nell's dismay: she abandoned her husband, Chester Arthur, in order to mate with a man of vigor and principle, yet when she returns to America, there that same man is as Chester Arthur. A most discouraging turn of events!

Just the same, he believes his own intentions have been above reproach. He has wished to spare her the turmoil of the campaign months. When quieter times came—and himself in Washington—he would have been eager for her to return to him. Now that he thinks of it, he has been missing her more and more as the weeks and months have gone by. Flown by, really. He has been on the point of telling her everything by letter, and inviting her, nay, begging her to return.

His sending Nellie to her may have been with this unspoken intention. Yet Alan was partly right: he has not handled it very well, that part of it. But he was only human. Mistakes were made in '65 as well. The slippery Lincoln eluded their grasp half a dozen times because of silly errors they made. But they finally got him. Other errors led to the scaffold and the dungeon for most of his valued troops. Well, all of them. Even his landlady was hanged.

The only consoling possibility—one that he now mulls over—is that perhaps Nell has not returned from France after all. Instead, Alan, and others, have created an illusion, a piece of theater. The woman made up to look like Nell has been caused to appear at a time when he could not immediately go to her; then she would vanish, tantalizing him with the question of whether it had really been she. He remembers a play that went something like that. Perhaps a letter would yet come from Nell in France that would have the effect of undoing their subterfuge.

The effort to convince himself is as useless as it is painful. If he has lost her forever, to whom can he truly utter that he loved honor more? Only if he came face to face with her would that be possible.

Unsettled, he grabs his hat and coat and heads out into the still damp streets, half determined to try to find her even though he has not the least idea where to look. Besides, he needs to walk in order to calm himself.

Striding quickly uptown from Gramercy Park, he is aware there are nearly as many people on the streets as earlier in the evening, although they seem now in a more unpredictable mood. Listening to them, he detects a new edge in their speech and in their laughter. Many of the passersby are talking about the visit of Garfield to New York and about the rallies they have attended; up near 24th Street, Booth can hear the distant sound of the band playing again. Eternally it is "The Battle Cry of Freedom," alleged to be Garfield's favorite.

He heads in that direction, aware that men are still giving speeches, as late as it is. Many in the crowd, stimulated by the earlier excitement, seem nearly out of hand. Young men run by, laughing and holding flaming torches high. Booth shields has face from view as they pass, but their reckless spirit somehow emboldens him. He remembers a part of himself that he freely indulged in his younger years. The commerce of the street changes after ten P.M.

Booth recalls that among the final speakers at the 24th Street rally is to be the Janus-faced Mr. Ghetto. To hear an address by that madman at such an hour seems appropriate to him. At the rally the young workingmen of the city would forgather to hear the political speakers who were furthest from the salt. Booth wishes suddenly that he were attending in some role other than Arthur—Götz Dörfer perhaps?

He promises himself that he will recover one of his older identities for at least a night sometime soon. Meanwhile, he will relax. He smiles to himself. The walking stick picked up in his impulsive departure from the house is the lethal one. Not he, but Raymond, has fashioned it that way. Nevertheless, the stick makes him smile a second time as he thinks how stolid and respectable he must look to people noticing him in the street.

He feels himself that he is dangerous.

17

FROM *The Compass*

STRANGE VISITATION TOLD BY WELL-KNOWN MYSTIC

Nyack—The strange ghostly appearance of a figure that resembled Mrs. General Chester A. Arthur, deceased wife of the Republican Vice-Presidential candidate, was reported Sunday in meeting by Mr. Oscar Labadee of R. R. #1. Mr. Labadee, a spiritualist and friend of the noted evangelist Dwight Moody, told a congregation in Nyack Sunday that several acquaintances of Mrs. Arthur, who passed over last January, observed the strange phenomenon at a political rally for The Boys in Blue in Madison Square. General Arthur, along with General James A. Garfield, the Republican candidate for President, spoke at the rally.

Mr. Labadee, who had for a time been a member of the Mendelssohn Society, a musical group to which Mrs. Arthur belonged, said that the apparition seemed to move in and out of a shadow next to a carter's wagon stopped near the terrace of the Fifth Avenue Hotel, where her husband was speaking. Members of Mrs. Arthur's family refused comment on the report, which they termed "impious nonsense."

18

THE HOFFMAN HOUSE

While Mr. Ghetto waits at a table in the bar of the hostelry, he nervously fingers a worn *Argosy* magazine, which someone before him has left on a chair. It seems to him incongruous to have found such a periodical—usually read by young people of the lower middle class—in so elegant an establishment. Several times he looks about the barroom to see if anyone is spying on him, but the tempo of the conversations seems unaffected. He speculates on what he will do if a claimant appears. Perhaps slip the magazine into his coat: possession is nine points of the law.

Surreptitiously, he skims the book advertisements in the back pages of the magazine: *Life in Utah, or the Mysteries and Crimes of Mormonism, Being an Exposé of their Secret Rites and Ceremonies,* by J. H. Beadle, Elegantly Bound in Extra Fine English Cloth at $2.75 per copy. And then *Sexual Science Including Manhood, Womanhood, and their Mutual Inter-Relations, Loves, Its Laws, Powers, Etc.,* by Prof. O. S. Fowler, Bound in Fine Leather (Library Style) at $4.00 per copy. Also, more familiarly, *The Light in the East, A Comprehensive Religious Work, Embracing the Life of Our Lord and Savior Jesus Christ and the Lives of the Holy Apostles and Evangelists,* by Rev. John Fleetwood, D. D., Elegantly Bound in Fine Morocco Cloth at $4.00 per copy.

He knows himself to be too sophisticated for appeals of such a nature. At the same time he senses that some gentlemen at the bar are glancing in his direction. It is none of their business what he is reading. That he does not wear expensive morning coats, starched Irish linen, or blocked derby hats does not mean that he lacks power of the mind. Few of the men here, he is willing to wager, know much about anything but business and finance. None, he judges, has any appreciation of the Fine Arts. Take the painting of the "Three Graces," for example, which hangs illuminated across from the main bar. He doubts that more than a man or two in the room would understand that the three maidens represented there have a strong connection with the Classical Tradition.

On the other wall, a mounted moosehead watches him with neutral expression.

"Mr. Ghetto?"

"Sir?"

The bearded gentleman staring down at him seems at first to Mr. Ghetto some kind of dandy, not much doubt of it. He does not like the man's looks, but he manages to shove the magazine under his coat as he intended. While his left hand does this business, his right shakes the hand extended to him.

"My name is Dörfer," the man says. "Are you comfortable at this table?"

Mr. Ghetto looks around suspiciously. "You are from the central committee?"

"Of course. . . . You were kind to wait for me before ordering."

"Ordering what?"

"You wouldn't be a temperance man, would you?" asks Dörfer.

"I am a Stalwart, sir!"

Dörfer seats himself. "As am I." He looks around the room for a waiter; it is rather crowded for early evening.

Mr. Ghetto says, "I see you are looking around d' room. I understand. You feels skeptical that I am what I say I am—a Stalwart!"

"Not at all."

"I stood with Grant. I stood wit' d' t'ree-hundred-six at Chicago."

"Excellent."

When the moustachioed waiter arrives, hands on hips, saying nothing, Mr. Ghetto says to the waiter, "Senator Conkling is d' finest man that walks."

"Should we order now?" Dörfer asks. "What would you like, Mr. Ghetto?"

"Draft beer. I do not put on airs."

Mr. Ghetto stares down the waiter. Perhaps it is not clear to others that he has a simple sense of honor and is unimpressed by false show. But when Dörfer also orders draft beer, Mr. Ghetto wonders briefly if it might not be a form of condescension.

"The vice-presidential candidate is a fine man too," Mr. Ghetto adds. "I discussed my speech wit' him, you know."

"I heard your speech. It was very effective."

Mr. Ghetto points out that first and last he is a party man. Still clutching the magazine under his coat, with his other hand he now makes the motion of a tree swaying in the wind. "I do not sway wit' d' wind," he says. "D' point I made about d' Rebel matter I have been making since 1872." Mr. Ghetto scowls as the beer arrives at the table. "D' speech was formerly titled 'Grant and Greeley.' In order to remain true to my principles, I had to support Greeley at dat time. Regretfully he lost. Dat did not sway me. At d' canvass in seventy-six I delivered d' same speech for Hayes, who, of course, was victorious, but—"

Mr. Ghetto is here interrupted by the appearance of a friend of Dörfer's at the table, a chap who looks like a waiter. Mr. Ghetto can recognize the type.

"Dörfer!" the friend exclaims. "You vanished so suddenly from Delmonico's that we thought—"

"Yes, yes, I found a position out of town. Do excuse me for not—"

"We were hoping nothing happened to you," the friend persists. Mr. Ghetto finds the manner aggressive, especially when the individual asks if he can join them.

When the intruder is finally gotten rid of, Ghetto leans across the table confidentially.

"May I give you a word of advice, Dörfer? I have had experience wit' confidence men, and you should not assume dat a man like dat is as he pretends to be. If I wagered, I would wager dat dat man is not a friend."

"What is he, do you think?"

Mr. Ghetto will not say. Still with his left hand inside his coat, he raises his beer glass with his right; having smeared his beard with foam, he sets down the glass and nervously wipes his mouth.

Dörfer edges forward now and says that the members of the party committee who sent him were impressed with Mr. Ghetto's "personal acuity."

"Yes, my personal qualities," Mr. Ghetto agrees. "My personal honor. I have a sense of honor."

An explosion of laughter at the bar makes Mr. Ghetto turn his head sharply.

"Other men," he says pointedly, "do not have my sense of honor and loyalty. I worked for a time as attorney at law. I had a practice, you understand. But now I have focused my attention on politics and government service."

"So far you have not received the kind of appointment you wanted," Dörfer reminds him.

"No. I have been hoping for Vienna."

"Vienna?"

"D' trust I once put in d' false Hayes I now put in Gen'ral Garfield. As a Stalwart, I must follow Gen'ral Arthur and Senata Conkling. If dey have faith in Garfield as a man of honor, so must I."

Dörfer murmurs that Mr. Ghetto must be persistent.

"Yes," Mr. Ghetto agrees. "I must. It pains me when wort'less men who have contributed no idea, no speech, nothing to d' campaign sue for positions dey have no qualifications for. And receive dese positions!"

"I see you have been shunted aside before, Mr. Ghetto, and do not mean to let it happen again."

Mr. Ghetto looks earnestly at his companion. Abruptly he pushes the beer stein out of the way and moves both hands imploringly into the middle of the table, thereby dropping the magazine from beneath his coat. It hits the floor with a thump, but Mr. Ghetto ignores it in his impulse to beseech a still fuller understanding with his new companion.

"Are you a married man or a single man, Mr. Dörfer?"

Mr. Dörfer says that he is a single man.

For a moment Mr. Ghetto makes no reply. It takes a great effort of will to push down the sensations that he feels; he is not exactly sure where they are coming from. But he makes the effort, and by biting his lip, he is able to go on.

"You may count yourself fortunate then," Mr. Ghetto says, "for I was a married man, and could not find loyalty even in my marriage. It grew so—so bad dat I had to lock her in d' closet when I went to work in d' morning. People said dat I could not do dat, and if she reported me to the police, dat I would go to jail. And, Mr. Dörfer, I said, 'Very well, I will go to jail if it is necessary. Holy wedlock is to me a covenant, and although I am not a religious man, I know what loyalty and honor mean, and dey are more to me dan all d' domestic ordinances in d' books.' Do you agree?"

Dörfer says, "We all define honor in our own way."

They later share a carriage for downtown. After leaving the Hoffman House, they discover that their business takes them in the same general direction, and Mr. Ghetto, for his part, expresses his thanks for the rare encouragement that Mr. Dörfer, as a member of the party's central committee, has given him. Mr. Dörfer, in his turn, advises Mr. Ghetto that in the last analysis, determination always pays off. Every book, every article, every story that one read, concurred on that point. They must meet frequently and talk more about it.

Mr. Ghetto agrees; he has never met a man, he thinks, with whom he has such an affinity.

PART FOUR
STEALING
the SCENES

For Garfield and Arthur   *For Hancock and English*
4,449,053 popular votes   4,442,030 popular votes
214 electoral votes   155 electoral votes

1

DELMONICO'S

"If we're goin' to be interrupted," Thurlow Weed says, "I'd just as soon not get started at all."

Booth has guided the two of them into a steward's pantry off the main banquet room. It is less than thirty minutes before the last great victory dinner is to begin, the final celebration before Lent. Inauguration is less than a month off.

"Have a seat; the captain doesn't use this pantry much," Booth says. With his old steward's key he opens a high cupboard, and in an expansive mood brings down some rare French wines, the labels of which he reads off for Weed. Beyond the closed door they can hear shouts arising from early guests in the hallway outside the dining room. There are cries of glee and triumph for the arrival of Senator Dorsey, the guest of honor. The election was "Dorsey's coup," as some have called it. He managed the race they won by a hair in Indiana. New York was almost as close.

Weed takes rum, having turned down the fancy wines, and says,

"I thought you oughta know the fat may be in the fire on Miss Victoria Coventry. She seems to have vanished from the face of the earth."

Booth pours a glass of rum for himself. "I daresay she merely left New York."

"Could be," says Weed. "But now her pater has turned up on Park Row. He grows apples near Waterford, and is worried about his little girl, who has not returned to Waterford and has failed to get in touch with him. The family's name is Kappenhalter, by the way, not Coventry."

Booth studies his own reflection in the glass door of a cabinet—the ruddy cheeks, the shaped white whiskers. "A woman of that stripe does not go home to Waterford once she has been given independent means."

"Neither her brother-in-law, nor her gent—they both live in Manhattan—knows what became of her either." Weed sits stiffly in his chair, resting his glass on a pier table. Gaunt, he fixes Booth with his gaze. "Dun says you asked him where she was workin'. You wouldn't have dropped an anonymous note to Latham's, would you, that they had a spy workin' for them in their factory?"

Booth says that New York is full of missing persons.

"Yeh, but this is one you say you paid to leave town. Old man Kappenhalter doesn't know that part of it."

"Does Bennett know?" Booth asks. Abruptly, he downs the half-tumbler of rum he has been holding, taking but two gulps.

With a forlorn air, Weed laughs and changes the subject. "No. Drink like that, and I can see why they paired you with General Grant at dinner."

"Why, Grant is said to like me."

"Yeh, you'll like Grant too. He's the easiest person in the world to talk to. Not the most fascinatin', just the easiest." Weed sighs, purses his lips, falls silent.

"The girl will turn up," Booth says. He is not afraid of the Victoria Coventry matter. He is rather more troubled about the banquet and, for some reason, about the speech he will be called upon to deliver. It is bad enough to be back at Delmonico's, where every last waiter and cook is familiar to him. But on top of that he has been experiencing a sense that he has been losing the characterization in the last few months. Ever since Nell's defection—and his lapses into Dörfer—he has felt shaky. In the intimate setting of this particular banquet, where he must be matey with the others, the platitudes of the campaign trail will not altogether do. He has been trying to think what the proper tone should be. Prince Hal, possibly?

"I hope you're not going to turn out to be an imbiber at this late date," Weed remarks cheerily. "You know they never forgave it when Andy Johnson turned up drunk on inauguration day."

Booth drains his glass and gets to his feet.

"The funny thing about Andy Johnson," Weed goes on, reaching for the stool beside him in order to help boost himself onto his pins, "is that he lacked the common touch. Born poor as dirt, but he didn't have the touch. Always put on some kind of airs."

Simple enough for a fully matured actor to manifest a common touch, Booth assures himself. But a prince with a common touch. Not a waiter. As he guides Weed down the service hallway to the banquet room, he eyes the familiar ambience with deep suspicion. He sniffs the air as though even the cooking aromas might turn him back into Götz Dörfer. Waiters are passing down the hallway, laden with trays bearing bisque, cold salmon, palmettos. One of the men he knows like a brother, and he swiftly drops his gaze.

As the waiters continue through the swinging doors, Booth pauses with Weed, appraising the decoration of the banquet room. The floral displays seem to have been ordered from the cheaper florist; the better of the two catered the banquet for Senator Jones last year, at which Booth decanted the wine. The present evening's flowers, from past experience, would wilt before the soup course.

Over the speaker's table, a bas-relief map of Indiana is done in flowers, complete with a rising sun over a prairie, and a "pioneer" looking at a buffalo; probably the decorator thought that Indiana was part of the Wild West.

But the guests have spotted him. First there is a ripple of applause and then some healthy cheers.

"Hurrah for General Arthur!"

"Hurrah for the Vice-President-Elect!"

While Weed trails in behind him, a ring of men approach and surround Booth, clapping their hands. His eyes meet theirs with forced warmth and merriment. But then he sees that their own regard seems genuine. He is not sure who all of them are, but at least he does not feel like a wine steward. He begins shaking hands, smiling back, calling those whom he knows by name. Senator Jones, for example. Senator Jones was once very short with him when a flat bottle of wine was served to the Senator in this very room. Now Jones, with whom he has become friendly in the new role over the past few months, is pumping his hand with gusto.

Tom Platt, now a Senator-Elect, emerges from the group to give him a dutiful handshake. No Roscoe tonight: he has gone to Mentor, Ohio, to chisel a cabinet seat or two out of Garfield there. Dorsey, the guest of honor, embraces him to a chorus of rousing cheers. As Dorsey pounds him violently on the back, Booth stares over the top of his oddly coiffed head toward the stone-faced waiters, in phalanx primed for labor. He spots wrinkled John Bradwell among them and wonders how Maggie's consumption is. Also, he sees Carrier, the waiter he ran into at the Hoffman House the first night he was with Ghetto there.

When General Grant pushes his way through the throng to offer the final warm handshake, Booth recognizes that his own credentials have been fully validated. In a few minutes he will be dining in tandem with The Yankee Butcher, who has become an "easy" conversationalist now that he is no longer fighting the war that made him notorious. Only he, Booth, continues to fight in that cursed war, and still in the enemy camp, where his post seems eternally to be.

The "easy" conversation: as soon as they are seated at the speaker's table, Grant, on his left, makes jokes about the engraved bill of fare each diner has received. The French language amuses Grant.

"Now, what's this?" he whispers to Booth, leaning confidentially.

It is, in fact, "*chapon farci aux truffes et marrons.*"

"Capon, I think, General," Booth says, trying to muster a smile. He knows Delmonico's menu as well as Grant knows Vicksburg. But he must avoid condescension.

Grant quickly identifies the word "*rotis,*" chuckling hoarsely through his whiskers. "It wasn't all bullshit when you boys told 'em I learned something on my trip abroad. I bet Garfield doesn't know what 'ro-tees' means."

Now he roars with laughter, and Booth, for politeness, offers one of his "common-touch" laughs. While just a touch princely, it is less theatrical than the royal laughs he used to do in Shakespeare. In his time, he won some fame for those laughs.

Grant, reminiscing, recalls place-names.

"The French Riviera. Nice. Monte Carlo. . . . Now that's a hell of a nice place."

Booth nods his large, rubicund head. As he contemplates the next three hours or so ahead of him, he wonders if he will be able to manage it all. Instead of the boredom and fitful anxiety that he feels, he could be relaxing on the Riviera with Nell. But even she, however temporarily, has made that impossible. Ah, once—in time forgot—woman was the patient sex!

"No pun intended," General Grant adds slyly. And when Booth looks blank, Grant explains.

"Nice—neece. No pun intended!"

Booth nods, clenching his teeth.

Three hours later, when it is finally his turn to speak, he is in a mellower mood. Delmonico's has not skimped on the wine, although the new wine steward has proved a perfect imbecile, absent when both the entrée wines and the dessert wines had to be decanted.

As the applause rings out for "General Arthur," he feels emboldened to try a bit of candor in his speech: essence of the common touch. With the echo of the introduction dying in his ears, he looks into their receding faces. He feels a bit light-headed, and he tries to look very squarely at Platt. Then he looks at Weed. He wishes Roscoe were present, for he is absolutely unafraid of Roscoe. The "campaign" must be his subject, but who the hell is he? In the cigar smoke, it feels more like Shrewsbury than Agincourt. Prince Hal is not right. Richard Three is closer to it. Richard Three talking familiarly with his subordinates after their common deviousness has achieved a success! No airs in Richard Three, not with his men.

"I don't think we had better go into the minute secrets of the campaign so far as I know them," he is saying, "because I see the reporters are present, who are taking it all down; and while there is no harm talking about some things after the election is over, you cannot tell what they may make of it because the inauguration has not yet taken place, and while I don't mean to say anything about my birthplace, whether it was in Canada, or elsewhere"—this is a jocular reference to Democratic charges, never proven, that Arthur was born in Canada, rather than Vermont, thus making him ineligible for the office. Booth is pleased when his listeners laugh and applaud—"still, if I should get going about the secrets of the campaign, there is no saying what I might say to make trouble between now and the Fourth of March."

Someone in the audience calls out "Hear! Hear!" More applause and laughter. Booth feels himself falling into a tempo, stimulated by the applause to deliver what none of the others in the long, boring evening have had the talent to give. He gestures toward the bas-relief map, with its pioneer and buffalo.

"The first great business of the committee was to carry Indiana. That was a cheerful task."

They are laughing and applauding at anything now. But he reminds himself that the wit must be a shade lumbering. Mercutio without the meter. Still, he does not have to add, as Grant would, "No irony intended."

"Indiana," Booth says, "was really, I suppose, a Democratic state that might be carried by close and perfect organization and a great deal of—" He pauses for a moment, catching the perfect nuance, and in the audience there are delighted cries of "Soap! Soap!"

He has gone as far as he might. It is a benighted era he lives in, not the Renaissance. "I see the reporters here," he says, "and therefore I will simply say that everybody showed a great deal of interest in the occasion, and distributed tracts and political documents all through the country."

His listeners love all that he says. He has the common touch. Only the greatest actors have it.

"If it were not for the reporters I would tell you the truth, because I know you are intimate friends of the Republican party."

Men of the world they are, pledged to each other in frankness: "We happy few . . ." Booth remembers that speech, too, wants to give it, realizes it would be too dangerous. Perhaps he has gone too far already. Abruptly, he sits down, another trick of the theater—the off-tempo ending.

He has the audience rollicking with cries of "More! More!" He stands up again, as though taking a curtain call, all of it done without stepping out of character. General Grant himself has finally to raise his hands in order to quiet the multitude.

Henry Ward Beecher, the theologian, is next introduced. Beecher allows them one more good laugh as he declares that it is well "for some he could name" that he is not present on this occasion in his role as a clergyman. Booth contributes a laugh as hearty as anybody else's, and then he relaxes in comfort as Beecher modulates into loftier regions, calling on them for "dedication" and what not. Booth is aware that he is the star of the evening, and reflects that that is some consolation for the three hours of boredom he's had to endure.

Presently, while Beecher drones on, Grant leans over and whispers to him, "General Arthur, I wish you'da been with me in the Vicksburg campaign instead of sittin' on your behind here in New York." He winks his eye. "You got nerve. Eight years in the White House and I never talked that straight when there 'uz reporters aroun'."

*

Grant is prescient. The notices on the speech turn out to be bad. "Cynicism in Second Highest Office in the Land," one journal headlines it. "Saturnalia at Delmonico's!" cries another.

Booth feels hurt. It is as though they are reviewing a play other than the one he was in. Moreover, the men who laughed loudest at the banquet are coldest to him now. Platt is like ice. Dorsey avoids him. Even Roscoe, back from Mentor, moans that one newspaper has called for articles of impeachment when he hasn't even been inaugurated yet.

"Raymond," Booth says heavily one afternoon while the servants are packing some of the items that will be sent on in the move to Washington, "perhaps the trouble is that I have become alienated from the core of my being."

Although he does not say it to Raymond, he knows that for an actor there is a difference between true believers—that is, those who strengthen the core of one's being—and the claque of the fickle, who are propitiated at great risk. In '64 and '65 he neglected to communicate with some who would have been sympathetic with him. As a result he lost spiritual nourishment. What use, he now must ask, is the second-highest office in the land—or even the first-highest—if he lacks fellow believers.

The fickle press, of course, need not be courted. And one can do without such false friends as the barbarous Tom Platt, or even poor Roscoe, a man fading out of fashion. But it is disconcerting to have been careless with hard-won friendships such as those with Weed and Dun, both of whom disapprove of what happened to the woman reporter, who, if she had only stayed in Waterford, using her good mind to help her father in the orchard business, would have gotten into no trouble at all.

Thinking of one woman reminds him of another. The most painful of the defections is Nell, who sacrificed her very identity for him, and now, failing to understand his new part, turns her back. He feels a lump in his throat, a new spasm of guilt over it. While he cannot lower himself to press Alan again about her whereabouts, to be estranged from her is the same as being estranged from the spiritual part of his own nature. With that side of him gone, he is no different from all the others who occupy high office soullessly.

"If only I could talk with her for ten minutes!" he bursts out to Raymond, morosely leaning on the bare desk in his office. "Without her a half of me is . . . putrescent."

Booth sees a look of astonishment on Raymond's face; of course he has cursed the woman to Raymond, damning her to eternal fire for having come halfway around the world for the single spiteful purpose of once gazing on him from a contemptuous distance.

"If ye wanna talk with her," Raymond now says hesitantly, "could she be stayin' in Virginia with her cousins?"

Raymond's face has flushed. Booth sees at once that it is far more than a wild guess on Raymond's part.

"You *know* where she is!" Booth cries, and he moves forward with such passion that Raymond, in fear of being struck a blow, cowers near a teetering stack of cardboard file drawers.

"When Miss Nellie's clothes was being picked up, I sneaked into the delivery wagon to see the address." Raymond risks a glance. "But ye said ye never wanted to know where she was. Ye damned her!"

"I did that!" Booth agrees. "I did." He steps back, relieving the pressure on Raymond. "You see, it was what she deserved. But I—I now realize that that isn't the whole question. . . . Never mind, Raymond. I commend you, I do."

Looking uncertain, Raymond blinks. Booth is already donning hat and topcoat, having resolved on an immediate trip to the telegraph office. Brodie Herndon can be trusted to answer a direct question from one who lived as his vassal for four years. Everything was becoming clear again: all the resources were not dissipated. Raymond, for one. Still, it should have been self-evident that the only place for Nell and Nellie to have gone was the Herndons' in Virginia. Where else was sanctuary?

"How will you like to see Miss Nellie again, Raymond?" he asks the lad exuberantly. "How will you like to see the light of your life, as I will see mine? And in God's Country! Prepare yourself."

2

FREDERICKSBURG

As the two of them step down onto the windy platform at Fredericksburg, each carries his own valise. There is no one at the station to meet them, although Brodie has wired his willingness for them to come. At once Booth engages a wagon to take him and Raymond out to the Herndon homestead. For himself he would have preferred to hire a mount from Collins, the local stable keeper, and leave the bags on the station platform for Brodie's servants to fetch later.

But horseback will not do for Raymond, who is gotten up in a fawn-colored coat, with contrasting trousers, fitted by Booth's own tailor just before they left New York. With his stiff-crowned hat, he has the anxious air of a lad arriving at Eton or Harrow for the first time. Partly, Raymond seems unsure as to how dangerous the Rebels still are. For the rest, he brings his young Dulcinea a special gift.

"Gettin' warmer," the driver says, once the valises have been loaded in the wagon and the newcomers brought up onto the seat.

"The wind is warm," Booth replies agreeably as the horse starts forward. He is content not to be recognized as the Vice-President-Elect, although he is dressed today much as he was on his campaign posters. Not many years ago they would have pegged one dressed as he is as a carpetbagger. In his heart he wishes he could have come to town in ragged gray with cavalry boots, and sixty pounds lighter; some of them would have welcomed him as the intrepid Captain Boyd, famous hunter for the Herndon household.

The first crocuses are poking out of the grass along the riverbank. Raymond sits easily with his hat on his knee. Booth unbuttons his own coat, a nervous gesture. It is bold of him to have come to Nell not as Captain Boyd or as Götz Dörfer, but as Chester Arthur, the role to which he has committed himself. All roles are risks of a kind, he will tell her. Perhaps he will mention his brother Edwin's recent decision while on tour in London not to open with the safe choice, *Richelieu,* but to beard Irving in his den by performing *Hamlet* at the Princess Theater. Nell, he will say to her, we are used to certain people in certain roles, but art and morality constantly make new demands.

Why should an actor not impersonate a public man? An actor must act.

As the Herndon house finally appears through the trees ahead, Booth feels his heart jump with the pleasure of recognition. It is just as he remembers it: he has loved this place, loved the people. What a happy chance if he be now welcomed as family; with the power he is about to gain in Washington he can restore to people such as these something closer to the noble life which they have lost.

These reflections put a special importance on his expected meeting with Nell. In a haze of excitement he jumps from the wagon as soon as it comes to a stop. A fresh-painted wooden fence has been thrown around the huge front yard; the house itself is freshly painted too. A black man is leading two horses by their bridles down toward the river. When Booth knocks at the front door, he is delighted to see a black face there too. For the years immediately following the war, help had been hard for the Herndons to come by.

"The doctuh, he not in," says the black woman who answers the door. When she sees the luggage being unloaded onto the veranda, she asks, "Be you de gen'l'min spected by de doctuh?"

"I am," Booth says. "Is anyone around?"

"De doctuh, he in town wi' de missus, Aunty Lew from Richmon' en de li'l missy." She looks at him coolly.

"When do you expect them back?"

"Din' say."

Lifting his head to the heavens, Booth declares that then he must borrow a horse, and find these people he has come so far to see. No, he does not propose to return to town in the wagon. "You must tell Dr. Brodie that I have borrowed a horse if I do not happen to locate him. What is your name?"

"Ah Peregrine and dat Henry wit' de horses, he bringin' dem back up from de waterin' trough."

In a flash Booth is running down the path and through the wooden gate toward the black man leading the horses. Raymond and the woman watch from the veranda. In no time Booth has transacted with Henry and the large sorrel is saddled; astride he comes wheeling down from the pasture area at an accelerating gallop.

Raymond's eyes fairly pop. Horse and rider seem one. So fluid is the action of the man on the animal that in the time it takes Booth to disappear from sight, the force that propels them seems beyond nature. Even Peregrine and Henry watch with astonishment.

Some minutes later Booth meets along the road a familiar wagon coming from the direction of town. He reins his horse into the shade of a large grove of willows and waits in the saddle. Neither of the persons in the wagon is Nell. Brodie, with Nellie beside him on the seat wearing her fur-collared coat, pulls his horse up alongside Booth's and gives the rider a long appraisal.

"Should I believe mah eyes?" he finally drawls. A smile flickers across Brodie's lips. Others who have encountered the new General Arthur usually pretend to see nothing at all different, either because they do not trust their own perceptions (Booth supposes) or because they fear social embarrassment. He is pleased to have the reaction of generous amusement from an old friend.

"Good afternoon, Brodie," Booth says in his best Chester Arthur voice.

Brodie says nothing for a moment. Then he looks down at Nellie, who is gazing at Booth with a china-doll impassivity. "Do you know this man?" Brodie asks her.

"Yes," she says. Her legs shoot stiffly out in front of her, then quickly relax again. "But I didn't know he was coming—"

"I wanted to surprise you, Nellie," Booth says. He remarks to Brodie that the servant woman thought that "the missus Aunty Lew" had gone into town with them.

"No," Brodie says, "she won't go into town."

"I hope she's well," Booth says. "Is your Aunty Lew well, Nellie?"

Not a wrinkle appears on Nellie's smooth forehead. "I guess so."

"Raymond has come to Fredericksburg with me," Booth now tells Nellie. "He's at the house with a present for you."

Nellie shrugs at that information.

"Your lady's staying in that old slave cabin," Brodie informs Booth. "Better go see her and find out if she's gonna let you remain around."

"The slave cabin?" He feels dismay to think of Nell quartered in such a place, as though she, rather than he, has a penance now to pay.

"You know the one."

Immediately, Booth pulls the horse's head around and with an air of urgency wheels the mount into a full gallop, hardly having the time to give a wave to Brodie and the little girl.

"I'm ready foah you! I'm ready foah you!" Nell cries.

She has answered the door of the slave cabin, but with such a look of terror in her eyes when she sees the image of her late husband before her that she involuntarily raises her hand, in which she holds a large spoon.

"Nell, my dear—"

"I'm ready foah you!" she shouts again, moving three steps backward. Then she throws the spoon at him.

"Nell—"

The spoon hits him in the chest and falls harmlessly. At once she dissolves into tears. "I . . . am ready foah you," she gasps.

Still at the threshold, he is nonplused by the violence of her reaction. As she turns her face from him in shuddering anguish, he contemplates the plain cotton dress, the hair laced into a knot at the back of her head.

"I know it is a shock to you, my present appearance," he says, keenly aware of how he must look to her, his sideburns precisely trimmed, his facial structure accurately modeled. "You must get used to it."

"You look nothing like him!" she declares.

"Nonsense."

"Chestuh had kind eyes," she says in a hollow and despairing tone. "He did'n' have a wax-dummy face."

The remark stings him. But he steps forward through the door, ducking his head under the lintel. When he lived here, his head cleared the door, but now in boot lifts, he is inches taller.

"Why did you leave him, then," Booth asks, "if he was so kind?"

"I thought . . . somebody else loved me moah."

Since she begins weeping again, he seats himself on a bare wooden bench next to the familiar table. A kettle of water is boiling on the stove. With a large iron she has been pressing a dress for Nellie.

In a quiet voice he asks her, "Do you really suppose I enjoy pumping myself up like this in order to look the respectable man? Do you think I would not prefer to be in the south of France with you?" Since she has pulled out a handkerchief and turned a profile toward him, he continues more boldly. "If you don't believe it, expose me then!"

"You fool, what can I do?" she retorts. "Mah own son is a party to the mockery. Even mah cousins here think it is some great joke that Chestuh is no better than a closetful of coats and trousers that somebody else can step into, and right away be a big Yankee politician."

Her chin stiffens as she talks. He says, "All of them make the best of it."

"Oh, the best of it? Poor Chestuh is killed, so why not make the best of it?"

Booth says that Chester was not killed.

"Yes, you ah going to tell me he died of shock, I know!"

"I was going to say he died of a weak constitution from too much dissolute living!"

As he jumps to his feet and begins pacing, she glares with contempt.

"I suppose just as Mistuh Lincoln died from too much dissolute living."

He knows he must not respond to the cruelty of her remarks. "Nell, I can restore the name Arthur to respectability, even as I restore the name Booth!" As his pacing quickens, the specific things he will do in order to vindicate himself come to him as in a vision. "Once I am in Washington, I will locate the Fredericksburg File. I am convinced it exists, Nell; men have seen it. I will find it no matter where Stanton left it!"

"Then you go look for it," she says suddenly. She has settled herself in a chair, gazing levelly at him. Her hands are clasped together in her lap, and her breasts have stopped heaving.

"But I need you at my side," he says earnestly. "How can you stay on in a slave cabin, Nell—"

"Easily! I have shown myself a slave!"

In his agitated course of movement, he now stops directly in front of her, recognizing that the scene must reach its denouement soon.

"Nell, you can be reborn! As I have been. You would make a—"

"No. No more Madeline Ushuh for me."

His need for her has become fierce. The thought of her having lived in the slave cabin for so many months where he once lived acts like an aphrodisiac. Probing for an angle, he says, "Nellie cannot be happy isolated here."

"I don't want to go to Washington! I nevuh did! Why don't you go lookin' for that Senatuh's daughter from New England if you ah so needful of a woman in Washington!" She has moved to the stove, puts the stove lid back over the fire, and says that she does not want the water to boil away while she wastes her time talking.

Sighing long and poignantly, Booth settles down into a half-broken rocker. "When they hold my trial," he says deliberately, "I'll do my best to keep the scandal away from Alan and Nellie's names. With Alan planning to start at Princeton, and Nellie having gone through so much, I wouldn't want to cause them any more—"

"You devil!" She turns so abruptly that he believes for an instant that she is going to throw the whole pot of water at him; he refuses to flinch. "If you turn on mah children now," she rages, "after all they been through with you, you just watch out for me! That's all I have to say."

She does not throw the pot of water.

"If you don't want to come to Washington," he suggests, "why

not come back to New York? I'll only be in Washington while the
Senate is in session. But when I'm back in New York, we can all live
together at the house as a family. That's where you belong."

She says nothing for a moment.

"What would you tell Bridget if I did?" she asks at last. "That I
am the madwoman livin' in the attic? Like Mr. Rochester's wife?"

Booth says that they could discharge Bridget and get another
cook.

"She's the only good servant we found in twenty years!" Nell
exclaims.

"Then tell her what you want. Tell her you're Auntie Lew. She
won't turn on us. She loves us. Just as the children do."

"I won't make a fool of mahself to Bridget!"

Booth sighs for the last time.

"Nell," he says, "after all these years, after all I've undergone,
don't you think I deserve at last to become a family man?"

Her eyes stare in disbelief. "I *had* a family man, Mistuh Booth!"

She adds that it is her final word on the subject, and that she
expects him and whoever is with him to leave at once and stop bothering the Herndons, who, Nell truly feels, have offered him hospitality
enough to last an ordinary person a lifetime.

Still, she consents to walk with him up the path to the big house.
Dabney and Brodie, Junior, she says, are both away at a medical
convention in Richmond.

"Remember me to them," he says politely.

"I'm sure they wish they stayed at home so you could explain to
them how you ah purifying the Yankees of all their venal sins."

He lets that pass. Truly, she is a woman of infinite variety, and he
is encouraged by the stubborn passion in her. He begins talking about
the crocuses blooming early this year, and hopes they can expect a
warm day in Washington for the inauguration; also, does she remember that blissful afternoon when they first became aware that five-year-
old Alan's fever had broken, and——

"Oh, hush," she says.

They can see Nellie flying back and forth against the sky, poised
with legs outstretched and skirt flowing full in the breeze as she is
pushed on the rope swing suspended from the great oak in the Herndons' front yard. Peregrine and Henry, through for the day, are walking across the veranda, dressed for town. Raymond, sturdy on the
ground beneath the limb of the oak tree, abides each stroke of the

pendulum, waiting as the child Nellie returns through the air to him and he can touch her momentarily and thrust her out, free of earth, his expression rapt with concentration.

"That boy looks foolish," Nell says to Booth with distaste. "She is too young foah someone to look so foolish about."

3

THE CAPITOL

And so he is inducted into high office, a slushy day. Booth experiences a sense of anticlimax in it. While there are thousands of faces pressing upward from below the Capitol portico, he feels little of the dramatic excitement he felt at the Lincoln inauguration when, with Lucy Hale's father's credentials in his pocket, he leaned with heart beating rapidly against the balustrade over Lincoln's head, daring himself to fire at the grotesque figure standing below him, but never finding the opportunity. The nearer he came the more exciting . . .

His own oath he must mouth, as custom prescribes, in the presence of the Senators in their chamber: "I, Chester Alan Arthur, do solemnly swear . . ." The name trips across his tongue by this time, but it lacks the satisfying resonance of, say, a name like Coriolanus, or Richelieu. Moreover, on Roscoe's advice, and as a way of offsetting the bad press he received after the Delmonico's speech, he assays a humble approach: "I come as your presiding officer with genuine solicitude, remembering my inexperience in parliamentary proceedings. *Blah, blah, blah!* I cannot forget how important, intricate, and often embarrassing are the duties of the chair . . . I rely with confidence upon your lenient judgment of any errors into which I may fall. In return, be assured of my earnest purpose to administer your rules in a spirit of absolute fairness. . . ."

Roscoe tells him afterward that his speech has been well received, having himself led the huzzahs and applause during the remarks. How proprietary Roscoe now seems! Hundreds of people line up in the corridor outside the chamber, most of them at Roscoe's behest, to greet the new Vice-President. Afterward, Roscoe shoulders him through to the picture taking with Garfield on the Capitol steps. "I have made progress with Garfield on appointments," he whispers, lodging himself in the second row so as to appear prominently in the memorializing photographs of the ceremony.

That night, with odd phrases from old plays going through his head—none of which he dare utter—Booth stands in the receiving line at the inaugural ball. The fete is held at the National Museum, where a huge plaster replica of the Statue of Liberty occupies the rotunda, holding high a torch illuminated by Edison's recent invention, the incandescent light. As soon as the guests have admired its dazzling candlepower, they pass on inside to shake the hands of Rutherford Hayes and his wife, Garfield and his wife, outgoing Vice-President Wheeler, and himself. Now I could drink warm blood, Booth hears in his head, but his face is a mask of perfect complacency.

Three hours they stand shaking hands. The pansies on Mrs. Garfield's satin dress wilt by the end of the first twenty minutes. Moreover, she looks sickly to Booth. The rest of the crew—veterans all—might have stood there three more hours. Lemonade Lucy, as Mrs. Hayes is privately known, looks as if she could last three days. The orchestra meanwhile plays Civil War songs, songs from both sides in an ecumenical spirit. Wheeler says that he even sees a few southerners around.

Booth sees no southerners at all. Indeed the one man he looks for—Mr. Ghetto—does not appear, and his crushed fingers are so badly swollen by the handshaking that when he gets back to the suite he is sharing with Roscoe, he has to soak them in a basin of water. The ring he has foolishly left on one of his fingers produces excruciating pain at a point where the dilated blood vessels are most constricted.

Sleepless, he has to find a blacksmith the next morning in order to get the cursed ring filed off his finger.

Some days later, while the Senate is trying to organize itself, Roscoe draws him into one of the cloakrooms and earnestly whispers, "You're not presiding with enough directness. Do at least concentrate when there is a deadlock and you have to cast the tie-breaking vote."

Booth says that by the end of a roll call he sometimes forgets whether their side is voting "aye" or "nay."

"My God, man! It's entirely along party lines at this stage," Roscoe pleads. "Vote the way I vote."

Booth shrugs. His mind keeps wandering between the first act of *Macbeth* and the third act of *Hamlet*, both of which concern the subject of regicide. In the meantime he longs for the proper election of a president pro tem of the Senate, who could sometimes relieve him in the chair. The august body, however, is divided with exactly thirty-seven Republicans and thirty-seven Democrats, along with one grossly obese Senator from Illinois named Davis, who calls himself an Independent, and a runty little snake-oil merchant from Virginia named Mahone, who is something called a Readjuster. If the two unaligned Senators would only jump the same way, the immediate tedium would be over and the body could go on to picking committee chairmen and so forth.

But it is not easy. As soon as the fat Senator hints that he will vote with the Democrats, little Mahone proposes to deadlock things for the Republicans again if they will but favor friends of his for certain posts.

"Do I vote 'aye' then for Mahone's appointments?" Booth asks in confusion.

"Of course!" Roscoe explodes. "Why, most Vice-Presidents go through an entire administration without being able to cast a single vote. You could cast many."

"And if I vote 'aye' here, then we'll be able to get on with the real business?"

"Well, yes, unless—"

Ominous voices in the corridor. Roscoe's practiced ear catches the fatal intonations. Then Booth, too, hears what his colleagues are chattering.

"Filibuster!"

The Democrats have decided to filibuster. It will continue to be a play without an argument, and his life a continuing holding action.

4

WASHINGTON

My dearest,

Alas, I've already lost track of the days. How stale, flat, and unprofitable does it all seem when I have no assurance of when I will next see you. But, believe me, this letter will contain no new appeals. Still, if Brodie passes this missive on to you (which I enclose in my thank-you letter to him for his kind hospitality) I must assume that he has some shred of respect for what I am trying to accomplish.

Alan promised to write you his impressions of the inauguration. This was his idea. He appears to find the whole process educational, and his opportunity for close observation of the executive branch may help him at Princeton.

My tireless pursuit of my honor takes place only when I find myself free of Senate business. So far, as a beginning, I have had my loyal Raymond bring me from the Library of Congress all the Stanton papers they have in their possession.

However, to conceal my true objectives, I have also asked for the papers of certain other former government officials, including, as it happens, those of Hannibal Hamlin, Lincoln's first Vice-President. Imagine my chagrin when the librarian exclaimed. "But, sir, Mr. Hamlin has left no papers for he is alive and seated in the Senate to-day!" An embarrassing—if amusing—error, for I spend a large part of the afternoons looking directly down on Hamlin's mane of white hair and have conversed with the man a number of times.

Roscoe provides me with much advice. In fact, when we reach our rooms at night, he likes nothing better than to talk to me for hours. Perhaps it is because he is disenchanted with everyone else.

The Collectorship in New York is what is left at issue. Should this post go to an enemy—such as Robertson—that could be the end of his hegemony. Poor Roscoe.

Probably you will think it strange that I waste sympathy on such as Roscoe Conkling, and his aggrandizements. In truth, I do not. I am occupied with the demands of a role I have chosen, and for the time being, it controls me more than I am able to control it. But time and destiny are on our side.

Would that I could tell you when I am going to be back in New York. You could then be sure of avoiding me if you should come there. If you want to bring Nellie up and meet Alan there, I know that you will make arrangements in spite of me.

Of course I have no time for a social life of any kind. In my continuing pursuit of the Fredericksburg File, I next delve into War Department archives, an enormous task complicated perhaps by the fact that the new Secretary, appointed by the President, is Robert Lincoln of Illinois. What fate shall my quest have in the den of the cub of the hyena?

My love to Nellie. For you, I entreat you to remember

Your Eternal Husband

5

THE SENATE CHAMBER

The obese Senator, Davis—having voted with the Republicans after all, and become "acting" pro tem—is dozing on the dais. While a western Senator holds the floor with logy incoherence, further up the aisle—Republican side—a pot begins to simmer. Half a dozen Senators, gathered near the desk of Senator Platt, have looked on something that causes consternation. Senator Platt himself clutches for support from the desk before sinking back, white-faced, into his chair behind it.

"Robertson!" he says in disbelief.

"Robertson," the Vice-President, standing with him, sonorously confirms to the others who have not yet seen it in black-and-white.

The list of new appointments, just sent over from the White House, contains the unthinkable—Robertson for collector of the port of New York! Roscoe Conkling, who has already been shown the list, sits speechless at his desk, rotating his head from side to side, as though helplessly turning the other cheek.

Other Senators begin assembling. The delegation grows at Senator Platt's desk. Some glance aghast from Platt to the Vice-President.

"Not Robertson?" one asks.

Steely-eyed, Platt nods.

"But for the collectorship?" another gasps.

As microbes move to a spot where a wound has been made, near half the members of the distinguished body swarm toward the desks of the two New York Senators. Even members on the Democratic side venture closer to see what all the excitement is about.

The Vice-President alone seems able to speak coherently. "Yes," he says in all solemnity, "the President's new list of appointments contains the name of Robertson for collector."

Men blanch at the news. Although some may feel that the arrogant Roscoe Conkling is due for his comeuppance, all are awed by the terrible silence in which he sits.

The western Senator continues to orate.

Platt is saying, "Only yesterday the President"—but his voice breaks.

"—strongly implied that Merritt would finish his term," the Vice-President concludes. The Stalwarts would have been willing to go on accommodating fusty old Merritt, Hayes's appointee.

"And now," Platt chokes, "it comes to this!"

The first distinct syllables begin emerging from the throat of Roscoe Conkling. Strangled and unintelligible at the start, the words (or, to be accurate, the "word") defines itself more and more emphatically as the Senator's auditors lean closer.

"Per-fi-dy . . . per-fidy . . . Perfidy! PERFIDY!"

What a fine Shakespearean actor the Senator would have made, Booth reflects.

6

WASHINGTON

On the evening of the fourteenth of April, Booth and Raymond enter a carriage in order to keep an appointment with the President. It is just past dusk when they set out, and although they are in an open barouche, Booth has dressed down for the occasion and thus is not widely recognized by passersby walking along the sidewalks or crossing the muddy streets.

Once under way, Raymond asks if they might not drive past Ford's Theater in case something is going on there. The newspapers have been writing of the anniversary of the assassination of Abraham Lincoln.

Booth, holding his hat on his lap, shakes his head. "It is poor taste for a Vice-President to visit a site where a President has been killed." Besides, the theater has since been converted to an office build-ing; Raymond would see nothing at all.

"Was Lincoln a greater man than General Grant?" Raymond asks.

Booth sighs in disdain. "Just tell me if you have read your eti-quette book so as to know how to address President Garfield if he should shake hands with you tonight?" Booth has given Raymond Mrs. Dahlgren's book on Washington etiquette, already in its fourth edition.

"I shook hands with him before," Raymond says. "In New York. He was with you."

"But you met him before he was President."

"I wasn't gonna call him Your Excellency anyway," Raymond sniffs. "He's not no royalty."

Booth commends Raymond for his skepticism. "Character and purpose are what count in a man, not high office. Anyone can hold high office."

Were that not true, Booth silently reflects, the President would not be summoning him tonight to talk about the ongoing hysteria over the Robertson appointment. A sad commentary that the two top lead-ers of government must discuss which scoundrel should dispense patronage in New York rather than considering serious social issues. There was no such thing as principle anymore. A lad could grow up without ever being exposed to models of selfless behavior. Pygmies one saw instead.

"Raymond," Booth says impulsively, "how would you like to go on a mission for me in about a week's time?"

"Where?"

"Back to Fredericksburg. Would you like that?"

Raymond nods and blushes.

"It will be a moral tonic for you," Booth says, "to be with the Herndons for a bit."

Their carriage has meanwhile reached the oval drive leading to the Executive Mansion. The horses move smartly up the drive to a spot near the porte cochere at the north entrance, where footmen and the doorkeeper see the gentlemen inside.

Garfield's young secretary, Mr. Stanley-Brown, meets them in the reception hall and leads Booth and Raymond quickly down the central hall to the Red Room. Along the route Booth glances into the Blue

Room, whence he hears conversation issuing desultorily. He is taken aback to see as many as twelve to fifteen men sitting and standing inside the room, smoking cigars or reading. Spittoons are clotted with cigar butts, and on the carpet, matches and other litter lie in the vicinity of spittoons where smokers have missed their targets.

In the Red Room, three more of the tribe have sequestered themselves and seem to be unpacking bread and sausages, probably with the view of protecting their provender from the larger throng in the other location.

Mr. Stanley-Brown addresses the picnickers.

"Do you mind, gentlemen? This room is being held for special use tonight."

"No trouble at all," says one of the men agreeably. He is tall and thin, of a build that has come to be called "Lincolnesque." A second man reminds Booth of Mr. Ghetto, but is far too closemouthed to really be him. Presently the group rolls up its food, whispers good-evenings to the Vice-President, and shambles back into the hallway, no doubt to finish their dining in the corridor.

After they have receded, Booth asks if they are office seekers.

"What else? Day and night. The President has taken to seeing them evenings so as to be able to get his work done during the daytime."

"I shall try not to keep him long," Booth says.

"No, he is expecting you," says Mr. Stanley-Brown and adds that if they will be seated in the Red Room, he will inform the President of their arrival. Booth notices that the upholstery on the furniture is threadbare, and that paths are worn in the piling of the carpet.

"Not done with much style," Raymond whispers after a moment.

Booth must agree. The lad is, of course, used to the elegance of the Fifth Avenue Hotel, and to 123 Lexington Avenue, where taste and tidiness have remained watchwords even with the lady of the house departed.

When Mr. Stanley-Brown returns, they are ushered at once into the family room, where the President is by himself, completing his evening repast.

"Ah, Mr. President!" Booth exclaims jovially as they enter. "Please don't get up."

For Garfield has risen from his meal and come forward to welcome them. A many-globed gas chandelier casts an aura of light over the dining table. But the fireplace is cold, and the room seems very dark, papered as it is in navy blue.

"That's all right, General . . . I hope you'll join me for what remains." Shelves stocked with gimcracks and vases filled with pussy willows loom in the shadows of the room.

"No, thank you, we've dined. I hope you don't mind my bringing my—"

"Yes, your aide," Garfield says, shaking hands with Raymond. "I believe we met in New York."

Booth beams. "How do you like that, Raymond?"

"I'm most honored, sir," Raymond says to the President.

Booth feels pride at Raymond's instinct for proper masculine response. Mrs. Dahlgren has been transcended.

It takes another few minutes to get Raymond sent off with the secretary, and then for Booth to commiserate with Garfield over the eternal nuisance of the office seekers cluttering the anterooms and the corridors.

"They reach for me as I go by," Garfield says. "It's as though they want a piece of me; perhaps it will ward off the plague for them. Come, sit down. I think they would as lief dismember me and share the pieces as they would obtain a job."

"I can believe it," Booth says.

Garfield offers a wry laugh. "You see, if we don't reform the system, sooner or later the President will be dismembered."

"We agree on that," Booth says cheerfully.

Puzzled perhaps as to what has been agreed to, Garfield frowns and offers brandy. They light cigars and Garfield says that he assumed the two of them had once agreed on the Robertson appointment as well. "You know, I am dismayed at the virulence of the reaction from Senator Conkling and Senator Platt in this matter."

"Ah, yes," says Booth.

The President puffs smoke from his cheeks. "When you and I last spoke, you indicated to me that, given the other appointments I was recommending, you thought a balancing appointment in the collectorship favorable to the other faction might be tolerated by the Senators."

"Yes, I thought that," Booth concedes.

"Well, it hasn't turned out like that, has it? Now I find we have a very serious schism on our hands unless I withdraw my nomination of Robertson."

Amiably, Booth says nothing.

Garfield says, "As you know, I am a cautious man by nature. I was not eager to do something that would be inflammatory to Senator

Conkling and to his followers. Can you speculate on how we went wrong, General?"

"Perhaps Roscoe will calm down yet," Booth offers offhandedly.

Garfield considers the answer for a moment, then says, with a brief smile, "Well, if he doesn't he should be advised that it's too late for me to withdraw the appointment. I'd look like a fool if I did."

"Nevertheless," Booth says (knowing that the rest of the scene is bound to play well), "I am under obligation strongly to urge you to do just that!"

The agitation commences to roil in Garfield, who gets to his feet. "Good Lord, General, you sing a different tune than you did a week ago! Are you in communication with Senator Conkling at all? Today I read in the paper that the Senator thinks I promised to retain Merritt—"

"Because we know you are in favor of 'merit,' and not 'spoils,' " Booth says, unable to resist.

"Really, General!" says the President. "Puns?"

"Well, bugger me," says Booth, affecting petulance. "If I offend you, do get a graver go-between, you and Roscoe—one who is equal to the two of you in stubborn pride."

"I proud?" Garfield expostulates, pacing to the cold fireplace and back. "I have wanted to talk to the Senator face to face a dozen times. He is the one who disdains!"

Readily Booth concedes that the Senator is often disdainful.

"I cannot see your purpose in misleading me," Garfield continues. "The Senator cannot want this fight; he lacks the votes. Do *you* want it?" Abruptly, Garfield has come to a stop and with a hand resting on the marble mantelpiece he looks down at Booth still seated in the Andrew Jackson rocker.

"I?"

"I wonder if you are what you seem," the President says.

Booth does not raise his eyes. He has an intuition that Garfield's sudden suspicion of him has arisen from sources not related to the immediate discussion.

But heaving a sigh, Garfield returns to the previous subject. "Well, they have chosen the fight, not I. If they mean to destroy themselves, I cannot stop them. For I have the votes to win, General."

"Yes," Booth says, "if one takes the short view."

There is a new watchfulness in Garfield's eyes, but Booth has grown tired of the contretemps. Garfield is a trivial man. If he were not trivial, he would not be spending so much time trying to satisfy everybody, including the maenads filling the hallways outside.

"Thank you for receiving me, Mr. President," Booth says, getting to his feet.

Garfield seems loath to let him go. He clears his throat. "Your own position will be awkward in all this, I should judge."

"I only hope it will be honorable," Booth replies.

"Perhaps there is still a way out."

"Perhaps."

Incongruously, Garfield flashes a smile, as though the "perhaps" encourages him. A man is very trivial when the emptiest piece of optimism can raise his spirits.

"I am grateful you were candid with me, General," Garfield says, still eyeing him.

Booth lets himself out, and while he loiters in the corridor looking for Raymond, who seems to be in none of the public rooms, he glances once more into the Blue Room, where most of the job-seekers are still hanging about. He hears a voice from within that he recognizes.

Not Raymond's, but Mr. Ghetto's.

Fortunately, Mr. Ghetto's back is toward him, and Booth is able to escape the area without being dismembered. Mr. Ghetto, from behind, has looked patient, all in all. But patience has its limits, does it not, Ghetto, when yet another faithless leader's perfidy is about to be exposed?

7

UNION STATION

The import of Garfield's probing speculation, "I wonder if you are what you seem," quickly slips from Booth's mind over the next few days. With Capitol intrigue so heavy, he diverts himself to the need for sentiment in his life. Hence, thoughts of Nell, for whom he has designed a gift to remind her of the object he bought her one memorable afternoon in the Yankee Notions department at Stewart's. That he should be using an intermediary to help him with his wooing adds to the interest: it is somehow Shakespearean.

As he and Raymond stand on the railroad platform, where the Virginia Limited is about to depart, Booth hands the lad not only a small billfold of banknotes for his expenses, but also a wrapped package that fits snugly in the palm of the hand.

"This is a favor for the lady," Booth says of the latter. "It is unique and expensive, and you must be careful of it. On the other hand, enjoy yourself when you get there. Give me a good report if you can. Let the lady know that I am ever her humble servant."

It amuses Booth to imagine how the unpredictable lad might elaborate on the theme.

"I understand, sir," Raymond says. "I will guard the package with my life."

"Oh, a package is not worth your life," Booth says. "Only your honor is."

As the conductor begins calling "All aboard!" Raymond jumps onto the steps of the nearest Pullman car. Other people push past him onto the car, and a few look curiously at them. Booth is getting used to being recognized occasionally as the Vice-President. God knows, more people recognized his face after a split week in Richmond or Charleston than in the months he has spent in public life.

". . . and Raymond, don't spend all your time with the child," he calls. "Try to make yourself useful to the Herndons, whom you could not do better than to school yourself to."

"I will, sir!" Raymond cries as the train pulls forward, the sounds of the great locomotive echoing against the station walls.

While Booth awaits word from Fredericksburg of the progress of his suit, he works diligently over the Stanton papers in a private room in the Library of Congress. Most of the papers from the war years are stored in thirty-five separate boxes.

Not a scrap escapes his attention. Since the so-called Fredericksburg File may no longer be intact as a unit, he has hope that at any moment he may come across the lost pages of his diary, or the left-behind letters of marque that he had been authorized to carry for the Confederacy, and which were the evidence that he was a soldier and not a madman. As he works, he remembers Poe's tale "The Purloined Letter," in which the crucial paper was lodged, without evident concealment, among wholly innocuous documents.

In his mind's eye, meanwhile, Booth has a clearer and clearer image of the last act, once he locates the file. He rather fancies he will be President by then, and, as such, will have proposed a restoration of the Confederacy. On the closing day of his term in federal office, he will point out to the country that while there was passion on both sides, killing on both sides as long as the war lasted, there was no madness. Behold: John Wilkes Booth, who has been leading the federal government in Washington in the guise of another, is not mad, but rather an image of harmony. Let them listen to their President, who is proof that the soul of the Confederacy can but inspire and create. Deathless idealism can never be a threat to the federal republic.

He will have many things to say. Let the government at Richmond rise again, and if Booth blood be needed to seal the new secession, he will accept the will of the people. If the execution of Lincoln, and whatever other sins they may hold against him, are too great, then let them drum him to the scaffold! He can subscribe to their justice, once they have the facts.

A farfetched scenario, some might say. But let the skeptics scoff. What has already happened from the coup in the theater to this very moment has been unlikely in the extreme. With destiny's help, it has come to pass because a higher power desired it. Hamlet says, "There's a divinity that shapes our ends, rough-hew them how we will."

So Booth deliberates over box after box of Stanton's papers and returns them, one at a time, to the aged employee of the library who has been put at his call. The old man, white of moustache and standing no more than four and a half feet tall, gasps at him after all this research, "Not since Thomas Jefferson have we had such a scholar in the Vice-Presidency!"

8

MISS HAVISHAM'S

The hot weather moves in during the next few days, and Booth arrives restlessly one evening back at the suite of rooms that he and Roscoe occupy. Not only has Senate business grown tedious, and his efforts among the Stanton papers gone unrewarded, but Raymond has not returned from Fredericksburg and has sent no message. Some would suppose, by now, that Raymond has fled with the money and the jewelry entrusted to him, but Booth fears something worse.

His apprehensions are not quieted by the news that a military officer has called on him while he was out. Miss Havisham offers the information; she believes Senator Conkling may have spoken to the military gentleman, too, and the Senator could be found belowstairs where he was "engaging in his exercises."

Booth at once descends. For the Senator's sake Miss Havisham, a lady of means, has equipped a cellar room with a prizefighter's punching bag and other athletic apparatus, there having arisen lately a fad for "the manly art of self-defense" among Washington gentlemen, a fad that will soon dissipate, Booth believes, with the summer heat. Roscoe, after his embarrassing set-to with Kate Sprague's husband (the encounter advertised as his defense of Kate's music teacher), has decided to develop his muscles even though he has given up on Kate.

Tonight, however, the sound of thudding leather against leather already seems to be faltering in the stygian darkness below, a sign perhaps that Roscoe's depression over their futile maneuvers in fighting the Robertson confirmation is increasing.

As soon as Booth penetrates the dank cell that is redolent with perspiration, Roscoe's haggard eyes are upon him. The sweat runs down Roscoe's sideburns into the wispy beard on his chin, matting it. Blotches stand out on his ribbed underwear.

"There hasn't been any word from my aide, Raymond, has there?" Booth asks him.

Still breathing heavily, Roscoe shakes his head. "But your brother, Colonel Arthur, came calling this afternoon while you were out."

"Good God, what did *he* want?"

Roscoe settles down onto a low bench, on which stands a dishpan containing a block of melting ice. Putting a hand onto the ice—having removed one of his boxing gloves—he says dolefully, "The colonel will see you in New York, where he is to be stationed."

Booth leans against the calcimined wall. It comes to him that Roscoe has long supposed that the man masquerading as Chester Arthur can in truth be none other than Colonel William Arthur, Chester's only brother. The colonel's visit makes that theory an impossibility.

"Your brother resembles you very little," the bruised Senator says, removing his other glove and laying that hand on the ice too.

"Yes, very little," Booth says, not having stepped into the illumination of the sole gas fixture in the room.

Roscoe peers earnestly in that direction.

"Oh, Chester," he suddenly bursts out, "is it really you after all? Is it some kind of trick you've been playing?" He lifts his hands from the pan of ice, and with the saddest and most vulnerable of expressions, he starts to his feet. "Who are you? Who could you be besides Chester, my old friend?"

Then stopping himself abruptly, Roscoe bites his lip.

"Why, I *am* your old friend Chester," Booth says quietly, not moving from the shadows. "Damned if I'm not."

Roscoe advances no further. The corners of his mouth turn down, and for a moment Booth imagines he might be going to cry. But the Senator simply turns and walks away, his shoulders stiffening in pride and ignorance.

Upstairs again, Booth finds a Special Delivery letter lying on the pier table in the hall. It is addressed to the Hon. C. A. Arthur; he recognizes Nell's hand and regards it as an encouraging sign that she is ready to address him under the new name.

But the letter tells a different story.

Fredericksburg
April 27

Sir:

I take this means of communicating with your rather than the telegraph as a means of protecting privacy, not yours, but that of my daughter. She has gone off with your emissary Raymond, and has left me a note that they are bound for New York.

As far as I am concerned, this is a case of kidnapping, and whether it is at ground your scheme, or whether it is Raymond's, makes no difference to me. Raymond is a degenerate, and that you could not see that his interest in a ten-year-old girl is unnatural astounds me.

My cousins Brodie and Dabney Herndon have set out for New York. They have also informed the N. Y. P. D. that Nellie has returned to New York against the will of her Virginia relatives and they should see to it that Raymond be put under arrest at once.

My advice to you is to get yourself to New York as soon as possible and to aid the hunt. I hope they are staying at the Lexington Avenue house, but in any case, if Nellie is not returned to me safely by this week end, I will expose you everywhere, no matter what the cost. I will write the President directly, as I did anonymously during the campaign. At that time I advised him to beware of his running-mate, that he was not what he seemed. This time I will be more specific.

That you should send an ugly piece of jewelry along with a kidnapper appalls and revolts me. Do you think I am some starry-eyed jeune fille *who waits for betrothal?*

I returned the item to your henchman and now dread the thought that the money they could get for it from a pawnbroker would give them half the world to travel in, and elude us forever.

Rest assured I mean what I say about finishing your masquerade forever if my daughter is not returned to me at once.

The Woman With No Name

Disgusted, Booth wads up the letter and shoves it in his pocket. "That cursed boy!" Quickly he buttons his waistcoat just as Roscoe comes up the stairs, puffing from his physical exertions.

"Something is wrong," says Roscoe, seeing the stormy look on Booth's face. "Is it the Robertson matter?"

"It assuredly is not."

Roscoe, his hands blue, holds a towel over his skinny shoulders, "You must not fail us tomorrow. The vote—"

"A dressmaker's dummy will do as well as I in the chair," Booth retorts on his way out.

He passes the night in a room at Willard's Hotel downtown, having wired ahead to Dun for assistance in New York. Since there is no train north until the morning, he can do little more than brood. For Raymond he reserves his blackest thoughts. It now seems possible that Nell is right, and Raymond is nothing more than a sexual degenerate. Given the circumstances under which Booth ran into him that night on the streets of New York—and then what Raymond confessed to him afterward—what kinder epithet could be applied?

Booth brings to mind the rough young men with whom he has worked before. Payne was an overgrown clod, Atzerodt a drunkard, Herold a mischievous puppy, but all of them were transformed from no-accounts into immortal martyrs of the Confederacy.

Raymond might be of a different breed. What did one know, after all, of ineradicable corruption? On the surface, Raymond with his ambitions and his good manners seemed a far better prospect for the higher values than did the men who were with him in '65. But those men, for all their dirty fingernails and their illiteracy, would have understood that there were some practices beyond the pale, some things that just were not done.

And while Raymond had the excuse of hunger and fear that first time—Booth must concede it—for having sunk into sodomy, there could be no excuse for transporting a maiden of ten years of age from her mother's arms to the streets and alleys of Manhattan. For a terrible moment, Booth considers the possibility that Raymond has sold Nellie to the same establishment where he was himself a prostitute. Shuddering, he dare not dwell long on such thoughts.

9

NEW YORK CITY

The following day Booth descends onto the platform in Jersey City and takes the connecting ferry across the Hudson to Manhattan. He here directs the first carriage he can find for hire to take him to Lexington Avenue, where he has asked Dun to meet him. He has traveled in virtual dishabille from Washington, having carried by hand a small satchel purchased that morning near Willard's in order to hold the razor with which he shaved aboard the train.

The drays and wagons and cabmen's hacks seem thicker than ever on the downtown streets. With the warming of the weather, there are also more of the wealthy out on the broader avenues, taking the air. Booth urges his driver to find the least traveled route, so intent is he to try to get on to the house of prostitution if he does not find Raymond and Nellie at home. He scarcely notices a somewhat disheveled man approaching him when he at last reaches his residence and is paying the fare to his driver.

"Greetings, General," the man says. "I am Kappenhalter of the *Herald*."

The name Kappenhalter jolts Booth, but he dare not let on that he knows it to have been the vanished Victoria Coventry's real name. Her father here? But no, he looks far too young.

"Kappenhalter of the *Herald*," the man repeats in a much louder voice. Clearly he is no orchardist; his hands are soft as a woman's. Beyond that he bears little resemblance to Victoria.

"Well?" Booth asks.

"You have left Washington?"

"As you see."

Kappenhalter asks if that means there is a break in the stalemate over the Robertson appointment.

"I am on private business," Booth declares. "Please allow me to pass, Mr. Kappenhalter."

"We have heard," the reporter says, "that there was an arrest at your residence this morning. Police arrested a young man."

"But I have just arrived from the station."

At that moment, the front door of his house is opened with a burst, and there, to his surprise, stands Nellie shielding her eyes from the sunshine. Immediately behind her is a colonel in uniform, who looks devilishly familiar, but whom he cannot place. For a crushing moment, he wonders if the entire scene is to be denouement: revelations to be made! The noose tightens.

Not so, for suddenly Nellie breaks loose from the handhold of the colonel, and comes careening down the steps, her arms outstretched.

"Father! Father!" she calls to him, and in the most piteous of voices. What astonishing expressiveness! "Father!" she moans, reaching up to him with directness and enthusiasm.

Booth himself misses half a beat before reaching intuitively and lifting her from the ground in a tender embrace. "My little Nellie!" he exclaims. "How your welcome pleases me!"

"Oh, Father," Nellie says. "Uncle William has come to visit. . . . Your brother!"

Ah, she is a little trouper!

"William!" he cries. Of course! He has seen William's photograph. The imperious colonel, stiff in his Union Army blue, comes down the stairs and gingerly shakes hands. The colonel's eyes are nervous, but playacting has its own momentum.

"This other gentleman is a reporter," Nellie reminds everyone.

"Yes, yes," Booth says to her. Just another reporter with a long name. "We mustn't overexcite ourselves." As he sets her down, he immediately begins shooing her up the steps. And he shoos William, too, lest their amateur standing become evident.

"But was there no arrest?" Kappenhalter calls after them.

"I shall send you a message later today," says Booth, not turning, "if I find any basis for that rumor."

Safe haven. He slams the door and is alone with his family.

Nellie is petted for a while, fed strawberries and cream, finally sent up to bed for a nap. At last Booth is able to sit down in the parlor with Dun and Colonel Arthur—whose appearance on a day of such turmoil is pure coincidence—so that he may hear the strange circumstances of Raymond and Nellie's journey from Virginia to New York, and of the summary arrest of Raymond, now in the Tombs on a kidnapping charge.

Booth has poured a round of Madeira, the household servants having been let go when the house was closed in March. Even now no one has taken the trouble to remove the coverings from the draped furniture, and the men loll carelessly about, drinking and smoking cigars.

"It is not clear how the two of them managed to get into the locked house here," Dun relates. "But in any case, the little lady was . . . not molested by the young man. She was—I believe thoroughly —examined by Dr. Brodie Herndon after . . . after we severally arrived."

"Ah," says Colonel Arthur.

Booth says, "Still, it was beastly of Raymond to have subjected her in this manner."

"And he has already begun to pay!" Dun says with some satisfaction. "It was Alan who arrived first, you know, having been telegraphed at Princeton. He burst into this house, found them, and thrashed the young man within an inch of his life. When the police followed in a few minutes, you can imagine that they added to Raymond's grief before hauling him off."

"Tush, tush," says Booth.

"Well, we have telegraphed Fredericksburg with the news that Nellie is safe." Dun drains his glass. Even now Alan was out helping the Herndons obtain reservations to take themselves and Nellie back to Virginia.

"Although Nellie does not wish to go back there," Dun says, with a smile.

"Your man Raymond . . . seems to have turned her head," the colonel remarks. He is a cadaverous individual with a painfully deliberate way of speaking.

Booth looks thoughtful for a moment. Nellie would, of course, be returned to Fredericksburg, he tells them. "But I am distressed, William, that your arrival here—by way of Washington, where I was sorry to miss you—should occur on a day of such terror and disturbance."

"I . . . am used to . . . disturbance," the colonel replies, closely taking in the facial features of the man who now hands him more wine. "Used to . . . bereavement."

Booth wonders if he means the war, suspects he means poor Chester. "Alas, so are we all."

The colonel decides to speak his mind.

"I . . . do not know what to say . . . of your bold attempt . . . to . . . help this family. . . . While it is unorthodox . . . it is also most . . . most . . . audacious."

Either maimed in the war or a born stutterer, Booth reflects. An elderly actor whom Booth knew in Boston talked in this manner and was always cast as a very wise man. "Success does not always go to those who use orthodox methods," Booth observes.

"That is more and more . . . the common opinion," Colonel Arthur agrees. His large, wrinkled lips form a sly smile.

Booth compliments the colonel on the audaciousness he showed when confronted by the prying reporter.

"In the military"—the colonel speaks while leaning forward as though with some ineffable sentiment to express—"the world knows . . . the world knows . . ." But he cannot say it. "I am only glad . . . I . . . do not face . . . your . . . problems."

Booth sighs, glances at the narrow-eyed Dun to see if he has profited from this philosophical interlude. Booth feels respect for the colonel. Only a military man could so promptly distinguish hard duty from easy, and so implicitly indicate he wanted no part of the more difficult assignment.

Booth believes they will see rather little of William Arthur.

Upstairs in her bedroom a short time later, he finds Nellie lying placidly under sheets and a blanket, the collar of her lacy nightgown pulled up to her smooth chin. She gazes at Booth without anxiety.

"Well, Nellie," he says briskly, moving to the bedside, "you have had a strenuous time. Are you feeling all right?"

"Yes," Nellie says, shifting her weight to one elbow, "now that I'm in my own bed."

Booth clucks his tongue. "But later on you're going to have to be returning to Fredericksburg with your uncles."

Nellie folds one hand over the other. Her expression, always slow to develop, has melted into a frown. "I know it. Raymond and I were hoping *she* would come after us."

Booth says, "Raymond had no business taking you from Virginia to New York without telling anybody."

"But we left them a note."

Booth nods. Looking down at the round face, now relaxed again, he cannot make up his mind whether the child is normal. She does not behave as the Herndon children did, always wanting him to fix their wagon or their dolls.

"Raymond was in an orphan asylum for a while," Nellie says.

"Well, you don't need to worry about anything like that happening to you."

"I know," she replies with vehemence. "But I like to be in my own home, and I don't like reporters and nosy people coming around. Do you?"

"No. You're right. We agree on that."

He beams at her with all the paternal benevolence at his command.

"Raymond is . . . peculiar sometimes," she ventures. "He listens to everything I say. And I try not to say very much."

Patting the hem of her blanket—tucking her in, he supposes it could be called—he says, "Perhaps Raymond sees through to your soul, Nellie."

On the way downtown to the Tombs he is of half a mind to stop the carriage at the *Herald* office in Park Row and demand from Bennett, or someone there, that the Kappenhalter family be directed, once and for all, to stop bothering him. But on thinking it over, his better judgment is to hold off for a time lest he connect himself with the Victoria Coventry disappearance in some irreparable way. Perhaps, if Raymond were available to him—instead of languishing in jail—he might cause inquiries to be made at the *Herald* by means of the lad. But, shorthanded as he is, he can undertake little on his own.

It is disgraceful that a Vice-President of the United States should be provided with no staff. And no political protection. Colfax, one of Grant's Vice-Presidents, even wound up getting indicted. How would one like that? Booth can only hope that some day, when he is President, he will have hundreds of flunkies at his beck and call: the Kappenhalter matter would then be like a gnat, too small to bother with.

In the meantime he must—under threatening skies—do his own business. The facade of the Tombs reminds him of dead pharaohs. Quickly he pays the driver and mounts the steps of the building, carrying a large package that he wrapped at home before leaving. One crossed to the male compound of the jail on an elevated gallery known as the Bridge of Sighs, named as such ever since condemned criminals used to pass across it on their way to the gallows in the courtyard below.

The storm Booth feels in the air he knows to be within him as well as without. He has meditated long and hard about how to deal with Raymond's irresponsible escapade with Nellie. Alan has argued that Raymond ought to stand trial for kidnapping. "Do you think he will remain silent," Booth asks, "no matter what torment we put him through?" And yet the offense was clear: if Raymond learned there was no penalty for violating his express commission in Fredericksburg, he would soon be as arrogant as Alan.

At the great door of the male compound, a uniformed keeper, who has been properly alerted, touches his hand to his forehead, and says: "I shall watch your package, sir, while ye find the prisoner you're takin' custody of."

A turnkey leads Booth down the gloomy central corridor of the compound, flanked on galleried walls by cells with iron-barred windows behind which, here and there, the faces of inmates can be seen.

The smell is nearly overpowering. Weak illumination penetrates from skylights over the lofty central hallway, and two large potbellied stoves stand at opposite ends of the compound, one of them being cleaned out by a potbellied inmate in gray prison-issue.

On the ground floor in front of the range of cells that the turnkey is leading Booth toward, a woman and a little girl wearing a beribboned straw hat are talking to an inmate. Next door, as the key is being found, Booth catches sight of Raymond, his hands coming through the bars on the door. The lad does not speak. His wide eyes, as he fixes them on Booth, seem not so much candid—as Booth has usually thought of them—but haunted and fearful. While the turnkey is unlocking the door, Booth can see back in the shadows of the same cell three or four burly men of various ages and sizes.

"I t'ink his lordship is leavin' us now," one of them says. They all begin laughing vulgarly.

The turnkey gives them a hostile glance, and as Raymond steps out into the corridor and waits, the turnkey says, "Year be-un released in the custody of this here gen'lman. Ye was not mistreated here now, was ye, lad?"

Booth sees to his shock that Raymond has bruises all over his face and bared forearms. Silent and white-faced, Raymond shakes his head.

In the most sugary of tones, the turnkey says, "See, sir, we treated him well. His own say-so."

Perceiving that he is expected to give the turnkey a gratuity, Booth fishes into his pocket for a coin and with silent contempt gives it to the man. The men in Raymond's cell are sniggering faintly.

"Farewell, your lordship!" someone in a cell across the court now calls, and there is general laughter. Shamefaced, Raymond looks at the floor and marches out, side by side with Booth, the turnkey grinning now too. The two visitors—woman and child—glance timidly at Booth, but from other cells harsh Irish voices are calling "Fare thee well, your lordship!"

At the gate that leads back across the Bridge of Sighs, Booth stops to retrieve his package.

"Be ye the gen'lman with the package?" the keeper asks loudly.

Booth already has his money out and redeems it.

"Much obliged, gov'nor," the keeper says. He gives a reproving look to the miscreant.

Across the Bridge, Raymond's pace seems to quicken as though he is apprehensive he may yet be detained inside the Tombs. It is not until he is safely out into Centre Street that he stops and looks up at Booth.

"Well, have you nothing at all to say?" Booth asks him.

Raymond puts his palm up to his chin, and Booth sees that he spits something into his hand.

"Whew!" Raymond says. He seems considerably relieved as he hands the object to Booth. It is the piece of jewelry that Booth entrusted to Raymond for Nell.

"Your lady give it back to me!" Raymond says, panting. "She would not take it!"

"So I was told," Booth murmurs, pushing the item into his watch pocket.

"I never thought I would get it out of there!" Raymond exclaims. "The men in the cell took my money. They turned me upside down and felt through all my clothes. Three times they done it!"

Raymond is breathless. His voice rises in pitch as he talks excitedly, drawing the attention of people who pass. Noticing as much, he starts to whisper.

"They suspicioned it right along," he confides. "That I was hiding something besides the money."

"Was that why they hit you?"

"Naw, they just felt me," Raymond replies. "It was Alan who hit me. And kicked me in my—tender parts."

They have moved under a tree to get protection from a light rain that has begun falling. Booth, holding the large package by its wrapping twine, looks around them as though in torment and indecision.

"I sure was glad to see you," Raymond says. His right cheek is swollen and discolored. "Another night and they woulda got the brooch for certain. They was raggin' me more and more, callin' me your lordship . . ."

"Raymond, why did you disobey my instructions and bring Nellie to New York?"

The blood rises in Raymond's face, matching the color of some of his bruises. "I never fondled her," Raymond says finally.

"But you were my intermediary, and how did you help me?"

Raymond clenches his fist and looks out into Centre Street, where men hold their hat brims and hurry across against the rain. A noisy horse-drawn trolley is approaching.

Raymond says, "I thought the lady would come after us to New York."

"What has happened instead is that you have aroused the whole family against you, and I am more alienated from my beloved than ever."

Booth heaves a sigh. At the news, Raymond assumes a putty-lipped expression so wretched that Booth scarcely has the heart to go on. But one of his faults in '65 after all was laxity; thus the master plan went awry in a hundred directions. And who suffered? The men in the ranks, unfortunately. Not the chief strategist, but the men—inadequately drilled, inadequately disciplined.

"Do you wish to remain in my service, Raymond?" Booth asks.

"Yes, sir," Raymond says, still not looking up.

"You believe that I can help you grow as a man of honor as well as a provider?"

"Oh, yes, sir."

"In the military, the disobedient get court-martialed. In the church they do penance. . . . Would you open that package, Raymond?"

There is a moment's hesitation, then Raymond sets to it, squatting against the tree trunk, tugging the twine over the corners of the package. "Them in the cell took my pocketknife," he tells Booth. As he strips away the brown wrapping paper, the shape revealed is but a wooden box, painted black.

"Why, it's a bootblack's kit," Raymond says in puzzlement.

"Correct," Booth says. "I purchased it from a boy on the street, gave him a good price. I give it to you now as a tool of your trade. The boy I bought it from had developed a strong back and a deal of humility, both of which can be valuable in a man's coming of age."

"You mean I'm to take it back to Washington with us?"

"I mean," Booth says, "that since you took the spending money I gave you and spent it on train fare for you and Nellie, you can now earn your way to Washington by working your way back."

"I'm to shine gentlemen's shoes?" Raymond asks with an expression of shock.

"Until you have enough for the fare to Washington. A few months perhaps. I will hold your place. . . . Or do you think yourself demeaned by such labor?"

"You make me a bootblack!" Raymond shouts. "When all I did was try to oblige you!"

Raymond's eyes are blazing now. He kicks at the bootblack box with his foot, and were it not for the rain, people hurrying down the street would no doubt have longer marked the dignified, well-dressed man remonstrating with the bruised but once well-dressed youth across a bootblack kit. Passengers on the slowing trolley look over at them.

"And I saved your damned brooch too!" Raymond declares, kicking the box again.

His outburst unnerves Booth, who is both regretful for the need for the sentence and apprehensive that he might be recognized as the Vice-President, particularly at a moment when Raymond could perhaps not be relied on for discretion. He wavers. The rain goes on falling. Then, just as he is of more than half a mind to revoke Raymond's banishment, an even more unsettling thing occurs.

Among the people who have come off the trolley are two women, one very old, the other perhaps a generation younger. Their path leads directly toward Booth and Raymond, and while the two ladies are hurrying past, paying them no more than brief attention, Booth feels a shiver go through him that leaves him totally shaken.

The two women are his mother and his sister Rose.

Neither of them pauses or shows any sign of recognition. The expression on his mother's face has been a neutral smile, the kind she habitually fixed on any stranger whose eyes met hers. Rose has kept her head down.

He has no impulse to speak to them; he feels fear, shame, and horror. His mother has aged hardly at all, but his sister has aged a great deal. He does not look after them. Indeed he does not stay riveted to the spot very long. Without the least farewell to Raymond, he grips the brim of his hat and goes hurrying across the street so rapidly that the conductor on the trolley car, which is just starting up again, hesitates an extra moment on the platform in order to help him up onto the car.

Wet and depressed, he spends the next hour at his tailor's, and when ordering three new suits of clothing seems not enough to lift his spirits, there is nothing for it but to require the tailor to come with him to Washington that evening—expenses paid, of course—in order that he have the leisure to select the rest of his summer wardrobe as he grows more in the mood for that sort of business.

10

*Office of the President
Executive Mansion
Washington
May 5*

Confidential

My dear Mr. Weed,

As one of the most deeply respected party men in the state of New York, as well as one of its most candid, you are the individual whose opinion I trust best on a delicate matter.

Not long ago, I received a letter, unsigned, alleging that the Vice-

President was "not what he seemed." A crank letter, one naturally supposes. But I have been sufficiently baffled by the Vice-President's behavior in the matter of the Robertson appointment—in which he has helped neither Senator Conkling nor myself—that I cannot comprehend what I am dealing with.

Have you heard anything that might be useful to me? As one of the greatest of our publishers and editors, and now sufficiently "above the fray" you may be able to call on immense resources.

Believe me, Mr. Weed, when I say I do not undertake this inquiry for advantage within the party. The struggle presently going on in the Senate over confirmation of the Robertson nomination I feel certain I can win in spite of recent threats from the Stalwarts that letters written by me during the heat of the campaign would be released unless I back down. The letters purport to portray my interest in getting campaign monies to Indiana as excessive.

Let the letters be released. I HAVE NO INTENTION OF WITHDRAWING THE ROBERTSON NOMINATION.

Trusting your discretion in this, I am

Yours faithfully,
Jas. A. Garfield

Mr. Thurlow Weed
12 W. 12 St.
New York, N. Y.

✣   ✣   ✣

New York
May 6

Confidential and Urgent

My dear Mr. Vice-President:

The President has lately written me inquiring as to my knowledge of whether you are "what you seem." No doubt he is angry and nervous over threats being made to get him to withdraw Robertson.

Nevertheless, it would be stupid of you, for your own sake, not to try to cool down the warfare at once.

Why not get Conkling and Platt out of Washington before they get licked in the showdown? Around the Manhattan and Union Clubs we hear talk that both Senators have spoken about resigning their seats in order to be "vindicated" through re-election in Albany.

You ought to be able to promote this idea to them. For Conkling it will seem a showy, Roman thing to do. Platt may also be easy to convince since sources tell me that for considerations he promised months ago not to vote against any *Garfield appointment. Believe it or not.*

Hoping, for your sake, you will not disregard this letter, I remain your constructive critic,

Thurlow Weed

P. S. There is no reporter named Kappenhalter working for the Herald. *One would have thought a relative of the missing Victoria would have approached you with more direct questions.*

The Hon. Chester A. Arthur
The Senate
Washington, D. C.

✤   ✤   ✤

<u>Confidential</u>

12. W. 12 St.
New York, N. Y.
May 17

My dear Mr. President,

Your letter of the 5th instant, postmarked the 9th, came here during my absence on the 10th. My daughter Harriet then forwarded it to me in New Jersey on the 13th, and the space since then I trust you will not think too long for due reflection on the question you have raised.

My answer is that I have heard no rumors of the sort you describe. It is the kind of query worthy of a professor of philosophy, is it not, for which of us is what he seems? Nevertheless, I have taken the Vice-President for as much as I would take any man. If he is not what he seems, perhaps he is better than he seems. All of us maintain that hope.

My congratulations on your having obtained the confirmation of the Robertson appointment. While New Yorkers have felt a sense of shock at the simultaneous resignations of both their Senators (the newspapers have naturally made much of it), a historical precedent may have been set to the benefit of the Chief Executive. Or perhaps it is too soon to say.

In any case, your fear of being embarrassed by the Vice-President must have diminished by this point. The struggle may be nearly over.

Your friend and servant,
Thurlow Weed

His Excellency,
the Hon. James A. Garfield
Executive Mansion
Washington, D. C.

11

The Baltimore and Potomac Station Washington

"Seven minutes late!" Senator Jones exclaims as they are waiting to board, his eyes on the large clock. Then: "Ten minutes late!" And: "Going on twelve minutes."

"My dear Jones," Booth sighs from the next bench. Mightn't one expect that a railroad executive—Jones, like all senators from west of the Mississippi, being one—would try to conceal from others that the system did not always function to perfection? Not so.

"Do restrain yourself," Booth says, for he wants the quiet in which mournfully to consider how best to lift the exile he imposed on poor Raymond outside the Tombs last month. The two travelers— Jones and he—are Albany-bound. With the Senate now adjourned, they are pledged to rush to the side of the resigned pair, Roscoe and Tom Platt, who have already set up shop at the Delavan House in the campaign for their vindication by the legislature.

"High time! High time!" Senator Jones now remarks, for a perspiring stationmaster has hurried over, making small apologies to them. The Limited is "nearly ready" to board.

Picking up a hand valise (the rest of his luggage having been checked aboard by Phillips), Booth brushes himself off. Truly, it was imbecilic to have left Raymond with a bootblack kit and the pious hope that he could reach Washington on his earnings. In a special case, Booth supposes it might be possible. But, in general, having given the matter more thought, he realizes that no bootblack could earn more than his food and shelter, let alone railroad tickets. And if Raymond should try to get over to the house on Lexington Avenue, the Pinkertons Alan has hired would probably garrot him on the doorstep.

A conductor waits ahead at a private gate near the tracks. But the ladies' waiting room, through which Booth and Jones are passing, is unpleasantly crowded. Out of the corner of his eye, among the females and their numerous children, Booth notes a man rising from one of the benches. The air is humid.

To his astonishment, Booth feels a blunt object prod him purposefully in the small of the back. Turning at once, he raises his stick in a defensive posture, even while his facial expression has been regulated to one of affected calm.

The personage he turns to look at, the one pushing at him with the rounded end of a walking stick, is the fiercely glaring Mr. Ghetto. Booth is surprised to feel his heart jump although Mr. Ghetto is now trying to smile, a smile that includes Senator Jones, who strains to drag Booth forward. Food stains are on Ghetto's lapel, even on his moustache.

"A black day, Gen'ral!" Mr. Ghetto says, looking about him as though for eavesdroppers.

Booth has stopped. He feels a chill crawl up his back. Didn't he use the phrase once himself—"A black day, gentlemen!"? Something like that?

"Sir, you catch me by surprise," Booth says.

"We are all surprised," Mr. Ghetto says. He looks thin as a consumptive. "We are all betrayed by d' Judas in d' White House."

Senator Jones, growing red in the face, says, "If you have business with us, sir, please state—"

"The gen'ral knows me well," Mr. Ghetto replies, ignoring Jones. But he makes an odd movement with his heels, then ducks his head, as though in deference to Booth. "I have taken no nourishment since d'resignations of d'senators."

"The President did not offer you the Austrian mission then?"

Mr. Ghetto confides that he would have settled for the Paris consulate, but that Secretary Blaine had him thrown bodily out of the State Department building. "Such is our reward, Gen'ral!"

Booth sees that poor Senator Jones is beginning to look apprehensive at the way Ghetto keeps raising his eyes while lowering his chin. Jones sputters: "Sir, if you have no business with the Vice-President—"

"And who should you be?" Mr. Ghetto hums. As Booth goes through the farce of presenting Jones, Ghetto, in turn, begins delving in his card case, a battered relic. He delivers his card to Jones with a flourish.

"I am a Stalwart, sir!"

"Humph!"

Jones pockets the card and stalks off.

"Senator Jones is a Stalwart too," Booth whispers to Ghetto. But now the Senator and he must repair to Senator Conkling's side in Albany, where all will stand as at Armageddon. There is not a moment to lose.

"You are right, not a moment," says Mr. Ghetto. The face is ferretlike; his lips part, showing small irregular teeth. Then he wheels, like a grenadier, sweeping his hand so that Booth may pass. Striding away, Booth casts one backward glance, but Ghetto is already facing away from him, one shoulder up, one shoulder down, a scarecrow in an old coat.

Later, when they are settled in their drawing room, Senator Jones looks at the calling card he has been handed in the station. "An 'attorney-at-law,' he claims to be," Jones says. "More likely a Bedlamite."

Booth says nothing. For a moment he has the impulse to defend Mr. Ghetto's sanity as though he were defending his own. But then he remembers he has himself called Ghetto mad. Has he not nurtured that madness?

"The political life!" Senator Jones suddenly exclaims. "How full of pests it is. And other inconveniences."

He fidgets his buttocks into a more comfortable position in the prickly upholstered chair as the train begins moving. A young woman with a swelling on her neck is standing on the platform waving goodbye to someone.

"Yet we choose it," Booth says.

"Ah, I do my duty," Jones declares.

His duty to Union Pacific, Booth supposes. He has picked up the calling card that Jones has laid down on the sill of the window.

.... **Art to come** ....

The name as it reads on the card, seems in some way more sinister than the name did as it has been spelled in Booth's mind for so long.

12

123 LEXINGTON AVENUE

In New York, Booth decides not to continue immediately to Albany after all. Senator Jones is beyond bearing: he looks at his pocket watch more often than the rabbit in *Through the Looking Glass*. Besides, Booth's thirst to find Raymond—while there is still time—grows irresistible. He savors the search: Götz Dörfer can use an airing. If Dörfer cannot find Raymond tonight, then Dörfer will look again tomorrow. Albany will remain.

Arriving in the receiving hall of his residence, however, the presence on a silver tray of a calling card more sinister than Mr. Guiteau's diminishes his good spirits considerably. A name, and nothing more, appears on the card: "K. Kappenhalter" embossed in Gothic capital letters.

Tossing down his hat, Booth looks around for the Pinkerton operative who admitted him to the house, but the man has disappeared. The continuing presence of Pinkertons unnerves him; he will speak to Alan about getting rid of them. To be engaging the agency that guarded Lincoln approaches farce. He does not need Yankee counterspies in his own house.

When Alan now appears from the direction of the rear parlor, his face seems more flushed than usual. Booth can hear the voices of other young men conversing in the room Alan has left. Somewhat furtively, Alan motions him toward the stairs.

"Come, I have something to show you," Alan says.

"Home from Princeton for the weekend?" Booth asks him.

"For the summer. Some of my fellows have dropped in."

Booth follows Alan up the steps, carrying the valise. "Would you have been at home when a man named Kappenhalter called?"

Alan behaves as though he has not heard.

"Perhaps he described himself as a reporter?" Booth persists.

Alan's silence is beginning to seem insolent to him. They have arrived in the upper hallway directly outside the sewing room.

"I cannot permit Pinkertons to be maintained indefinitely—"

Alan knocks briefly, throws open a door to the room. Inside, a figure is reclining on the chaise under a lighted lamp. It is Nell herself, who looks up almost casually. She is dressed in a pastel blue, but her hair is gathered in a tight knot at the back of her head, more severe than he has ever seen it.

"I b'lieve I've been invited to return to this house, where I once resided," she remarks. Her color is high, her features sharp.

"Nell! At last!" he exclaims, starting forward, but not without reprimanding Alan for having guests in the house on the day of Nell's homecoming.

She puts up her hand in a way that halts him. "Do not be concerned about that," she says. "I have given mah permission." Her tone is dry. She waves to Alan that he is to go. Booth detects a simper in the scoundrel's face as he withdraws, shutting the door behind him.

"Mah little girl was not happy in Virginia," she informs Booth. "So I have brought her here; we ah all together again."

"My dearest, darling Nell . . ." He is most moved to see her.

"Not Nell, but Auntie Lew, the invalid." She stares at him without expression. "That's as you wish. I oblige when I can. Alan has hired a new staff, and perhaps I will send menus down."

"The new people are Pinkerton men!" Booth declares. "I mean to get rid of them."

"But we will not get rid of them," Nell replies. "Without them, I would not be here."

"My dear love—"

"I do not propose to live with you as man and wife, Mistuh Booth, if that was your idea."

He says nothing. If it is true she will have nothing to do with him, he wonders why she has prepared herself in this most enticing way. The warm color of her skin is complemented by the burnished glow of the lamp. Her long, tapering fingers touch the fabric of her skirt, the rough satin of her sash, then play with the collar over her bodice. Her arms are bare and soft.

"You have shown you do not wish to live abroad," she says. "Very well. As long as you maintain us, maintain mah children, I will not betray you. You want to be Chester? You go ahead."

"Nell, I love you."

"There will be none of that. And no more ugly jewelry either. No presents!"

He throws out his arms in bewilderment. "But I am one step from the highest office in the land. Does that suggest to you that my business has been frivolous? What if destiny permits me to take the final step?"

"You needn't lie to me anymore."

"I could restore the Confederacy, Nell!"

"As you did when you killed Mistuh Lincoln?"

He is shocked to hear her say these words. He looks at her face, but it registers no particular anguish to have spoken so bluntly.

"I *tried* to restore it by that deed."

"Nevuh mind, it did not happen the way you said." Her voice rises a little as though her rage at him might yet find expression. "You lied. You lied about Major Rathbone. You said he was Colonel Rathbone. I've now read about it. And you said he was armed. He—"

Booth clasps his hands together. "In the theater box that night do you think I could ascertain his rank? And in that moment what caliber arms he—"

"No caliber ahms!" she exclaims. "No ahms at all!"

"Says the Yankee newspaper!"

She has one more volley to fire.

"And remembuh that attack on you, Wilkes, from the carriage outside A. T. Stewart's depahtment store that aftuhnoon. That was in no Yankee newspaper, that lie!"

Booth says, "But you saw them attack me!"

"That was no attack! That was playactin'!" She flings it at him, her breasts heaving. "Your tool Raymond—the degenerate one—wrote me a letter after you abandoned him on the streets of New York with nothing but the clothes on his back. He said he wanted to apologize to me for running off with Nellie the way he did. And apologize for deceivin' me in front of A. T. Stewart's that afternoon!"

"You believe a degenerate!" Booth exclaims in scorn.

"He told it exactly as it was. He wasn't lyin'. You wuh!"

Booth says nothing for a moment. The thought that Raymond has betrayed him, too, deflates him utterly. Curse the boy: let him starve to death in the filthiest alley in the Bowery! Götz Dörfer would not go abroad tonight.

"You understand why I don't want any more jewelry from you!" she says.

"That ugly jewelry," Booth intones, "had seventeen cut gems in it, all forming a design to remind you of the warming pan I bought you at A. T. Stewart's that day you—"

"Warming pan! You had a piece of jewelry made to look like a warming pan? What is there beauty-ful in a warming pan!"

Her eyes are so venomous that Booth is too paralyzed to respond.

"You get out of here, now," she says. "You go to Albany for Conkling, or wherever you got to go. Do like Chester would. It's what you want."

Booth picks up the valise he has left at the door. By God, he would win his honor back, no matter what. Had he ever let the bold self-regard of loved ones interfere with his purposes?

"By the way," Nell says to him as he reaches the door, "Bridget's preparin' to go to Washington to cook for you there. Alan talked her into it."

"She's to be your Pinkerton woman in Washington, is that it?" Booth sneers.

"Don't flatter yourself," she snaps. He glances at her disdainfully as she picks up a bound octavo volume beside her on the chaise and opens it.

Then he slams the door behind him. The Kappenhalter business is probably her doing too, he reflects. Hers. And Weed's. And Raymond's. They all think he caused Victoria What's-Her-Name's disappearance. Let them.

No matter if his heart is breaking, he will still give a performance in Albany. He will do his work.

13

FROM THE *Albany Journal*

(May 24)

THE FIGHT FOR VINDICATION BEGUN

VICE-PRESIDENT ARTHUR AT THE SIDE OF THE
NEW YORK "SENATORS"

(May 31)

ONLY 35 VOTES FOR CONKLING ON FIRST BALLOT

29 FOR PLATT, FAR SHORT OF MAJORITY

OTHER VOTES SPLIT AMONG
20 CANDIDATES

(June 7)

WHERE IS GOVERNOR CORNELL NOW THAT CONKLING NEEDS HIM?

RIFT IN STALWARTS DENIED
BY VICE-PRESIDENT ARTHUR

(June 14)

DEPEW FORGES AHEAD OF PLATT

STALWARTS HINT DEPEW
PURCHASED HIS VOTES

STILL NO CANDIDATE
WITH A MAJORITY

(June 28)

EX-VICE-PRESIDENT WHEELER RUNNING AHEAD OF CONKLING

ARTHUR PREDICTS TIDE
WILL TURN BACK SOON

(July 2)

PLATT WITHDRAWS!

14

THE NEW DELAVAN HOUSE

A large domestic pigeon, brown and white, is feeding on the sill outside the window of their suite. Booth is feeding it; he has taken an interest in the animal life of Albany. He also keeps a small black cat in the suite, whom he is careful to isolate from the feeding birds. When the cat falls asleep in the morning heat, Booth fingers out crumbs from the breakfast dishes for the pigeons.

"You are an ass," Roscoe is telling Platt, who has just come in to join them. The news stories of Platt's withdrawal are already in the papers, although without the embarrassing details that necessitated it.

"Oh, bullshit," Platt says. He starts chewing on their leftover biscuits, looking as happy to be out of the race as Roscoe is miserable still to be in it. Booth, who was awakened at daybreak in order to be informed of these events, yawns.

"You should have waited until Tuesday to withdraw," Roscoe says peevishly.

"I withdrew when I heard them at the transom," Platt says, and he guffaws.

The circumstance is that Platt has been observed in carnal embrace with a woman of the town. Those observing—none of them his political friends—have accomplished it by means of the transom over Platt's hotel room door. When French and Wheelhorse, the corridor sentinels, were seen leaving for a saloon, those peeping at Tom took turns standing on a ladder brought into the hallway.

"I don't give a damn anymore," Platt says. "I just want to go home."

Roscoe snorts. Roscoe and Booth both have some of their luggage piled near the door, where the bellman will pick it up shortly; they will spend their Fourth of July weekend in New York before returning for the contest that remains.

"If you'd waited until Tuesday," says Roscoe, "we could have got a quid pro quo."

"You mean my seat for yours? Not on your tintype."

Booth turns from the window. "It may still be possible."

"Is *that* your opinion, Chester?" Roscoe inquires bitterly. "You have had precious few, considering that you are the one who dragooned us up here six weeks ago."

"I did not dragoon you up here," says Booth calmly. Having, for half the night, occupied himself among crates of Stanton papers, he feels comfortably detached from Roscoe's pettiness. He feels shriven. Roscoe, on the other hand, looks more and more to have lost his grip on reality: if Booth isn't William Arthur, then Chester Arthur he must be with all Chester's old obligations to him.

By the time the bellman knocks and steps in to collect their hand luggage, they have said nothing further to one another.

"My train for Oswego doesn't leave until noon," Platt now remarks, forking up a piece of the breakfast fish. "I'll stay here and finish eating, if you don't mind."

"Sure, why don't you?" Roscoe says. A cold smile is directed at the bell captain, then back at Platt. "Give my love to Ellie. She'll be relieved to have you back running the drugstore."

In the middle of the morning, halfway down the Hudson River, Booth is drowsing lightly in the stateroom they have engaged. Roscoe has gone promenading on the deck.

Asleep, Booth dreams not that he is President, or even Vice-President. No, he is a humble clerk. Has he not always accepted humble fare? In the office where he is employed, he learns that the file for which he searches is to be found in the safe in his employer's office. Although it is forbidden for him to enter the safe, he has found out the combination for it, and when there is nobody around, he throws caution to the winds. Quickly he spins the dial. Will the door come open for him before he is discovered? Will he pluck honor from the bosom of the safe?

A loud report from off the ferry awakens him. He jumps from the bed in surprise, and goes to the cabin window. He flings it open and gazes up and down the churning green river, hazy in the sunlight. On the Poughkeepsie pier someone must have set off a string of holiday firecrackers. He thinks the sound came from that direction. He can hear nothing for sure.

15

THE BALTIMORE AND POTOMAC STATION WASHINGTON

Across the floral-patterned carpet of the ladies' waiting room come President Garfield and Secretary Blaine, walking arm in arm. Blaine is here to see the President off to a reunion of his college class at Williams in Massachusetts. The President's two sons, already aboard the train, are going to travel with him. Mrs. Garfield, not in good health, remains in Elberson, New Jersey, where she is spending the summer at the seashore.

As Garfield and Blaine make progress toward the gates, they talk about the news of Platt's withdrawal in Albany. Robert Lincoln, another member of the Cabinet, is also just arriving by carriage to see the President off for the holiday. In the meantime, however, a shabby-looking man of medium height suddenly moves up behind Garfield and Blaine. Drawing a small revolver, he fires it twice at the President, shooting the second time after Garfield has already fallen to one knee.

Cries of dismay and fear ring out in the station. Innocent travelers see that a man has been shot and that another man stands with a gun still pointed at the floor, sidestepping uncertainly away from the victim. A pool of blood has begun to form underneath the President on the carpet of the waiting room. Blaine kneels to hold the President's hand when the latter tries to speak. A matron who works in the station comes to Garfield's side, too, and cradles his head in her lap. Robert Lincoln, hearing the commotion from a distance, comes forward, sees what has happened, and with anguish etched across his face hurries out to where his carriage is being held for him. He gives an order that the surgeon general be summoned at once. The horses are whipped to a frenzied gallop down the middle of Pennsylvania Avenue.

The shabby-looking man has meanwhile eluded the grasp of a ticket agent, but he runs out the door of the station—still holding the weapon—into the embrace of a city policeman, who has hurried toward the building on hearing the shots.

"Stop! You are under arrest!" gasps the policeman, clinging to his quarry.

"All right," replies Guiteau. "I did it and will go to jail for it. I am a Stalwart of Stalwarts, and Art'ur will be President!"

*

When the physicians arrive at the Baltimore and Potomac depot —three of them in rapid order—they have Garfield carried on a mattress into the stationmaster's office, where they undress him to the waist. One of the wounds is superficial, but the other is not—a cartridge has embedded itself in the President's back. Each of the doctors probes in turn with his fingers in the wound, but none of them finds the projectile. A sweeper, very small of stature, tries his luck probing the wound because he has little hands. Blaine, who has seen the angle of the gun barrel, urges the man to push in a different direction than the doctors have done. But the effort, most earnest, produces no bullet.

It is decided to take Garfield back to the Executive Mansion at once.

"You know how I love you, Blaine," Garfield says, looking faint, but reaching up to embrace Blaine.

At the perimeter of the crowd around the President, his two sons, lips clenched, stare across at him, as does Robert Lincoln.

16

THE WINDSOR HOTEL
NEW YORK

"Great God, Mary, try to sleep."

Edwin Booth stands over his moaning wife, who lies feverish and mistrustful, her small head falling backward between the two silk-covered pillows on her bed. She has started up, looking fearful, when he entered the bedroom of the suite, then sank back again, her face a scowl.

"Get out o' here, get out o' here," she whimpers in her throat.

"I am, I will . . ."

He tries to soothe her with his voice. It hardly ever does any good. She has been affected with a brain fever that the doctors in England were unable to treat, and which has grown worse. The Booths are barely off the ship; their steamer trunks are still unpacked in the sitting room. One doctor has already seen Mary since their return. Another is expected within the hour.

Now from the other room Edwin Booth can hear a loud knocking at the door to the suite. Mary's frail body in white nightgown thrashes upward again uncomprehendingly. She is stronger than she looks. "No, Mary," he says to the bright, hollowed eyes, holding his hand against her arm. He hears his daughter Edwina, who has answered the door, admitting people to the suite. Mary's head falls back onto the pillow.

When, presently, he finds a moment to leave the bedroom and see what the disturbance is, he discovers himself confronted by a group of reporters.

Edwina, a tall, pale girl of nineteen, says, "Father, the President has just been shot."

"What President? What are you talking about?"

One of the reporters addresses him. "President Garfield has just been shot in Washington. Do you have any comment, Mr. Booth?"

The actor says nothing for a moment; he is outraged by the intrusion. Mary could go into one of her screaming tantrums at any moment.

"I'm shocked to hear it," he says finally, controlling himself. "But why come to me? My wife is very ill, and as you can see, we are hardly off the ship from England."

He points to trunks and suitcases around the sitting room. Edwina, who has been helping to unpack them, dabs perspiration from her forehead.

One reporter asks if Booth can anticipate the Vice-President's reaction to the shooting.

"Vice-President!" Edwin Booth exclaims. "I'm blessed if I know who the Vice-President is, sir. We have been in England the past year and a half."

"Why, Arthur."

"Arthur? I don't know any Arthur."

The reporter says that Mr. Booth and General Arthur are members of the same club.

"*That* Arthur?" Edwin Booth flings up his hands. "Why, how should I know his reaction? I scarcely know the man. . . . Please, I implore you to leave the premises; my wife cannot be troubled with any excitement."

"Can you tell us if President Garfield was admired in England, Mr. Booth?"

"Will you please leave? Or must I—"

"The assassin is a man named Guido, Mr. Booth. Is he a member of your club?"

"I know no Guido!" Booth storms.

Outraged, he grabs two of the men by their arms and pushes them into a third, presently propelling all three out the door and into the hallway. Slamming the door, he returns, shaken, to Edwina. "No more, no more."

He sinks into a chair and puts his head into his hands. He does not know a Guido, does he? The name Guido is a waiter's name, and the last time he saw his cursed brother he was a waiter. But Guido was not the name he used. Edwin rubs his forehead in anguish.

"I'm sorry, Father, I thought it was the doctor at the door," Edwina murmurs, tears forming in her eyes.

"You cannot imagine in your wildest dreams what it's like when they begin," he groans.

And not even Edwina knows that Johnny is still alive. No one in the family knows. Surely Johnny cannot be involved in this one.

A voice screams out from the bedroom, Mary's voice.

"Don't kill me!" she shrieks.

And he runs to her. She pulls the quilt over her head when she sees him, her whimpering sounding piteously from beneath the cover.

17

THE YONKERS PIER

"Wait for the rider!"

The call comes from the riverboat passengers to the deckhand who has begun raising the gangplank at the Yonkers pier. They have seen a single horseman galloping rapidly down the river road from the south, the direction in which the ferry is headed. They watch him bring his panting horse to a stop; he could be a westerner, judging by his large, brimmed hat.

"Is General Arthur aboard?" the rider calls out to the deck officer.

Informed that he is, the horse is entrusted to one of the company agents on shore, and the gangplank is lowered so that the perspiring rider may come aboard. He has no luggage of any kind; his manner is grimly dignified. He has no words for any of them. The ship's officer leads him to the stateroom deck where a door is knocked on.

"Why, Jones!" Roscoe Conkling remarks in some surprise.

Still silent, Senator Jones steps into the cabin where Booth is lolling, boots off, on the made bed.

Jones shuts the door behind him. "President Garfield has just been shot in Washington. The news arrived in New York by telegraph not two hours ago. I have ridden here to warn you."

Booth looks up, eyes fierce. "What is his condition?"

"Not clear. One report says 'survived.' The other not."

"Good Lord," says Roscoe.

"From the calling cards on the man's person," Jones continues, still breathing hard, "it appears he was shot by a man named Guiteau, a lawyer. G-U-I-T-E-A-U. Do you know him?" Suddenly Jones's face grows pale. "Wait, it's the man in the station!"

"Who?" Roscoe asks in puzzlement. Booth looks at his fingernails. Outside the open window, holiday firecrackers are still going off along the shore as the ferry leaves the slip.

"The most disturbing matter, I fear," Senator Jones now tells them, "is that as soon as he was apprehended he is supposed to have said, 'I am a Stalwart. Now Arthur is President!' "

Roscoe glares at Booth. "Do you know this man?"

"I know him as much and as little as you do," says Booth. He has begun pulling on his boots.

Jones sits down. The three men contemplate each other in silence. "I don't like to say this," Jones goes on after a moment, "but some of the ignorant may believe we are responsible for this attack—"

"Inconceivable!" Roscoe Conkling exclaims.

"Not at all," Booth murmurs. "After Lincoln's death, there were mobs in the streets—"

Roscoe scowls with alarm. "Mobs?"

"At the very least there will be a mob of reporters at the dock in New York," says Jones. "We must be prepared—"

Booted now, the Vice-President rises to his full height. He is a handsome man, gentle-featured when he assumes the right expression. His slight corpulence scarcely conceals that he still moves with agility. "I will handle this," he says to them.

"But what if—" Roscoe begins.

"No, I will handle it," Booth says. "I will find a tone." He suggests that the one precaution they should take in New York is to leave the ferry at different ends. For the Vice-President to be seen in the company of the arch-Stalwart at so sensitive a moment would be taste-less.

"Will you disembark fore or aft?" Booth asks.

"My God, think of the shambles in Albany after this," Roscoe groans. He says he will disembark aft.

"Then I will go fore, gentlemen," Booth says. His voice has taken on some authority. "Believe me, we need only react with ordinary humanity in this situation. Fate, not any of us, has dealt the hand."

In boldface headline: "THE PRESIDENT LIVES!" Below the banner: "Sorely Wounded," but attending physicians hold out hope that the bullet inside him may yet be located with the help of instru-ments.

By the time Booth reaches Washington to call at the White House the following day, he has found his tone: distracted, like Titus An-dronicus. The tone occurs to him instinctively while talking to the reporters on the dock in New York. He senses that if there are mobs threatening, he must seem at least as deranged by grief as they are by anger. While there are no mobs in evidence, the newspapermen react sympathetically to the version of distraction that he offers them.

"In my heart . . . what injustice . . . no, I cannot speak . . ."

At the Mansion, he is not allowed to visit the bedside of the stricken President. Only the family and the probing physicians may. But he is plainly distracted in the presence of the ailing Mrs. Garfield, who looks sturdier to him than she did on the night they stood in the reception line at the inaugural ball with the wilting flowers on her dress.

"You are so kind," she says, shaking his hand. Then, bucking him up: "We must be brave and hopeful now, General."

He heaves a deep sigh. "And . . . and trust in the Lord."

Later, the press quotes Senator Benjamin Harrison, who is also present: "The Vice-President showed deep feeling and seemed to be overcome with calamity."

Booth quarters himself in Senator Jones's home, waiting. Some of the Stalwart papers have already called the jailed Guiteau "an obvious madman," although no interviews with the would-be assassin have as yet been permitted.

Pacing restlessly in the guest bedroom, windows open to the warm and damp Washington night, Booth ponders the obstacles that may still lie in destiny's way. He has faith that they will be overcome.

Destiny must be aware that he will sound finer chords as a President than he has as a Vice-President. After all, Presidents were more like kings, and he has played many kings.

Once he is President he will have unlimited resources with which to find the evidence that will restore the honor of the Booths and stop the Kappenhalters forever. But at the same time he resolves to be President of all the people, north and south. How soon he can announce himself as Booth ("I Am Myself Alone!") is anybody's guess. But the people will be made to see that the death of Lincoln, their ape god, had a predestined significance, and they will accept its necessity.

With the file revealed, perhaps he will pardon Weed as well as the others, even if they don't deserve it. He may need men like Weed and Dun in the day-to-day business of running the country, particularly since Roscoe is now a dead mackerel. He needs other men to restore the morale of the South, to cancel its war debts, and to run out any fag-end carpetbaggers.

One effort he will make for Garfield's sake: get rid of the spoils system! Garfield's death can be made to have nearly as much transfiguring inevitability as Lincoln's did. Without it, none of the great redeeming events that destiny envisioned for the Republic could take place. If Garfield survived the wound, for example, it would all go for naught. But Booth does not believe in a destiny so unresponsive to opportunity.

Two days later, however, Garfield has improved a bit, and while he is not out of danger of blood poisoning, the Cabinet gives advice that the Vice-President might as well return to his home in New York if that is his wish. Booth senses at once that the period ahead (very nearly an interregnum) will be important. He takes leave of his host, Senator Jones, then pays a last call on Mrs. Garfield, on Blaine, and on the other members of the Cabinet, behaving with so fine a sense of misery and distraction that they seem thawed to a large extent.

He sets out then for New York, where he means to deal decisively with Raymond and whatever other obstacles might lie in destiny's rough path.

18

A House on Madison Avenue

"You do not realize how much misery we are sparin' you, dear Raymond," says Mrs. Gauley. She is an elderly woman with thin hair and ample bosom who manages the kitchen staff. "You oughten ter complain."

Raymond does not look at her. He is standing over a sink, scrubbing pans, for he has become a scullery boy at the house of assignation where once he worked in a more responsible role. The humiliation he is complaining of at the moment is not that of scrubbing the pans, but of having to set out a meal in the dining room for the misbegotten boy who has succeeded him upstairs.

"We oughten ter make the young women nor John Thomas ter serve the meals ter theirselves," Mrs. Gauley goes on. "It's fer the staff ter do."

"I could do John Thomas's work upstairs well as he," Raymond grumbles.

"Not for me ter say," she croons. Inspecting the lamp chimneys that still have smudges on them, she returns a few to the drainboard for Raymond to wash all over again. "You're too old fer that kinda work. Can't you see now you're too old?"

The reek of the washing powder makes Raymond sneeze. He wipes his nose with the back of his sleeve. "Not so old as some of the young women, I bet."

Mrs. Gauley clucks her tongue. Doesn't he feel he's a full-grown man now who "oughten ter" liken himself to boys and young women? "Honest work don't hurt you," she tells him. "I alleez worked. I come from a pioneer family."

While he is drying his hands and getting John Thomas's half-cold chop and turnips on a plate, she tells him about her "pioneer family." He has heard it before, how the family went to Pennsylvania and then to West Virginia, where some of them built a town that they named Gauley Bridge. Raymond is not impressed. He doubts all stories these days.

In the dining room he sets the plate down in front of John

Thomas, who is staring solitarily at the wallpaper with a napkin under his chin. He is tricked up in his best linen and knickerbockers. But there is nothing much that they have been able to do about the way his ears stick out.

"Where uz my milk?" John Thomas asks sulkily, blue eyes gazing.

Raymond scowls at him, and when he goes back to the kitchen, he takes a slug of milk right out of the pitcher when nobody is looking before he pours a glassful for John Thomas. Probably Mrs. Gauley is right, Raymond thinks. He doesn't want to do what John Thomas does anymore. He wants more and more each day to be back with the general. There is where the excitement and the travel was. Sodomy was a childish and disgraceful thing, not much better than scrubbing pans or blacking boots.

Raymond knows that the general is back in town, and will probably remain all summer, or as long as it takes for President Garfield to recover from being shot. Why shouldn't Raymond drop over to 123 Lexington Avenue soon and throw himself on the general's mercy? Except he is afraid to do it because by now, more than likely, the general will have found out about that letter Raymond wrote to Miss Nellie's mother, telling her about the trick played on her in front of A. T. Stewart's. That kind of thing the general would look on as real betrayal, more serious than running off from Virginia with Miss Nellie. Servants who worked in great houses just didn't tell the master's secrets. Raymond has read enough books to know what a sin that is.

In the dining room he gives John Thomas his glass of milk. Meanwhile, a young lady, neatly and fashionably dressed, can be seen in the parlor across the hall, having entered from the street. Since she seats herself as though she is waiting for someone, Raymond wonders if she has come in response to one of the newspaper advertisements. He has seen some of them: "Rooms in a strictly private family, where boarders are not annoyed with impertinent questions." Or "A handsome room to let, with board for the lady only."

Since no one is troubling to attend, Raymond takes it upon himself to cross the hall and speak to her.

"Do ye wish to see Mrs. Stonerudder?" he asks pleasantly, naming the woman who currently manages the establishment.

"Nooo, thank you," the young woman says without warmth. She seems not to like his butcher's apron and rolled sleeves. But she is lovely-looking under a large bonnet, her ash-blond hair discreetly enclosed. She has the look of the ladies of fashion on the brand-new Dresden-blue wallpaper in the room.

"Would ye like something cooling to drink?" he asks, showing off his gentility.

But before she can reply, Jenny comes into the room, greets the newcomer familiarly, and takes her hand. Jenny, no friend of Raymond's, is being kept at the house by a wealthy stockbroker, a Mr. Van Rensselaer by name. The two adjourn so rapidly from the parlor that Raymond is left in the silence, listening to John Thomas across the hall masticating his chop.

It is beginning to get dark. All of us are ensnared in the web of the powerful, Raymond is suddenly aware. These women, although they dress smart and snub him, are caught in it just as he is. He has never thought of it in this way before. Take, for instance, Victoria Coventry, the woman reporter, who was probably betrayed by the general when she was trying to get the story on the hoopskirt factory. She disappeared. She had elegance, but she was consumed in the web of the powerful.

John Thomas's chewing stops. He stands up, near to six feet of him, and peers toward the kitchen, looking for Raymond to bring him more milk. Jesus, Raymond would like to go back to blacking boots rather than be John Thomas's slop boy. But you couldn't even shine shoes out there nowadays without paying Tammany for a territory. He found that out when he tried to set up near the Astor with the general's box. Two Tammany roughs came along and gave him the bum's rush. Even his customer got pushed. A person was at their mercy, all right.

John Thomas spots him now. "More milk!" John Thomas demands, nasty and high-pitched. He is skinny and gangly as a grasshopper.

"Ye get too fresh," Raymond tells him, passing through to the kitchen, "and I'll push your face in."

It does not occur to Raymond that John Thomas is also at the mercy of the powerful.

"Ah, shet your face too," John Thomas sneers.

Raymond pours John Thomas's milk in the kitchen. "Sodomite," he mutters under his breath.

19

123 LEXINGTON AVENUE

The regular servants are off for the evening, a Saturday. Young Nellie has gone to bed early with the catarrh, uncommon in such warm weather, and Nell has been moving back and forth between the child's sickroom and her own sewing room with frequency.

Booth, while dressing to go out, has deliberately left his door ajar so that she can see him before his mirror as she passes in the corridor. The icy contempt that she has directed toward him these three months he believes is beginning to crack with the heat. Constantly agitated, she seems to watch him all the time. Her remarks grow more barbed, her threats more desperate.

Earlier this evening, for example, clad in a light silk dressing gown, loosely tied, she confided in the hallway that she expects to visit Philadelphia as soon as Nellie is better in order to consult Dr. Weir Mitchell "foah his advice" on her "nerves."

"All right," he replies. Both of them know that Mitchell, for all his self-regard, will possibly remember her as Nell Arthur.

She studies him for a further reaction, but gets none.

"What if the President should expire while you ah out?" she ventures. "What would I say?"

"Alan will take care of things downstairs till I get back."

Holding the tie on her robe, she sniffs. "Do forgive me if mah walkin' around troubles you here upstairs."

She is waiting to get another look at him tonight, he knows, as Götz Dörfer. While searching the city after dark for the treacherous Raymond, he has gone forth regularly as Dörfer. Although he has extra flesh now (the adipose of the public figure), he corsets himself well in an old tuxedo and blackens his hair with greasepaint. The glimpses she catches of him must be tantalizing to her. In the mirror he is no longer Chester but the person she made love to in Paris that spring.

When he is ready, he deliberately waits until he hears her passing. He sweeps out into the hall, complete with silk-lined evening cape and his favorite walking stick.

Nell draws in her breath as she looks at him. She clenches both hands just below her breasts.

Unsmiling, he stares into her eyes.

"Come out with me tonight, Nell," he says to her in a quiet, determined voice. "I will dress you myself, if you let me."

He speaks with such unexpected feeling that she seems shocked. Her eyes cloud. She shudders. It is as though he has suggested a *Walpurgisnacht* orgy.

"Never! Never again!" she gasps.

Blindly, she continues toward the child's room as, undismayed, he leaves by the back stairs, the route by which he avoids both the Pinkertons and the occasional tireless reporter outside on the street. Of the two, he is more wary of the press. Anonymous letters have lately appeared in two papers, one of them the penny-rag *Evening News,* claiming that the Vice-President is "not what he seems." No doubt it is only the vindictive Nell, inflicting new jeopardy on them. But the language is strangely oracular, like a voice from beyond the grave in a ghost story by Poe.

Outside in the warm, humid night Booth strides with purpose two blocks down and one block over. The freshness of the air is a relief after the cramped confines of the house and of Chester Arthur. Ironically, in these uncertain days, he is safer as Dörfer than as Arthur, the man some think conspired to kill the President.

The Pinkertons are charged with guarding Arthur from the vengeful. Booth laughs, for the further irony is that Arthur has no Constitutional successor in line for the White House. Since the Senate has neglected to choose a permanent pro tem because of their eternal filibustering, and the House will not be able to choose a Speaker until December when the new Congress sits, only Garfield's organs, probably growing gangrenous, and he, John Wilkes Booth, keep the country from having no President whatever.

"The Bowery, my man," he calls to the cab driver, spinning his cane as the carriage pulls up to let him get aboard.

Having had no luck finding the elusive Raymond in any of the fashionable places that bootblacks worked, Booth has decided to try the part of town where the German burghers, who liked a high shine on their shoes, lingered on summer evenings.

On the ground floor of the Atlantic Garden, Booth shoulders his way among friendly beer drinkers. This grand saloon opens into an alfresco park planted with trees and flowers, blooming and fragrant.

Inside, under the great curved ceiling, a restaurant and a noisy shooting gallery resonate from the balcony level. A monster music box, called an orchestrion, adds to the din with oompah music.

Booth orders a glass of wine and settles himself at the end of a long table. Perhaps later on a young bootblack or two would wander in, looking for business. At the far end of the table where Booth is sitting, two lads in knickerbockers—neither of them much younger than Raymond—are sitting and eating with their parents, amiably talking in German.

When eventually the father gets up and walks off with one of the boys, the other boy pulls a paper-covered book out of his back pocket and reads it while his mother scrapes table crumbs into checkered napkins. Booth recognizes the volume as one of the kind Raymond once read: *Ragged Dick, Mark the Match Boy, Phil the News Boy.* The memory gives Booth a lump in his throat, for most of the time Raymond was as plucky and brave as Horatio Alger's lads were. No task suggested to him was too heavy or onerous for him to attempt.

And yet he broke discipline. Not only that, but he turned his coat. The secrets he revealed condemned him. The Cause was at stake, survival was at stake, and there would be no easy way to take care of Raymond once Arthur became President. No President could prowl the streets of New York in disguise, searching for a lost bootblack.

Booth sips his wine without enjoying it. He has never wanted to kill. He has merely wished to serve his Cause with tongue and sword. And he has persisted when lesser men have quit the fray.

Later, walking restlessly along Eighth Street in the direction of Bellevue and the morgue, where first he met Raymond, Booth comes upon a group of young roughs lolling outside one of the shooting galleries. Some of them have bootblack kits, but they are smoking cigarettes and look to be intoxicated.

One of them shouts at Booth, "Shine, mister? How 'bout a shine?"

They look so erratic and uncouth that he shakes his head.

Then they begin mocking him.

"Gee, ain't he hot stuff!"

"He's a dandy masher, ain't he?"

Booth twirls his cane and thinks about giving one of them a surprise. But the streets are so crowded with people he isn't sure how easy it would be to get away.

"Well, what's eatin' ya?" one of them says when Booth seems to take too long to saunter past them.

Booth moves on. The neighborhood reeks of booze and beer. He has come to realize that a youth like Raymond, once touched by the finer things in life, could never long exist in a world of bootblacks anymore. It has been a total miscalculation. Of course Raymond would abandon the box and go back to work he was more accustomed to. Seeing the German boy has, for some reason, already sent Booth in the direction of the morgue.

But by the time he reaches First Avenue, he is not so sure of his idea. The vehicles rumbling down First are rickety wagons and peddlers' carts. A police wagon passes: by its pace it is probably a Dead Wagon transporting a corpse found in the lower harbor up to Bellevue. He casts his eyes downward. The thought that is troubling him relates again to the German boy. It is the knickerbockers. He sees Raymond wearing knickerbockers.

How galling is that presentation to his mind! He knows now that Raymond would not have returned to honest work at the morgue; given his pusillanimous character, he would have hurried over to that house of assignation where they had once before put boys' breeches on him, and where, Booth fears, he would let them do so again!

The breath of the river seems fetid; he does not continue up First Avenue but turns crosstown again, determined to find the house in which the base coward, damned beyond redemption, must have sold himself without shame for yet a second time. No mercy is possible if such be the case.

By half past one in the morning Booth has picked up a "waitress" from the Chatham Street concert saloon, which he occasionally patronized when he worked at Delmonico's. A few drinks and he feels mellower. Mabel has a good head on her shoulders, although her face is no longer what it was. She is an old-timer, as Letty was. Letty, for whom he had true affection, knew everything about the neighborhood. But Letty passed on a month ago, he is told, only thirty-two. Well, Mabel knows things too.

When he stops to buy a newspaper—the *Herald,* just off the press—she says, "Ain't cher comin' back with me, then?" They are heading for the familiar bed house that she and Letty always used.

"Sure I am, Mabel. Hold on a minute." The *Herald* story says there is no change in the condition of the President: Booth can spend the night relaxing as Dörfer.

"Thoughtcher was gonna read—"

"Not when a girl like you wants to give me a tumble."

"Ye want a tumble, ye devil?"

Nonchalant, he throws the newspaper away in the street as they move off, a comforting decision. On page six, had he kept the paper, he might have noticed, sooner or later, the annoying by-line, K. Kappenhalter, signed to a story about the drainage of the city sewers.

20

THE UNION CLUB

The next day, the young and well-dressed Mr. James Gordon Bennett, Jr., owner and publisher of the *Herald*, happens to be lunching with Weed and Dun at his club on 21st Street and Fifth Avenue. At a point during the soup course, Bennett pats his mouth with a napkin and says, "I'm really trying to put a stop to the matter you inquired about last month, Thurlow."

"The Victoria Coventry Society?" Weed asks, glancing at Dun.

Lighting a cigarette, Bennett pushes his soup aside. "It's the young reporters. They've gotten together and *each one of them* is calling himself Kappenhalter, the girl's true name."

Weed says that he doesn't see their point.

"A strange bit of defiance," Bennett agrees. "You remember that old man Kappenhalter came down from Waterford, looking for her. And that he pleaded with our legmen, asking them to help him find her."

"Do they think you know something about it?" Dun asks.

"Oh, they suspect I had her working undercover," Bennett acknowledges. "But acting like schoolboys over a pawky girl reporter, can you imagine it? Printing up calling cards, sneaking a by-line into the paper! I wish I could fire them all."

"You can!" Weed declares. "Your father would have."

Bennett laughs uneasily. "If I fire them, who would find out the answer . . . if there is one?"

"Hell, you already got a good story this summer, a dying President . . ."

Bennett shakes his head as the waiter enters with the fish course.

The frosted windows overlooking Fifth Avenue are open, and through the baffled wells at the bottom, traffic noise is audible. A revolving ceiling fan is stirring the air, for a hot spell has gripped the East. The morning bulletin from Washington says that Garfield may be weakened by malaria, since he is showing symptoms of the fever and chills.

When the waiter leaves, Bennett says, "You know what I wish you two could tell me: that Miss Victoria Coventry is being maintained in comfort somewhere in the city, and if she knows what is good for her, she will inform her father and brother-in-law she is all right. Then I could get my reporters back to their proper business."

"Well, I wish we could, Jimmy." Weed's fish has been filleted for him, and he gropes for his fork.

Bennett looks right at him. "Thurlow, you put me up to hiring this girl. She must have had somebody behind her who wanted it."

"Ah, martyrdom would fly out the window if she were somebody's uptown tootsie."

"Better that than foul play at the hands of Latham's!"

Weed concedes it with a harsh laugh. Let the rumor of foul play get around and, tarnation, there'd be suicidal women rushing into every newsroom in America, demanding jobs.

Bennett shakes his finger. "You don't take me seriously!"

"Well, hell, Jimmy, I gave your sainted father all my readers, my most secret files. What more do you want?" Weed exclaims. "Give us a little executive privilege."

Bennett scowls. "It wouldn't be the Vice-President who's keeping her, would it?"

"Why, what done give you dat idea, Massa Jim?" Weed keeps his eyes off Dun.

"Some talk that she was looking for him in Albany, and again in Utica."

"Oh, my," Weed says.

"He could be keeping her right in his home in Gramercy Park. He's got Pinkertons there thick as fenceposts. And from what we hear, a strange woman upstairs."

"A real white slaver."

Bennett's left eye flickers, but he says nothing.

"Drop it, Jimmy," Weed says. "If Garfield dies, and you pursue this, we're off to a great start, ain't we, in the new administration? Tammany'd love it. Besides, let me assure you Victoria Coventry is definitely not in residence at 123 Lexington Avenue. Right, Dun? Dun's eyes are better than mine."

Dun says, "If Latham's found the girl out, and there was foul play, the body will turn up sooner or later."

"Christ, then I have an authentic martyr," Bennett groans. "And I'm the one who let her go to Latham's."

"Fire your reporters!" Weed says. "Kick Old Man Kappenhalter and his dog-catcher son-in-law down the damned staircase! If it was a man who'd gotten into trouble doing an undercover story, would you put up with this slop in your city room?"

Bennett is beginning to look thoughtful.

Later, under the royal blue Union Club canopy, Dun, holding Weed's elbow, helps him into the carriage and, when he is beside him, says, "Maybe she's not dead after all."

"Oh, you think not? Even her room was stripped."

The two men settle back against the cushions of the carriage as it starts down Fifth Avenue. The sound of an elevated train passing on Sixth obliterates for a moment other traffic noise.

"Some days I just see the damfool side of all this," Weed admits.

"You think Booth betrayed her to Latham's?"

"We could send some Kappenhalters of our own at him if you really want to try to find out."

Dun shakes his head in dismay.

21

A House on Madison Avenue

Since neither Mrs. Gauley nor Mrs. Stonerudder are near, the ringing doorbell is answered by the new girl in residence, Miss Isabel Manton. She has come down from her bed-sitting-room suite on the third floor front because it always seems to be cooler in a heat wave nearer the ground. She is less reserved and lofty than she first appeared to Raymond and others, and indeed has been eager to be helpful in little ways around the house.

Still, she is careful and noncommittal when the visiting gentleman with cape and cane asks at the door if a young man named Raymond could be found in the house. Isabel thinks the gentleman to be rather too flamboyant for daytime; besides, she is unsure of the arrangement when a member of the kitchen staff is requested, even though the gentleman says that he only wants to chat.

She seats him in the parlor. He is smiling so benignly, gloved hand on gold-headed walking stick, that she grows more mistrustful by the minute. Hurrying off, she encounters Mrs. Stonerudder, fan in hand, ascending from the back lavatory.

"A gentleman is in the parlor asking for Raymond, Mrs. Stonerudder."

"Then send him up to John Thomas, dear."

Isabel smiles uncertainly. "Oh, but he said he just wanted to chat."

"I'll take care of him, dear."

Isabel watches the lady, still fanning, go off to the parlor. On her own she hustles into the kitchen to inform Raymond, who seems to have been in an argument with the iceman. She has heard thirty seconds of foul words, then a huge clatter. Disheveled and shirtless, Raymond is staring at a fifty-pound block of ice that for some reason the iceman seems to have thrown in anger onto the floor against a wooden cupboard door.

"Oh, goodness, are you all right?" Isabel asks.

"God a'mighty, God a'mighty!" Raymond exclaims. He is trying to surround the block of ice, so as to lift it into a galvanized tub, but a puddle of water is already rapidly forming. Moreover, Raymond is smeared with grease all over, on hair, on face, even on the buttons of his underwear top from having been cleaning the grease trap on the kitchen stove.

"My goodness," Isabel laughs. The spectacle of poor Raymond lifting the cake of ice with slippery smeared hands and arms is more than a little hilarious. But she has to admire his persistence.

When he finally has the ice safely in the tub, she tells Raymond about the gentleman who asked for him, and as she describes the man, watches the gamut of expressions on Raymond's face.

"Is he a—you know?" Isabel asks. "He never looked like one."

Raymond shakes his head. "Naw, I used to be in—uhh—service with him. And his family."

Isabel says that Raymond should certainly see the gentleman then, greasy or not; otherwise, there would be embarrassment when Mrs. Stonerudder sent the gentleman up to John Thomas.

"Did you notice if he was carrying a cane?" Raymond asks suddenly.

"He was." As Isabel describes the cane, she watches Raymond's eyes get very large. With the hair on his chest, he looks so adorable that she resolves to get him to take her out some night. Not, of course, when her own gentleman is in town. But some other time, just for diversion.

"Don't let him find me!" Raymond starts looking around, as though for a way out.

By the time she asks him what the matter is, he is at the steps leading down from the pantry. "Tell him I don't live here anymore, Isabel!"

"You take me out sometime, and I will," she says, laughing.

But there is no chance to see what he thinks of that, for he has run outdoors, then around the corner, stumbling toward the cellar steps. She continues to laugh. Of course she will help him.

First, she hurries back toward the lower hallway, where one of the housemaids mentions that the gentleman is already upstairs, Mrs. Stonerudder having thus divined his most secret wishes. Now if Isabel is any judge—

Yes, here he comes down again, the gentleman! With his hat on his head, and his cane held like a riding-crop with which to whip a horse, he descends the stairway with an air of total indignation. His face is aflame. He looks neither to the right nor the left.

As he reaches the bottom, the party who may have given offense —John Thomas himself—in belted knickerbockers and with a few buttons of his waistcoat undone—appears at the upper balustrade and calls down to the gentleman, "Good sir—uh—good sir—"

But John Thomas cannot think of what more to say, and besides, the gentleman does not stop to listen.

"I am dreadfully sorry, sir," Isabel Manton declares as the gentleman hesitates a moment, trying to find the front door.

"Is or is not Raymond a resident here?" the gentleman asks in an immoderate voice.

"Is not," says Isabel promptly. "Unfortunate that you was misunderstood."

"Unfortunate that you do not believe that men mean what they say." The gentleman glares. "Men of honor."

"This way out," says Isabel, pointing the way.

22

THE EXECUTIVE MANSION
SEPTEMBER 6

Shortly after daybreak, with the sun vast and warm in a cloudless sky, six men, moving deliberately, bring President Garfield out of the Mansion on a mattress. They carry him down to the horsecar tracks, where fresh sawdust has been spilled to cushion the passage of the express van drawn up to transport the invalid. The people in the crowd who have come for a look hardly recognize the President, he has shriveled so much. But he moves his head once in a while to watch how the bearers are loading him.

Once he is set inside with attendants, and the commotion is allowed to settle, the horses start up. Some of the crowd are able to follow the van a short way, the horses move so slowly. On Sixth Street the van shifts with a perceptible bump to tracks specially laid by the railroad company for the occasion. By the time the van reaches the station, many are on hand to witness the transfer of the President to a private Pullman car, equipped, it is said, with special devices to regulate heat and light.

As soon as the physicians and other attendants have joined the party on board, the locomotive begins moving. No whistles or bells are sounded on the train. Early morning traffic has been cleared aside by Washington police officers, and bystanders are admonished not to cheer or call to the President.

He is heading toward a better place. A cottage at the temperate seashore in New Jersey has been selected so that he can get out of the heat of Washington and can see and hear the ocean every day. In New Jersey tracks have been laid from the railroad station right to the door of his cottage. The President is encouraged by the move, it is reported, although some say that his fevers are still a matter for concern.

The doctors continue to be puzzled about where the bullet has lodged in the President's body. Not even Alexander Graham Bell has been able to find it. Bell brought to the White House his electric induction balance machine. When connected to a telephone, the machine was supposed to be able to detect metal objects in the body by breaking a circuit, but as the machine was rubbed over the area of the President's abdomen where the doctors guessed the bullet had probably come to rest, Mr. Bell heard nothing.

23

NEW YORK CITY

Raymond and Isabel Manton have spent an afternoon in the central park. For ten cents they have been rowed around the lake in a canopied boat. They have visited the meteorological observatory in the Museum of Natural History and have looked at all the zoo animals and birds outside, part of the collection of the former Archduke Maximilian. The caged lions, even though they are asleep in the heat, give Isabel a queasy feeling. Raymond watches them indifferently and with a preoccupied air. He keeps glancing away, over his left shoulder or over his right shoulder, at the people in the park.

Isabel can't tell what is the matter, but when she mentions to him with an offhand laugh that no act of crime "or lawlessness" has ever occurred in the central park in its entire history, he seems not to hear her.

Given his remoteness for most of the day, Isabel is surprised when Raymond invites her to his room on their return to Mrs. Stonerudder's. It is well after dark, but since Mrs. Gauley, the only other resident besides Raymond who lives belowstairs, is away for the weekend, she consents. He has "cigarettes" that they can smoke, and it is the coolest part of the house on warm and humid nights.

Isabel, sitting down uneasily on the one straight chair in Raymond's chamber, removes the hat from her ash-blond hair and makes an approving remark about the rug in the room. The gas illuminates the room cozily. Raymond sits on the bed and starts rolling cigarettes for them. He has a nice can in which the tobacco is kept, and the papers look fresh and white.

Raymond asks, "Is your friend, the—the—coming back one day soon?"

"Not as I know of," Isabel replies coolly. "But sometime."

Raymond licks the paper and seals in the tobacco. "He's out of town a lot."

Isabel manages a sigh. "You think I put on airs, don't you, when he's around?"

"I don't mind that at all," Raymond declares.

She is a bit puzzled how to take his remark. But his inscrutability attracts her. He is very good-looking and well-proportioned, although he is not much taller than she. Around the bedroom there are some free-library books, lying on the table and the floor. One of them is *Ivanhoe,* another *Knights of the Round Table.* Since she suspects that such books are down on smoking and women, she decides not to try them as a subject for conversation. But she realizes how intelligent he must be to want to take books out of the free library.

Raymond looks up suddenly. He seems to have heard something from the street. A high window is open onto the alley.

"Did they call 'Extra'?" Raymond asks.

"I didn't hear a thing."

"I think I heard 'Extra,' " says Raymond. "I bet the President died."

"Oh, what do we care?" Isabel exclaims. To relieve the tension she feels, she gets to her feet and goes over to the bed, ready to receive the second cigarette from him when he finishes rolling it.

Presently, his eyes return from the window to the business of the cigarette. He spills a few flecks of tobacco on the blanket as she impulsively sits down next to him on the bed, but in a moment the end is twisted and he hands it to her with a smile. He now finds a match and, igniting it against the friction strip on the box, lights first her cigarette, then his own.

She inhales carefully. "My goodness, the first time I had one, I really coughed," she admits. Sophisticated people were all smoking cigarettes these days; her gentleman friend initiated her. She can imagine that Raymond must have been exposed when in the service of that dandy that he worked for.

"You know, they don't smoke cigarettes anywhere but in New York and Europe," she suddenly declares.

"Have ye ever been in Europe?"

"Uhh—no."

"Neither have I."

"I bet you'd like to sometime."

They are half sitting, half lying across the bed, the backs of their heads against the paint-peeling wall. She has never been anyplace but

New York and Yonkers, the latter being where she grew up and met her gentleman friend after her father married a woman younger than his daughters were.

Raymond says, "I was on my way."

"To Europe?"

"No." This time there is a note of palpable sadness. "Just on my way."

Isabel's patience is not endless. When the smoking shows signs of entrenching his melancholy, she arranges to turn her face sharply at the same time he is reaching across to the ashtray. Their foreheads and noses collide.

"Goodness," she cries, fiercely rubbing her forehead, watching his eyes compelled to focus again on the real present, the real company. "You must want to rub noses?"

She lets her boldness overwhelm him. Laughing, she holds her cigarette out away from her, and leaning her hand on his leg, she pushes her nose back and forth against his nose.

"Wild Eskimos kiss like that!" she exclaims.

But he does not react much; he does not laugh, or do anything but look surprised. She leans her head back against the wall, smoking again. Of course, he was employed as the "boy" of the house in his previous service. Supposing he liked that stuff!

"What are you thinking about?" he asks suddenly, his eyes fixed on the mask of her face.

"Not a thing."

Before she knows it, he has grabbed her in a fierce embrace and begins kissing her with urgency. She reaches for his leg again and runs her hand up into more sensitive areas. Disappointed at the absence of anything dramatic there, she is excited some by not being able to breathe. She waves her hand holding the cigarette, sure that she is dropping hot ashes on the blanket.

At last Raymond releases her. They put their cigarettes down. While there remains a determined look on his face, it seems to her more like an animal intent on his prey than a man wanting to make love.

Even after she loosens the buttons on the bodice of her gown and slips her arms quickly out of the sleeves, allowing him to admire the prospect of her breasts under the cotton fabric of her chemise, she senses that it is all in his head. She embraces him, caresses the outside of his thigh with her one hand and with the other lifts his chin so as to kiss him on the cheek in a sisterly fashion.

"What's the matter, Raymond?" she asks, fondling him. "Is there something wrong?"

He says nothing for a long time; she wonders if his mind is out the window again where they could be yelling "Extra."

He finally blurts, "Afraid of . . . infection."

Unexpectedly, she laughs.

"Oh, Raymond."

She leans back, her arms dropped to her sides. He sits erect, stiff as a marionette.

"You read too many books," she says. "That's a terrible thing to say."

Raymond looks shamefaced.

In a way, she is sorry for him. "Never mind," she says. "Do you know a nice love poem? You read poems too, don't you?"

His chin juts forward. As she retrieves her cigarette, he begins.

"Uhh . . . It was many and many a year ago, In a kingdom by the sea, That a maiden there lived whom you may know, By the name of Annabel Lee, And this maiden lived with no other thought, Than to love and be loved by me. . . . I was a child, and she was a child, In this kingdom by the sea, But we loved with a love that was more than love—"

When he pauses, she looks at him, waiting for him to continue.

"I and my Annabel Lee," says Raymond. His eyes have glazed over.

"Is there any more?" she asks.

"Don't remember it," says Raymond. Abruptly he gets to his feet, and she begins to realize she has lost him for good. He seems to be listening for something.

24

DISTRICT OF COLUMBIA PRISON

The assassin in his cell is not troubled by the future.

But he looks up quickly when his visitor, seated on the other side of a small writing table, tells him that the President is "sinking."

"Ah," says the assassin, his beard trimmed, his face fuller. "Say dat I have much pity for Mrs. Garfield and d' children."

The man he speaks to—who is both his brother-in-law and his legal counsel—gazes dolefully at Guiteau, leaning forward now.

"It was inevitable," says Guiteau. "All men pass. D' guards just told me that General Burnside passed away. Is dat correct? All go to dere reward, some soon, some later—"

"You must think seriously about your defense, Charles."

"Yes, indeed," says Guiteau. He gestures at the papers on the writing table, the stub of a pencil lying on top of some of the pages. "I am at work on my autobiography. D' newspaper is publishing my life story. I am at work to finish it before d' trial."

"The plea of insanity is very difficult—"

Guiteau waves off his brother-in-law's words. With regular meals over the past two months in prison, his gestures are no longer as shaky as they were. "I am legally insane," he asserts. "It is completely clear. *Legally,* I am insane."

"You should not be overconfident in this matter, Charles."

"By and by, you will see," Guiteau tells him. "Gen'ral Art'ur is still not in control of d' government. When dat occurs—sooner better than later, we should hope—it will be said dat I am legally insane." Seeing the flicker of skepticism in his brother-in-law's eyes, Guiteau says, "I am legally insane because I shot wit'out passion! I dare dem to bring out a witness to show dat I shot wit' passion!"

The mind of the assassin, whenever famished, nourishes itself with a new idea. Guiteau rises and begins pacing.

"You will see," he continues. "After a period of mourning President Art'ur will make a favorable judgment in my case."

"You will go to trial, Charles."

"Of course!" Guiteau throws up his arms. "Garfield has many friends. Dey have to be pacified now. But dat is—dat is everyday politics! Do you suppose Gen'ral Art'ur does not know how to make arrangements!"

"I think you fool yourself."

"I have written to Art'ur! He knows me, I tell you. His agent talked to me many nights in d' Hoffman House."

"But you said yourself you decided to do this thing while lying in bed one night."

"I will produce dese witnesses!" Guiteau shouts, clenching his fists above his head. "You feel certain my letters are reaching Gen'ral Art'ur?"

"I think they are."

"James, the postmaster gen'ral is a Stalwart," Guiteau says, more calmly. "He will see to it my letters go t'rough."

25

UTICA

Alfresco in the tree shade on his fenced property, Roscoe Conkling sits, looking down John Street toward the Mohawk River. His activities have become circumscribed since President Garfield began sinking. No one is interested in his life story, and he sits behind the trunk of a tree, out of view of those returning from Sunday services on foot. As he throws the Utica paper down on the green lawn, his shoulder feels cramped.

Although he has long since withdrawn from the Senate race, he wishes he had a New York *Herald* to read. Or any New York paper. Even the *Times,* a recent betrayer, would do. The *Times* has decided, after the shooting in Washington, that the state was "not well served by Senators Conkling and Platt." He forgives them. He is beginning to experience himself as a thing of tremendous noble dignity. Seneca, opening his veins, could not have had the dignity that Roscoe more and more feels himself in possession of.

At the black iron gate to the walk, his wife Julia and her friends exchange parting words. She opens the gate and walks past him within a few feet, carrying her hymn book. Although her nose is high, her shoulders do not have as much of the old reproachfulness, he believes.

She suspects, of course, that he will be summoned to Washington by the new administration, when and if there is one. Personally he doubts it. He will be staying in Utica. Possibly he would be staying in Utica even if it were the same old Chet Arthur about to assume high office. Not that he is sure, day in and day out, that it isn't old Chet.

Some of the old guard—such as French and Wheelhorse—have gravitated toward the man, whoever he may be. They see signs of his being able to take over the reins. He has struck the right note, and nobody wanted George Washington anyway.

The visible prospect down John Street has grown unnervingly dead. Roscoe gets to his feet. It's not as though the old Chet were irreplaceable. The fact is he *was* replaced. The new man is no impostor on any count; he is surely the man who has served as Vice-President, the man who was nominated and who campaigned for the job. Roscoe is surprised to realize how just and benign it all seems.

When he opens the front door, he is somewhat relieved to see that Julia is standing in front of the mirror over the pier table, still unpinning her bonnet. He is feeling lonesome and ready to converse with her; he steps inside.

Her voice dry as an owl's, she says to him, "Keep the door shet, Roscoe, so all the heat don't come in."

26

123 LEXINGTON AVENUE

In an ominous mood, Nell has sneaked right into the master bedroom as soon as she has heard Booth descending before dinner to his office. The dying President is the last thing on her mind. Boldly she takes a seat in front of Booth's sumptuous dressing table, and, shaking out her black hair, begins an inventory of his makeup cases. Never has she been this close to seeing how he performs his alchemy. A rainbow of rouges, powders, pomades, greets her eye. She sorts through tweezers, pencils, swabs, false hair, jars of putty, and cream. Some of the fancier cosmetic containers have French names on their lids, and one of them —a strange-smelling concoction that she is unable to identify—has been imported from London.

The idea of practicing his special sorcery, while using his own potions, has come to her this evening with a rush of sensual pleasure. Earlier, for no reason, she had been thinking about a certain Parisienne who had been stopping in Nice for the season, and who dressed with such a liberated imagination that Nell felt envious. At the time she was trying not to be noticed; besides, in respectable circles one did not dress in such a manner. But now, what was there to stop her? She would not stay hidden in the house the rest of her life. After dark, in the right makeup, she could be as bold as he when they went out. Nay, bolder. There was no social role for her to play, as there was for Götz Dörfer. She could give her impulses free rein.

A scissors clips her hair in a way she has seen women of fashion wear it. She puts a tweezers to her eyebrows, then adds a discreet beauty mark to her cheek. She dusts a faint white streak into her hair. In her wardrobe, meanwhile, she has found a gown that is low-cut with narrow clinging lines. She bought it in Paris and never wore it; *"La Dame aux Camélias,"* Booth said of it at the time. The color is orchid with a trace of something darker in the weft.

Back in her own room her toilette continues through the dinner hour. Once or twice she glances out the window and notices a few more carriages than usual parked on the street. But she pays little attention. She anticipates the moment when he will come upstairs after his dinner, transform himself into Götz Dörfer, and head off toward the back stairs into the night ahead.

His footsteps going past her room tell her of the moment when he has reached the second story; she listens for a door to close, trusting that she has restored the tubes and jars in his makeup kit with such care that he will suspect nothing of what she has done. Of course, he may have given up on asking her to join him on his prowls; he may even suppose she is on her way to Philadelphia.

But having to think in such a way makes her angry. She does not wish to be enslaved to his expectations, whatever they are. He has made her commit adultery, then he has killed her, then he has betrayed her by not appreciating that she gave him more than any woman ever gave a man before.

She does not want to be angry. She simply wants to show him that she will make her own choices now. When the door from his room opens again, she makes her decision. She steps from her room into the corridor. She stands, the *cocotte,* silent and unsmiling.

But when she raises her eyes, he is not the cavalier in cape and opera hat. He stands before her, tall and rubicund, fawn-colored coat buttoned over his stomach. Only the momentary glint in his eye, his lips silently forming the words *"La Dame . . ."* betray that this is anyone but Chester Arthur.

She appraises him only for a moment.

"I seem to be in the wrong play," she says.

"The President is near death in New Jersey. I am not going out tonight." He tries to call her name as she turns back into her room. "Nell—"

No, she cannot abide the humiliation. She will not. Furious, she spins away and slams the door behind her.

Booth deliberates knocking, wanting to lavish praise on her. She has learned well how the dead prepare to walk abroad. How promising for the future! But French and Wheelhorse are waiting for him in the parlor downstairs. Like draft animals they seem to have a sense of when it is time for them to be worked. They need no bulletins from New Jersey to govern their arrival.

But at a noise from the street he moves to the second floor window. Another carriage has drawn up below; reporters have been back and forth all day. As he looks down, he sees that this time it is Alan, dressed like a mortician, climbing down from the cab and paying the driver.

With the carriage moving off, Booth is next astonished to see a foreshortened figure rushing directly at Alan from the dark stairwell of the service entrance. The figure, moreover, carries a cudgel of some sort, and with no warning to Alan, who is frozen to the spot, levels a blow with the club directly at Alan's midsection. "Ohhh!" Alan cries and falls forward immediately. Good Lord, Booth gasps, was it possible that the family members of national leaders were now going to be struck down?

But in the blink of an eye, just as Booth is about to shout down to the street to get help for Alan, a Pinkerton man issues from the front door and heads directly toward the short assailant, seizing him and forcing him to drop the club before he can hit the fallen Alan a second time.

Oddly, it is not until Booth is hurrying down the stairs to add his weight to the fray that it occurs to him who the villain is. No one but Raymond! He must not be allowed to get away!

When Booth reaches the street, two burly Pinkertons have Raymond in their grasp, but Raymond is still kicking out at the body of the prone Alan, who has crawled painfully onto the bottom steps. He is still gasping for air.

"Don't let him loose!" Booth cries out to the Pinkertons. "Hold him fast, now!"

Similar encouragement is coming from the open entrance door where French and Wheelhorse have emerged, each holding a glass of whiskey, and grinning.

"Hold the bugger fast!" one of them calls out.

The good counsel is needed, for Alan, threatened by the flailing legs, grabs on to Raymond's ankles with a burst of energy that wrenches him away from the Pinkertons. Then Alan himself loses his grasp, and the wily miscreant is for a moment completely free.

But not long. Before Raymond can run, Booth, who has been standing on the third step from the bottom, takes a flying leap down to the sidewalk, a jump such as he has not attempted in sixteen years. He half expects his ankle to collapse on impact, but when it does not, he tackles the astonished Raymond with such ferocity that both of them go crashing to the sidewalk with Booth securely on top.

Alan, sitting up, has recognized his assailant now, and starts in roundly: "You peasant! You scummy peasant! You coward!"

The Pinkertons are attempting to look to the Vice-President, who is systematically twisting Raymond's arm behind him.

Raymond pants for breath. "You damned snob!" he shouts shrilly at Alan.

"Watch out, sir!" one of the Pinkertons calls. "He may be armed!"

But Booth can take care of that matter. In the straining proximity to Raymond, his hand on the lad's windpipe, holding the lad's trunk in a full-armed embrace, he feels surges of strange impulses inside him. One of the impulses is to close off Raymond's breathing right there, to terminate him as a hazard while this chance yet remained. The unwarranted attack on Alan would in itself justify him—if he did not somehow find it hard forgetting the way that Alan had once beaten up on Raymond.

What a nagging sense of justice he has!

"Let me have him . . . Father," Alan now cries, for with his wind back, he has gotten to his feet and is prepared to strike Raymond with the same plank that was used on him.

"No," Booth declares. "We'll have none of that." He has by this time glanced around them, and a coterie of eight to ten onlookers, all of them male, have formed an interested audience. Relieved that none of them are reporters, he says to the Pinkertons, "Take this lad inside, I want to talk to him. . . . And let none of us speak of this undignified business."

Among the onlookers Booth now notices a heavyset man sitting astride a black horse. He believes for a moment that the rider is a city policeman whom he is about to wave on with promises that the peace has been preserved. But the gaze riveted on him is so solemn and the man so formally dressed that Booth pauses.

"Be you General Arthur?" the rider asks him.

"Yes."

"I am the district superintendent for Western Union, sir. President Garfield has just expired in New Jersey."

The black horse paws the ground. For a moment there is silence, then among the people on the street a ripple of exclamation.

Booth lifts his hand to his forehead.

"May God be with him," he intones.

A few feet away, not having heard the bulletin, one of the Pinkertons is struggling up the steps with Raymond, who is caterwauling, "That holy snob! That ape!"

The audience gasps at the desecration of the moment. With Alan having vanished indoors, perhaps to tell Nell the news, one of the onlookers threatens Raymond with a shaking fist.

The Western Union messenger meanwhile departs, and Booth gives rapid orders to French and Wheelhorse, who look suddenly embarrassed to be holding whiskey glasses and cigars in the doorway.

"Go," he tells them. "French, find Judge Brady. Wheelhorse, look for Judge Donahue. . . . We need a judge here to administer the oath of office to me."

At last they move. As Booth hurries up the steps back into the house, people in the crowd call to him: "God be with you, Mr. President!" "Good luck, Mr. President!" Booth can also see some reporters scrambling toward the house from the park, pocketing their flasks.

He makes it inside, slams the heavy door behind him, and breathing with brief difficulty hastens into the parlor, where he orders the Pinkerton outside. Raymond stands in one corner of the room with his back to Booth.

"Shall I call the police to pick him up here, sir?" the Pinkerton asks.

"Did I tell you to call the police?" Booth inquires ominously.

With the room emptied of all but the two of them—Raymond and himself—Booth turns the key in the door, pockets it, and pulls the drape.

"There is no point in trying to run, Raymond. You'd just be put in the Tombs again."

Raymond's nose is smeared with blood from their wrestling match. He wipes it on his sleeve as he turns to look fixedly at Booth.

"I'd sooner ye kill me this time!" says Raymond with defiance. "No one can stop ye if you're President."

Booth seems to consider. He has a pistol in the drawer of the gateleg table. It would be a simple matter to say that Raymond tried to attack him, or that he made an attempt to escape.

But instead he searches the lad's eyes for some sign of compunc-tion. "Let your tongue make your plea," Booth says at last. "The time now is short. I say that when you joined me you pledged your life, fortune, sacred honor. Am I correct? I say you betrayed that pledge."

"By God, sir, I took Miss Nellie to New York for your sake, and all I got was a bootblack's box."

"We are speaking of letters you wrote since that time, revealing secrets."

"But was I not punished enough?" Raymond cries. He has clasped his hands behind him like the drummer boy charged with espionage, as seen in the old lithograph. "Alan beat me up, they beat me up in the Tombs, then ye left me on the street with only the clothes on my back. Didn't ye think, sir, that I had personal keep-sakes in Washington that I wouldn't have no more when ye abandoned me here in this city?"

"Personal keepsakes! Is that to the point, Raymond?" Booth rises now and begins pacing back and forth with some agitation. When there is a knock at the locked door, soft and tentative, Booth calls out, "Later! I am not ready now."

"Then kill me," Raymond says as Booth turns the fierce gaze on him. Raymond stands with remarkable dignity, a thread of blood dry-ing under one nostril, an eyelid twitching. "Ye go 'head. I'm not much worth. Ye prob'ly got your trick walking stick around here. Ye could stab it into me and not have to answer to no one—uhh—to anyone."

Booth bites his lips. To the end, the lad tries to improve his grammar. "Raymond, why did you come here tonight?"

"I'm no good," Raymond repeats, his chin jutting out, his shoul-ders back even further. "I'm a Judas and a degenerate. No one but you can save me. . . . I—I was wrong, sir."

Booth straightens. What is he hearing if not repentance? he asks himself. The trembling, the rigid jaw, betray Raymond's sincerity. When the lad goes on to say that his hope was to see Miss Nellie on this night, just a glimpse, Booth believes.

"And then that holy snob Alan shows up!" Raymond expostu-lates.

Again they are interrupted by a knock on the door and a firm call.

"Mr. President—"

"One minute, gentlemen," Booth intones. "I am still preparing myself." Now he turns to Raymond. "Raymond, you are from this moment put on probation. Since there is not time for you to finish your plea to me and say all the things that are in your heart, I shall let your future deeds in my service make judgment. I restore you."

As Raymond bows his head, his neck and face suffused with a flush, Booth, in a feeling of great euphoria, slaps folding money onto the gateleg table. "Here, take this . . . fare to Washington." He grabs Raymond's shoulder. "Await me there at Senator Jones's. I will inform him that you are to be not a servant but my aide-de-camp. Do you agree?"

Tears are forming in Raymond's eyes. Booth sees with satisfaction that the lad feels great compunction, and he is moved by his own mercy.

"Now, out the window with you, Raymond! The administration you are about to serve will be like no other in history!"

Booth has pulled open the drape; then he unlatches the window and opens it. Leaning forward into the warm midnight, Booth sees no one immediately below, and so he signals to the lad. Raymond grabs him in an embrace.

Briskly, Booth pats the lad on the shoulder, feels the warm tears against his neck.

"Now off with you!" he says again.

Still Raymond fails to release him.

Booth clears his throat. "Enough!" He is beginning to grow embarrassed.

"God be with ye, Mr. President!" Raymond calls. He climbs to the windowsill and leaps off into the street. A few bystanders ranged near the front steps see him, but no one follows as he disappears into the darkness.

The knocking at the door persists. Booth has located a gilt-edged Bible among the family knickknacks. He hears French call "Judge Brady is here, Mr. President, to administer the oath!"

"So is Judge Donahue!" cries Wheelhorse.

God be with me, Booth prays, turning open the key in the lock. I am about to belong to the ages.

"Enter, Your Honors!" he calls out.

PART FIVE
LIVING
the PART

THE EXECUTIVE MANSION

·Stanley-Brown stares.

Once the late lamented President Garfield's secretary—and loved by that man, he believes—he is at work in his shirt-sleeves, packing boxes in the executive office, when the new President's aide, the one called Raymond, sticks his head in and says, "You just go on with your work, Mr. Stanley-Brown. President Arthur will come by here when he's finished inspectin' the house."

Stanley-Brown can but stare. The wretched runt disappears before receiving a reply. But it is useless to expect protocol from a President who employs aides fit only to be court jesters.

As Stanley-Brown works, his spectacles high on his forehead, he faces down the same corridor where in sacred memory the seated line of office seekers used to wait for President Garfield on folding chairs. Others of their number waited on the more comfortable furniture in the Blue Room. Damn them all, the ones on the folding chairs, and the others too! Damn them!

He has been packing Garfield's souvenirs from the war—the large ceremonial sword with its bedraggled tassel, the epaulets, the framed record of his commissions. Some of the smaller mounted photographs, taken while on bivouac, lie in piles on Stanley-Brown's desk. Perhaps it is natural that he feels resentment toward President Arthur for having gained advantage from a madman's crime. But his hurt feels deeper than that, more as though some clever pretender had succeeded to power rather than a legitimate heir.

When the pretender and his aide are at last sighted approaching down the deserted corridor, both of them are wearing marten-trimmed topcoats, custom-tailored. Stanley-Brown wonders if he will be able to keep a civil tongue in his head.

"Please go on with your work, Stanley-Brown," the new President suggests, once they have shaken hands. "Mr. Gilpin wanted to show us around, but I preferred finding things by trial and error."

Almost at once, his gaze falls upon the mounted photographs of the field scenes from the war. "Interesting, most interesting," the President hums, as he picks them up one after the other from the desk. Soon he has seated himself on a straight chair, casually lifting his boot onto the rung of another chair while continuing to murmur comments.

"We are, of course, shipping the photographs back to Mentor, sir," Stanley-Brown says crisply after a while. They were not a prize of war.

"Well, you needn't hurry with the packing up around here," says the new President. "Mrs. Garfield must take whatever time she requires. I don't plan to move in for months."

That surprises Stanley-Brown. "I'm afraid you won't be able to put off the work that long."

"The work I'll do elsewhere," the President says, still absently studying photographs. "But the Mansion needs to be cleaned up and redecorated. It's like a sty, you know."

"I say—" Stanley-Brown mutters, offended.

"Look at the place," says the President. "The carpets are threadbare. The draperies are dark and musty—they must be filled with colonies of moths. And the goddamned spittoons! The Blue Room and the Red Room look like Bowery flophouses! You said so yourself once."

"But the men wishing to see the President must wait there," Stanley-Brown objects.

"They won't wait for me there, or anywhere else in my house." The President slaps the photographs back onto the desk. "Do you think distinguished members of the Cabinet should have to wait for bums and idlers before they can take their turn to use the lavatory?"

Stanley-Brown grunts, glancing at the young aide, among the first to be redecorated for the new regime. Perhaps the nation would soon have a Cabinet member named Raymond.

"No reflection," the President goes on. Quite the contrary; Garfield and his predecessors were the unfortunate victims. "But changes must be made." He gets to his feet, strangely supple as he moves back and forth. "I am in no hurry, we need a period of mourning. But then we have to have new things. New furnishings. New ideas."

Stanley-Brown flexes an elastic sleeve garter with his spread fingers. "As for the furnishings, you will find some handsome articles from previous administrations stored in the Mansion basement."

A restrained grimace crosses the President's features. "Rather looks like the prop room of an old theater down there, you know." He has seen it and given orders that the whole rumpus be sold at auction.

"But we'll let you know particulars about that, won't we, Raymond?"

Stanley-Brown has withheld an audible gasp to hear of the auctioning of the heirlooms of the forefathers. Is Abigail Adams's pewter mug to be knocked down to some Italian barber for display among bottles of tonic water and jars of moustache wax?

With Raymond presently dismissed in order to call up the carriage, the President sees fit to begin snooping in a file of letters. "I fear that is not official correspondence, sir," Stanley-Brown protests. "Merely personal."

Naturally, the President goes on reading. When he finally looks up, his eyes focus on a broken spot in the ceiling plaster. "Another idea, Stanley-Brown," he says. "Has thought ever been given to installing a large screen just inside the north entrance? It would afford privacy when we are passing down the main hall."

"Such as a wooden partition, sir?"

"Hardly that," says the President. "I was thinking of something in stained glass. Wooden partitions are for public toilets in railroad stations."

Stanley-Brown clamps his jaws. To talk of a wish for privacy while rooting around in a dead man's personal letters is nerve unmatched. Ohio in the White House might have been backward and old-fashioned, but never two-faced.

Soon President and aide depart, the aide mumbling deferences that only prove his gutter origins ("Pleased to have met ye again," and so forth). Stanley-Brown takes out his feelings later when Phillips, the new President's secretary, arrives to offer him help.

"Please, Phillips," he hisses, barely able to keep from weeping, "I must insist on being allowed the privilege of gathering up the last shards here before the new broom sweeps us all clean. *If* you don't mind?"

The humble Phillips naturally looks embarrassed and perplexed.

2

THE CENTURY CLUB
NEW YORK

Needham lifts the steel-pointed dart up near his right ear and from a stiff-legged stance spins it toward the target. "Bugger," he mutters. Just off the bull's-eye.

He looks around the crowded room. A horsefaced man, father of seven, Needham dresses sets in the theater for a living (his wife is wealthy), and he has produced some elaborate *tableaux vivants* for society balls. It is a busy day at the club, and rather noisy.

"Lot of these new chaps," he grumbles to the man he is playing with. "I don't even know them. I didn't vote them in, did you?"

The other man, who is not good at darts, shakes his head. He has been in Europe until recently and has not voted on anything for ages.

"Seems to me they act like schoolboys," Needham says. "Probably come out because Arthur's dropping by later."

"Arthur who?"

"Why, Chet Arthur, of course," Needham says. "Were y' in England so long that y' failed to notice that one of our number has become President of the country?"

Of course he has noticed, the other exclaims in disgust, for it is Edwin Booth playing at darts with Needham. "Don't you imagine every reporter south of Hudson Bay has grilled me about it?"

Needham clucks sympathetically, then adds that he likes Chet. "Chet cuts a fine figure, y' know. Always has. Remember when he used to do 'Cotter's Saturday Night' in the old days?"

Edwin Booth scowls silently. As he lifts a dart for throwing, his hand trembles. Not, Needham trusts, from recollections of Chet reciting Robert Burns. No, the poor chap is on the wagon, and his wife remains ill. Ill mentally, they say. And yet his show goes on each night, no matter what effort and strain it costs.

"Why isn't Arthur in Washington if he's the President?" Edwin Booth asks.

"Oh, you know Chet," Needham chuckles. "Prob'ly needs to visit his tailor. . . . Some say he's also seeing Conkling; others say no, that Conkling is *de trop*, so Wall Street must be the attraction."

"Oh, spare me!" cries Edwin Booth. "Let politics stop for me at the War of the Roses!"

Indeed, when the game is over, Edwin sends the boy for his hat and cane. "I think we should make ourselves scarce," he says to Needham, "before some invading reporter presses me into face-to-face confrontation with Arthur."

But bad luck intervenes for Edwin Booth. As he and Needham are slipping down the backstairs on their way to dinner at the Astor, an empty-headed dandy, coming up the stairs, buttonholes poor Edwin with profuse compliments on his performance as Richard. Nothing will do but that Mr. Booth *must* take on Hamlet next. Oh, he has already done Hamlet? Indeed? What a show that must have been. The fencing alone must have been worth the price of admission.

While Edwin Booth's admirer detains him on the stairs, the President, with three others, mounts the same staircase from the bottom, it having become the fashion since the assassination of Garfield for the chief executive to use back entrances when possible.

As the President reaches Edwin Booth and the other two men blocking the stairs, he stops dead as though the encounter particularly startles him.

Needham does his best. "Mr. President," he says in a voice that he hopes is unconstrained, "you remember Mr. Edwin Booth."

The President is grasping the railing to steady himself. "Ah, yes," he says in a strangely artificial tone. "Back from England, I see." Needham watches Edwin Booth's eyes narrow incredulously as he stares into the President's face while the President continues: "You must bring your Richard to Washington some time, Mr. Booth!"

The color begins draining from Edwin Booth's cheeks. Needham watches him in alarm as the President says a few more words: "Of course we are in mourning during this—"

Disconcerted, the President stops. Edwin Booth's knees have seemed to grow weak as he puts his hand to his head, tipping back his hat. His cane falls from his hand and goes bouncing down the stairway.

The President seems least taken by surprise at Edwin Booth's fainting spell. Or at any rate he is the one who catches the actor and steadies him, helped out by a youthful aide of small stature. One of the President's other attendants goes running after the cane, and Needham takes hold of Edwin's hat. Edwin meanwhile bends over the railing to restore the blood to his head. Presently, while all watch anxiously, he starts breathing with regularity and composing himself.

"Shall we return upstairs so that you may lie down?" Needham asks him.

"I should advise it, Mr. Booth," echoes the President.

Members of the club who have been watching from above now begin descending to see what is going on, and Edwin Booth whispers harshly to Needham, "Get me out of here."

He is helped down the stairs. The President, remaining where he stands, is reassured—Needham hears the members whispering—that Mr. Booth was "sometimes like that." All actors were high-strung.

The President's words penetrate to the foot of the stairs.

"But such a fine actor!" the President says resonantly. "One of the two greatest actors in the world today."

As Needham helps Booth into the carriage, he hopes Edwin has not heard the last remark. Was the President referring to the rivalry with Irving? But how tedious to recall it at such a moment!

"Shall I tell the driver the Astor still?" Needham asks.

Edwin Booth shakes his head. "Home." He stares straight ahead. "Tell him home—where demons are bred!"

"Edwin," Needham cries, "you must tell me what has brought this all about!"

"Unpack my heart? No." The eyes look haunted, although the great profile is etched as sharply as that of a savage chieftain. "Deeds, not words, are needed," says Edwin Booth.

Try as he will, Needham can get nothing more from him. As he sends the carriage off, he hopes the scene played was mere theater, for the passion itself is as puzzling to him as the first act of *Richelieu*.

3

IN THE PRESIDENT'S CARRIAGE

An hour later a brougham bearing Booth the Younger leaves the Century Club bound for his residence on Lexington Avenue. The brandy and conversation—with two members of the Stock Exchange board—having gone down well enough, he is thinking seriously of the nature of the Presidency. Seeing Edwin again has tempted him to draw comparisons with the theater. He expatiates to the only other occupant of the carriage, his youthful aide.

"Ambience is always crucial, Raymond," he declares, gesturing with a finger. "When the curtain rises—as it were—everything must look well. Elevated. Refined. Moral idealism is to be expressed by means of design. Before the 'argument' can ensue—that is to say, the inevitable struggle—representations of the ideal must suffuse the audience's consciousness. Otherwise all struggles are purely creatural."

While Booth talks, he begins drawing a rough sketch on a pad of paper he has picked up at the club. Even though the carriage jounces at moments on the paving stones, he is able to limn a geometric pattern that once served as the backdrop for an avant-garde production of *Phèdre,* which he saw with Nell in Paris. Paradoxically, it was a gesture of his brother Edwin's on the stairs of the club that reminded him of a similar gesture from the leading actor in *Phèdre.* The striking decor of that production has come to his mind as the perfect motif for the screen he is intending to order for the north entrance hall of the Executive Mansion.

"This is what I have in mind, Raymond, for the entrance hall screen." He hands his sketch to the lad. "When you go to Tiffany's for me tomorrow, tell them to commune with Aristotle and Euclid. I do not want to see the likenesses of previous chief executives on my screen."

To have yet another image of Lincoln in his living quarters, Booth reflects, would be irony compounded.

Raymond stares at the sketch with such innocent puzzlement that Booth laughs. "Is't not brave to be a President, Raymond?"

"This part looks like the Rebel flag to me," Raymond says, scratching his head.

Booth whistles in surprise. "So it does!" he cries. "We'll have to keep that in the motif for certain!"

By and by, he has plans to design a presidential flag for the country. Something more representational will do for that, he believes. He loves the rampant dragons on European coats of arms and would like to have an eagle on the flag for his high office.

Apathetically, Raymond has torn the sketch for the screen design off the pad and solemnly installs it, folded, in his inside coat pocket. Booth feels disappointed that Raymond does not look happier. For the first time in his life Raymond is wearing imported tweed and shoes of the finest cordovan, and carrying a cane and hat that are as fine as any sported in the clubs.

But Booth can guess what the problem is. Although the carriage is even now drawing onto Lexington Avenue, Raymond has been forbidden to visit the lady he loves.

"Ah, but Raymond," Booth sighs, "she is only ten years old."

"She is virtuous, pure, calming in spirit," Raymond says, "capable of gaiety, profound in faith, incor—incorruptibly feminine. The men of the Round Table had such ladies even though others thought the ladies too young, or not remarkable."

Booth is astounded.

"Also, she will soon be eleven," Raymond adds. "And eventually older."

"You are certain this is love?" Booth asks.

"As certain as you are of the love of your own lady!"

Booth contemplates his own love. Since the night of his accession, when she wore her "camellias" dress, she has refused to see him. From her point of view, she has once more felt herself to have been spurned. He can see that. He is sensitive to how she feels about the affronts he appears to commit.

But it is no less love. Love is a thicket of difficulties. Lovers are forever being parted. Faith must transcend, transcend even the grave, as he and Nell have often said. Their love has transcended both their deaths, and given such a miracle, how could she, or he, ever betray it? Alas, even a love beyond the grave has seemed to require long separations—briefly interrupted by bliss—but that is what helped make it love.

Moved by his thoughts, Booth declares, "Raymond, as you have tried to help me with my lady, I shall help you with yours if I can."

At this, Raymond reddens. "Would ye give her a present from me?" he asks with painful intensity. "I—I cannot, as you did, give cut gems."

"I should think not. What is it?"

It takes Raymond five anguished blocks down Lexington before he reaches into his vest pocket and hands Booth a small box. Half uneasily, Booth opens it.

The box contains a mother-of-pearl locket of rather large size for a child. Inside, pressed against one of the surfaces, is a miniature orange sachet, perceptibly fragrant. On the other half is an oval photograph of Raymond—three-quarters view—dressed up in his new clothes. He must have visited the studio as soon as the tailor fitted him.

"Yes, indeed," Booth says, more or less approving.

"Put that in her hands," Raymond implores, "and I will be your slave for life."

Booth clears his throat in embarrassment. But when they reach the house he keeps his promise. With Alan off at school and "Auntie Lew" pointedly absent, Booth locates Nellie in the back parlor and spirits her away from her governess on the pretext of taking her for a short walk. He then delivers her to Raymond, still in the carriage.

"Do not abuse the privilege," Booth says to them. "A half hour ride, no more."

Nellie wears a look so distant and remote in its fatalism that Booth cannot be sure whether she relishes the opportunity to deal with Raymond's urgencies yet another time or not. He thinks that he is growing uncomfortable to have so inscrutable a child.

"I swear! I swear!" Raymond is blustering, with his eyes alight. "I swear no more than half an hour."

Booth waves them off, fanning himself with his high beaver hat.

Among the calling cards Booth finds on the silver tray in the vestibule is one from Robert Dun. He turns it over to read a written message on the back: "Sorry I missed you. Truly I am convinced I cannot accept the Treasury portfolio, thank you. I am not a politician. Robert."

"Flippant," Booth says aloud. Of course he may himself have been too flippant when he mentioned the job to Dun. A President must ride as though much weight is in the saddle. Such is the tradition, and for his own sake Booth must continue to grope for more gravity of manner.

Yet how is it possible when his mind is just now teeming with ideas and insights? The Fredericksburg File flashes in his brain, and his thoughts begin to focus on a different member of the Cabinet—the Secretary of War, Robert Lincoln. Like the other members of Garfield's Cabinet, Lincoln yesterday submitted a resignation from his post.

Booth cannot understand why he is suddenly trying to recall how Robert Lincoln looked as a boy. Somehow, the locket portrait of Raymond, which he just viewed in the carriage, has reminded him—perhaps because of its sepia tint—of a studio photograph from the Stanton archives colored in the same way. This photograph, which Booth presently locates in one of the boxes he keeps, shows three unidentified youths seated side by side against a painted backdrop. The young man on the left Booth knows to be the late Edwin Stanton, Junior.

But the youth in the middle, Booth now realizes, is probably Robert Lincoln, then sprouting a moustache on a face since obscured by a full beard. If it is indeed Lincoln, mightn't the presence together of the two scions imply a friendship that would have made possible confidential discussion between them about the Fredericksburg File after the elder Stanton died? Eventually, could not Lincoln himself have become heir to the file?

To try to confirm that the youth in the photo is who he thinks it is, Booth searches out another document that he's kept: an illustrated article about young Robert's "brush with death" on a railroad platform in New Jersey in 1861. In that year Robert, traveling with his father just before the first inauguration, lost his footing on the platform next to a moving train, and but for the quick intervention of none other than Edwin Booth, who was preparing to board with members of his theater company, might have been crushed beneath the wheels.

How the illustrated papers loved the divine irony of that coincidence in the years after the assassination! Wilkes has saved a clipping of one of the accounts of the episode in his "Booth Vindication Folder," and soon finds it.

There can be no doubt. Despite retouched graphics on yellowing paper, the pie-faced likeness of Robert Lincoln in the newspaper feature is the same countenance that appears next to that of Edwin Stanton, Junior, in the studio photograph. A head so round, a face so bland that it defies one to remember it. And yet how destiny would love it if Stanton's son bequeathed the file to Lincoln's son, and thus caused him to be the final arbiter of its disposition!

Thurlow Weed, of course, pretends to think that the file is no longer important.

"The file!" Weed jeered at him only yesterday. "Is that why you went to all this trouble, becomin' the twenty-first President of the United States, just to go on digging up the past, like a dog?"

"The file is my integrity," Booth says, face to face with the portrait of the archbishop. "Still, I will not use it to bring you grief. I will be judicious."

"Oh, thank you," Weed says with sarcasm.

The two of them are sitting in the near darkness of Weed's library. Weed is looking feeble again. Booth sits at the kneehole desk, dipping a steel pen in the inkwell. "I am incomplete without the file. I have a duty to myself as well as to the state."

In a hoarse voice, Weed says, "But why should I bother recommending men for your Cabinet if all that is in your head is—"

"I said you had nothing to fear from the file," Booth reminds him. He has come to Weed for names. "Would Frelinghuysen be good? And if so, where? I am serious. I shall have a sound administration, I promise you that."

"And what do you want to accomplish in this sound administration?"

For the first time, Booth realizes that the question is no longer an idle one. Can he rise to the occasion? Can he say that he wants to convey his sense of rectitude? "I expect to help the South," he says.

"All right."

"I don't want ambitious men," Booth goes on. He is glad to be off the idea of restoring slavery, restoring the Confederacy. That would take ambitious men.

"Think about Frelinghuysen for State," Weed suggests. Since the man has been out of things for so long—first, in Morocco, then with the gout—he should be flattered to be asked.

"I don't want interfering people," Booth says.

"If Frelinghuysen won't do for State, think about him for War."

Mostly he wants old men, Booth realizes.

To a knock on the door of his office, Booth calls out, "One minute, please," and hastily puts away the evidence he has been examining. He is expecting to be called upon by a representative of Frelinghuysen, to whom he will offer State. Robert Lincoln he is determined to keep on in War.

"Come in," he calls.

Raymond's voice pipes up from beyond the door.

"It's only us, sir. Me and Nellie."

"Well, what do you want?"

Booth opens the door to see them standing there, Nellie with one of her more insouciant expressions, looking to have grown another couple of inches since noon.

"Here she is," Raymond says.

"Does a doctor have to examine me again, like the other time?" Nellie asks abruptly.

Raymond chokes in alarm, sputters, puts his hand to his forehead. "I swear—" he stammers.

Nellie says, "The doctors thought last time he might have a contagion."

Booth waves his hand as though at insects and shuts them out.

4

THE EXECUTIVE MANSION

"Would you mind coming as far as the greenhouse with me, Mr. Lincoln?" Booth asks in a honeyed voice. "As a former resident in these walls, your suggestions can be more valuable than anyone else's I can think of."

Mr. Lincoln says, "My brothers used to play shooting games in the greenhouse. No longer a fitting use, I'm afraid."

Booth smiles and leads the way. While Lincoln is a bit tense, he seems pleased to have been invited to give on-site advice on the redecoration of the White House. Also, he has creditable judgment about wainscoting and wallpaper, which is more than Booth can say for the Union Pacific's Senator Jones, the only other person to have made the tour of inspection. Given the fact that Lincoln stood with the 306 for Grant right to the end, one might have supposed that he had no imagination at all.

As they approach the humid environs of the greenhouse, Booth begins to venture into a topic of more testing importance.

"You know, I did a very embarrassing thing while I was in New York," he says.

"And what was that, Mr. President?" Lincoln strokes his beard. Perhaps the beard is to make him look more like his father, who was as tall and gaunt as the son is roundheaded and stocky.

"Well, I hesitate to tell you this . . . but I ran into Edwin Booth, a fellow member of the Century Club, and I said to him I hoped he would consider appearing in Washington again after all these years."

"You were quite right. I have been aware that he has stayed away since the assassination." Robert Lincoln's eyes blink several times. "You never met my father, did you?"

"Not formally," the President replies.

"He was a great lover of the theater. Moreover, he admired Edwin Booth, who you may know saved me from a serious accident on a railroad platform in—in Jersey City, I believe it was."

"Indeed?"

As they enter the conservatory, Booth identifies some of the plantings there, and discourses on the wildflowers of Maryland and

Virginia, about which he has an astonishing amount of information for a New Yorker.

"You know, Mr. Lincoln," he says at last, "you must see how impossible it would be for me to accept your resignation from the Cabinet. Your long experience in this city, your—uh—manifest qualifications. Why, your very name is synonymous with War!"

"You are kind, Mr. President," Robert Lincoln says.

"We know the great days of the party were the days of Lincoln. Who does not know that?" Booth allows a pregnant pause and risks going into the register he used on stage. "Not only are *you* wanted by us, but let me say your father's great friend Judge Davis is also wanted as a friend of the administration."

The last remark is designed to pique Lincoln's interest, inasmuch as Davis—the fattest man in politics—has been a second father to Robert Lincoln, and as an independent has been a natural choice for the role of permanent presiding officer of the Senate. Ah, the weary days that Booth spent presiding over that stalled engine, the Senate. "We have decided to throw our support to Senator Davis for pro tem," he says, "and thus he will be next in line for the Presidency should anything befall the present occupant. That is, myself."

Booth chuckles airily, watching the impassive Lincoln.

"You will forgive me," he concludes, "but to have a Davis without a Lincoln would be like a—like a—like a cart without a horse."

"It is true," Robert Lincoln muses, "that my wife and I have regretted having to return to Illinois when we were scarcely settled in Washington, but our inconvenience is nothing compared to the tragedy of—"

"Since you—ahem—mention 'tragedy,' Mr. Lincoln," Booth cannot resist saying, "my further endeavor will be to reopen the inquiry into the murder of your father. We have seen that the nation is no longer going to consent to having its leaders done away with, and not to get to the bottom of it."

"An inquiry?" Robert Lincoln narrows his eyes and looks considerably nonplussed.

"Dear me, dear me, I do not mean to upset you," Booth says, "but it has sometimes been—uh—said that the attack on your father was directly condoned by northern business and political leaders who sponsored the endeavors of—of damned southern infiltrators, who . . . This is grievous, is it not? I go too rapidly to the heart of the matter for you."

Robert Lincoln opens his mouth and then closes it. "But, Mr.

President," he finally says, "we still have the Guiteau trial immediately before us. How can we—"

"Yes, yes, that is true." Quickly Booth turns away, then back again, looking at Lincoln with a somewhat injured air. He takes several deep breaths. "I perceive you think me yet another vile exploiter of your father's murder. Not so. Believe me when I say I should not let one word of my investigation reach the public until I had collected every scintilla of evidence."

Booth now withdraws some distance away, and he contemplates the autumn blossoms on their loamy beds with a mournful air. He holds his cane perpendicular to the cinder path—an upright statesman. Quite a distance away, well out of earshot, two colored gardeners are working over rows of struggling new shoots.

Robert Lincoln says, "Of course, I did not mean to offend you, Mr. President. But it is naturally a painful subject for me and mine, particularly since you do not speak of specific new evidence—"

"Mr. Lincoln, have you ever heard of the Fredericksburg File?"

Booth turns, full-face, and believes he detects Robert Lincoln suddenly casting his eyes toward the ground.

"Ah, I see you have heard of it," Booth continues. Secretly his heart lifts. He senses he has struck gold.

Lincoln speaks haltingly. "Such a file—has been rumored for years."

"Containing information of the sort I describe?"

"Mr. President," says Robert Lincoln, raising his eyes, "why should you wish to expose such information to the public—if it exists?"

"Perhaps I will not do it, no, no," Booth says. "But do you know where the file is?"

A gamut of emotions seems to pass over Robert Lincoln's features. For an instant Booth believes that Lincoln is going to speak frankly of what he knows, but in the next moment he draws out his pocket watch, and with trembling hand, studies the dial.

"I believe you are sincere, Mr. President," he says at last, but I confess that right now I am too shaken to discuss the matter further."

Booth scowls in frustration. As President, can he not compel Lincoln to answer him? But no; he must temporize.

"I am not an impetuous man," he says at last. "I move like a turtle. We will talk about it another time."

As they proceed down the cinder path, the two gardeners have begun to give ground eagerly and to duck their heads in nervous deference.

"Good—good—good aftahnoon, Mistuh President," the younger one stutters.

"God bless you, Massa Lincoln!" exclaims the other.

Lincoln stares vacantly.

Later, as Booth is handing his troubled guest into his carriage, he says, with great warmth, "You are loved here, Bob. By one and all. Perhaps we are destined to help each other, you and I, as only true friends can."

But he senses that Lincoln does not care for him.

By the date of the first formal reception at the redecorated White House, Booth has had to assign Raymond the job of getting acquainted with the staff at Lincoln's residence in Washington. Lincoln himself has not referred to the file again. While he has withdrawn his resignation from the Cabinet, he appears as indifferent to bringing his father's murderers to justice as the most venal of the moneychangers. Booth wonders if a shameless burglary of the Lincoln residence will be necessary, assuming that Raymond can get accurate information as to where the file might be kept.

The receiving line at the reception, meanwhile, tests his flesh. Attired in impeccable tuxedo, he counts one hundred fifty hands shaken even before the Congressmen and their wives are begun. To help fortify himself, he makes a silent bet on each woman's bust measurement just before she comes around the corner on her husband's arm.

When he is far off—as he has just been with Mrs. Green of Indiana —he compels himself to pay the forfeit of spending an extra minute or so with the couple before he passes them on to Mrs. McElroy—a sister of Chester Arthur's—who has come down from Albany, or wherever it is she normally resides, in order to help out as the White House hostess during the social season.

"May I present Mrs. McElroy?" Booth will say to a couple such as the Greens, and then his "sister" will explain how Mr. McElroy is doing back in Albany under the care of their two lovely daughters. Not that Mrs. McElroy is without additional accomplishments. Every woman in Washington appears to know that she attended that most brilliant of finishing schools—Emma Willard's Academy in Troy, New York—*ergo propter hoc* became hostess at the White House.

Gracious for a Yankee, she responds with heartiness to the guests' admiration of his new decor for the Executive Mansion. Clearly, he has a triumph. Pale olive shades, and squares of gold leaf, dominate the walls of the main lobby, where the reception line winds in from the cold outdoors. The ceiling is decorated in gold and silver, and "USA" is interwoven throughout the motif in different colors. A brass frieze done in India, and selected by Booth, has won quick acclaim from the guests, while a full-color sketch of the proposed presidential flag is prominently displayed to the awe of the diplomatic officers, who savor the heraldry.

"Congressman Wood and Mrs. Wood, also of Indiana," says the protocol officer.

The President smiles. He has whispered "Thirty-six" to himself before her entrance and is not far wrong. Mrs. Wood is, in fact, such a breath of fresh air that he is tempted to converse about Indiana with her even though he has no forfeit to pay. Many of the women offer him most disarming looks. And why should they not, given the lack of a wife to monitor him?

Following Mrs. Wood with his eyes as she begins mingling, he sees that, of all people, Mr. Sousa is the one lucky enough to engage her in discourse. Such a stiff man. He conducted stiff, and the Marine Band played stiff under his direction. But people seemed to like it all the more; perhaps it was a quality Booth should strive for in himself.

In passing, he wonders how his dear Nell would bear up at a reception such as this one. Alas, not well. The realization troubles him. In spite of her fine upbringing, she was never interested in showing off her social graces. His heart is sickened to have learned—through Alan —of her most recent aberration in New York. She is taking instruction in the Roman Catholic faith. In disguise she goes forth, not as his lady of the camellias, but as humble penitent to visit a blind priest in the Bowery. So says Alan.

If only the damned boy were the one to have turned to religion, Booth's worries might be fewer. Since the reopening of the White House, not a weekend has passed without Alan's having arrived with innumberable chums from Princeton. One or more of them has always wound up drunk in the wine cellar, no matter that the administration was still in mourning for Garfield.

The protocol chief is saying, "Mr. President, may I present the Honorable Mr. William Chandler and Mrs. Chandler?"

Booth turns to Chandler, whose dryness he remembers from the time when Chandler was running the Blaine campaign in Chicago. A rumpled New Englander, wearing pince-nez, he shakes hands with a detached air.

Mrs. Chandler's gaze, on the other hand, is forthright. Booth swallows. A warm-featured blonde, she seems to hesitate as her amazed eyes probe his own. Good Lord, Lucy Hale—she to whom he was "betrothed" in '65—Senator Hale's daughter!

In hopes that his voice will not provide a clue to trigger her memory, he refrains for a moment from speaking. Still, when Mrs. McElroy takes the hand of the gentleman, he is forced to murmur, "May I present Mr. and Mrs. Chandler of—"

At this moment Lucy Hale Chandler still has her own hand in Booth's, and his voice, plus the touch of his flesh, seem to seal it for her. One more quick look into his eyes. And plainly, she knows.

Sighing, she turns white, and falls in a dead faint.

Seldom—maybe never—has Booth seen so honest a swoon. He reaches out his arms, trying to cradle her.

"Why, the poor dear!" cries Mrs. McElroy while two footmen and a member of the Marine Band rush to the scene.

As they bear Lucy off to one of the adjoining rooms—followed by the imperturbable Chandler—Booth removes a kerchief from his breast pocket and begins wiping his forehead.

5

THE EXECUTIVE MANSION

His senses quickened by the note he receives from Lucy the following morning, he schedules the Chandlers for a private audience right after lunch. While her handwriting is nearly illegible, he savors certain phrases: ". . . quite embarrassed, Mr. President, by what happened. . . . You resembled someone I once knew . . . someone I perhaps felt ill-treated by. . . . My husband understands *perfectly*."

Given the provocativeness of all this, he is less attentive to Raymond's report on the Lincoln residence than he otherwise would have been. They lunch together—President and aide—in the private dining room, one of Booth's favorites in the redecorated Mansion. Pomegranate plush is the dominant fabric, and he recalls his pleasure at the effectiveness of the crimson glass that he has had installed around the fireplace. Haddock Delmonico and asparagus hollandaise are served them, the recipe for the former having been given to Bridget by Booth some time before.

"Lincoln, he pens up his police dog in his side yard," Raymond relates. "The dog, he barks all the time. I seen one servant. The Lincolns theirselves was at your reception." Neatly attired in suit and cravat, Raymond sips on white wine, a glass of which has been poured for him. His fingers poke through a dish of blanched almonds.

"Yes, yes," Booth says. "Well, you must befriend the servant, have drinks with him. Maybe you can find out where the Lincolns keep their valuables." To avoid admitting to Raymond that a President may be contemplating an ordinary burglary, he says, "Who knows but that a presidential writ of *certiorari* may not be the procedure to take if—uhh—we can but find out where the file is located?"

Abruptly pushing his food aside, Booth excuses himself and retires to the privacy of his quarters. How can he concentrate on the file until the Chandlers are quite squared away? Restlessly, he paces his bedchamber. As he sinks onto the bed, he ruminates on Chandler's political experience. Have not the newspapers been saying that the new President needs a political "power base"?

By the time the Chandlers are announced, Booth has dropped off to sleep, then awakened, feeling refreshed and more presidential. Truly, his trouble is dissatisfaction with his Cabinet choices: with the exception of Lincoln, dotards all. Walking toward the Red Room, he carries with him the sheaf of papers that he can pretend to read from while passing through the halls. Salesmen and high-class beggars continue to infiltrate the Mansion, and he feigns trances in order to elude them.

"I do hope we haven't drawn you away from your lunch, Mr. President," Lucy says, as he greets them. Her china-blue eyes easily meet his. A faint pulse seems to throb in her graceful neck.

"Not at all," he says calmly. "I am glad to see you looking so well." In truth, she has dressed like a *Harper's Bazaar* model in feathered bonnet, close-fitting jacket, and faille skirt. As a girl, she did not give a fig for clothes.

"Good aftanoon, Mr. President," says Chandler, adjusting his pince-nez nervously.

"Good afternoon, Bill," says Booth, shaking hands. "May I call you Bill?"

As the flesh is touched, Chandler blushes deep red from the base of his neck to the top of his forehead. Perhaps then he does know all. Most women would not be so frank with their husbands. But then most women—knowing what this one knew at the time—would not have given Booth the stolen passes for the second inauguration. Had he shot Lincoln then, she would have been in some trouble.

"Please sit down," he says to them, determined to get quickly to the point.

"Bill, a stroke of luck it was, all considered. I've been looking for somebody for the Navy Department. By God, when this happened with Mrs. Chandler yesterday, once I realized she was going to be all right . . . not long after, I began thinking, what better man for Navy than you." Hunt was as easy to move out as anybody in the Cabinet, especially since there were embassies open in Europe.

"Goodness, Mr. President," Lucy interrupts. "I believe we came to make our sincerest apologies to you. Perhaps if you are going to get into—well, I am nearly embarrassed—into weighty—"

"Navy?" Chandler suddenly asks with a note of doubt. "Navy?"

"Ah, all New Englanders are seafarers in their souls!" Booth proclaims.

Brushing what might be chalk dust from his coat, Chandler now recalls the President's noble family connections with the Navy, and when Booth looks puzzled, Lucy remarks at once, "Your wife, Mr. President . . . your late wife came from a naval family . . . did she not?"

"Ah, yes. Commander Herndon," Booth says, getting to his feet. He forgot about Commander Herndon. Well, what difference did it make? He shoots a mesmerizing look at Lucy, the kind that worked when she met him after matinees and they walked discreetly along the Boston Common to his hotel. Her figure has not altered much in the intervening years.

"The Herndons!" Booth echoes, perceiving now his true direction. "The Herndons, and people like them, are the flower of the South, are they not?" With Chandler reacting slowly, Booth says, "All New Englanders have feelings about the South. As my adviser, you share, I hope, my progressive feelings about the South."

The temptress fiddles with her gloves. "Oh, the South," she murmurs, almost inaudibly.

"I believe," Chandler says staunchly, "that the South should not be consigned in perpetuity to the Democratic party."

"Bravo," says Booth.

"I believe," Chandler goes on, "that *all* the people of the South need to be considered, not just the Bourbon interests."

"Yes, all the people of the South," Booth affirms. He thinks of the

Herndons in Fredericksburg, he thinks of all the people in the audiences in Richmond who applauded him on stage, in Charleston, in Atlanta. . . .

"That is encouraging to hear," Chandler says. Both men's eyes follow Lucy to where she has moved near the window overlooking the south lawn. The winter sunshine streams in over her shoulder.

Suddenly she turns and laughs. "My husband is most progressive," she says.

"As am I," Booth hears himself saying. He is not sure what a "progressive" is, but he believes that Chandler has defected from Blaine on that score. Perhaps Chandler would want to back the Virginia Readjusters, some of them tobacco-chewers like that half-pint Mahone. But if the President is going to take political advice from the man, then he needs to have some faith in him, does he not?

By the time the Chandlers are ready to leave, the conversation has drifted to the "beautiful, magnificent" restoration the new administration has achieved. Lucy claims herself to be enchanted by it.

"The midwestern taste is impenetrable," she declares of the old regime. "Truly, it is no taste at all."

Since Chandler has gone ahead to the lower entrance to see if the stablemen have come back with the horses (one of them having dropped a shoe), Lucy says to Booth, "You must come to our home for dinner next Saturday evening, Mr. President. Alas, we entertain simply. No guests other than yourself."

"Can you bear so much of me?" Booth asks.

"Since you are a man of honor," Lucy says. "The gentleman you remind me of also valued honor more than love."

"Were we talking of love?"

"Goodness, no," Lucy says. He thinks there is a tremor in her voice. Perhaps not.

He kisses her hand in the Continental way; she gives him one more look before allowing him to lead her out to her husband.

6

The Executive Mansion
Washington
December 18

My dearest Nell,

With what heartfelt emotion I think of you during this Christmas season! The next time I get up to New York I will call again and this time I hope

✤   ✤   ✤

The Executive Mansion
Washington
December 18

Dearest Nell,

Is there a chance that you could come down for a visit during the holiday season? I realize, of course, that you are taking instruction in the Roman Catholic faith. But in this happy season is it not well to put differences aside for the sake of the family? Alan I am told is already visiting you in New York but

✤   ✤   ✤

Executive Mansion
Washington
December 18

My dearest,

Another Christmas apart! Alan has perhaps reported that I will be up in New York again as soon as I can make it, and perhaps at that time we can work out our remaining differences. I realize

✤   ✤   ✤

Executive Mansion
Washington
December 18

My dearest,

It is the Christmas season, and I long for my Nell—my lover, my friend, my political adviser. If you only could be here with me in this residence to help me during my time of need. While you could not preside at the social functions which seem to take up more and more of my time (without my willing it), you could certainly do so many other things. Alan, for example, is almost beyond control, and, if you were here, you might

✤ ✤ ✤

Executive Mansion
Washington
December 18

Dearest,

My love, ever greening, to you and to Nellie in the holy season ahead.

Ever yours,
W.

✤ ✤ ✤

Executive Mansion
Washington
December 18

Dr. Brodie Herndon, Sr.
Fredericksburg, Virginia

Dear Brodie,

Is there any chance you would accept a political appointment in the administration? I need somebody whose advice I can trust. What, for example, does the term "progressive" mean to you in terms of policy toward the South? Good? Bad? You would be my right-hand man.

If you can't consider it, I understand,

Best wishes for the holiday season,
"Captain B."

7

Christmas comes and goes.

In the weeks that follow, Booth suddenly finds himself teetering on the brink of debauchery. After but three Cabinet meetings and a treaty signing he takes to drink, he gorges himself with food, he makes fatuous overtures to Lucy Chandler, who teases worse than a plantation belle when all she really wants is to give parties for the President.

Tardily, he realizes how low he has sunk when one evening well into the social season, as he is being squeezed into his dinner clothes by his new colored valet, Raymond comes to his dressing room, bearing news.

"You can go for your writ o' search-a-rory," the lad says pertly to him. They have not conversed much lately.

"What? What are you talking about?" he wheezes. The valet is cinching a corset that Booth wears next to his skin. Without it he would be as gross as the maharajah of Jaipur.

"I found out where Lincoln's safe is—ye know—for 'the writ.' "

"I can't bother with that now," he finds himself saying.

The sapping of his finer nature he can date from the night of the private dinner between himself and the Chandlers at their home on I Street. Here he has learned that Lucy's ambition in life is not for "simple entertainments" at all, but for creating occasions so grandiose in their design and execution that they might be talked about even as far away as Fifth Avenue in Manhattan. As a "Cabinet wife," Lucy hopes to use the White House itself as her venue. Nor has Mrs. Mc-Elroy, to Booth's surprise, any objection. The two Yankee ladies will work in happy tandem, advancing the social reputation of the Northeast.

At first, all of it is no harder for him than getting ready for a performance in the theater every night. Since Lucy wishes to observe the proprieties of the mourning for President Garfield, she begins by scheduling musicales, usually of a religious nature. Soon there are sopranos too, but not the sort that will offend dedicated mourners, if there be any.

Put to the test, the capital responds as though Garfield died in the

Van Buren administration; Booth finds himself spending more and more time with tailors and protocol officers and social secretaries, who want him to initial his approval on their swatches and menus and guest lists. The parties themselves become as strenuous as *Hamlet* or *Lear*. The dinner in honor of General Grant lasts ten hours. Later, the Hanging Gardens of Babylon dinner stuffs him with twenty-one separate courses, including seventeen different wines. While his head spins, he watches an enormous revolving centerpiece with the largest floral display ever seen—carnations, roses, honeysuckle, and rare blossoms from "the nunplant."

Is it any wonder that the regimen makes him wanton? After being teased, then rebuffed, by Lucy in reception line and at table, when released he takes up, usually half-drunk, with any convenient woman present. The unmarried ones have to linger at his pleasure, not only because he is President, but because he is "eligible" as well ("May I venture a joke that is entirely fit for mixed company?"). Several times Secretary Frelinghuysen's vapid daughter puts up with him patiently until Mary McElroy brings an end to it since it is being whispered in the state dining room that he has proposed to the child.

His sensual nature is most stirred by a girl who appears under the personal imprimatur of Lucy Chandler. Dark-haired and an enchanting conversationalist, Miss Sackville-West, Booth learns, is the illegitimate daughter of the British ambassador, her mother having been a Spanish lady of so distinguished a family that she is accepted socially. He rather pursues her. The girl and her father have stayed very late, and while Chandler is talking to the old man, Booth shows the daughter some of the rooms where the guests do not usually go. Probably he says something to her that she thinks disrespectful. ("Do you never have a wicked impulse, my dear?") Given her background, she is sensitive to that kind of thing. He even apologizes for it, later to fall into bed too drunk to take off his clothes.

One afternoon, when he is most affected by headache (the appearance of Raymond in his dressing room having occurred the evening before), Booth keeps an appointment that is supposed to concern his "power base."

"A most successful reception last night," Chandler observes, having taken a seat.

Booth is at his desk. "Saturnalia," he mutters.

Chandler says, "The capital is not straitlaced. The capital enjoys good society."

Booth grunts. Was the President's function simply to oblige? He wonders often why there are not more bills for him to sign, or veto. Whenever one comes over from the Hill, he does his best to make a sound decision on it. But nobody in Washington seems to ask him for advice in advance, not even his Cabinet officers.

"They will come to you if they get into trouble," Chandler has reassured him. But lacking a "power base" (much like not being one of the Elect), he will lack automatic deference.

Chandler now says, "As far as the Conkling matter goes—"

"Oh, do forget it," Booth says, getting to his feet. He feels strangely impatient with Chandler today, anxious to get back to Raymond so as to discuss how they may proceed with the Fredericksburg File.

Taking off his pince-nez, Chandler repeats that little may have been lost, in power base terms, by having failed with their gesture to Conkling.

"Yes, yes," Booth sniffs. An appointment as associate justice of the Supreme Court was offered Roscoe, and—with the vestige of a sneer—Roscoe turned it down. So much for Roscoe. "As far as New York is concerned, remember I have Dun and Thurlow Weed there."

"Ho-hum," says Chandler.

Booth goes to the window. In the sunshine, the half-finished shaft of the Washington Monument is visible. "Why isn't the South my power base? If it isn't, why do we keep inviting that foul toad Mahone to the Mansion? He chews tobacco like a chimpanzee."

Chandler says that since Mahone is not a Republican or a Democrat, but rather a Readjuster, his power base is very small.

"Well, let's help him make it bigger," Booth urges. "And why haven't I made any inroads with the reform crowd? We are helping to sponsor a civil service bill, we are prosecuting that great rogue Dorsey—"

Chandler says, "I feel uncertain about the Dorsey matter."

"Tush," says Booth. It was one thing for Dorsey to steal votes in an honest cause (the party honored him for that), but quite another to knock down millions of dollars by reselling franchised mail route contracts at a thousand percent personal profit. "Why am I given no credit for moral fiber?"

Chandler looks circumspect, has little else to say. Indeed, the only further communication Booth receives from either of the Chandlers that day is a written note from Lucy reproaching him for his conduct toward Miss Sackville-West, the ambassador's daughter. Most gentlemen, she says, outgrow such innuendo when they reach an age of dignity.

Wet snow falls on Washington for the next four days. It is the time for the beginning of the Guiteau trial. For some reason Booth has overlooked the prosecution. It has seemed to him as though "Mr. Ghetto" would remain in the District of Columbia prison indefinitely, like a caged ferret living out his life.

But with the matter now unavoidably coming to a head, Booth feels he cannot move on the Fredericksburg File until later. One assassination at a time.

He tries to use the interval to refurbish his relationship with Raymond, to whom he realizes he has offered little guidance in recent weeks. Booth and Raymond take several lunches together, one on an afternoon—the coldest of the year—when all the fireplaces are blazing, the coal deliveries having failed throughout the District. Booth makes some sober suggestions about the developing course Raymond's attentions to Nellie might take in the years immediately ahead.

"At fifteen, she may be considered a woman," Booth tells Raymond; a girl of Nellie's build will surely be a woman at fifteen.

"Till then," Raymond says, "I place flowers before her portrait every day."

"Flowers at this time of year?" Booth asks, but is impressed. What a useful symbol of fidelity!

When Raymond supplies the florist's name, Booth promptly puts in a daily order of his own. To set fresh-cut flowers before his late wife's portrait is a better way to reaffirm his profound spiritual connection with Nell than anything else could be.

The Guiteau trial does not restore social restraint in the capital, as Booth has hoped. On the contrary, Washington finds that parties are a particular necessity during the court hearings. No topic becomes so fascinating as the legal question of the assassin's sanity. For historical precedent, it is noted that a young man who shot twice at President Andrew Jackson some years before (he missed both shots) was quickly judged insane. Those who take advanced views go so far as to suggest that perhaps anyone making an attempt on the life of a President is, prima facie, insane, an opinion that disturbs Booth.

Guiteau's own contribution to the argument appears daily in the newspapers. He turns out essays, plays, autobiography, or whatever seems to strike his fancy. Much of his writing seems "mad" to most people, although those with less advanced opinions think that he might be shamming it, or even that somebody else has written the material for him, perhaps a fully certified lunatic. The assassin adamantly regards himself as technically insane, and given his vast legal experience, demonstrated by the frequent use of Latin words (such as *replevin* and *mittimus*), he cannot see how he can be gainsaid.

Booth reads this all. He is insulted that the newspapers will print such drivel when not a one of them would publish the beautiful and incisive letter he wrote in '65 explaining his own motives. Yet he feels he must pick through the dross to make sure that the mills of Guiteau's brain do not grind out anything that will provide someone with a clue to a larger pattern. Nightly, very late, he sits beside the lighted gas jet in his bedroom, wearing his long quilted maroon robe, reading and reading.

Letters from Guiteau requesting a presidential pardon arrive now and then at the White House. Guiteau's crime—"altogether dispassionate"—was recommended, the assassin claims, not only by God, but also by such friends as "yourself, Mr. President Arthur" and "that slender young gentleman (I have misplace his name)" who was sent to meet Guiteau in the bar of the Hoffman House in New York. Seek that young gentleman, as well as others "too numerous to mention," and the parade of witnesses for Guiteau will be longer than those who marched at Garfield's funeral. "Insane," "insane," "insane," they will all testify. The mad are nearest to the gods.

But no witnesses are located. And in spite of all the ballyhoo, when the lawyers' summations are over and the judge's charge given, the jury is out only an hour and five minutes. They find Guiteau "guilty as indicted," and adequately sane for execution.

That night, to celebrate the verdict, a small party is given at Willard's Hotel by a Senator who was a special friend of President Garfield. As things go, the new President is invited to attend the affair.

Booth gets there around ten P.M., a normal hour for him, as host and guests are all aware. He is greeted expansively; most of the men there have been drinking for two or three hours, but they are good-natured and ready with orotund toasts to the prosecutors in the Guiteau case, to the judge, to anyone they can think of whom they feel well disposed toward. Booth feels tired and uneasy, surprising himself by the lack of facility with which he joins in.

"To Senator Dorsey," someone cries jovially, "who goes on trial next week for mail fraud!"

"To Dorsey, without whom some of us would not be here!"

"Sir?" Booth says with a piercing look. He puts down his glass. His own Justice Department is prosecuting Dorsey, who is a wanton profiteer. Booth is reminded that he cannot be one with these men. When he tried it some months ago at the Delmonico's party for this very same Dorsey, he saw what a dangerous and corrupting exercise it was.

"I cannot drink to that," he says with gnawing sobriety. A few minutes later he picks up his hat and leaves.

8

Executive Mansion
Washington, D.C.

My dear Mr. Lincoln,

I trust you may have been able to be with friends of the late President last night, as I was, in order to share the solace and celebration attendant on the conviction of his assassin. One of the things that makes life worth living is the satisfaction of seeing justice done. I hope you agree with me.

While Secretary Chandler and I will be away in Annapolis for the dedication of the Herndon memorial (the Commander was my late wife's father, as you know), when I return it would give me pleasure if you could attend a private luncheon here on the 12th. In this last effort on my part, I assure you we would move with the greatest deliberateness in assessing the guilt, or lack of it, of any man—be he high or low—involved in perpetrating your father's murder.

There is less that one can accomplish as President than I would have imagined before I attained this eminence. Let it be said that you

*and I stood for justice; there is no better way that I would like to be
remembered.*

*Faithfully yours,
Chester A. Arthur*

*The Hon. Robert T. Lincoln
Department of War
State, War, and Navy Building
Washington, D.C.*

9

THE NAVAL ACADEMY

Booth has hoped that getting back to his home territory, his Maryland,
might refresh his spirits, but sitting on the reviewing stand, listening
to the remarks of the other officials (previous to his own remarks)
proves no great restorative. The weather is suddenly warm for the time
of year, and there is a drone of insects that seems to have drifted over
from the stables nearby. The midshipmen, standing in ranks at parade
rest, look a little glassy-eyed in their postures on the trampled ground.

Across the aisle from him in a folding chair, seated with his neck
drawn in, is one who is equally glassy-eyed: the hero's grandson, Alan.
At four A.M., not ten hours ago, Alan was released from the Washington jail after having been arrested with the crown prince of Siam for
swimming nude in the White House fountain.

Booth supposes that it was Raymond who called the police on the
naked Alan and the heir apparent, inasmuch as Booth happened to see
the serene expression on Raymond's face when Alan was returned to
the Mansion just before sun-up, wearing stable-boy breeches and a
shirt way too short for his arms. The crown prince, falling-down
drunk, had been bailed out a number of hours before.

The real sinner in the matter, Booth suspects, may be himself. He
has been unforgivably lax with Alan, who has been permitted to bring
Princeton friends home on nearly every weekend when Lucy had noth-

ing scheduled, and on some occasions when she did. Whereas chaperons of the young ladies invited to meet the Princeton boys at first put their charges in the way of the young men, Booth has since learned that they whisk them off well before eleven so that if one of the girls is taken out "in the trees" by a ravening youth, better it be early than late, when intoxication reached epidemic levels.

As soon as the females go home, the young men come indoors (if it is not swimming weather). On the most recent occasion when the entire Princeton glee club was present, tenors, baritones, and bassos played leap frog in the East Room over half the night. Moreover, Alan commanded a midnight supper for the crew, and then another, complete with champagne, at half past three.

Is this the reason he, Booth, developed a political conscience, and strove to be a force: in order to offer bacchanal to college boys?

Booth lets his eyes travel across the aisle, where Lucy is sitting next to Chandler, whose remarks are already concluded. She is wearing a large floppy hat, and she smiles at him with such wanton innocence that he is ashamed for her. Abruptly, her smile fades as the Marine Band strikes up a hymn, said to be "one of Commander Herndon's favorites."

Nellie sits beyond the Chandlers, accompanied by her Aunt Regina from Newtonville. The child grows more implacable by the month. She is bundled to her chin in a coat, and yet she does not perspire.

The single face that does not depress him in some fashion on the other side of the aisle is Brodie Herndon's. In the very wrinkles of the man's face there is purity of judgment, there is maintenance of principle. The cut of Brodie's coat, the style of his shirt, the length of his hair, are not in the Yankee fashion. But the commander was Brodie's brother, and Booth has been gratified to see due deference being paid to Brodie. While he has had no success at persuading Brodie to help him in Washington, he means to have an earnest private conversation with him immediately after the ceremony.

As Mr. Sousa and the band members finish with "A Mighty Fortress Is Our God," Booth opens the palm of his hand to take a last look at the notes he has penned on a card held there. He will not speak long. Indeed he has developed a reputation for brevity, which has been well received. Left to himself, he would perhaps speak longer, but the reedy Episcopal-clergyman voice that Chester Arthur long affected is hard for Booth to sustain over extended stretches.

Waiting for Rear Admiral Hooper to introduce him, he supposes the other reason he never speaks at length is the nagging fear that Nell might turn up in the crowd again to listen. Recalling that terrible moment when his eyes fell on her while he was speaking from the terrace of the Fifth Avenue Hotel, he is uneasy that the dedication of this statue to her noble father might give her reason to venture forth.

Nervous, he focuses again on all the people on the reviewing stand, and on each face he can distinguish among those seated below. Why does he fear Nell above all people?

"Ladies and gentlemen," says Admiral Hooper. "The President!"

He rises, smiling, to warm applause. Good God, what if she has hidden herself on the pedestal of the monument itself? When he pulls the cord that lowers the silken sheath, will he find her instead of the heroic replica of her father? His conscience!

Absurd, of course. Still, he hurries through the speech, dazzled by the theatricality of what he has conceived.

He is partly disappointed when there is nothing after all under the sheath but Commander Herndon himself.

Later, he talks candidly with Brodie Herndon as the two of them stroll along the high banks of the Severn. Booth has excused himself from the others and led Brodie up through wooded lanes that Booth has known from the days when he brought young actresses to walk with him here. Then as now, one encountered midshipmen in uniform walking these same paths, sometimes accompanied by women of the town.

Booth has begun describing, with a certain earnest passion, some of the physical symptoms he has experienced: "dryness of the throat, a sense of confusion, loss of energy." He salutes a passing midshipman, who salutes him. To Brodie he says, "I conceive that these things have come upon me only in the last few months, and I believe that the number of pounds I put on this frame by frequent, heavy meals may produce lethargy, vertigo, and possibly—"

"You ah under great strain."

"Why should I be under strain?" Booth replies. "I began my administration feeling a great rush of energy. The newspapers have continued to be favorable to me, for the most part. The country is prosperous."

"Then I would say you are afflicted by a mild case of melancholia."

The word does not fall on Booth's ears pleasantly. It is a condition often associated with his brother Edwin. He has always believed it comes from letting one's anger simmer too long without taking action. He thinks of it as a form of paralysis; one might be better off dead.

"I *cannot* act to suit myself!" he now declares to Brodie, standing stock-still, staring over the revealed vista of the river. "I am blocked at every turn. No one helps me in my endeavors. No one—"

"But surely—"

"Even you!" Booth exclaims. "I offer you the most powerful hand in the country, offer it to you in the interest of our beloved South, and you write me that you are too busy to come to Washington."

Brodie's eyes narrow. He turns from the panorama of the river to look directly and steadily at Booth.

"Do not reproach me, Cap'n. I did not set up, I remind you, to be the savior of the South, or any othuh republic."

A bit abashed at the tone he has been taking, Booth says, "Yes, you are right. You are entirely correct. The truth is, I had those symptoms weeks ago. Lately my condition has degenerated into sloth and drunkenness."

Brodie observes that he has never seen Booth slothful.

"Sloth and drunkenness, I tell you!" Booth whispers harshly. "And lust, lust for another man's wife!"

Brodie says, "It is the nature of the times. Still, you ought to resist such feelings."

Another midshipman—this one accompanied by a sweet-looking young lady—has drifted onto the esplanade overlooking the river. Booth shields his face by turning his shoulder, in order not to be recognized by the young couple. Sotto voce, he murmurs to Brodie, "I do not have advisers, I have obfuscators. My Secretary of War defies me in spite of my noblest efforts. My Secretary of the Navy and his temptress of a wife subject me to parties worthy of Nero. My dear Nell snubs me for a priest. Her son is a scandal to me. . . . And my slightest move toward justice is taken account of, anticipated, and pronounced hopeless."

"You do well to avoid the Secretary's wife," Brodie ponders.

Booth's momentum plunges him onward. "I try to help the South, and the only man I can find to take my help is a chimpanzee. When I try to bring Dorsey, that supreme looter of government treasuries, to the bar of justice, what happens? The jury acquits him, and some blame me for fixing the jury."

"Perfect justice is difficult to achieve," Brodie says, "given the human condition. No man is perfect."

Cold comfort, Booth wants to say, but, behold, he has been

recognized. The midshipman—tall and towheaded—has thrown himself into a fearful brace.

"Sir! Mr. President!" he screams out, going red as a beet.

The young lady looks frightened too.

"Please be at your ease, midshipman," says Booth with civility. Elegantly, he takes off his hat and looks to be presented to the lady.

"Sir, Miss Amelia Brownstead!"

Booth presents Dr. Brodie Herndon of Fredericksburg. The young lady is sweet and modest. But the young people are nervous, and Booth lets them go after a moment. When they have left, he says to Brodie, "You see, I should derive satisfaction, should I not, when young people treat me with respect, the respect due me? Instead, instead, I can only think of those who do not treat me in this way."

"Come, come," Brodie says, putting his arm on Booth's shoulder. "I will talk to Alan for you, if that may help. I will remind him that he is by way of bringing his Herndon forebears to disgrace."

As they start down the path together, Booth is silent. He takes off his tall hat and turns it in his hand, moved by Brodie's offer to help him.

"I follow the news reports of the government," Brodie remarks. "You seem conscientious at your work."

"Although I accomplish nothing?" Booth asks tremulously. "Although I have no power base?"

"You must continue to try to do right," Brodie says earnestly, looking into Booth's eyes. The men are near the road where the carriage is waiting for them. "You acted very boldly, I thought, in vetoing the bill that would have forbidden the Chinese people from entering the country. A stirring message!"

"The Chinese civilization," Booth murmurs, "is two thousand years older than our own."

"No doubt, no doubt," Brodie replies. "I commend you." The two men approach the carriage. Salutes are exchanged between Booth and a sentry from the academy as they climb in.

"A great pity," Brodie observes when the horses have started up and their conversation is once more private, "that the Congress passed the act over your veto."

Tears are running down Booth's cheeks. He looks straight forward, his lips tight. The makeup is streaked.

"Come now, my friend," Brodie says easily, patting Booth on the shoulder.

10

THE EXECUTIVE MANSION

A thunderstorm strikes the capital not ten minutes after the President reaches his office following the trip to Annapolis. En route from the station he has seen the great dark plumes moving in rapidly from the west, turning midday into a hushed twilight. A vast stirring of wind has followed. Booth has just begun sorting his mail when the tempest hits.

Most of the letters are appeals for mercy in the case of Guiteau. Booth thrusts them aside uneasily. He has relighted and turned up the gas illumination that was blown out by a draft from the outer hallway. He closes the door, and watches the rain descend in sheets against the windows.

Quickly he opens a letter from Robert Lincoln, marked *Confidential*. But he soon tosses this aside too, for the letter advises that during "his mother Mrs. Lincoln's illness (as yet undiagnosed)," Mr. Lincoln will not be able to address himself to "the grave matter" alluded to by the President in his recent letter.

A second confidential missive is from a physician in Albany, whose name he does not recognize.

My dear Mr. President:

You will forgive my presumption but since your new duties seem to have prevented your visits to my office here, I can only hope that you are continuing your course of treatment with a physician in Washington City.

May I respectfully remind you that your condition (Bright's disease) requires vigilance. For the benefit of those now in charge of your case I note the medication that was prescribed by me for you on your last visit—now well over a year ago.

Rest assured that what I write is in the strictest confidence, but if I can be of any use to you and your doctors, please advise.

Respectfully yours,
R. F. Schock, M.D.

Enclosed, Booth finds a scrap of paper bearing a medical prescription in Latin. Flipping open the lid of his inkwell, he takes up one of the steel pens.

My dear Dr. Schock:

Thank you for your concern. My condition is much improved.

Cordially yours,
Chester A. Arthur

Writing the letter sets him to thinking. Suppose he should throw up the game after all and have "President Arthur" succumb; good God, if one couldn't accomplish anything, why remain self-condemned to this thankless role? Surely, the President might fall ill to one of his recurrent attacks of Bright's disease—whatever that might be—and sink rapidly. Very rapidly. At some time or other Dr. Schock could be pushed forward—sometime after the funeral, that is to say—in order to confirm that the President had long been a secret sufferer from the condition.

The matter that gives Booth most pause in this pleasant fantasy is the thought that the Presidency would fall to that fat Lincoln-lover, Judge Davis, now entitled to succeed by virtue of being president of the Senate. How could it be abided: to surrender to the whelp Robert and that three-hundred-pound blob of a man, as grossly obese as Father Abraham was cadaverous?

Disconcerted by the prospect, Booth now opens the third of the confidential letters in the pile, this from the Department of Justice, which must soon make a recommendation on whether or not Guiteau's death sentence should be commuted. And why not commute it? Booth thinks at moments. It is part of the self-destructive mood that has gripped him of late. Save Guiteau!

In the present report, however, his eye lights on the name Dörfer, "just recalled" by the assassin. The investigator appends a note: "Dörfer may at one time have been employed at Delmonico's as a wine steward. He dropped out of sight under suspicious circumstances; it is possible he plotted with Guiteau at the Hoffman House. An eyewitness, employed at Delmonico's, once saw the two men in close conversation."

"Dropped out of sight for good," Booth says to himself. He is surprised to have pronounced the words aloud, and rather like a death sentence. No more may he slip into that *très joli* disguise; all the Pinkertons in the East will be looking for Dörfer, his favorite role in a way. He feels a little as his brother Edwin might feel if he knew he could no longer play Hamlet.

On a strange impulse, he marches to the outer office, where he utters a command. "Have my carriage brought around, Fred." There is still mud on his shoes. He notices he has tracked mud onto the carpet next to his secretary's desk.

Fred Phillips looks up and raises his eyebrows. Does he wish to wait until the storm is over?

"I am going to the District prison, Fred. Right now," Booth declares. "Am I not charged to judge for myself . . . this assassin!"

Minutes later, in the driving rain, Booth steps from the shelter of the porte cochere at the north entrance into the shuddering carriage, atremble in the gusts of wind and blowing rain. Not even the large umbrella held over his head as he ascends keeps the raindrops from misting his face. Quickly he settles himself. A servant is holding the traces and trying to calm one of the two matched bays, made tense by the storm. The footmen wear heavy leather capes; the Negro driver sits severely on the box, the back of his collar protected by a fabric draped from the back of his hat.

Booth folds a lap robe over his knees, his fingers touching the silken monogram CAA in one corner. He signals he is ready, the door is closed, and the bays fairly leap forward. One would think that Guiteau were to be hanged in the next ten minutes and he was on his way to stop it.

The tree limbs wave and eddy; the coach wheels strike puddles and send water splashing high. The high-tension springs on the vehicle bounce him gently up and down and he looks out at the familiar streets, now almost deserted in a premature twilight; here and there, people who have taken shelter under trees or building cornices watch with interest as the President's carriage passes. The carriage is something to see, especially in the rain. The doors are faced with morocco and heavy lace; the chassis is painted green, trimmed with red, made shiny by the wetness.

Once when his comrades, Payne and Herold and the others, were but a day or two from the gallows, he dreamed of arriving in a fine carriage at the prison where they were held; wearing white gloves, he would descend and ask to be shown to the governor of the prison. When ushered there, all lowly men deferring to him the while, he

would present to the governor a reprieve for all his friends. He
dreamed of the clothes he would wear, the name he would take, the
office he would hold that would so hypnotize his audience that at once
the shackles would be unlocked, the heavy doors opened wide. All this
he dreamed while he was hiding at Brodie Herndon's farm.

Why should a lunatic like Charles Guiteau be reprieved when the
brave young men who made up his own band were not?

A peddler's cart drives pell-mell through the street, heading in the
opposite direction: there is other traffic on the thoroughfares. He wonders why the people don't stop and take shelter. But they don't. The
thunder and lightning are scarcely diminished, and the rain is still very
strong. A lone horsecar, partly filled with passengers, has come to a
stop and looks prepared to wait out the storm.

Booth finds himself coughing. The phlegm in his throat feels more
like bile. He wants to spit but is closed in and will not spit on the
carpet. Perhaps Raymond would have a kerchief for him if Raymond
were along. But, feeling protective, he has told Raymond not to come.

A brief scene in the north lobby: when the carriage was summoned, Fred Phillips—out of habit—summoned Raymond too. As
Booth emerged from his quarters, Raymond, his familiar, was waiting
beside the Tiffany screen, garbed in layers of houndstooth, his hat in
one hand, an umbrella in the other, all on ten minutes' notice.

"From the look of you—" Booth started to say, then waved him
off abruptly. Seeing the disconsolate expression in Raymond's eyes, he
added, "This is business I will do for myself." Not usual.

The truth must be confessed. In the prison scene ahead he has
imagined himself Sidney Carton. He would enter the cell, he would
change clothes with Guiteau. Guiteau would leave as the President.

That is why Raymond could not come along.

As the carriage reaches the end of the horsecar line, Booth leans
over and wrenches open the door in order to spit. The rain flies in his
face, but he hawks up the phlegm and coughs it out into the void. It
flies back to hit him squarely in the eye, a great dripping gob. Even a
President cannot spit into the wind.

Startled, he pulls shut the door and reflexively wipes the mess on
his coat sleeve. On the nervous verge of laughter, he leans back into
the cushions, turning the offending side of the sleeve away from him.
The pace of the horses has not slackened; the sound of the wheels
against the packed earth, however, resonates less loudly than on the
paved avenues they have left behind.

The prison, a large, ugly building, stands on a bluff overlooking the Anacostia River. Although Booth knows they are fast approaching it, the mist is so thick that it is doubtful that the driver will be able to see the structure well. Across the river on a fair day, the Maryland countryside would present itself. But all vision is obscured by the rising blasts of wind and rain. Faster, faster, a small voice in Booth urges. On so foul a day, why, the Carton trick can truly be worked!

As the gait of the horses is slowed from a gallop to a trot, Booth can hear the driver calling to the horses in a rough, unintelligible voice. They must be approaching the outer wall of the structure. A walled yard surrounds the prison; from one of the guard stations on that gray wall, newly installed to protect the assassin, a sergeant took a potshot the other day at Guiteau when the latter's face appeared at his cell window. Lamentably (some thought) he missed. Lamentably (some felt) the sergeant was taken into custody.

Booth pulls back the curtains on his right side. The fortress looming solitary on the edge of the cliff seems in the storm like the last outpost on the road to hell. He has lost his appetite for the renunciation scene in the careening drama of the ride itself. The stone prison looks impenetrable in the roiling fog two hundred feet above the river.

"I have changed my mind!" he calls to the driver when the horses have been brought to a stop. "We shall return to the Mansion at once."

He closes the door and wipes his sleeve on the cushions of the carriage. Perhaps that is what has made him change his mind: to dress the condemned man in stained raiment was to afflict him with the knowledge of good and evil. Guiteau's escape would come on better terms.

"About! About!" he cries.

"Gipp, gipp," he hears the driver call to the horses.

11

1421 I STREET

On the eve of Guiteau's execution, Booth, now much calmer in spirit, goes privately to the Chandlers for an informal supper. Earlier in the day, in order to escape the Quakers—who seem to believe that no

crime is a capital offense—he and Raymond drove out into the countryside, where they inspected a vacation residence for the President on
the grounds of the Soldiers' Home not far outside the city. As it was
a pleasant, balmy day, the trip turned out to be refreshing, although
the interior appointments of the large frame house that would serve as
the summer "cottage" struck Booth as rather too flouncy and feminine
for a widower President. The decorator, a man with polished fingernails, registered no expression as Booth entered certain objections to
the furnishings and draperies; if anything, the creature seemed flattered
to hear a responsive judgment from a man of affairs. Ordinarily, perhaps, he dressed "love nests" across the river.

"Is 'decorator' a trade a man may have?" Raymond asked on the
ride back.

"In the theater it is common," Booth replied. "But I hope it is not
a trade you are thinking of for yourself."

Hearing no answer, he narrowed his eyes.

The Chandlers receive him at twilight. Neither of them mentions
Guiteau, and he tells them a little of the summer cottage at the Soldiers' Home, how it is ample for long visits from Alan and Nellie, how
a Bell telephone is going to be installed for direct communication to
the White House. "The wires are already laid."

His eyes fall on Lucy's white shoulders. She is wearing a gown of
low-cut watered silk, and he finds himself nettled once again by the
frankness of her charms. The long, humid parties in the White House
had inured him to her presence, he believed. But tonight, closer to her,
he can see a trace of perspiration on her neck; he finds himself reacting
to the way she moves. The three of them are served a dry sherry, and
remarks are exchanged about Chandler's trip south. By chance,
Chandler will be leaving the following day to inspect naval stations in
Virginia and the Carolinas at about the same time that the assassin will
face the hangman's noose.

French doors leading to a small balcony stand open. When
Chandler leaves the room for a moment, Booth says to her, "You now
admit the open air. When I first knew you, you believed windows
should be shut at all times."

"But that was in the North," she replies easily. "Washington has
a sultry climate."

He says that none of his predecessors in the White House seemed
to have noticed the climate, for he is the first to ask that electric fans
be installed. ". . . although they have not been shy about bringing in
other furnishings," he goes on. "Grant had the whole of a dismantled

steamboat saloon moved from St. Louis, you know. Wanted to bolt it to the floor of the East Room."

"Goodness," Lucy says, laughing. "And where will you have the fans installed?"

Booth takes a sip of the sherry and says, "Why, they are already operating in the living quarters. You must come over and see them while your husband is away."

She sets her glass down on the marble top of a pier table. "Oh, I doubt if I could do that."

"Come tomorrow," he says, standing and moving closer to her. "I want you to."

"You shouldn't speak like that."

He continues to fix his gaze upon her without remark. Of course she has seen him on the stage do the same thing.

"My husband—" she nevertheless begins.

"This does not concern your husband."

"You are reckless still, are you not?"

"Never mind what I am. What do *you* feel, Lucy?"

She does not like bravado, she says with propriety. "You think—"

"Come to me tomorrow night," he now insists. "You will be alone. I will be depressed after the day."

She neither nods nor shakes her head.

"Come to me tomorrow," he repeats. Suddenly, he has put his arm around her waist. His lips brush her warm neck.

At this moment, tentatively, the drawing room door is opened, but before entering, Chandler intrudes his dry, scholarly voice. "My dear, Cook says that dinner is served."

Booth cannot see Lucy's face as she pulls away from him.

Later, after a goose pie larded with bacon (the Chandler cook was once employed by the British embassy), Chandler pursues a rather desultory political speculation. He says "certainly" many times: "certainly" the Readjusters in Richmond will need full support, "certainly" the planters in South Carolina have gained ascendancy, but "certainly" he will do what he can.

With very little luck, Booth tries at table to catch the flitting gaze of Lucy. Opposite her, Chandler looks like her younger brother with his glasses and his scraggly trace of a chin whiskers. He never seems to have aged. Lucy, on the other hand, has a fully ripened figure, her breasts firm and round. Strange that she is childless, while the wispy Chandler has fathered three babes by his first wife.

"Your wine is excellent," Booth exclaims.

"Manzanilla," says Lucy evenly.

Chandler pushes on. Booth notices that the words "power base" are not stimulating him tonight. He is trying to remember the explanation Lucy gave years ago (in Boston?) when telling him that she could never bear a child. Did he himself want one then?

"With the depressing event in the prison yard that is scheduled for tomorrow," Lucy says not too much later, "we should not keep our guest too long, Bill."

Chandler shrugs. A late breeze ruffles the brocaded drapery in front of the open balcony. Booth measures Lucy's tone; a southern drawl seems to have crept into her voice, whether from living in a sultry climate for so long or for other reasons he is not certain.

Still, he must devote the remaining minutes of departure (since the carriage is called) to wishing Chandler godspeed, to assure him of the importance of what he is undertaking. Tacitly, Booth has decided that Lucy will come to him whenever he sends his driver for her tomorrow. Is it perverse of him to want her on the very day that Guiteau will climb the scaffold?

Their eyes meet ambiguously one more time. On either side of the entryway just outside the front door two glass globes illuminate the eight stone steps to the sidewalk. The footman has run up to escort him down.

"An enjoyable evening, Mrs. Chandler!" the President calls.

"So glad you liked it, Mr. President."

Booth cannot sleep. On the way home in the carriage, one of the horses threw a shoe and there was an unconscionable delay until a properly shod horse was located at a stable not half a block away. Then, under the porte cochere of the north entrance he was forced to brush past a delegation of never-say-die Quakers, who writhed at him like the damned of Dante's hell, imploring mercy for Guiteau. He has a theory about Quakers: they are frustrated thespians all and relish playing agony—or underplaying it.

But his larger thoughts are elsewhere. In his bedroom he pulls off his own boots, having dismissed his valet. He shuts the blinds. Pacing back and forth, shrunken without the lifts in his boots, he contemplates his situation. With his Nell almost certainly lost to the Romish priests in New York, what choice does he have but more adultery?

In a corrupted age, a monarch settles for his female courtiers. While the trap springs on the scaffold below, the king finds diversion with his mistress. So things go. What does it matter if she is married to one of his counselors? He knew her first.

At least Booth is now aware who is responsible for his behavior. At the time he confessed his self-disgust to Brodie Herndon, he was blaming Lucy and others for his drunkenness and his sloth. No more. Sin envelops him because he is too cynical to transcend it.

It was ever so. Even in '65, what was he but a drunk and a lecher, except for one exalted moment when he burst the bonds at Ford's Theater to declare his principles! In that moment he, too, had principles. He was more than a drunken fancy-man!

The lamp burns late that night. Smoking cheroot after cheroot, he paces until at last he yields, fully dressed, to exhausted sleep on the chaise longue in his dressing room.

12

PRISON YARD

"D' President has sealed his own doom and d' doom of d' nation!" the condemned man shouts when he learns there is no reprieve. "He and his Cabinet are possessed of d' devil. Dey oppose God's will and power. Dey will be paid for dere cowardice, dere treachery, and dere ingratitude!"

But on the scaffold at noon, with his shoes freshly blacked and an elegant full-course meal in his stomach, he offers with great dignity a reading from the book of Matthew. The audience—reporters, prison officials, some political figures—listen politely.

He has reached the verse "Except ye be converted and become as little children, ye shall not enter into the kingdom of heaven." Then, with eyes bright, he unfolds a slip of paper in one of his bound hands, and holding it, announces: "I am now going to read some verses which are intended to indicate my feelings at d' moment of leaving dis world. If set to music, dey may be rendered very effective. De idea is dat of a child babbling to his mamma and papa. I wrote it dis morning about ten o'clock."

The condemned man has now raised his voice to an unnatural falsetto:

I am going to d' Lordy, I am so glad!
I am going to d' Lordy, I am so glad,
  I am going to d' Lordy,   5.5
Glory Hallelujah! Glory Hallelujah!
  I am going to d' Lordy
I love d' Lordy wit' all my soul,
  Glory Hallelujah!
And dat is d' reason I am going to d' Lord,
Glory Hallelujah! Glory Hallelujah!
  I am going to d' Lord.
I saved my party and my land,
  Glory Hallelujah!
But dey have murdered me for it,
 And dat is d' reason I am going to d' Lordy,
Glory Hallelujah! Glory Hallelujah!
  I am going to d' Lordy!
I wonder what I will do when I get to d' Lordy,
I expect to see most glorious t'ings,
Beyond all earthly conception,
When I am wit' d' Lordy!
Glory Hallelujah! Glory Hallelujah!
  I am wit' d' Lord.

In the last stanza he reclaims his own hearty voice for the final "Glory Hallelujah! Glory Hallelujah! I am wit' d' Lord." Moved by his own poem, he struggles to hold back the tears.

Now, however, as he falls silent and braces himself, the hangman covers his head with a black hood that blots out his vision. He drops the manuscript of his poem, calling out loudly, "Glory, ready go!"

With a sudden grinding of gears, the trap snaps open and Mr. Ghetto dances on air.

13

THE EXECUTIVE MANSION

During the evening of the same day—sometime before ten o'clock—a closed carriage draws up at the north portico with windows tightly curtained. No one emerges from the interior, but word is sent via the driver that a guest has arrived. The night doorkeeper, a relic from the Grant administration, summons the President's aide Raymond.

While Raymond is waited for, the horses stand quietly, half in shadow, half in torchlight. June bugs flutter in the moist heat; occasionally a carriage is heard passing along the avenue below, but no movement stirs inside the one parked before the Executive Mansion. The driver holds the reins patiently.

Raymond emerges from the Mansion, the fingers of one hand suavely in the pocket of his waistcoat. The other hand smooths back his hair. His sharp eye quickly detects the hem of a lady's gown caught in the bottom of the carriage door; then behind a briefly opened curtain he catches sight of the white face of a woman. He speaks to her sotto voce: "Ye will be received in a few minutes."

He gives an order to the driver to continue around the Mansion to a side entrance. For his part he has little doubt of the urgency of the case. The President this morning mentioned the possibility of a late visitor, who was to be received discreetly. Then he isolated himself, and after the execution at the prison, he failed to appear again.

Raymond hurries upstairs to the President's living quarters.

Booth, sitting in darkness except for the light of a dying fire in the grate, scarcely hears the knock at first. He sits with his linen loose, staring down at a tumbler full of whiskey in his hand. Although he has not drunk much, he is feeling low.

As the rapping on the door comes again, he rises in some irritation. He is expecting no one; the note he thought he would send Lucy, letting her know when he would send over his carriage, he never wrote. Even after the sleepless night, he spoke at breakfast with Raymond about the possibility of a visitor, but then his melancholia, as Brodie called it, took over. Because of the execution of Guiteau, all business was canceled.

Now, flinging open the door, he stares into Raymond's narrow gaze. "Can I have no peace?" he thunders.

"A lady in a closed carriage has arrived at the side entrance."

Booth tightens his grasp on the tumbler. Can she have come brazenly in her own carriage? Very well, he is revived.

"Clear the footman, the doorman, whoever else is about from our path," Booth commands Raymond. "Say, 'A matter of state.' "

While Raymond moves to do his bidding, Booth turns momentarily back into the bedroom. He straightens his garments and throws the contents of the glass into the fire.

He does not tarry long. Striding with purpose down the steps, he notes by the silence in the hallways that his order has been carried out. His route proceeds along the great stained-glass screen from Tiffany's, no less eloquent a backdrop than it was at the *Comédie* in Paris.

Booth descends a winding flight of steps, finds the door to the outside standing open, and just beyond it he sees the waiting carriage. Not a soul is in sight. Booth leaps lightly to the carriage step, raps on the door, and speaks in a voice full of *vibrato,* "I adore you."

The door opens. But the woman inside is not Lucy Chandler. It is Nell, and sitting across from her, like a bedazzled child in a picture book, is Nellie.

"Husband?" Nell murmurs, peering up at him, unaware that he has mistaken her for another. She is wearing a long pelisse, a hat bound with a ribbon. Her hand touches the door handle and she looks about cautiously.

For a moment he is too stunned to speak. But almost at once he begins to experience the moment as divine intervention. Such moments transcend the pleasure—or the disappointment—in them. The miracle of the timing always baffles or amazes him, but he never fails to see how providence restores him to his purpose. He will not be allowed long to yield to the claims of the mundane. Hundreds of times he has imagined that his high aims were about to be undermined—often by his own mortal weaknesses and deficiencies. Now he knows he is destined to recover his honor again, no matter how many pitfalls lie in his way.

"Nell!" he says. "And my Nellie too. Come!" He helps each of them down to the ground; from the distant darkness frogs croak in the swamp. "Tell me how you were able to come."

In the dim light, Nell seems oddly to close her eyes for a moment. "I have been wrong to have abandoned you," she says. "I will be wife to you from now on if you shelter us heah."

"Wife indeed, and Nellie my daughter too," Booth says hoarsely, embracing them. "No one but you shall be sheltered while I am master here."

Moments later, as they pass down the deserted hallway, single file, Booth sees Raymond, half concealed and watching, his eyes glazed with the same holy calm that Booth knows must be in his own face.

PART SIX
The
FREDERICKS-
BURG FILE

1

"And then what happened?" asks Thurlow Weed, his pet dove perched on his bony shoulder, his sightless eyes focused straight ahead on his visitor.

"I'm not tiring you out, am I?" Dun inquires.

"On the contrary. What happened?"

"Why, she joined him in Washington," Dun replies. "From what I hear, he took her in at the White House, and as soon as Congress adjourned, he installed her in the summer cottage on the grounds of the Soldiers' Home, where he is staying himself now."

Thurlow Weed nods in satisfaction. "We've reunited them—the two lovers. Like a fairy tale. 'Death' could not manage it, but we did."

"We must give Brodie Herndon some of the credit," Dun says.

Weed asks if there was any trouble with Nell's priest. Accidentally, the blanket has slipped from his knees.

As Dun moves to retrieve it, he keeps an eye on the large white dove whose random flights around the library leave him unsettled. "I told the priest an entire window would be given in offering," Dun says, "in appreciation for the guidance and instruction he had given our friend. But I explained that she had a husband in another city. Would he not advise her that her place was there?"

"This was the blind priest?"

"Yes, blind . . . but he saw."

The laughter from Weed comes in a single spasm. He is partial to jokes about blindness. While Weed blinks his watery eyes, catching his breath, Dun keeps his own gaze on the imperious bird.

"And I decided to tell Nell," Dun adds, "that the lady at the President's right hand was the former Lucy Hale. She took notice."

"Did she?" Thurlow Weed exclaims, this time with such vigor that the bird is startled and takes wing in the direction in which Dun is sitting. Feeling threatened, Dun sinks to his knees on the carpet and bending his chin to his chest, clasps both hands over his head. The bird flies on to settle on a bust of George Washington next to Weed's heroic portrait of the archbishop.

Weed, too blind to notice his guest's distress, extends palsied fingers toward his empty shoulder. He says, "Looks like the market's straightened itself out too, doesn't it? None of this boom-and-bust stuff we had with Grant."

Dun agrees that Grant was too anxious to do favors for people. "The market's happy now."

The two men fall silent for a moment. Weed says, "I think we might leave him alone now, let him find his own way. Of course it is a shame that he has such a violent, unstable nature."

"A nature you once took advantage of."

"Good Lord, I'm done with that, Dun. . . . Do you hear if he's still lookin' for his goddamned file?"

Dun says that he has heard it.

Weed says: "That's a hopeful sign. Don't you think? As long as he resumes huntin' for the goddamned file . . . Was that my bird?"

Weed's bird has left the bust of Washington and languidly flown back into its cage.

"Your bird is home," Dun says.

2

FROM *The National Star*
JULY 25, 1882

STRANGE VISITATION
AT SOLDIERS HOME IN WASHINGTON

G.A.R. VETERAN SEES APPARITION

An unearthly manifestation of the Other World was reported at the Soldiers Home near the capital city of Washington, D.C. one morning last week. Corporal Hezekiah Broadhead, Grand Army of the Republic, who resides at the Home, claimed to have seen an apparition of the late wife of President Arthur on an upper portico of Anderson Cottage, where the President has been in residence this summer. Mrs. Arthur died in 1880.

Corporal Broadhead said he was directly below the Anderson Cottage at dawn and when he looked up he saw a woman in a nightgown, whom he identified as "the true likeness" of the President's late wife, whom the Corporal met a number of times, he says, when he served in an honor guard unit under the then-General Arthur in New York during the War. Corporal Broadhead knocked on the door of the Cottage to describe what he had seen to the aide who received him. But by the time others reached the place where Corporal Broadhead saw the manifestation, what he had seen had vanished.

Corporal Broadhead has a reputation for sobriety, although he is over eighty and lost a limb on the battlefield at Gettysburg. "Her spirit seeks to keep him from marrying again," Corporal Broadhead ventured in explaining the apparition.

A similar manifestation was reported in New York near the Fifth Avenue Hotel during the campaign where General Arthur was giving an address prior to his election as Vice-President.

Booth lays the newspaper next to the breakfast tray and steps into the adjoining bedroom, where Nell is sleeping soundly. The single sheet she sleeps under is tangled oddly about her legs, and a film of moisture lies across her forehead, but otherwise she seems tranquil enough in her nightgown with its fine embroidered collar. The tightly screened window admits as much of the morning breeze as exists, although Booth, two days before, has had to switch bedrooms with her. He has taken the one with the access to the upstairs porch so as not to repeat the incident that lately troubled Corporal Broadhead.

Booth is not upset by the newspaper account. None of the real newspapers covers such incidents, inasmuch as they cover nothing about the government during the summer. Booth has nevertheless consulted with the household staff, all of whom realize that the corporal has seen the invalided lady known as Lew, whose presence at the cottage the President has seen fit to remain discreet about.

As for "Lew" herself, Booth has found her most gentle and amenable since her return to him, although he has been forced to discourage her from calling him Husband when the servants are about. His and Nell's bedrooms adjoin the same morning room, a large and cheery chamber with cross-ventilation.

"Is there any reading matter you would wish, dear?" he asks while she is eating and before he goes downstairs.

"I do not read much anymore since I accepted the true faith," she replies.

"May I send out for more yarn, then? Do you have all the colors you need?"

"All the coluhs of the rainbow," she answers. "Do not trouble yourself."

"Not at all," he says. His patience has been rewarded. His fidelity to her—that noblest part of himself—has revived his idealism on every front.

On some afternoons Nellie attends her mother. A melodeon occupies one corner of the morning room, and on occasions Nell will play a selection or two on it. Raymond reports that once he heard both their voices joined in song behind the closed doors. But the musical offering, to Raymond's regret, was not of long duration.

"I'm glad you enjoy things like that, Raymond," Booth says to him. "The ladies seem to have everything they need here, don't you think?"

Raymond, who is looking more like a man, less like a boy these days, nods. His taste in reading matter has progressed from Scott to Dumas in recent weeks.

On the morning in question, after leaving Nell, Booth finds Raymond sitting on a stone bench in the garden beside a monument with a fountain. He is smoking a small cigar. Further ahead, along the cinder path, Nellie has perched herself in the pergola at the confluence of paths. She is reclining on a wooden seat, having leaned her cheek on her hand while reading a book. Raymond is observing her.

"Good morning, Raymond," Booth says, sitting on a bench across from him. On the way outdoors he has picked up his morning mail, which he leafs through. "I trust Corporal Broadhead has been comfortably resettled in a new hospital, as we discussed."

"Yes, sir. In Philadelphia."

"That's a good hospital. Old. But good."

"And closer to his home too," Raymond says.

"Oh, where is his home?"

"Montpelier, Vermont."

"Really?"

Booth straightens on the bench. He sees that one of his letters is from Robert Lincoln, and he peels away the wax that seals it. At first the letter seems a conventional expression of thanks for the President's condolences on the death of his mother, Mrs. Mary Todd Lincoln. But Robert goes on to say that in his bereavement he has reached the conclusion that as long as his mother need no longer bear the pain of certain "revelations," he will discuss the President's request for the Fredericksburg File "most seriously" when he finishes with his mother's affairs and returns to Washington.

With trembling fingers Booth folds the letter and puts it inside his coat. He has curiously confused feelings. He had hoped to stimulate Raymond by helping the lad form a plan for extricating the file from the Lincoln safe. It was the kind of enterprise Raymond needed in order to burn away the dross of idleness.

But Raymond will have to be otherwise inspired. Down the path the morning light offers a magical quality at the spot where Nellie languishes with her slim leather-bound volume. She is wearing a pale peach-colored frock, with one white-stockinged leg bent at the knee and propped against the bench in a most beguiling way.

"She looks like a fairy princess there, doesn't she?" Booth remarks, wanting to give sympathetic echo to Raymond's enchantment.

For a moment Raymond says nothing. Then he takes the cigar out of his mouth. "If there'uz one who wished to violate her," he says, "I'ud kill him . . . slowly!"

"Yes, well—" Booth murmurs.

He advises Raymond to undertake setting-up exercises in the mornings. Dumbbell exercises too. One must not savor thoughts of killing people "slowly."

3

THE PRESIDENT'S PRIVATE RAILROAD CAR
NEAR HARTFORD, CONNECTICUT

"At long last," says Robert Lincoln, with smiling countenance, "I feel I can talk to you frankly about the documents in question."

Having just boarded the train five minutes before at the Hartford stop, he has made his way back to the President's car, where a guard at the rear of the last public Pullman passes him through. When Lincoln has pulled the door shut behind him, it muffles the rattling sound of the wheels against the track.

The two men are alone. Lincoln takes the large plush chair that Booth indicates, dons spectacles, and draws out a piece of paper from his coat pocket.

"You would not have brought the file with you, would you?" Booth asks, feeling the train rapidly gathering speed. He is wearing dark Scottish tweeds with a belted coat. Tweeds imply his discretion.

"No, I have not," Robert Lincoln says soberly. "However, these are notes about the documents, which are secured in a safe in my home."

Ah, then he was correct about the safe, Booth thinks gleefully. But he folds his hands in his lap, patient as a clergyman.

On the other side of the windows of the speeding Limited, the leaves of the maples and oaks have just begun to wither and burnish. The two men are en route to the centennial observance in Massachusetts of Daniel Webster's birth, where they will offer brief remarks. It will be the first official appearance of the President in the fall season. Like an actor who has been off the boards for a time, Booth has been working hard in private to get himself up for the part again.

"But the material you have," Booth asks, "belongs to the so-called Fredericksburg File?"

"Yes, so it has been called," says Lincoln, touching his beard with a disarming candor. "I must reiterate that I myself believe it to be not . . . prudent or fair to reopen an inquiry into an assassination after seventeen years have passed."

"I understand your view."

Lincoln draws a deep breath. "That said, I do advise you that the evidence I possess consists of the missing pages of Booth's diary.

Secretary Stanton excised these pages—according to his son—because he felt that Union leaders who were implicated did not deserve to be disgraced on the word of John Wilkes Booth."

With coolness, Booth suggests that Stanton's true motive may have been a self-serving one. "He consolidated his power, you must be aware, by holding this evidence over the heads of the conspirators. Northern speculators—were they not?"

"They were," Lincoln says, looking out at the autumn countryside. "But during the war it was common practice for men with financial interests to negotiate with the other side. Sometimes an objective, such as replacing the President, might be discussed without the specific means being defined."

"Ah, that definition, when it came, was a cruel one!" Booth intones. "Your father was taken at the very prime of his life!" He feels the emotion in his own voice at the thought of the prime of the life that was taken.

Bowing his head, Lincoln says, "As to that, President Arthur, my father's physicians felt him to be an ill man at the time he went to Ford's Theater that night. God might well have taken him soon had the assassin failed."

"Truly?"

"Booth's act is not mitigated on that account."

Booth licks his lips. "Ah, no."

"You look pale, sir," Lincoln says.

"It is a distressing episode," Booth replies sharply.

The train meanwhile has drawn into a village along the route, hardly more than a flag stop. Some children wearing overalls and large straw hats stand near the rails, and they wave blindly as the cars roll past them.

"And yet in Stanton's behalf," Lincoln says, putting his hands together, "perhaps he withheld the diary so as not to cloud the issue at the trial of Payne and Herold and the others. If half the Union were said to be in on the conspiracy to kill, how could anyone's guilt be clear?"

"Then you think it was better to let the onus fall on the poor?"

With conviction growing in his voice, Robert Lincoln presses his forehead. "Nay, I have forgiven the poor conspirators as well as the rich. Men were poorest in that time who did not have a uniform to wear." He looks out over the ripe farmlands. "I know. Whenever I arrived in Washington from school, I felt so ashamed not to be in uniform that I wanted to kill anybody or anything just to prove I was no coward. Finally, I prevailed upon my father, and once I was in service, I began to relax. After being under fire with General Grant, I never felt murderous again." Lincoln bursts into a mild laugh. "Or is that a damning admission for a war secretary to make?"

As the train slows to a crawl entering a railroad yard, the President swivels so as to put his back to the window. "I cannot believe that you wish to blame no one but Booth for what happened."

"Oh, for a long time I blamed my father," Lincoln says. "I resented it that he was so careless about protecting himself. . . . Yet perhaps he cared little because he knew he was ill. Or he could not bear all the men dying in the war while he continued to live. But his fatalism literally drove my mother insane."

Lincoln's confidences have begun to make Booth uneasy. He turns again and looks out the window. Standing alone on the station platform, staring as the train passes, is a single, tall, middle-aged man with gaunt features. Booth is so close he can watch the man's jaws work as he chews his tobacco. The man stares without recognition.

Lincoln says, "I blamed my father most as he lay sprawled out diagonally on the narrow bed in the room at the top of the stairs."

Not the memory Booth has. He remembers the dark shape of a man's head against the plush of the high-backed chair; and that was only for a second, everything went so fast.

"Still I made my peace," the other man declares. "I saw my folly at last, I think, in the depot with Garfield lying shot on the filthy mattress they had brought down from the stationmaster's office; that started to cure me of my conviction of the victim's complicity. Garfield did not want to be shot, I promise you."

As the train picks up speed leaving the yards, Booth sees a knot of children wearing sweaters and caps, oddly huddled in three clusters. Not leapfrog or crack-the-whip.

Lincoln says, "I am going to release the Fredericksburg File, Mr. President. I am not going to pass it on when I die to yet another bewildered soul, as Eddie Stanton did to me, and force that man to make the decision."

Hearing this, Booth folds his hands. "And are there other documents in the file? Official papers of Booth's perhaps?"

A muted assent, and Lincoln is suddenly asking if he may be excused, since their talk has, after all, "spent" him.

Blinking his eyes rapidly, Booth lets his chair swivel forward again. "Perhaps the evidence will show that Booth was supported by a network of rational men, some patriotic, some venal—men as different as those around Brutus when Caesar was slain."

A wide conspiracy, Lincoln agrees, his eyes downcast. "Do you know why it is called the Fredericksburg File, Mr. President? Because there is evidence that Booth was not the man killed in the tobacco barn, and that he escaped and lived for a time with a well-to-do family in Fredericksburg, Virginia. After that, his trail vanishes."

"And is this family mentioned by name?" the President inquires after a moment.

Lincoln replies that he does not think so. "But with the clues given, it should be possible to work it out. If one wanted to."

"We must be merciful," Booth says, "to those who offered refuge. ... When will you give me the file, Mr. Lincoln?"

Gathering his memoranda, Lincoln murmurs, "You mean when will I release the documents?"

"Why, I assumed you were going to release them to me, so as to properly winnow—"

A look of disaffection crosses Lincoln's face as he rises. "Do excuse me, Mr. President. I wonder if there has not already been enough selective winnowing in this case. ... It seems to me we have reached the point where it must be all or nothing."

4

THE EXECUTIVE MANSION

Raymond now drives The Maid—Miss Nellie—to school each day. She attends the Franklin School, where one of President Andrew Johnson's children used to go. With The Maid now living at the White House so as to be near her school, she is separated from the President's lady, who continues to reside at the cottage on the grounds of the Soldiers' Home. But once a week Raymond drives the phaeton out to the Soldiers' Home so that Nellie can pay a visit there. Raymond and the lady occasionally listen to Nellie recite lines that she has committed to memory at school:

Birds in the high hall garden
When twilight was falling
Maud, Maud, Maud, Maud
They were crying and calling.   **9.5**

Later he drives the lady to St. Mary's Catholic Church and waits outside. Whenever she takes longer than usual to do her religious duties he becomes nervous, because he knows it is his responsibility to watch her. He supposes she goes in there to confess; he knows people confess their sins to priests inside the church. But he is not sure what to expect of the lady anymore. With the President not visiting her so often, she dresses in black, wears veils when she goes out, and declines to talk much. Raymond felt more trustful of her when she used to be angry with him; since becoming a Catholic she has gotten quiet as an old dog.

Back at the Soldiers' Home, where the GAR veterans sit around the grounds chewing and whittling, she sits in her room, knitting and doing needlework. She makes her samplers in the room where Old Abe—as the veterans call him—signed the Emancipation Proclamation.

Raymond wonders if sometime he will run for public office himself when he gets older. He has had valuable experience already for one as young as he is. He has lived in the President's house, the Fifth Avenue Hotel, the Grand Pacific Hotel in Chicago, the Delavan House in Albany. It nearly wearies him to think of it all. A couple of times his career was nearly smashed to smithereens. Once—the time he took Nellie to New York—was when he was trying to help his employer out and his action was misunderstood.

He does not read Horatio Alger anymore. In those stories a young man's initiative was always praiseworthy. In real life it was sometimes misunderstood. One had to be cautious about pursuing one's deepest ideals. He originally thought, when he first attached himself to the President—once the general, earlier the count—that his employer was bold like himself and that he prized initiative. Alas, Raymond now sees that a real gentleman—rather than a mere merchant—does not always like initiative, does not even get into much action. Between the feats of chivalry that the knights in armor did (if they did them as Sir Walter Scott says), Raymond now concedes there must have been long stretches when they stayed around the castle satisfying the king. During these times each of them could improve the adoration of his lady.

Raymond has himself used the weeks just before Nellie moved

from the Soldiers' Home back into the White House by purchasing little presents, which he leaves in her room—a secondhand music box, a delicate bud vase, an ivoried comb with a pastoral scene painted where you hold it. Since some of Nellie's clothing has been sent over in advance of her arrival (and has been unpacked and placed in wardrobes and chiffoniers), Raymond's additions blend in with what has already arrived.

Lately, Raymond has been reading the Frenchman Dumas—more avidly, he believes, than any author he has ever read. The French are base. Brave men capture, and are captured by, other men; they savor their enemies' humiliation, or they writhe in agony when strapped on the rack. Raymond shudders to think of it, and is not surprised to be assigned physical exercises to perform as penance.

One midnight, shortly after the President's return from the Webster centennial—the President never went to bed before two A.M.—Raymond, while sitting alone in his room devouring *The Count of Monte Cristo*, hears a light knock on the door. He is wearing a robe over his shirt, for the weather has turned cooler, and when he answers the door, there stands the President, also in his shirt. He seems to be holding something behind his back, but he is smiling faintly. His body has a different contour late at night when everybody has gone to bed but himself.

Raymond asks if anything is wrong, for the President rarely comes to the servants' wing.

"Nay," the President says, winking his eye. He steps over the threshold into Raymond's room and closes the door behind him. "Look what I discovered down in the Garden Room." From behind his back he produces two matched fencing foils of well-tempered steel.

Raymond's eyes grow large. "The real thing?" He has just been reading about sword fights.

Booth laughs. "General Sheridan and I were poking about in the souvenirs from the war. There are barrels of arms down there. When I found these, I challenged him to a bout. But the coward fled." He tosses Raymond one of the foils. "What do *you* say to a 'go,' my squire?"

Remembering his misadventures with the sword-cane, Raymond takes the foil uneasily. But the smooth hard curve of the shaft feels irresistible in his fingers. "Are we to do it now?"

"The East Room will be our ground," Booth avers. The carpet has been torn out and the furniture removed. "If anyone hears us, they will think it is the decorators working overtime."

The two of them, each with his foil, tiptoe down the narrow hallway that leads out of the servants' wing. As they pass along the main corridor (where Nell's portrait hangs, flanked by roses), they are concealed from the night watchman by the Tiffany screen. At the far end of the corridor there is a cluster of furniture blocking the entrance to the vast and drafty East Room, the final project in the redecoration plan. Mahogany chairs and great circular ottomans, installed in the Grant administration, have been removed for disposal on Booth's order. The thick Brussels carpet, five hundred yards of it, has been rolled up against one wall.

As Booth turns up the gas, the East Room shows its bare boards, thick-textured drapery, and low-hanging chandeliers.

"Next month electric lights!" Booth exclaims. "But for now, pull shut the curtains, Raymond, on Thomas Edison, and Wall Street, whatever is out there."

Obediently, Raymond moves from one great window to the next, unloosing the ties that hold the draperies open. The great swaths of fabric descend, one after the other.

"Aha!" Booth cries as Raymond turns about with the last of the draperies having fallen to. *"En garde, Monsieur!"*

Raymond poses gracefully with his weapon, as he has seen it done. Booth's wrist flicks so quickly at him that Raymond does not have time to move. He feels his shoulder touched by the button concealing the point of the foil. "You must call *touché!*" Booth cries.

Raymond grunts. He lashes back at Booth a little half-heartedly.

"Here, let me instruct you," Booth says. "It must be an art if it is to be a sign of breeding." Booth explains the positions of the feet. "The success comes in the footwork, you see, and the flick of the wrist." He demonstrates with a couple of sudden thrusts from various postures. "Take off your dressing gown, for God's sake," says Booth. After Raymond does so, Booth says, "Now try to touch me. Expect a riposte—that is, a hit from me—when you open yourself."

Raymond launches several thrusts at Booth, but Booth easily repels them. A couple times Booth replies with answering thrusts, from which Raymond has difficulty in protecting himself. There is a fierce intensity in Booth's behavior that belies the bemused smile on his face. He gives advice. "Now, think before you attack." Or "Stop slashing! You're not a windmill, are you? Or the kind of prizefighter who does nothing but throw punches?"

Raymond finds himself picking up the art rapidly. He is soon able to parry some of Booth's attacks. "Ah, Dumas would be proud!"

Booth exclaims at one ptint. There is perspiration on his forehead.

"We'll play a bout," Booth says. "If you lose, you must get me the Fredericksburg File from Robert Lincoln's citadel."

His tone is light. But when Raymond knits his eyebrows, Booth laughs uneasily and says, "I hope I am joking, *mon frère,* and yet he speaks of releasing the documents not to me but to the world. . . . *En garde.*"

So Raymond prepares. He finds that watching Booth's eyes help him judge when Booth is about to make an attack. The youth holds his foil high, and when Booth's eyes narrow in a certain way, he parries. Once he even tries a riposte—as Booth calls it—by conducting his own attack when Booth misses. But Booth pushes off the riposte with relative ease.

Backing off a moment, Booth says, "And if he releases it to the world, what then might happen to the Herndons? And when the family of the President's wife becomes involved, does not the President as well?"

Booth taps Raymond's foil to let him know that they have re-sumed. As they move in linear patterns down the middle of the bare floor, the foils strike off each other like flints. Booth, eyes riveted, says, "Did you know . . . Abraham Lincoln lay in state in this room, Ray-mond . . . in April of Sixty-five."

Raymond keeps his eye on the point of the foil. "I'ud rather see where he was shot. . . . In Ford's Theater."

"Alas, it's not . . . a theater anymore."

"I'ud like to see it anyway."

"There now! You must cry *touché!*" Booth has struck directly over Raymond's heart, a clean hit. Raymond looks abashed, and Booth says, "We won't count that one on the wager. Besides, I cannot engage you to attempt a burglary for me, can I? My eminence is too great."

The President is enjoying himself hugely. Raymond steps back, and as Booth's foil straightens again, Booth says, *"Autre temps, mon frère, en garde."*

Booth puts his foil against Raymond's. "Do you know what *mon frère* means, Raymond?" Raymond holds his ground, will not speak. "Ah, you're afraid you will lose your concentration. . . . All right. . . . *Mon frère* means 'my brother.' . . . Did you know I have a brother, Raymond, who is . . . an excellent swordsman? We have—"

"Touché on you!" Raymond cries, having with a sudden thrust caught Booth just below his navel. "I touched ye!"

"But too low. It's a foul, you know, below the waist."

"Ye didn't tell me that." Raymond stands back, drops his arm in disappointment.

"Of course it is a foul to strike below the waist!"

"Small difference it would make if they was real weapons," Raymond declares.

"They *are* real weapons. They make a real test of our honor, do they not?" Booth replies. "If we lose our honor, we take no pleasure in the kill."

The point is not argued by Raymond. Booth has raised his foil again, and although he is breathing hard, he goes on talking as he parries. "A strange thing . . . I dreamed the other night, Raymond . . . that my brother and I were dueling . . . all through this house. . . . We fought up one staircase and down another. . . . People stood below and watched us while we delivered the most incredible strokes."

"Like in a play," Raymond says. For two pennies a ticket, he has seen some of the plays put on in the Bowery.

"Very like a play." Booth gives a sudden cry, and he thrusts at once toward Raymond's breast. "A *touché*?" He stops and looks. "A hit, was it not?"

"No, ye missed me," Raymond says.

"Did I?" Booth asks. He seems puzzled for a moment, takes some deep breaths, and says, "Five minutes more, Raymond. . . . If you make a fair hit on me . . . I will . . . I will give you the hand of my daughter in marriage! Hah!"

Raymond blinks. His heart begins beating faster.

"I will take you on left-handed," the President declares. *"En garde!"*

Raymond speaks not a word. For a long half-minute, he holds himself like a sentinel, planning his attack. Booth stands almost idly; he offers no attack of his own. When Raymond comes forward once, then twice, he fends off Raymond's foil with ease. Raymond rights himself, tries again. He remembers not to rush it, he holds his ground, concentrating on how he will move. Still, Booth fends him off.

Five minutes pass, ten minutes. Booth says nothing. Raymond is beginning to feel desperate, anticipating that Booth will call time on him at any moment. But Booth stands with wrist high; his left arm extends his foil, pointing slightly downward.

At last, at last Raymond does it. The thrust is upward. Booth expects the thrust toward his waist, but the attack lands on his breastbone, along the collar line of his shirt. It is cleanly a hit.

"*Touché!*" Raymond cries.

Booth nods, puts his arm around Raymond, holding him by his side in a tight embrace.

"Excellent, *mon frère!* Excellent," Booth exclaims.

Raymond feels tears forming in his eyes. He fears he will break out into sobs, he is so proud of himself.

"Of course we must wait until the young lady reaches a marriageable age, eh what?" Booth says.

Raymond nods, wiping his hand over his face, and as Booth releases him, he puts down the foil. "I will look after her, sir!" Nellie is all that keeps him from being a monster.

As he later departs from the East Room to return to his bedroom, he leaves Booth behind still making shadowy passes with the foil at unseen opponents. For Raymond, his best illusions have been restored.

The President's spirits do not remain long elevated. First, there is the heavy in-and-out, in-and-out of many office appointments with congressmen and New York financiers. Afterward, Raymond sees him looking angry when state elections are lost in New York and elsewhere. What do we care about what happens in New York, eh what, he would like to hear the President say.

Then after a short illness, Mr. Thurlow Weed, a very important man, passes away.

The President calls Raymond into his office. He is applying sealing wax to a letter and seems quite beside himself with energy. "We can see now," he trumpets, "why Mr. Lincoln has been stalling about the file: Weed's illness. He wished to spare Weed the ignominy. Well, Weed has been spared." The sealed letter is handed to Raymond. Booth paces back and forth. "If there had to be a winnowing of Weed," Booth exclaims, "then there can be a winnowing of others!"

Shifting his feet, not understanding, Raymond asks where he is to take the letter. It is raining outside.

"Why, to Secretary Lincoln. Do you not see that I've written there his name? And you must wait for an answer." Booth grasps Raymond by the shoulder and stares fiercely into his eyes. "I am determined to see the file in question *before* he releases it to the newspapers. That is what I have written and what he must *specifically* reply to. Is that clear?"

Trembling at the sudden passion in the President, Raymond nods emphatically and takes his leave. In the outer office, while Raymond buttons his long coat and waits for one of the carriages to be brought up, Fred Phillips is preparing a condolence letter to be directed to Mr. Weed's daughter and is arranging for a floral tribute at the services.

Outdoors, on the carriage ride to the War Department, the rain seems at first not so bad as the wind. Some wire trash receptacles have blown over, and even Pennsylvania Avenue, the grandest thoroughfare in the city, is littered with spheres of crumpled newspapers, skittering about bad enough to scare the horses.

From Secretary Lincoln's office in the War Department, Raymond is directed to Lincoln's home. By this time the rain has come on in tropical force, but Raymond knows that the file that has been spoken of has to do with the President's honor, a serious matter. When he gets out of the carriage in front of Mr. Lincoln's home on Thomas Circle, he must hold tight to his hat brim between the street and the front door. The porch is uncovered, and it seems to take hours for a servant to answer his ring. Raymond's acquaintance on the staff does not appear. Instead, sopping wet, he must address himself to a parlor maid, who is too ignorant to ask him in and does not oblige his request to see Mr. Lincoln personally with more than a grunt.

When Lincoln at last appears, he looks sullen and unfriendly. In the vestibule Raymond drips water from his clothing onto the parqueted floor.

"You must answer this letter at once!" Raymond tells him excitedly.

Robert Lincoln looks him over. "You are close to being impertinent," he says.

Nevertheless, Lincoln removes himself to a room nearby, and while Raymond stands unattended beside the staircase, an answer is prepared. Forty-five minutes later, Mr. Lincoln hands a sealed letter back to him.

"Do ye have a 'specific answer,' sir, for the President in the letter?" Raymond remembers his charge.

"Now you *are* impertinent!" Robert Lincoln exclaims.

Raymond has no choice but to hurry back to the White House. Still wet through and through, he waits in the outer office while the reply is sent in to the President. Raymond anticipates that the letter will be found not "specific" enough, and the President in a rage will demand that he return to Secretary Lincoln at once.

The rage comes while Raymond is sitting there. From behind the closed door of the inner office there is the sudden fracturing of a pane of glass that Raymond at first imagines is a window broken by the gusting rainstorm.

But what follows in rapid succession is the startling impact of objects being hurled against the walls. At length, a sound of splintering wood suggests that a chair is being violently broken. Raymond and Fred Phillips look at each other anxiously, and when the tornado inside seems finally to have diminished in intensity, Raymond, although half fearing he will be the next target, rises bravely and knocks on the door.

"What do you want, you fool?" the President calls. But the door is flung open and the President stands aside to admit Raymond. Around the office wild destruction has been wrought upon the furniture. The President is breathing hard. Paperweights and partly filled inkwells have been thrown; a large pane of glass has been shattered, admitting a current of wind and a splatter of rain from the storm. The broken chair has been disintegrated into kindling wood—a shame, since it was from James Monroe, whose furnishings, Raymond recalls, the President has been partial to.

The President's color is angry red, except for his cheeks, which seem to have begun to melt, much as though a finger could now leave a print mark in the skin.

"Sir, is the answer not specific?" Raymond asks at last.

"Specific? Too specific!" the President shouts. "Mr. Lincoln says the Fredericksburg File has been stolen from his bedroom safe! . . . Once more the purpose of my entire existence goes unfulfilled!"

It is some hours later, up in the living quarters, that the President resolves to call in the Pinkertons. *In petto*—"that is to say, in secret" —they will inquire into the alleged burglary of the safe in the Lincoln residence. A fitting irony it will be, Booth tells Raymond, for the Pinkertons achieved their fame by protecting a Lincoln.

"Now," Booth declares, sniffing over a brandy, "if I find that Lincoln is lying to me, if he is suppressing public documents, I will bring him to the dock for treason, Raymond! Treason! Nothing less."

Raymond nods, relieved that the investigation will not be his job. Little Charlie Pinkerton, aged eleven, is in fact a schoolmate of Nellie's, and Raymond often drives the two of them to the Franklin School together. Raymond must hope that Charlie's social prestige will not be so enhanced by the new assignment from the President to Charlie's father's agency that Nellie's head will be turned. It is not easy to compete for one's lady with eleven-year-olds.

5

WASHINGTON AND THE SOUTH

One morning Booth picks up the mailed copy of *The New York Times* in Fred Phillips's office and reads:

PENDLETON'S BILL PASSED

ONLY 5 VOTES RECORDED IN THE NEGATIVE

A TEDIOUS DEBATE DURING WHICH CERTAIN DEMOCRATIC SENATORS ATTEMPT TO MAKE THE MEASURE RIDICULOUS

WASHINGTON—Dec. 27—After a day of tedious debate the Senate this evening passed the Civil Service Reform Bill by the very decisive vote of 39 to 5. As might have been expected, the five negative votes were cast by Democrats, Messrs. Brown of Georgia, Call of Florida, Jones of Louisiana, McPherson of New Jersey, and Morgan of Alabama being the only Senators who were bold enough to go on record as opposed to the reform measure. There were many other Democrats who would have been willing, if they had dared to record themselves in the same way. It is perfectly safe to say since it was plainly apparent to those who followed the debate that on . . .

Booth lays down the paper, feeling oddly depressed. The progress of the bill has been as slow-moving as the fifth act of *Tortesa the Usurer.*

"See, it is passed, this monument to Garfield, and we received no word of it, Fred, let alone credit." Booth looks down the empty corridor where once the shabby genteel vied for place. "At least we got rid of the toads."

"Yes, sir."

"No more office seekers! No more spittoons! No more damned folding chairs. Send the folding chairs back to the Chautauqua circuit, Fred!"

"Yes, sir."

*

In the following weeks there is arranged for Booth his first extended political tour as President. Having turned the confidential matter of the Lincoln "burglary" over to the Pinkertons (a more supercilious bunch than the ones he knows in the New York branch), he is restless to be traveling somewhere. If he wants renomination, Chandler advises that he must barnstorm the South, a prospect that suits him well. The paucity of White House entertainments since the redecoration of the East Room has left a social gap in his life.

He knows that Lucy must feel the same way.

"Do invite Mrs. Chandler to join us on the trip south," Booth tells Chandler. Lucy has been neglected of late.

"I believe she thinks the South too sultry," Chandler says.

Just as well, Booth thinks to himself. She would be wasting her time teasing him, now that Nell is back.

The southern tour begins in Fredericksburg on a note of triumph. The Herndons are prominent on the welcoming committee inasmuch as Chester Arthur has always been a favorite in Nell's hometown. Nor is it a snobbish community. Captain Boyd would still be popular here too, Booth believes, should the captain ever have occasion to materialize again.

In a private audience with Brodie Herndon, Booth confides that Nell is comfortably settled at the Soldiers' Home. Alan and Nellie visit her often. She plays the melodeon and sings.

Unfortunately, being busy, Booth has been seeing her somewhat less often himself. He does not tell Brodie that she wanders about the grounds in all kinds of weather, and although the old soldiers do not speculate about her since Corporal Broadhead's transfer, he has heard they regard her as some kind of war casualty. He has had to station Raymond behind at the home to keep an eye on her.

"And what will you do for the people in your second administration," Brodie eventually asks, "if you ah elected again?"

"Oh, we are building capital ships, we are changing the policy toward Guatemala—" Booth begins in a rush, and then strangely can think of nothing more to add.

As the tour proceeds toward Richmond, Chandler, rubbing his pince-nez, gives the President counsel about Senator Mahone.

"You comprehend," says Chandler, "that Richmond is not Fredericksburg? The Readjusters are the small businessmen of Virginia who resent being taxed to pay off the money which the dominion borrowed from the wealthy planters during the war."

"I comprehend the Readjusters," Booth says pertly. "I suffered Mahone in the Senate, didn't I, for all those months when he was the swing vote?"

"We must continue to suffer him," Chandler says. "The old blood is all Democratic."

On reaching Richmond, Booth is forced to wonder if there is any blood besides old blood in the dominion. First, he fails to get a reception at the railroad station, although the onlookers seem to know who he is well enough. Then, tardily, he and Chandler (and French and Wheelhorse) are fetched by a grizzled party hack, smelling of whiskey, who drives them behind an old cob to the "party headquarters," which resembles nothing so much as one of the frontier playhouses that Booth's father used to perform in out west thirty years before.

Mahone, when he appears, looks to Booth not so much a small businessman as a small confidence man; and his postmasters and collectors, duly pointed out, could be an outlaw band, the way they grunt their assent to his words of greeting ("uh-yuh, uh-yuh"). What Booth desires is that every one of them be shipped back to their saloons and livery stables as soon as the new Civil Service Commission gets busy. General Lee would rise from his grave if he knew the shame in the Cradle of the Confederacy!

Later, on the train, Chandler, sensing his disappointment, says, "You must get over the idea that you are something besides a Yankee down here."

Booth mentions the family ties to the Herndons of Fredericksburg.

"Yes, yes," says Chandler patiently, "but how can you expect the rest of these people to trust a Yankee belonging to the party that freed the Negroes? Even the Readjusters don't trust you. They want to take the patronage away, that's all, from the old guard."

Privately Booth wonders what Chandler has been doing all this time—besides cleaning his pince-nez—if everybody is still so suspicious of him. But he says, "It's all right. I do want to help the real people of the South, and not the privileged ones."

When they reach Florida, supposed to be the other "promising state," it is worse than Virginia. It is a pesthole, this time not so much because of the politicians as because of the mosquitoes, the sandflies, and the midges. It is the earliest spring in anyone's memory, and every time the men try to go fishing they are cannibalized by the insects until they have to go back to the railroad car, where it is like an inferno when the train is standing still.

In Tallahassee, a young reporter is admitted to the car. The bright-red color of his hair—rather like Victoria Coventry's—disconcerts Booth.

"What is your name, then?" Booth demands.

"Petuh Gordon, Sir."

"Truly?"

After the interview is terminated, Booth advises that the young fraud would have called himself Kappenhalter if he dared. "Let me see no reporters after this. . . . The people, yes."

But Chandler soon wears him out by making the train stop at every station platform on which more than three citizens are sighted who might want to shake hands with the President. The trip reaches a fitting climax in Savannah, where Nell's cousin Elizabeth Hull Herndon—now Mrs. Henry Botts—invites the President and his party for dinner.

During the night after the dinner with the Bottses, Booth comes down with the worst gastrointestinal attack of his life. From his cabin on the packet boat where the presidential party is quartered, at three A.M. he summons Chandler, who in turn calls a ship's surgeon. Booth is sure he has been poisoned, incredibly in the very bosom of the Confederacy while dining with a family he has always thought of as the South's finest flower. It is the worst pain he has experienced since childhood.

A week later, recovered, he recounts these events to Nell while pacing back and forth in the parlor of the cottage on the grounds of the Soldiers' Home.

"The Savannah shrimp salad, they said it was. In truth, it was arsenic!"

Nell, fanning herself, says nothing for a moment. She rests on a chaise longue near the scarf-covered melodeon, but her color is better than usual. A copy of "The Harp That Once Thro' Tara's Halls" lies on the instrument.

"I've not seen Elizabeth for years," Nell murmurs. "Somethin' on the tip of mah tongue I remember about her. . . . Hmmm. . . . Slender when a girl, she stahted to develop a fuller figure aftuh her weddin' . . ."

"Yes, she's immense," Booth says, scowling. "And she poisoned me in Savannah."

"Now I know what I remembuh about her," Nell says. "She

always had bad cooks. She did! Ever'body said so. You nevah could trust a meal at Elizabeth's."

Booth pauses in his pacing, considering whether or not to be mollified by the assertion.

"The Herndons have always loved you," Nell offers mildly. "If you wuh poisoned on purpose, it was surely done somewhere other than Elizabeth's."

"Yes, somewhere in the South! The South betrays me! I go to the South to submit my body and my soul to them. And I am betrayed!"

Nell folds her hands, sighing as though at his peevishness. "Well, you ah a Yankee."

"I do not want to keep hearing that I am a Yankee!" Booth retorts.

"You ah the Yankee President from New York," she declares calmly. "You ah a former general of the Grand Army of the Republic."

She unfolds her hands and places one on her bodice while the other travels down the length of her skirt, her eyes following it. Booth's eyes follow it too. He wonders uneasily how often she knows who he really is, and how often she does not.

"I have a mad impulse to bring you to the next reception at the White House!" he says with a sudden nervous laugh. "You have a right to be there."

"I could not do that," Nell says at once in a tone that is half serious, half mocking. "I am proud that Nellie and Alan have the opportunity, but we all know that I and politics do not mix well. We know that. I told mah confessor that we in the family had worked out othuh arrangements."

"And what does your confessor say to that?"

"He says, 'Stay away from wheah you do not belong,'" Nell replies.

Booth puts his fingernail to his teeth. He has removed his gloves earlier. None of the servants are around; a few bluebottle flies are buzzing in the shaft of sunlight coming in the parlor window. He glances in the direction of the staircase to the upper floor.

When they are in the bedroom, she whirls once. She holds her mouth in an odd way.

"Maud, Maud, Maud, Maud," she starts to croon under her breath. Her gown is quickly shed. She is dressed in light cotton underclothing, which she steps out of without the least modesty, gazing this way and that.

"From the look of you—" he begins, excited by her wantonness, stripping off his own garments.

"Yes, look, look, you Yankee!" she cries, turning her chin aside, and lying back. Wild-eyed, she hums under her breath. She can contain currents that have been dammed up inside of him.

"Nell, Nell, you are my love," he says with deep feeling, his flesh against hers, caressing her patiently until he feels her response, and freely enters . . .

Later, when he is preparing to leave, she says to him, "The fabric we ord'd for Nellie's gown has turned out not to be raht. You really ought to leave some extra funds in the household account."

"Good Lord, Nell—"

"She is the President's daughtah, isn't she? If I don't worry about her ball gown, who will?"

"All right," he says. Perhaps she is angry with him because he has been evasive when she asked how long he intended to remain President. Who could say whether or not another term would be necessary? The woman has lost awareness of the duty he bears to the South, let alone to the name of Booth. It is, God knows, not for himself that he runs.

While he is putting on his gloves, waiting for the carriage, she says again, in a more ominous way, "You will not forget the funds?"

"I said I would not," he replies, looking away from her. As he remembers, extravagance was the first symptom of insanity in President Lincoln's wife.

6

BALTIMORE

PRESIDENT CHESTER A ARTHUR
EXECUTIVE MANSION
WASHINGTON D C

HOT ON TRAIL OF PETERMEN KNOWN AS SOHO GANG
SUSPECTED IN WASHINGTON WEST END BURGLARIES
STOP EXPECT REPORT ON OUR PROGRESS SOON

PINKERTON

"Petermen?" Booth asks himself, scratching his head.

7

WORMLEY'S HOTEL

During the month his close companion Robert Dun has come to Washington, and Booth decides to pay him a visit in his local hotel suite. Passing strange, Booth thinks, that Dun has not sought to call at the White House, given their long intimacy.

He stations Raymond for a spell at Wormley's in the lobby, and then strolls over himself (the hotel is practically across the street) so as to make sure he will catch Dun. It is a warm day for a walk, but there are nevertheless many people on the streets, some of them riding bicycles.

Booth has begun to wonder if Dun's neglecting to call could be a portent of Wall Street's abandonment of the administration. The loss of Albany must have been annoying to them, and some even said that the failure to convict Dorsey was taken hard in the Street, inasmuch as probity and moderation have come into fashion again. Fastidious bankers still remembered Chet Arthur's old customhouse swindles.

In the lobby of Wormley's, Raymond indicates with a nod that

Dun is still in his suite. At the same time, Wormley's desk clerk—a most obsequious darky—has recognized Booth, and begins bowing and scraping and Mister-Presidenting him so that Booth takes off his hat three times before the man is willing to draw a breath. Wormley's is managed entirely by Negroes, an achievement that does not surprise Booth, whose respect for the race's talent in domestic service yields to no man's.

Booth has begun writing on the back of one of his calling cards: "Am in the lobby and wd appreciate seeing you briefly if at all possible." To the clerk he says, "Please send in my card to Mr. Dun."

A few minutes later, Booth is taken aback when Dun does not respond to his card by coming out to the lobby to greet him. Instead, the bellboy returns to say that "Mr. Dun is agreeable, sir." Booth taps his hat against the side of his leg and follows the boy down the corridor.

Although Dun answers the knock and shakes hands with him civilly, Booth feels aggrieved that Dun is not alone, but rather in some kind of meeting with a man of leprous complexion, whom Booth recalls as a local attorney. Legal documents are distributed around a walnut secretary in an alcove of the suite. It seems to take forever for the lawyer—an old and decrepit man—to absent himself from their presence.

"Would you care for a glass of water?" Dun asks when they are alone; he is coatless, and while he pours water into two tumblers, he invites Booth to doff his coat and have a chair. It is warm and close in the room although an overhead fan stirs currents of air.

While Booth takes off his hat and seats himself, he says pleasantly, "Indeed I had heard you were expanding your business operations to Washington. I hope it will not interfere with our fishing this summer."

"Alas, I fear it may," says Dun. He hands Booth the glass of cold water.

"Unfortunate," Booth says, looking into Dun's fathomless eyes. "But I, too, may be kept from our customary haunts. Some army officers and I are going to Yellowstone Park this summer. We leave the railroad at Rock Springs, heading overland by saddle horse, stopping at Fort . . . Fort What-is-it?"

Dun shrugs. "It sounds most stimulating."

When Booth adds that Secretary Lincoln may join them on the trip to Yellowstone, he watches Dun's reaction, for if it is not the New York election that has caused Dun's coldness to him, then it is a more serious matter.

"Dun, I must ask you a question," he says. "An item of some interest has recently disappeared from a safe in the home of Robert Lincoln. Now agents assigned to the case inform me they are pursuing in Baltimore, of all places, a most unlikely-sounding gang of safe-crackers." Booth takes a deep breath. "Could it be that Thurlow Weed, before he died, arranged for the theft of this item, if indeed it has been stolen . . ."

"The Fredericksburg File, I suppose?" Dun asks coolly.

"Ah, then it was Weed!" Booth exclaims. "Up to his old tricks!"

"Why, he was up to nothing that I know of," Dun replies.

"But I tell you it is Weed's sort of trickery!" Booth insists. In shirt-sleeves, he paces the thick carpet of the suite, alternately folding his arms and flinging them wide. "It's like the Kappenhalter trickery, pretending that the girl's relatives were pursuing me. He hired men to play roles and to leave calling cards with 'Kappenhalter' printed on them!"

Dun says, "In that regard, the girl has finally been found."

Booth pauses, his face apprehensive.

"Dead, of course," Dun continues. "I see you haven't heard. Her body was fished out of the river. She had been dead for some months."

"Victoria Coventry?"

Dun nods. "Bennett himself made the identification at the morgue and elected to keep what she was doing at the time of her death a secret. What all the Kappenhalters are going to do, if anything, I wouldn't know. Perhaps you should look out for them."

"I regret the girl's death," Booth says stonily.

Dun adds that a corset stay was wrapped around her neck, caus-ing strangulation. "Latham's appeared to want to warn off all other reporters from spying on them. Don't you think?" The flicker in Dun's eye is ominous.

Silent, Booth has a brief image of the bloated body of a red-headed woman lying on a stone slab.

"So she did not leave town as you claimed," Dun says. "What I regret is being the one who told you she was at Latham's."

"She chose work too dangerous for a woman."

Dun licks his lips. In a tense voice, he says, "You are a Pharisee."

"So be it then," Booth returns in a low and angry tone. He grabs coat, stick, hat. "You and your holy brokers! You use me to line your pockets. You used me in the war to do the same thing. Then you cry 'Foul! Foul!' when blood is shed. Never mind. I will locate the Fred-ericksburg File in the time left to me, no matter how short, no matter what the shell game that you and Mr. Weed and Mr. Robert Lincoln try to play with me."

The words hang in the air as he storms from Dun's suite in a haze of resentment and bitter uneasiness.

That afternoon Booth leaves word with Fred Phillips that if anyone named Kappenhalter, or with red hair, calls at the White House the doorman must be summoned at once and the person searched for weapons, no matter that he pretends to have a press card. "The identification will be false," Fred Phillips is told.

That done, Booth sequesters himself in the White House living quarters and barely ventures forth even to the office. At night he has uncomfortable dreams about Victoria Coventry. He does not go out to the Soldiers' Home. He does not fence with Raymond, or discuss his power base with Chandler. He wishes it were already time for his trip to Yellowstone, a trip on which he plans to take Raymond along and finally to teach him to ride. Alan must look after Nell during that month.

Two weeks without Kappenhalters, and Booth is just beginning to feel better.

But one afternoon in the confessional at St. Mary's, Nell goes into a fit of nonstop babbling ("I am the wife of the President, but untrue to him, untrue to him . . ."). An elderly priest, normally inured to monologues of all kinds, summons help.

A strange series of events follows.

A young physician happens to be in the church with his wife, and since no one present is aware that Raymond is waiting in a carriage just outside the front door, Nell is taken off through a side entrance under the physician's auspices.

"What is your name, Missus? What is your name?"

But a stupor has come on her after the babbling. The physician tries snapping his fingers in front of Nell's staring gaze, but that effects no cure. The frustration whets his appetite for stronger measures.

As irony would have it, the young physician has only that morning been listening to a lecture by the visiting nerve specialist, Weir Mitchell of Philadelphia, a man experienced with cases of dementia, neuraesthenia, and other delusional malfunction. Since the young physician has not been able to catch the older doctor's interest during the question period after the lecture, he sees it now as a point of honor to rush his interesting patient to the private clinic where Dr. Mitchell is supposed to be attending the staff physicians on their rounds. The young physician's wife, so astonished at all this that she forgets to tie her bonnet before entering the family buggy, has no further chance to tie it on during the ride to the clinic, so firmly does Nell take hold of the young woman's hand.

Later, when an uneasy Raymond discovers what has occurred within the church, he charges off in his own carriage, possessed of only a single clue from the priest: namely, that she was to be taken to a visiting nerve specialist named Mitchell. On his way into the city, however, Raymond stops briefly at the Soldiers' Home to see if by luck Nell recovered herself enough to ask to be delivered there.

What the abashed Raymond finds is another carriage just arrived with the President inside, along with Alan, who is down from Princeton for the weekend. Raymond is compelled to tell them what happened.

"You are an ass, and always will be," Alan says to him in his most aristocratic tone. "No matter what fine feathers they put on you."

Raymond shoots him a murderous look.

"We must try to head them off," Booth says, "for surely Weir Mitchell will recognize her."

"Still, the lady's not as she was," Raymond pipes up, "not as she looked in the old days."

"Really, scullery boy!" Alan retorts. "How would you know about 'the old days'?"

To keep the two of them apart, Booth sends Raymond off to pick up Nellie at school and turns the carriage containing Alan and himself toward the heart of Washington. He tries to think if Raymond is right about Nell's being no longer as she was: he remembers the once unlined features, the bright, dark eyes of the Nell who was with him in France for that brief sojourn. Her eyes have now become dull, her face weary; even her voice is changed, having grown toneless and without modulation.

As Booth, who is driving, slaps the horses' rumps with the reins, Alan says, "I never cared for her staying at the Soldiers' Home, you know. It is like a warehouse."

Booth hopes the accelerating vibration of the carriage will set Alan's teeth to chattering and silence him, but Alan simply sniffs and adjusts his hands on his long bony knees. He remarks that Washington and the White House are barely tolerable addresses, let alone having to reside in a warehouse.

"Because you have grown bored with Washington is no reason we need to be," Booth snaps. He has noticed—not without relief—that

Alan has stopped coming down from Princeton with his friends.

"It's not a matter of boredom," Alan says. "I've simply gotten in with a crowd that—well, rides to the hounds, you know. Also I row eights. A sport sometimes called crew."

"Keep at it."

"Why, may I ask, while I am so favorably placed, must my poor sister be in the day-to-day keeping of that street arab Raymond? It baffles me."

Booth hits the horses again. "She goes to school every day with the best people in Washington, with the Pinkerton boy—"

"The Pinkertons! My God, do you really believe the Pinkertons are anybody?"

"*I* am somebody," Booth replies without raising his voice.

"You are," Alan slowly concedes, "very close to being somebody."

Booth stares at Alan for a moment, then strikes the reins again. Alan keeps quiet the rest of the way, having to concentrate on grabbing hold of things in order to maintain his balance.

When the carriage reaches the Ebbitt House, where Booth feels Mitchell is likely to be staying, an inquiry produces the information that the eminent doctor is inspecting a private clinic, which is at the far west end of the capital, a discouraging distance for them, if that is where Nell has been taken.

Nevertheless, the two of them start off again. Many of the mansions in this quarter of the town are enhanced by sweeping green lawns that extend down to the Potomac River; here the Soho Gang is supposed to have operated, according to Pinkerton. Booth half expects that the clinic they are looking for will be similarly opulent.

In this he is disappointed. Although the clinic, when they reach it, is ensconced among tall leafy trees on comfortable acreage, an ugly spiked fence surrounds the building, which in its turn has the same kind of drab brick facade as do the commonest edifices in New York or Philadelphia. A drowsing gatekeeper readily admits them on Booth's advice that he is the President of the United States.

No other human being presents himself to them until after they have got as far as the main lobby by way of a large oaken door at which no one has answered their loud pounding of a brass knocker. A dog is barking somewhere. Booth has to wonder if he might one day wind up in such a place himself should he ever be tried and found insane.

Better the hangman's noose. There is an air of decrepitude, as well as an odor of mildew. Some patients—two rather young males swathed in heavy flannel and a young woman in street clothes, her bonnet undone—are seated forlornly on wooden benches in the corridor. Directly ahead, metal bars cast stripes in a square of light from a large arched window. It is not much better than Bellevue.

An attendant at last appears—a sturdy personage in a brown smock. "Whatcher business?" he inquires curtly. The President is not recognized as such, and Alan seems inclined to take a high hand at the oversight until Booth stops him.

"Has a woman patient come in," Booth asks pleasantly, "attended, we think, by a young physician, bringing her to Dr. Weir Mitchell? Is Dr. Mitchell visiting here today?"

By coincidence, the young physician himself appears in the corridor at this moment, a tall blond man with blue eyes, who advances on them with great alacrity. "This is indeed an honor, Mr. President," he says heartily. "We have just learned of the authenticity of the lady's connection with you."

"Indeed?" says Booth, a watchful look in his eye.

"And this must be your son, I judge?"

When Booth mumbles an affirmative, the physician signals to the woman on the bench whom Booth took to be a patient. "My name is Fitzsimmons," the physician informs, and when the female duly reaches them, with her bonnet laces still dangling, he says, "May I present my wife? Dear, this is the President and his son."

"I can hardly believe it, Your Excellencies," the lady says, curtsying.

"Your relative is with Dr. Mitchell," Fitzsimmons quickly reveals, and while leading them away from his wife to chairs in an empty office, he apologizes for having "snatched" the poor woman the way he did. "Is her name Nell or Lew or Maud? It wasn't clear."

Brushing dust off the chair he is offered before sitting, Booth essays a laugh. "*That* is confusion, is it not? . . . What a constant challenge your work here must present to you."

Fitzsimmons says that he does not practice at the clinic, he merely "consults."

"Splendid," Booth says. "How does a layman offer support to an institution such as this one, which appears to offer the unfortunate both sympathy and confidentiality?"

"My word, Mr. President, you ought to speak to the director."

"Why don't *you* speak to him?" Booth urges. "I must say I'd feel a good deal more confident about my support if you *were* on the staff here. Perhaps I'll write the director a note to that effect." Booth starts fishing in his pockets as though for notepaper, and he glances at Alan, who gives him a discerning glance in return.

By the time notepaper is found and the note written—with Fitzsimmons still stuttering his astonished gratitude—the doyen Weir Mitchell appears, having been summoned by the attendant. He is wearing riding clothes, for some reason; his beard is trimmed in a tighter, fussier way than when he fell out of the rowboat.

"My dear President Arthur," Mitchell booms, advancing effusively. "I scarcely recognize you without a fishing rod in your hand. But I suppose the trout are not running on Pennsylvania Avenue, eh what?" He shakes hands with both Booth and Alan. "Wretched place this, isn't it? You'd think it was some kind of charity ward. Ah, well, Fitzsimmons here is not responsible. And I've seen expensive clinics that are worse. Here they keep only ninety percent of the patients in the locked wards."

Fitzsimmons looks sheepish and bows himself out of the room, still holding his citation of merit. Mitchell meanwhile settles down to describe his patient's condition.

"She's resting now. Was in a hysterical trance, that's all," Mitchell declares. "I've seen it before. Woman of breeding. Who knows what causes it? Unhappy love affair, loss of money, the passing of maidenhood. Nothing escapes me. This woman is a cousin of your late wife, I believe?"

"Uhh—yes," Booth says.

Mitchell nods. "Some physical resemblance all right. This woman is older. Much older. . . . The fact is, during the seizure, part of the time she believed herself to be your wife. Of course she believed the President to be John Wilkes Booth!" Here Mitchell lets out a guffaw. "You must excuse me, I do not take hysterical symptoms lightly. But the delusions were most . . . bizarre in this case. Well, the life of a man has distinct aims and purposes which steady him as a flywheel does an engine. Women are not so fortunate."

"May we see her now?" Booth asks. He looks humbly at the knees of his trousers and holds his cane at an angle.

"Oh, I've given her something to relax her. See her tomorrow, why don't you? While I'm in town, I'll look in on her. It's a touching case."

Booth glances at Alan, who looks still to be in shock at having heard the name John Wilkes Booth. To Mitchell he says, "Aunt Lew is such a homebody. If this place is really wretched, should she not be restored to the environment she is used to?"

"Forgive me, but the medical literature would suggest just the opposite," Mitchell declares. "It is a change of scene that is usually helpful."

"A change of scene?" Booth asks.

"Now, I don't mean an asylum," Mitchell goes on. "Not at all. I mean a trip abroad. A rest cure."

"Ahh!" Booth says. "We'll have to do that. Indeed we shall."

"She mustn't go off alone," Dr. Mitchell now advises. He says that personally he thinks someone should go with her who sincerely cares for her. Perhaps there was no great hurry. Why, before falling asleep, she seemed nearly contented again, as though her little guilts were discharged. Confession that went beyond the comprehension of the priests, if one could put it that way.

Booth says, "Mitchell, I cannot allow you to spend any more of your valuable time on this case. I know you are busy with your novels and your poetry as well as your famous medical practice—"

Mitchell raises his eyes to the ceiling. "Not the half of it. I serve on constant boards and committees as well. I am fair committee'd to death."

"Then leave it to us; the rest cure is the answer!" Booth declares, and stands with such authority that Mitchell automatically rises, too, and proceeds as though he were the one who was leaving.

"If you do move her, let me know," Mitchell says. "Of course, I'll look in on her before I leave Washington." He nods at Alan, who is standing in a kind of slouching way, his eyes lidded.

"We'll post you how she is," Booth corrects amiably.

"By George, I believe we're likely to see each other in Newport in July," Mitchell says, donning his gloves. "At least I was told you were going to drop in at the horse show."

"I think it's on my calendar," Booth says. "I'm helping to dedicate the Brooklyn Bridge that month too, you know."

"A real feat of engineering," says Mitchell.

At last he is gone. When the door is closed behind him, Booth can feel Alan looking at him with an expression of frightened astonishment.

Alan's voice is tremulous, rather like a child's.

"Is my—uhh—Uncle Jim then in truth John Wilkes Booth?"

Booth returns the intensest of gazes.

"Find out where your mother is," he quickly orders. "And let's get her to the White House. The servants' entrance will be least conspicuous."

Alan, seeming cowed, moves at once. In the corridor he finds the attendant and tells him that the President must see the new patient at once, on Dr. Mitchell's order. In no time, they are at Nell's bedside.

She lies on a narrow cot near the window of a private room, dressed in an ill-fitting flannel nightgown. But her face is calm and the sun throws a warm light on her complexion. Her head, framed by the white linen of the pillowcase, lies so squarely in the middle of the pillow, and her hands rest so lightly on the top of the blanket that she might be in eternal rest. For a moment Booth wonders what would happen if he left her here for good. Not possible. He grabs her shoulder and shakes it abruptly to force her awake.

Nell does not stir at first but then her eyes slowly open, and as she looks at them, plainly recognizing each of them in turn, there is an expression of comprehension in the eyes. Calmly she reaches out one hand to each of them on opposite sides of the bed, and as all four hands are clasped, her eyes immediately close again. Booth feels a little unsettled at the expression on her face. Were she going insane, she might be dangerous. But if she were playing at it, she might be more so.

"Orderly!" Alan cries to the attendant. "This lady must be prepared for immediate release. Is that clear?"

The attendant at first looks puzzled, then disappears to check with Dr. Fitzsimmons, who Booth knows will present no problem.

But he grows aware, for almost the first time, that his destiny in high office is resting more and more in the hands of others, who are growing subtler in purpose and more determined to reach their goals than was true even of the office seekers, like Guiteau.

While they are waiting, Alan inquires anxiously, "Are you really going to Newport this summer?"

"Yes," Booth says.

"Hard to believe, I've never been to Newport, Mr. Booth."

"All right, I'll take you," Booth says, "as long as you do not ever call me that."

Blushing, Alan apologizes. The prospect of being presented in Newport, he says, "might—er—shake any man for a second or two."

8

THE LINCOLN BEDROOM

Having reached a difficult decision, Booth ascends the uncarpeted back stairway, carrying a glass of milk on a silver tray for Nell, who is quartered in the Lincoln Bedroom. Painful though it may be for him, he can see what needs to be done and he will do it. A gloomy Wednesday it is. Weir Mitchell, who has attempted to call on Nell, has already been turned away at the door.

Outside the bedroom Booth nods to Raymond, who is standing guard. He knocks twice and does not wait for an answer before entering.

Nell is sitting up in bed, brushing her raven-black hair. Since the personal maid Booth assigned to Nell is not around, he exchanges a kiss with her, still holding the tray. She wears a high-necked mantle with ruffled collar and cuffs. On a table nearby is a dish of half-eaten croissants and a bowl with the remains of breakfast gooseberries.

When he offers her the milk, she shakes her head. "I apologize," she says ruefully. "I behave like a child, so you bring me milk."

"Not at all, my dear."

Nell looks at him and continues matter-of-factly, still brushing her hair. "No, I behaved badly yesterday, Husband. Every once in a while I feel like I'm going to have a nervous breakdown."

"The milk I bring is to relax you."

"But I am relaxed now. I have slept well and am perfectly relaxed."

"Then perhaps *I* will drink the milk," Booth says. And he does. It fails to produce relaxation. She is right to shun it.

He says to her, "Nell, I have reached a difficult decision. But one I think you will commend me for. I have decided not to run for reelection."

"I am too great a burden for you," she says, looking decisively away from him. "I make you do things you do not want to do."

"No, that is not true," Booth says, sitting down beside her on the bed. "I have come to realize that there are times when one should think less about honor and public good, and rather more about the needs of one's family and friends. I have been deficient in the latter regard."

"Well, who expected you to be President?" Nell says graciously.

"I have let others down as well as you. Robert Dun felt my wrath the other day, although he was perfectly correct in saying I had done something mean and ill-advised." Booth has taken her hand in his with such insistence that she must turn and look at him. "Will you continue to live in this house with me until the end of my term? We shall go abroad after that."

With a testy glance, Nell shakes free her hand. "You do not need me here. You have hostesses aplenty. Mary McElroy, Lucy Hale Chandler . . ."

"You misunderstand about Mrs. Chandler," Booth says. "She is not a hostess here. For a brief time perhaps . . ."

"Oh, I read of her pourin' at the receptions. I read it in the papers." Nell fans herself lightly. "I s'pose that's why you were stayin' away from the Soldiers' Home."

Booth reaches for her hand again. He is somewhat encouraged by her display of temper; she is more as she used to be, full of willfulness and jealousy. "You will not go back to the Soldiers' Home . . . unless I am there too."

"But I prefer the Soldiers' Home," she murmurs, casting her eyes away from him again. "Do you care for the furniture in this room? It is very plain."

Booth tells her that she is in the Lincoln Bedroom, "as the sycophants call it." The name Lincoln, however, does not, to his surprise, produce the usual anger in him; perhaps he is already living in the future when the Lincolns will be no worse than shadowy ghosts.

"If it is Lincoln's furniture," Nell says archly, "I s'pose Abraham Lincoln brought it here all the way from Indiana, or wherever it was, and we don't dare lay a finger on it."

"Nell, you may have any bedroom in the Mansion, including my own!" he exclaims. "Do you think I am happy in this museum? I have but one hope for the rest of my term. To secure the Fredericksburg File, if destiny permits. But then, I promise you we are off to Europe. To fresh woods and pastures new!"

"With Alan and Nellie?"

"Of course." Booth says that he has asked the two children to come to the Lincoln Bedroom so that he can share with them his decision about the future. "We will want new roles. Fresh roles! Can you conceive that there are actors who will tolerate playing Richelieu, or Charles the Second, or some other single role for near thirty years? Imagine the numbness of it, never to change—"

While he is making discourse, the voices of the children are heard in the corridor outside. Alan's is fiercely audible ("Come here, you!"), Nellie's is muffled. Raymond's inflamed tenor calls out a challenge, and the next thing Booth and Nell are aware of is brief scuffling, violent enough to produce a shattering thump against the solid oaken door of the Lincoln Bedroom. Booth strides to the door and flings it open.

"Again? Again?" he cries.

Here stands Alan, six-foot-four inches of contorted smirk, rubbing a fist, and a few feet from him, brandishing a silver candlestick defensively, Raymond, his cheeks flushed, but with an expression that seems guilty more than it does defiant. Nearby, Nellie, in sailor dress with ankle-length skirt, watches implacably, Alice in her Wonderland.

"If you have no respect for *me*," Booth thunders at them, "do you have none for this revered house! You behave like you are in a Five Points saloon!"

"What is he doing here?" Alan demands.

"Why, I asked him to wait there. Do not wave that candlestick, Raymond!"

"He is not only a child molester," Alan declares. "He is a . . . never mind."

"I am no child molester!" Raymond shrills, but he looks disconcerted, as though Alan may have more to reveal. He puts down the candlestick and turns his back.

Alan says, "He is a sneak too. But never mind it. You will only take his part."

"He lies through his teeth!" Raymond shouts.

Pulling the door shut in order to spare Nell the unseemly scene, Booth says, "At least have pity for the good lady who lies beyond the door."

"My seconds will visit you, Mr. Arthur!" Raymond says to Alan.

"Don't be ridiculous," Alan scoffs.

In the mildest of voices, Nellie says, "Alan thinks Raymond went into his bedroom in the middle of the night with a clothesline."

"I suppose he meant to strangle me. I woke up," Alan says, adjusting his ascot.

"Ye liar, I wouldn't strangle ye, strangling's too good for ye!"

Raymond has stuck out his chin so far that Booth is half hoping that Alan will hit him just to improve Raymond's common sense. But when Alan turns away in contempt, Booth is forced to say "Raymond, get back to your quarters without another word."

Raymond clamps his lips together and sullenly goes. Booth says to Alan, "If you saw someone in your room with a clothesline, you were doubtless dreaming. But lock your door if you must have such dreams."

While Alan looks disputatious for a moment, Booth answers with so burning a gaze that Alan seems at last to remember to whom he is talking.

Nellie asks, "Did you—and Auntie Lew—have something you wanted to tell us today, Father?"

"No, I did not!" Booth thunders suddenly. "Why should I? What do my sacrifices mean to any of you?"

That is what is shocking to him: the generation to come is full of snobs and sneaks. He does not want to have to guess what Raymond was up to with the clothesline.

Later that day he gives orders that Alan and Raymond may never again sleep under the same roof. For the time being, Alan will be exiled to the Soldiers' Home.

9

PHILADELPHIA

PRESIDENT CHESTER A ARTHUR
EXECUTIVE MANSION
WASHINGTON

BELIEVE SOHO GANG WILL BE APPREHENDED HERE
SHORTLY STOP PROMISE UTTER CONFIDENTIALITY

PINKERTON

10

NEW YORK CITY

Booth submits no announcement that the President declines to seek a second term. With disappointment, he senses that the public has lost interest in him. Perhaps it is merely the result of summer doldrums, but he half wishes that a journalist like Victoria Coventry were still around. With patience and charm, he could in time have converted her negative suspicions of him into a positive interest.

But in the meantime he must be true to his promise to Nell by preparing for what lies beyond the White House. Should his precious file be retaken from the humbug Soho Gang (or, more likely, be wrested bodily from Robert Lincoln), perhaps there still could be apotheosis in the Capitol rotunda. Without the file he must make other plans.

"Dear Edwin," Booth writes. The taste of ashes in his mouth gives bitter satisfaction. "Dear Edwin Booth, When may I see you on a matter of some importance?" Edwin is back again in New York after having completed another tour of Europe. Before the tour began, a formal request from the President "for Mr. Booth to bring his distinguished company to Washington" was met with complete rejection. Edwin wrote of the emotional impossibility of ever performing again in a city where the burden of the past was too great. Ay, the burden of the past. . . .

"Dear Edwin," Booth writes, "when may I see you again? I will be in New York on the occasion of the opening of the Brooklyn Bridge. Can you receive me?"

While waiting for an answer, he goes down one night to the second cellar under the Mansion, the deeper one. Carrying a kerosene lantern, he makes his solitary way through the musty arsenal there, the barrels and crates of weapons and ammunition, all of which, Booth supposes, were once thought necessary to defend the house and its inhabitants. Musket balls are what he is interested in, the same ones he saw General Sheridan point out on the evening they stumbled across the dueling foils that Booth and Raymond later played with. He extricates six or seven of the round gritty objects from a crate and places them in a small burlap bag, which he carries upstairs to his bedroom.

No word arrives from Edwin until Booth reaches New York. There at the desk of the Fifth Avenue Hotel, in the company of Bill Chandler and of Raymond, Booth is handed a sealed note addressed to the Hon. Chester A. Arthur, Confidential: Mr. Booth would receive the President in Mr. Booth's suite at the Windsor "at the President's pleasure."

The communication lifts its recipient's morale. Indeed, the next morning—windy but brilliantly warm—he finds it difficult to give full concentration to the ceremonies marking the opening of the bridge, so fixed is his mind on the meeting with his brother. His first blunder comes during an introduction of the new governor of New York—a Democrat named Cleveland from Buffalo. "Delighted to meet you, Governor Buffalo!" he cries, a terrible gaffe. Cleveland, wearing a tall beaver hat, grumbles. Booth apologizes, they shake hands. Off to the races. Privately, Booth recalls playing both Buffalo and Cleveland in his youth, and has found the two cities to be indistinguishable.

Under the porte cochere of the hotel, the mayor of New York, an affable man named Edson, greets President and governor and joins them in a carriage at the head of a parade composed of equipages bearing many dignitaries, Chandler among them. On the way to the City Hall, Booth and Cleveland lift their beaver hats to the crowds that line both sides of Broadway. The cheering is affectionate. The people are fond of their own Chet Arthur, and Booth willingly waves to their applause.

The trees are in full leaf in City Hall Park. Here Booth leaves his carriage and joins the rest of the official party, who walk eight to ten abreast in the direction of the tower at the Manhattan end of the bridge. The wind is just strong enough so that Booth must hold on to his hat brim when the photographers take his picture. Cannon fire booms out from Governor's Island and the band plays "Hail to the Chief!"

The great stone towers of the bridge, rising from the river and joined by the mighty sweep of the vaulting cables, are a sight to behold. When the presidential party moves forward in order to take the crossing of the bridge on foot, reporters cry out to him for his reactions, and one reporter, who perhaps remembers the President's food poisoning in Georgia, inquires about his health.

"My health is excellent!" he cries, and sets a brisk pace even though others in the party, including the mayor, show signs of flagging very early. Soon Booth slows down, reminding himself that Chester Arthur must succumb to old infirmities very soon after leaving office.

Since he does not plan to run again, Booth must perform true to the tragic destiny of his character.

But what excitement envelops them! What a convoy of ships, scows, boats, barges, float in the harbor below! As the party crosses, all the boats begin tooting their horns and blowing their whistles. Booth waves his hat with enthusiasm. How like a curtain call being President is, with all the bows and postures that an actor alone knows how to perform! In the present case, the acclaim is due him, he believes, not just because Arthur is a native son, but because he has served unselfishly in his term of office.

As the party draws closer to the Brooklyn tower (conversation among the men having diminished with the need to draw breath on their lengthy hike), Booth supposes that sometime before the end of his term it would be appropriate that testimonials about his administration be solicited. He contemplates that, when older, he will set store by such clippings. In the theater, of course, there were people whose chief function was to drum up pithy endorsements. In politics, on the other hand, one had speeches. . . .

The speeches soon come. As Booth descends a ramp adjoining the Brooklyn tower of the bridge, the mayor of Brooklyn reaches up a hairy paw to clasp Booth's hand. The mayor is a short man named Low.

"Mr. President, the step you take today will be long remembered in the history of our great republic. . . ."

Two more hours follow of stultifying oratory, some of it his own.

The next day Booth awakens, experiencing pains in his abdomen and an increase in the beating of his pulse. He does not appreciate such a personal foreshadowing of the death of Chet Arthur, particularly not on the day he is to visit his brother.

Even as he endures the pain, he alters his makeup in front of the dressing-table mirror, for he has determined to appear before Edwin not as Arthur but rather as "Johnny," who was once one of the Booths. Under the greasepaint, however, which he removes for his rendezvous, his real face has its own symptoms of blemish. No matter his high standards of preparation, the years of applying paint and putty have mottled his flesh. As for the rest of his body, the weight that he added to his form in order to avoid the need of padding now makes him seem topheavy when he dispenses with the lifts in his shoes that have given him height. On his shorter frame, he looks stout, fit for clown roles at best.

Chandler waits for him in an inner room of the presidential suite but makes no comment on his changed appearance. Raymond, more used to such transformations, has settled himself on one of the divans. He will stay behind in order to deal with possible callers. Booth meanwhile lights a cigar and backs out of the suite as though he has just ended a visit there. He later meets Chandler at a carriage stand, and the driver is directed to a service entrance at the Windsor.

Here the two men climb the stairs to the second floor. At the door to Edwin Booth's suite, Chandler knocks in the rhythm that has been suggested in advance. The President feels the anxious beating of his heart again at the sight of the Roman profile of his eldest brother in the crack of the door.

He hears himself say, "Thank you, Bill," and takes something like a portfolio from Chandler's hands. Then he is inside, alone with his fiercely gazing brother, and Chandler is left outside in the corridor.

"Ted, I wish I could embrace you," Booth says to the white marble profile. Then he looks with shame at the floor. "But I see you do not feel that way."

"I cannot, I cannot," says Edwin.

In some ways, Edwin has not changed much at all; in others, he seems unrecognizably severe. His jaw muscles have tightened; his nose has become so thin and aquiline that it seems a face in intaglio.

"But come inside," Edwin says, tying the sash on the quilted dressing gown he wears.

He leads the way into the sitting room; the suite is empty of servants, and of any others. As the younger man seats himself, he notes the half-unpacked suitcases in the room.

"Your latest tour of the Continent was a complete triumph, we hear."

"Not complete," Edwin says as he sits down opposite his brother. "But some of the performances were well received." The company has been back in the States for only a few days; its prospects are not clear.

"And is Booth's Theater now shut down for good?" John Wilkes asks.

"It would seem so," Edwin admits. "I of course sold out my interest some time ago. But the actual closing happened while we were abroad."

"And Edwina was with you? How is she? Have you seen Mother?"

"Edwina is well," Edwin says shortly. "Mother is holding her own, although weaker."

When no further details are forthcoming, John Wilkes searches his brother's eyes. "And Rose? And—"

"Your concern for your family is a bit late, Johnny."

John Wilkes gazes at his brother silently.

At last Edwin says, "Besides, your visit, whatever its purpose, should not be allowed to interfere with pressing affairs of state."

"I have handled the affairs of state with honor, I think," the other replies. "You have been abroad so long you may not know the excellent reputation of my administration."

"Please spare me." Edwin raises his hand. "The murder of one President while you were a patriotic youth I could perhaps understand. But that does not account for the convenient elimination of a more recent President. I also shudder to think of how that good fellow, my clubman General Arthur, met his Maker."

"General Arthur expired of heart failure." Wilkes's voice is cold. "A consequence of Bright's disease." When Edwin says nothing, Wilkes adds, "To this day I protect and cherish his widow and children."

Edwin says, "The monstrosity of it is beyond imagination. Daily I wonder why I do nothing, why I lift no finger. Am I Hamlet in the flesh?"

Wilkes now leaps to his feet. "Judge my performance as a public servant against General Arthur's while he lived," he challenges. "If you like, I can bring you vouchers, receipts, correspondence, that show how this man bilked money from employees of the state and the federal government throughout his tenure as collector and after. Good God, his personal fortune comes from bribes and extortion. Is this the 'good man' you wish were President?"

"Enough, enough." Edwin clasps his hand to his forehead. "Tell me what you want of me, Johnny, and pray leave me in peace."

A tremor passes through the younger brother. He stops pacing the carpet, ardently wishing to touch the other's heart, even if only for a moment. On the brocaded divan where he has set the portfolio he brought with him he now casts his eye, and undertakes to explain.

"I am finishing my term of office," he says bravely, "and will not seek another. I want to go to Europe with Nell and the children, but I have had enough of Arthur. Let the children be Arthurs if they wish it; it is a harmless name. For me, I would earn my living in the way I know best."

He begins fumbling in the portfolio with a feeling of pleasure and excitement.

"As an actor?" Edwin murmurs.

"I—I would be uneasy," Wilkes stutters. His fingers have found what he wants in an interior pocket of the portfolio. "The cities make me uneasy. I relish the open road. My—my—the new shape of my body on the boards makes me uneasy."

Without warning he now flips something spherical into the air. As it describes an arc around his head, he throws up another sphere, catching the first at the same time that he throws up a third. Musket balls they are, the ones he has been practicing with ever since he secured them from the great cache of ammunition in the deepest cellar of the White House.

Soon he is juggling six, and then seven musket balls in the air.

"I thought of the circus," he says now to Edwin without missing a beat. "They have excellent circuses in Europe, and I thought you could give me a character reference. Do you not know a manager with a circus?"

When he has caught the last of the musket balls with a cheery "huzzah" and buried them in the pocket of his tweed coat, he is surprised to see Edwin looking pale and bewildered.

John Wilkes says, "You wonder, no doubt, what my family will be doing while I am juggling with the circus. A good question. They are not troupers, as the Booths were when we were young. But who knows?"

For a moment it seems that Edwin is going to open his mouth, then he seems to think better of it. At last, gripping the purple sash of his dressing gown with some tension, he says in a quiet voice, "Cannot this business—with the circuses—wait until you are really prepared to leave, Johnny?"

"Surely." Wilkes is heartened by his brother's tone. "I hoped you would see I was worthy of recommending. When the time came."

On this advice Edwin rises from the sofa and moves toward his brother. He touches him on the shoulder; they are at last almost of the same height, for Wilkes has done some stretching exercises in recent years that have made them near equals, even without the lifts in his shoes.

"In the meantime, Johnny," Edwin says, with tenderness, "it is not right for the President to vanish from the earth for hours simply because you feel like removing the makeup. Your position is a sacred trust. You must do it well."

"I will. I do."

"You must not act violently."

"I will get the Fredericksburg File," Wilkes says, now much moved. He is determined to maintain his brother's interest and approval. "I will get the file and prove to the world that the name of Booth—"

"Do not concern yourself about the name of Booth."

There is a moment, briefly, in which Wilkes, watching the expression on Edwin's face, feels that he is merely being humored. Carefully he takes one step aside and says, "Nay, it is all right. I will have the file yet. They are trying to lead me up the garden path with their Pinkertons. Someone. Weed? Dun? Robert Lincoln?" He attempts a laugh. "Kappenhalter perhaps. But I will get it."

Edwin's response is dangerously vibrant.

"I promise you, Johnny, if I hear, or even suspect, that one man more—be he a Lincoln or the meanest man in America—falls victim to your obsessions, I will act. *I will act!* I promise you that!"

For a moment there is silence. Then John Wilkes says, in a nearly flippant tone, "No harm will come to Mr. Lincoln."

Before Wilkes takes his leave, the two men embrace, and the younger speaks of paying the elder another visit some time in the future.

"I think not," Edwin says. "Since Mary's illness has become hopeless, Edwina and I are moving to a new home. In another state."

"I regret not being able to meet your daughter."

"Well, it is impossible."

They shake hands and the door closes. With his heart tripping again in his breast, Wilkes marches down the corridor. He promises himself that he will pursue the Fredericksburg File to his last breath and see to it that, once the Herndons are protected, the contents are published. He means to redeem the name of Booth, no matter what his brother's opinion is, and no matter what the cost to the ill-gotten repute of others. Even Abraham Lincoln's name would shine the brighter by comparison with the corrupted men who surrounded him.

So much the better if it does. Booth's respect for Abraham Lincoln has grown. He believes he has more respect for Lincoln than does Lincoln's own son, who long withheld the truth.

"Chandler," Booth says to his friend as they meet again up the hall from the suite, "let us not allow the rest of our time in office to be wasted. Let us hold in abeyance any announcement of my withdrawal from a reelection campaign and do our utmost to catch off guard those who would deceive us."

11

For the summer—the last one before he becomes a lame duck—Booth moves back to the cottage at the Soldiers' Home along with Nell and Nellie and a skeleton household staff. Raymond is left at the White House, where he must take daily riding lessons at the stables in order to be ready for the great western trip to Wyoming in August. Before that, during the time when Booth and Alan are in Newport in late July, Raymond will look after the ladies.

But in the meantime Alan, with perpetual frown, is showing new concern for his mother. After the mischance in the church, he has become aware that one more misstep by Nell could jeopardize his status at the Hunt Club and on the polo grounds. He does not let his mother leave the cottage unescorted. He takes her to church himself and goes with her to the door of the confessional. He gets up during the night to check with the watchman and make sure that all is well. Booth commends him.

As for Raymond, Booth cogitates much on the lad. Sitting alone on the terrace while the bees browse over the beds of fragrant sweet peas and colorful azaleas, he plans for the time when Raymond will be with them in Europe. Perhaps in the circus Raymond will truly have a chance to win Nellie's heart. Although the idea seems impossible, given Alan's view of the lad, and Nell's view, Booth believes they will grow mellower toward him. In the sweet democracy of a gypsy life in Central Europe, anything might be possible. Raymond might make a trapeze acrobat; he is small and supple. Alan likely would not be interested in circus life. Would he go off somewhere, find a position, and leave Raymond and Nellie alone? Then the rest of them could live in tents and wagons.

Booth has sometimes asked Raymond, "And what does Nellie say to you when you tell her of your lifetime devotion?" "She don't say anything" is Raymond's reply, and he seems satisfied with that. At least she doesn't laugh; perhaps she is too young to laugh.

One thing about the circus: the women who work in it look at men in a certain way. The rope dancers and the bareback rider. They have attractive costumes and are usually frank and unabashed in their manner. Booth remembers when the Vienna Circus toured America just before the war. That was a wonderful memory. He was barely old enough to take advantage of it.

He would not call them coarse women—they are artists of a special kind. But one of them might look at Raymond in a certain way, and perhaps Nellie would not matter so much to him. In the upstairs room of the cottage at the Soldiers' Home, at night when everyone else has retired, Booth sometimes juggles his musket balls and thinks of the women of the circus. They *were* frank and unabashed. But not like Victoria Coventry, who was only interested in spying on a man, and who would take her money for betraying any one of them she could.

One warm and somnolent morning shortly before the Newport trip Booth receives a letter in the mail which he reads over breakfast.

Confidential

To Your Excellency:

It has come to our attention that you may be interested in securing the Fredericksburg file which we may have in our posession. I would conduct negotiation for it with a business-like agent that you choose coming to the Ebbitt House at noon on Sunday next. For recognizing him your agent should wear a gardenia in his lapel and should unfold the umbrella he will carry partly open on the carpet beside him. Come in good faith or not at all.

Yr. obedient servant
The Gent

"This letter is a puzzlement, Raymond," Booth says later to the lad. He has gone into Washington for the purpose of joining Raymond at the latter's riding lesson. Afterward the two of them take their mounts far out Pierce's Mill Road along Rock Creek. Although the road is dusty, the vistas here are pleasant; a breeze rustles the leaves of the tall trees, and Raymond's confidence as a rider appears to be growing.

Having shown the "Gent" letter to Raymond before they set off, Booth's first chance to discuss it is when the horses have slowed to a walk on a trail near the rushing stream.

"Either I am the butt of an endless confidence game, Raymond, or we are slowly reaching the Day of Judgment."

"If ye want," says Raymond, "I kin get a gardenia and umbrella and meet him for ye."

"The letter does not ring quite true to me. It is supposed to be from a thief, possibly from a member of the Soho Gang, as they call it. But it is written in too fine a hand. The mistakes do not seem natural. Or the manner British."

"P'raps he hired a scribe to write it for him," Raymond says. Carefully he watches his horse step through the roiling water of a shallow ford in the creek where the trail crosses. To Booth he seems to sit the horse well. He looks trim in his new boating cap, ribbed jersey, jodhpurs, and polished boots.

"The Pinkertons sometimes set traps," Booth says darkly. "In the war that's what they did."

"The Pinkertons, they be working for you now," Raymond says.

The trail narrows here and goes upward so that the horses must form a single file. Raymond yields the lead to Booth, who at the top kicks his horse into a gallop through the trees. When he at last reaches the stone tower of Pierce's Mill, Raymond is not so far behind. The lad's boating cap flies off in the last sixty yards.

Booth laughs. "You are just about ready for Wyoming!" he calls.

Raymond has to dismount, hand Booth the reins, and go back to fetch his cap. "Will we see wild Indians?" he asks, flushed and panting a little as he gets his boot into the stirrup and pulls himself up again.

"We will see them do a dance for us at Fort Washakie," Booth says, handing him the reins. "Did you ever see the primitive races dancing? Their wildness is not far beneath the surface."

By the middle of the following day Booth determines to widen his investigation of the strange letter from The Gent. Nellie has been invited to a birthday party for her classmate Charlie Pinkerton: Charlie's father, the head of the Pinkerton Agency, is to be home for the occasion.

"Not in Philadelphia after all," Booth inquires rhetorically, "pursuing the Soho Gang?" He is addressing himself to Nellie, all dressed up in her wine-colored taffeta with a velvet sash around her waist. Grabbing the birthday present that has been bought and wrapped for Charlie, Booth volunteers to drive guest and gift to the party.

"So," he asks Nellie, once they are under way, "what are you giving Charlie for his birthday?"

Nellie sits comfortably in the phaeton beside Booth with the package in her lap. "Skates," she says, unsmiling.

"Does Charlie give such generous presents when he goes to a birthday party?" Booth asks. When Nellie shrugs, Booth says, with an air of mischief, "The Pinkertons are Scotsmen, if you did not know it."

In truth, Booth enjoys the leisurely ride in the phaeton back to the center of Washington. It gives him time to think how he will face down Pinkerton. The Soho Gang, the gardenia letter, belong to a farce. Yet how does Wall Street expect to gain from it? Or if not Wall Street, are there others in on the plot? Roscoe Conkling? James G. Blaine, who still aspires to the Presidency?

"Do you know Charlie Pinkerton?" Nellie asks him after a while.

"No," Booth says. At least Charlie is not in on the plot.

Nellie keeps her eyes on the horse's tail. "He writes good compositions."

"And what does he like to write about?"

Nellie says, "Next year we get to write compositions on a subject of our choice, if I could think of one."

The phaeton maintains its steady pace. "Subjects such as beauty and idealism are always appropriate," Booth says.

The traffic in the city seems unusually heavy for the hottest part of the day. Past the great Center Market at Seventh and Pennsylvania with its stalls of shad and herring and terrapin and its tall poles with red canvasback ducks, Nellie points the way for Booth to go.

When they reach the Pinkerton residence, Booth ties the horse to an iron hitching post and helps Nellie down from the seat with her package. "Oh, see the servants watching us," Nellie whispers as she and Booth go up the walk. Maid and waiter are consulting each other nervously over what they see, and three little-girl guests peering around the servants run back into the drawing room, crying, "The President is coming!"

By the time Booth is at last alone with William Pinkerton in the latter's library, he has shaken hands with the bashful Charlie, walked through a game of blindman's buff, and noted that Nellie is a head taller than any child present.

"Forgive my intrusion here," Booth says brusquely to his host, "but I learned you were not in Philadelphia on the Soho case."

"My honor to receive you," says Pinkerton. "I would have contacted you on the mor-row, sirrr." He is a tall man with pink cheeks, dark sideburns, and deep-blue eyes. He has the same rolling burr, but not the gray iciness of his father, the founder of the firm.

"The Soho Gang continues to elude you, I take it?" Booth asks wittily, settling in the upholstered chair he is offered. "They have not moved on, I trust. To Trenton? To Perth Amboy?"

"Come, come, Mr. President," Pinkerton says without dismay. He pours glasses of whiskey and water for the two of them. "Our operrratives stay in the field."

"No doubt I am skeptical of your project only because I am not a Lincoln," Booth says, accepting the glass of whiskey with a stiff face. "The Lincolns know you are infallible."

A puzzled look crosses the ruddy brow of the investigator, but he murmurs of the high admiration the Pinkerton family has for the Arthur family, "in parrrticular, the fairrr daughter of the President."

"You can submit some kind of written report on this case, I trust?" Booth interrupts. Good God, it is like talking with a Scottish hay merchant, not a detective.

"Yes, sirrr."

"This Soho Gang, having deprived their countrymen of all their valuables, took passage, *en bloc,* to this city in order to plunder the wealth of great Croesuses such as Mr. Robert Lincoln? Is that it? How much did Mr. Lincoln lose in this burglary anyway?"

Pinkerton says that he lost a secret file of important state papers, as the President well knew.

"And is that all?" Booth puts down the whiskey glass and leaps to his feet. "As Christ is our Lord, Pinkerton, I do not see why British safecrackers would be interested in an American government file."

"State papers are sometimes stolen by forrreign agents."

"But these men are thieves, not spies!" Booth ejaculates. Angry, he strikes the head of his cane with force on the rough finish of Pinkerton's writing desk.

Flushed, Pinkerton, who has risen too, takes an involuntary step backward. He asks the President please not to startle the children, who are but a single room away.

Booth focuses Pinkerton with a dazzling glare. "What if I told you one of the members of this purported gang may have written to me, offering to sell me the file?"

With deliberation Pinkerton nods. "Have you brrrought the letter with you?"

Booth utters a harsh laugh. "No, I have not." He shakes his finger in the air. "For I do not believe the letter is authentic. I do not even believe the Soho Gang is authentic!"

In silence, Pinkerton sits down behind his desk and rolls a cigar clipper about in his hand.

"Mr. President, I will submit a reporrrt to you on the mor-row, giving you the police records on these men from two continents. I will give you their vital statistics, their Bertillon measurements, and a studio photograph of two of the men." Pinkerton pulls some drapes shut on an open window where women are seen walking in the garden. "Why should we practice deception on you when Mr. Lincoln is involved, whose father's name is the foundation of the integrrrity of our agency?"

"God bless him, Massa Lincoln!" Booth drawls with old malice. Impulsively, he snatches up his hat. "Very well, Pinkerton. As you say, have the report on my desk tomorrow. . . . My compliments."

In five seconds he has hat and stick and launches out of the room, soon finding himself again among the players of blindman's buff, who have spilled into hallway and vestibule. God knows, the Lincolns controlled the Pinkertons, and always would! No doubt the agency would deliver a fancy report on the Soho Gang tomorrow; soon they might hire somebody to play "The Gent" and try to sell their President something called "the Fredericksburg File." They would tell him it was the real thing, and if he denied it, they would simply say, well, the real thing never existed in the first place!

"G'bye, Mr. President," freckle-faced Charlie Pinkerton calls to Booth as he pauses in the sunlight for the servant to open the front door for him. Nellie, he can see, is wandering around behind Charlie with a heavy blindfold over her eyes.

He wakes up sharply in the dark bedroom, sweating and mutely anxious, the pillow having fallen to the floor. Nell, white-faced, with her hair wrapped in a cloth, is hovering over him.

"Husband?" she is crooning. "Husband?"

She is like a mantled ghost poised over him in the thin moonlight from an open window.

"What is it?" he asks her. He guesses she must be wandering in confusion again. Sleepwalking perhaps. But the truth is, he is in her bed and cannot remember how.

"It's all raht," she says, her voice soft and lulling.

He realizes then that it was his nightmare, not hers, that disturbed the night. Abraham Lincoln—the same—came to him in a dream and said that he must pursue the Fredericksburg File in order to demonstrate to people that it was a universe of purpose, not of contingency. He tries to tell Abraham Lincoln how difficult it is all going to be, how costly. . . .

Then Nell has touched his forehead like a ghost and, after lying down beside him, has closed her eyes once again.

In the airless heat of the middle of the night he wonders if maybe the two of them—he and Nell—are both deceased after all, as recorded on the official rolls. Perhaps they are lying together in hell, condemned to this humid chamber forever, allowed only the dreams and nightmares that they sometimes took to be reality.

He could believe it, were it not for the banal itchiness in his hair and along his neckline, the result of makeup on his face over the years having made his skin flaky and raw. The sensation is unusually annoying in the close heat.

Getting out of the bed, he walks heavily to the open window, where a scent of magnolia drifts upward from the moon-drenched grounds below. Not in hell, then. He looks upward at the bright pinpoints of stars in the dark sky.

12

THE SOLDIERS' HOME

The next afternoon the President's tailor arrives at the same time as does the special report from Pinkerton on the Soho Gang. In a more receptive frame of mind, Booth finds himself glancing over the report at the same time that he tries on his new western riding clothes and fishing costumes. The tailor has also sewn him a Great White Father suit for the ceremonial visit to the Shoshone and the Arapaho at Fort Washakie.

Booth's eyes go over Pinkerton's report casually, almost as though he is compensating for the intensity of his earlier suspicions. With one arm raised for the tailor, he takes note that the "gang" has operated in London, Manchester, Brussels, Washington, Baltimore, Philadelphia. They have robbed jewelry from "certain establishments" on Bond Street after "forcing their way in," but usually admit themselves by means of false keys made "from wax impressions of genuine keys." Inside the building they lower the windows from the top about an inch to prevent the breaking of the glass from the explosion. The safe is then wrapped in blankets, et cetera, et cetera.

Booth models the white linen suit, letting the tailor take final tucks in the cut of the sleeve; and he reads that the "petermen" employ "bedchamber sneaks" for burglaries in the homes of wealthy people: "When they wish to obtain the keys of a dwelling, they come as visitors to the servant girls, and while they stand chatting with them, manage to slip the key from the lock, take its impression in wax, and return it to the lock unobserved by the girl." Such was the method used in the burglary of the Robert Lincoln residence while the Lincolns were in Illinois for a week.

According to the report, members of the Soho Gang have names such as Jenkins, Harvey, and Palmer; none of them, Booth notices, is identified with the sobriquet The Gent. Their most characteristic mode of operation is to move from city to city, thereby remaining "one jump ahead of the local police." Booth turns at last to a posed tintype, allegedly of two of the Soho Gang. Both men appear indecently young, solemn in derbies and checked suits next to a table holding a bowl of lilies, with a garish backdrop behind. One of them looks a little like Davie Herold as he looked early in '65.

"Do you fancy that the silk waistcoats will do for Newport, sir?" the tailor asks.

But Booth raises his hand and excuses himself for a moment. The image of Davie Herold has suddenly decided him. There is no reason to be afraid of the likes of Davie Herold. Even if the Ebbitt House meeting turns out to be a trick, Booth will be on hand himself to give Raymond aid, no matter what the young scamps—or their masters— are up to.

In his study, he writes a note to Raymond at the White House: "Get gardenia. Get umbrella. We will meet 'The Gent' this Sunday at noon."

"I am corrupted," Raymond is declaring. Sitting next to Booth in their closed carriage on the way to the Ebbitt House, he shakes his head, looks downward. "I am corrupted. Just as St. Augustine was."

"What are you talking about, lad?"

The church bells, tolling their counterpoint across the capital, seem to have caused Raymond to go into an unexpected fit of self-doubt.

"Ye call me lad, but you said, too, how corrupted I was, like what I done with the sword-cane in Chicago. Ye said it yourself." He is wearing a white gardenia in the lapel of his linen coat, but his eyes look haunted.

"What do you know of St. Augustine?" Booth asks. "You are not a Catholic."

"Your lady, she left behind the book *The Confessions of St. Augustine* in the carriage one day."

"That has nothing to do with you," Booth says. "St. Augustine is of the ancient world."

"But I have cruel urges. Do you not want me to reform?" Raymond asks, his candid eyes staring up at Booth. The carriage has stopped on F Street next to the Ebbitt House. Booth pats Raymond once on the shoulder. "Later," he says. And half reluctantly, Raymond takes up the rolled umbrella from the seat and jumps down to the curb into the bright sunshine.

Pondering, Booth continues around the corner in the carriage. Perhaps a good dose of the out-of-doors would help Raymond: clearly, St. Augustine did not apply.

On the 14th Street side of the building, where Booth stands down into the street, he is at once startled by an encounter with three tipsy-looking men who run into him as they are emerging from the service entrance of the hotel. Of course they are reporters; only newspapermen drink themselves into intoxication while church bells are fracturing one's eardrums.

"I cannot chat with you, gentlemen," Booth says with severity. The eyes of the man closest to him look rheumy. "You invade my privacy. Even the President has a right to privacy."

He puts on his hat and marches right past them, satisfied with the way he has handled it. They are still looking at each other vacantly when he glances back as he enters the hotel. None of them seems disposed to follow him.

Once upstairs in the mezzanine suite he has taken for the day, he settles down on a plush sofa to review the possibilities ahead. One, The Gent will require Raymond to leave the hotel with him; then Booth, alerted by the bellboy, must try to follow. Two, The Gent will agree to negotiate directly with the President in the mezzanine suite; then Booth will receive him, having made an effort to look both western and presidential. He is wearing buckskin vest and plantation coat; under his arm, hidden, he carries a shoulder holster containing a small-caliber revolver.

As the hour of noon nears, Booth takes a peek out the door of the suite down into the lobby below. Sunday is a quiet day in the Ebbitt House; there sits the troubled Raymond in his deep-dyed linen suit, the white gardenia in his lapel, the half-opened umbrella on the carpet beside the chair he is sitting on. From outside the door, opened onto the sidewalk, street sounds are audible: moving carriages, peddlers' carts (driven by Jews, no doubt, since it is a Sunday), and more church bells.

Booth's purest fantasy about the Soho Gang is that while talking to The Gent about the Fredericksburg File, he may somehow persuade these young men that he would be willing to engage them all as part of a presidential honor guard for the great packing trip through Wyoming to Yellowstone. He would like to say, "Look, you no longer need to think of yourselves as dregs from the foul streets of Europe. I do not offer mere money for this file; I offer you all an opportunity to rehabilitate yourselves in the noblest possible way. Just as my aide Raymond, plucked from the streets of a great city, learned to ride and to benefit from the life of the great outdoors, so, too, you can find new purpose and meaning in your existence."

What an opportunity he could give them! Deep into frontier country—deeper than a President has ever gone—he and General Sheridan and the others would lead them. He would show them great tribes of red Indians, pacified on their reservations; he would show them all the natural wonders of Yellowstone. When they returned to Washington as his honor guard, uniforms of some kind could be given to them.

Booth can further imagine that one day the Soho Gang might be the nucleus of his circus in Europe. He would not need to worry about finding someone else's circus to work for. Safecrackers and second-story-men, no doubt, had multiple skills that could be trained in Europe for more practical applications. Acrobatics they could surely learn; meanwhile around the Continent he could very likely pick up animal acts, strong men, and so forth. But he would have the nucleus of an Anglo-American circus. With his own special style as manager and ringmaster.

Perhaps by presenting himself to them in his somewhat exotic western garb, he will whet their appetites for the vigorous life that he will paint for them with his language.

"But don't worry, Father Abraham," he murmurs with a mute chuckle. "I will get the Fredericksburg File too. I honor my duty to the past as much as I do the one I have to the future."

With his hands crossed upon his ample stomach, he settles down in a tall-backed rocking chair. A faint smell of camphor balls touches his nostrils; the muffled whir of a ceiling fan lulls his hearing.

*

But the hour of high noon passes, and so does half-past. Booth leaves the suite long enough to take a searching look over the balustrade down into the lobby at about twenty minutes to one. There sits Raymond, the palm of his hand on one knee, looking around the lobby with some hint of restlessness. The gardenia he is wearing may already be drooping. Three middle-aged ladies, standing in a group near the registration desk, appear to be watching the lad with some apprehension.

Booth retreats to the suite.

When, by twenty minutes after one (his next emergence into the corridor) he sees no change in the tableau in the lobby other than that Raymond is now being watched by a feeble man in a wheelchair, who looks fit for embalming, Booth grabs his hat, buttons his buckskin vest and planter's coat, and unabashedly descends the central staircase of the hotel. With an unmistakable signal to Raymond, who gets to his feet at once, Booth passes in the direction of the desk clerk and the bellboy, to whom he gives honoraria. Without further comment, he and Raymond descend into the street, Raymond still carrying the half-opened umbrella.

While they are waiting in the sunshine for the doorman to secure them a cab, Booth hisses, "We are the butt of confidence men. Can you tell me why?"

With some vehemence Raymond offers the possibility that Booth's presence was detected by "The Gent" and seen as a threat to the gang.

Booth snorts. "There is no Soho Gang," he states. "There is no 'Gent.' There has been no robbery committed." He is about to say there is no Fredericksburg File either. But that would be too devastating to allow. Why, the file is probably still in Robert Lincoln's safe, where it has lain for years.

"Quickly now, Raymond," Booth says, for the inebriated newspapermen are, by annoying coincidence, again coming out of the service entrance on 14th Street at the very moment that the horse cab is slowly approaching. The nag is feeding from a nosebag, and the driver seems in no hurry to pick up his fares.

Pushing Raymond along ahead of him, Booth snaps at the hotel doorman, "You may tell those keyhole snoopers that I shall answer their questions after my return from Wyoming."

Once in the cab, Booth offers a concession to Raymond for the fiasco of the afternoon.

"We will make a last attempt to contact The Gent," Booth says.

"If you have your pencil on you, Raymond, you may take down this ad to be inserted in the personals column of the *Washington Daily News*." Raymond, having found a pencil, transcribes Booth's dictation on the back of a cardboard fan supplied on the seat of the cab.

"Thus," says Booth. "The Gent. Colon. You failed your appointment at the Ebbitt House Sunday. You have but one more chance. Do not fail me any further. Signed: T. P. That is T. P. for 'The President.' But it does not matter if he understands that. He will know he is 'The Gent,' and know who it is that is writing to him. . . . does that satisfy you, Raymond?"

"Yes, sir," Raymond replies.

"Then cheer up," Booth says. "Learn to live for the moment, as I do. Do not trouble yourself about the agonies of the saints of old."

13

FROM THE *Washington Daily News*

(National, page 2)

NEWPORT—The President and his son, Chester Alan Arthur, Jr., were the guests today of Mr. and Mrs. William K. Vanderbilt aboard the Vanderbilt yacht, *Alva*. In Newport for the season after the sumptuous opening of their Fifth Avenue home in March, the Vanderbilts gave a small reception for about 75 guests, following the annual Regatta.

The President will continue to Chicago from here, where he will be joined by Secretary of War, Robert T. Lincoln, General Philip Sheridan, Senator George Vest, and others, who will proceed by rail and then overland by saddle horse to Yellowstone Park in what will be an epoch-making visit.

(Personals, page 12)

T.P. Your agent was not alone at the Ebbitt House. If you are serious this time, send same agent to 20 Maine in dress of ordinary seaman to meet me exactly 7 days and 12 hours after previous appointment. No pranks this time. The Gent

14

MAINE AVENUE DOCKS

After dark the swamp mosquitoes get so bad that Raymond can understand why hardly anybody is strolling the cobbled streets around the
docks. By eleven o'clock even the barrooms look half dead. Save for
the waning moon and patches of brightness near the saloon entrances,
there is barely enough light for The Gent to see him walking here.

Raymond is dressed in a long-sleeved blue shirt and a mariner's
cap with a bill. He wears slop-chest trousers and limber-soled shoes, for
he knows how a seaman dresses. He wonders if his father still makes
port in New York every two years or so, and if he has looked for Raymond there of late, and not found him. Small worry for the Chief; he
can always find others to give him company.

In New York along the river there would be many deep-water
sailors taking the air. The air was often pleasant on a summer night
with the salt smell coming off the sea. Here the odor is foul with decay;
the swamps that produce the mosquitoes give off a fetid smell that near
knocks your hat off.

He stands outside one of the saloons for a while, deciding to roll a
cigarette. It is not yet midnight, and he feels a little nervous. Not that
he thinks it likely that The Gent will show up any more than he did the
first time. If he intends to, why would The Gent want Raymond to
wear the very same thing that the other men have on, riverboat sailors
that most of them are? All of them are! God almighty, even Alexan-
dria is a better deep-water port than Washington. The one time he was
down here before, he nearly burst out laughing: cargo sheds about the
size of market stalls, a couple of two-masters next to a dilapidated
pier, and a single paddlewheel heading down the river. It was pitiful,
compared to New York.

A couple of bruisers push out of the swinging doors of the saloon
and glance at him long enough to make him swallow quickly. But they
pass on. A concertina inside is playing an Italian song. If he were
standing around like this near the docks in New York, he'd have to be
alert and make sure he didn't get shanghaied. He'd heard of that
happening to a friend of a newsboy he knew. The fellow had drunk too
much, and then before he knew it he was on a ship to Morocco. They

made you do terrible things. Raymond dwells momentarily on what they might be. He doesn't know whether the shanghaied fellow ever got back to New York or not. If he didn't, probably no one would have known he'd been in Morocco.

Some other people come out of the saloon. They could be dock workers. Raymond supposes it must be close to midnight. He thought about bringing his pocket watch along, pinning it next to his skin. But he decided if he looked at it at the wrong time he might just get robbed. A lot of ex-Rebs hang about in Washington, and they are broke, most of them, and would not like him anyway, him being a Yankee. So he could get robbed easy. He wonders if he is softer than he used to be. Well, he is going to Chicago and then out west soon; that will toughen him up.

Wouldn't it be something if he could surprise the President in Chicago, when he got there, with the file that the President was wanting so much? Not that The Gent would simply hand it over at 20 Maine Avenue on the stroke of midnight. What would he want in exchange though? Money? But Raymond has no money. Raymond has come to the docks with nothing but himself. He has not even brought a revolver such as he knows the President had with him the first time they tried to meet The Gent. And that was in broad daylight.

The two bruisers Raymond has noticed earlier when they came out of the saloon seem to have stopped about fifty yards up the avenue, and are heading back in his direction. He thinks it might be a good time to stroll down the pier. Some other men are smoking there leaning on the pilings. Younger men with lazy-soft voices. One of them has a cigar that drifts sparks now and then.

Raymond wants to do the right thing tonight. He wishes he could have wired the President—who was going from Newport to Louisville, then to Chicago—but the ad in the personals didn't leave any time. If The Gent was to be met exactly at midnight Sunday at 20 Maine Avenue, Raymond had to take it upon himself to do it. Initiative is what it is called. Not that he reads Horatio Alger anymore. And he is tired of St. Augustine. Some day he will go back to New York.

As he strolls down the pier, on an impulse he calls out to the young men smoking around the piling over the moonlit river. He tries his best lazy-soft drawl.

"Evenin', boys."

For a moment none of them says anything, then one voice pipes up. "Evenin'."

"Been drinkin' a little, boys?"

"Keeps the skeeters off," one of them promptly answers, and they begin laughing. "You ain't an inspector, are ye, Shorty?"

"No," he says. He guesses that the inspectors try to stop men from smoking on the wharf. "Jus' like yourselves," he adds.

But they begin laughing again, and he becomes discouraged from trying any harder to befriend them. Besides, he has business to do; it must be close to midnight, give or take five minutes one way or the other.

At the head of the pier, the two bruisers suddenly step out of the shadows cast by some crates and barrels stacked there. Raymond knows at once that it is too late. Still he tries to cry out. But one of them steps behind him and puts a meaty hand over his mouth. The other leans forward, blinking rapidly, his face so close to Raymond's that Raymond can see deep-pitted pockmarks. But the man merely nods to the other one.

Raymond is struck over the head with paralyzing force.

He awakens very briefly some time later; his face is against a wet plank. He hears water beating against the plank. He is in a boat being rowed somewhere; he hears muffled voices. Hears the word "Kowloon." But when he lifts his head up, he is struck again a blow almost as hard as the first one and he sinks dizzily into oblivion.

15

CHICAGO

MR FRED PHILLIPS
SECRETARY TO THE PRESIDENT
EXECUTIVE MANSION
WASHINGTON

WHERE IN HELL IS RAYMOND STOP HE IS SUPPOSED
TO MEET ME HERE

ARTHUR

✤   ✤   ✤

WASHINGTON

HON CHESTER A ARTHUR
GRAND PACIFIC HOTEL
CHICAGO

NO ONE HAS SEEN RAYMOND SINCE SUNDAY NIGHT
STOP PERHAPS HE LEFT FOR CHICAGO EARLY AND
HAS BEEN DELAYED EN ROUTE STOP SHALL I TURN
MATTER OVER TO POLICE

PHILLIPS

✣ ✣ ✣

CHICAGO

MR FRED PHILLIPS
SECRETARY TO THE PRESIDENT
EXECUTIVE MANSION
WASHINGTON

NO KEEP STILL

ARTHUR

✣ ✣ ✣

CHICAGO

HON WILLIAM CHANDLER
NAVY DEPARTMENT
WASHINGTON

RAYMOND HAS DISAPPEARED STOP PLEASE CHECK
ON HIS ACTIVITIES OF SUNDAY LAST STOP WIRE
ME IN GREEN RIVER WYOMING STOP KEEP ALL
POLICE AND PINKERTONS OUT OF THIS

ARTHUR

✣ ✣ ✣

WASHINGTON

HON CHESTER A ARTHUR
CARE OF STATIONMASTER
GREEN RIVER WYOMING

BEST INFORMATION SUGGESTS RAYMOND ANSWERED
NEWSPAPER AD SUNDAY MIDNIGHT ON MAINE
AVENUE DOCKS STOP AD SIGNED BY THE GENT
STOP NO TRACE OF RAYMOND SINCE STOP SHALL I
DO ANYTHING

CHANDLER

✣ ✣ ✣

GREEN RIVER

HON WILLIAM CHANDLER
NAVY DEPARTMENT
WASHINGTON

I WILL DO ALL THAT NEEDS TO BE DONE

ARTHUR

16

WIND RIVER VALLEY
WYOMING

The spring wagons have been left behind at Fort Washakie, and each man now rides his own saddle horse. Stoically, Booth follows those ahead of him on the trail—Senator Vest, General Sheridan, Governor Crosby—toward a rough, bouldery plateau. Behind him, just beginning the climb from the bottomland across the river, Booth can see a part of the cavalry escort tending the pack mules. The cavalrymen will be bivouacked far enough away from the main party's tents, he believes, to present little problem to him later.

He is biding his time. A high, solid bank of clouds obscures the sun today, producing mild temperatures that accelerate the pace of the expedition. Getting into the rhythm of it quickly, Booth shows himself to be a veteran in the saddle. But the others—the greenhorns —are not expected to cover a long distance the first day. Just ahead is the initial opportunity to throw a fishing line into the river. "So thick with trout," Sheridan has declared, "it's really no challenge, gentlemen, if y' bait the hook."

Sheridan is riding up ahead with Lincoln, who is perhaps the weakest rider in the group, although in other respects he could be a physically vigorous antagonist, Booth senses. The outdoors has brought a ruddy glow to Lincoln's cheeks, and while he is not an athletic man, his stocky build is solid and supple.

But this awareness does not give Booth any pause. He can barely conceal his fury. No one but Lincoln—with the help of the Pinkertons —could have perpetrated the fraud of the Soho Gang, which eventually ensnared poor Raymond. Lincoln's motive remains obscure to

Booth: why kidnap (or, dare he think it, kill?) an innocent lad like Raymond?

From behind him, Booth hears Dan Rollins's horse move up as the trail widens. Although Rollins serves as a speech writer at the White House, he is nevertheless a strong and wiry young man, fitter than most. While Rollins has little personal loyalty, in a pinch Booth might be able to count on him.

"I'm going to ride with the general for a while if you don't mind, sir," Rollins calls. (They all lick Sheridan's boots.) When Booth signals assent, Rollins's roan canters past. Oddly, the sound of the river current seems louder up where they are than it did down below. Cottonwoods still conceal a clear view of the water.

Booth deeply misses Raymond. Can one believe motiveless malignity is responsible for Lincoln's cruelty toward the lad? Some kind of revenge? Obscure financial purpose?

The only other alternative—and this one perhaps more revolting —is that The Gent made certain indecent proposals to Raymond when they met on the Maine Avenue docks, proposals not concerning the Fredericksburg File. Booth knows that Raymond is vulnerable to "the English vice." If he succumbed, God knows where they might now be setting up shop, and whether or not Raymond put up any initial resistance.

To get such thoughts out of his mind, Booth must remind himself that The Gent in the Soho Gang was surely no real gentleman, and this fact makes the notion less plausible. Nay, the dog Lincoln must have taken Raymond; of that, Booth feels certain.

During these ruminations, Mr. Haynes, the official photographer for the party, has come riding up beside Booth, trailed by Lieutenant Colonel Sheridan, the younger brother to the general, who calls out:

"We're making camp, sir, in about an hour at just about the best fishing spot you could want." He is a large, handsome man with a handlebar moustache.

"Thank you, Colonel," says Booth.

"Jiminy!" Haynes exclaims suddenly, looking westward to where silhouettes of the higher hills are emerging from the cloud cover. "Can't you fancy five hundred redskins ridin' down on us from one of the passes up there!"

Colonel Sheridan says that there is no danger of that.

"Wearing warpaint!" Haynes exclaims hungrily.

Only the night before the Shoshone and the Arapaho greeted the President and his party in a full-dress ceremony at Fort Washakie.

Booth says to Colonel Sheridan, "We may not get five hundred, but I suppose a small raiding party is still a possibility, is it not, Colonel?"

When Sheridan laughs politely, Booth gives Haynes a shrug.

What no one knows is that at Washakie he covertly asked for a "souvenir" tomahawk from one of the Arapaho chiefs.

The tomahawk now rests in Booth's saddlebag. If such a weapon were to be found in Mr. Lincoln's skull tomorrow at sunrise, surely wild Indians would be blamed, whether the Sheridans had expected any or not.

In the hour before darkness Booth puts on his public face and commences a fishing contest with Senator Vest. The President and the Senator find positions on separate boulders that extend into the running river, and as General Sheridan has predicted, they have no trouble pulling one speckled trout after another out of the water. A grizzled sergeant named Monroe strips Booth's hook for him, and a lively debate among all concerned ensues. Vest has the edge in number of fish caught, but Booth protests, "Weight is the only fair way to determine the winner, Senator."

"Very well," Vest calls back.

In a stake-all mood, Booth lands an eight-pounder, but as the contest wears on, he loses one and then another fish off his hook. It nettles him that Vest, an inexperienced angler, appears to have the lead.

General Sheridan, Lincoln, and Haynes come down from the camp area, where most of the tents have already been pitched in a grove of tall trees.

"You must be the judge, General," Vest calls. "You have to say who is the victor on the basis of weight."

"Not on your life!" Sheridan laughs, his voice echoing down the trail. Along with him is one of his aides, Major Forwood, a company medical officer.

Gunfire is heard at a higher elevation. Booth looks up sharply and asks if Haynes has his wild Indians at last.

"Merely antelope," Sheridan replies heartily. "Provided by the men, if God wills."

"Ah, then Senator Vest and I are *not* going to have to feed the whole company!"

From the other side, Lincoln shouts, "Nay, you must learn to relax, Mr. President! You have too keen a sense of responsibility for us all."

As Booth thumbs the catch on his fishing reel, he glances idly at Lincoln, who tries to look innocent of innuendo. Well for him that he sticks to Sheridan like glue.

"Maybe y'd like to try some huntin' yourself tomorrow, Mr. President," Sheridan says. "I notice you carry a sidearm."

"A small sidearm," Booth admits. "I'd have to borrow a rifle, of course. In Virginia for a time—" He stops himself. No need to boast he'd provisioned the Herndon family in Fredericksburg after the looters in Sheridan's army had laid Virginia waste.

Some of Sheridan's men have now brought up a mule, and having unloaded two fifty-pound bales of dried buffalo meat for use as a counterweight, they set up a makeshift scale out of a felled aspen trunk with a rock as fulcrum. When the fishing is over, the catch for the day is bundled in a large piece of canvas. A cheer is raised, for on the scale it outweighs the buffalo meat, certifying that the catch is over one hundred pounds. The contest between Vest and the President is declared a draw.

Haynes takes his pictures at last, and Lieutenant Colonel Sheridan vows to feature the fishing in his daily report on the expedition.

The men in the ranks cheer the President and Senator Vest again as the pictures are being taken. Then Booth walks up through the area where the tents have been pitched, noting their locations. Smoke from the campfires wafts acrid aromas down toward him. He is annoyed to see that the tents of Lincoln and Sheridan are so close together that any attempt to enter Lincoln's tent tonight would be foolhardy.

But he tries to put his anger out of his mind. Later, as he and Rollins, apart from the others, are washing up over galvanized pots containing water that has been heated, Booth starts to speak to Rollins about the grandeur of the landscape.

Instead, he hears himself saying "Lincoln and Sheridan are closer than lovers!"

Rollins looks shocked and says nothing; in fact, he walks away rather quickly, leaving Booth alone. The reaction hardly surprises Booth: generals were expected to have intimates. Were not Presidents to be allowed the same privilege? He thinks, wrenchingly, on his loyal aide Raymond, who had completed his riding lessons, who had been fitted for his wardrobe, who had made his plans for this expedition.

On a tree trunk over one of the wash cans hang a small looking glass, into which Booth now stares. Nay, for as long as it takes, he must be true to the sculptured image he sees there. He must shave every morning and give careful trim to the pattern of his sideburns. The smooth-planed cheekbones must be guileless as a baby's. Until he strikes, he must do nothing to correct that impression.

The next day Booth makes his first attempt at shooting antelope. One beast he comes close to hitting, but he soon realizes his eye is not what it was in the Fredericksburg days. How skillful he must have been as a hunter for the Herndons, considering how much less plentiful the game was in the Appalachians than it is in the West.

The party spends another night at the riverbank site. Booth has declined to fish at sunset, remarking that after his failures with a rifle that afternoon, he fears the planets are against him.

Senator Vest replies with an indulgent chuckle. "Perhaps you will brave it tomorrow. We would not have you begging off, lest someone say to you, as Casca does, 'The fault, dear Brutus—' "

"Ah, but it is Cassius, sir, rather than Casca," Booth protests. "And the line which precedes the one you quote is 'Men *at some time* are masters of their fates.' Note that Cassius says *'At some time,'* sir! Not at all times."

"Oh, but I think it is not the same speech that I refer to, Mr. President."

"Sir, the lines go, 'Men at some time are masters of their fates; The fault, dear Brutus, is not in our stars, But in ourselves, that we are underlings.' "

After a moment Senator Vest nods sagely. He considers the manner of the President's delivery with some solemnity. Then he says, "Well and good, well and good." He has his fishing pole in his hand. "And this speech rather precedes the assassination?"

"Of course," Booth replies shortly.

"Well and good," Vest murmurs again. As they catch sight of Lincoln and Sheridan approaching, Senator Vest looks downward, indicating that the subject of assassination is not appropriate in Mr. Lincoln's presence.

Early the next morning, back in the saddle, the party of horsemen and mules moves by stages to higher ground. The mountainsides are covered with spruce and mountain ash and great Douglas fir. The air is crisp and giddy in the early morning hours. The party can observe the snow-covered peaks above the timberline, great glacial troughs leading downward into meadowed valleys and small lakes dotting the breathtaking landscape. Lieutenant Colonel Gregory and Mr. Crosby, the territorial governor, prove interesting commentators on the scene and what the group may expect ahead.

What a noble country it could be, Booth reflects, with vistas such as this. One can almost become philosophical about the venality of man when it is compared with the magnificent handiwork of God. But, no, he will not fall into that trap. Just because the landscape is fair, he will not allow a lad such as Raymond to be sacrificed on the altar of greed and fear.

Still, he knows at last how the Kappenhalter family must have felt when Victoria was missing. His retribution is just.

That night, under gathering rain clouds, the expedition halts in a grove of towering pines. In this hushed natural cathedral, the party is widely dispersed in tents among the knolls and rocks of the great rolling upland. The horses are fed and tethered below the main camp. The men in the ranks bed down below in bedrolls and build a fire away from the stands of timber in order to heat water and to cook.

Robert Lincoln has begun to look bilious. While most of the party seem weary after the long ride, Lincoln, the weariest, speaks hardly a word, eats practically nothing, and retires to his small tent before darkness has fully descended. The other men of the main party—the officers, the President, the Senator, and Governor Crosby, along with Haynes and Rollins—sit up talking and smoking until darkness is total. Sheridan and the President both drink coffee from tin cups; earlier on the ride Sheridan offered Booth a shot of whiskey from a flask that he carried, but after Booth politely declined, Sheridan made no second offer.

As Sheridan holds forth to the party with some military anecdotes of the war, Booth silently assesses the general's qualifications for appointment as chief of staff. His intimacy with Lincoln is no recommendation; also he drinks too much, or so it is said. But drink has become essential for a general of the armies ever since Grant. All knew what Robert Lincoln's father is supposed to have said about Grant's drinking during the war.

Good God, how he would have liked to decimate the whole bunch of them in '64 and '65!

"Well said, General, well said!" Senator Vest now exclaims. Booth laughs with the others although he has lost the point of the anecdote. Others of the company, he notices then, are looking a little glazed, and since the protocol seems to require he withdraw the soonest, he says, "Gentlemen, I beg you to excuse me. I must rest my weary bones."

The younger men immediately start to rise deferentially, but Booth waves his hand. "No, we'll please not begin that." So they sink back, smiling. He seems to put them all at their ease. Quickly he strides off toward his tent.

He hopes they put his absence to good use by increasing their drinking. When the rain begins, very gentle at first, he no longer hears their voices, but he continues to lie on his cot fully dressed, for he has noticed earlier that General Sheridan's tent this night is not immediately adjacent to Lincoln's as it was at the previous site. If the rain increases in volume, he expects to make his move soon after everyone else is asleep.

An hour and a half later, the time seems right. He is just lighting a cheroot given to him by General Stager during the Indian rain dance at Fort Washakie when the precipitation gains real force and volume. Still in his boots, Booth pops to his feet. He ducks his head when it comes in contact with the canvas ceiling of the tent, then he sidles his way around a table holding an unlit lantern, and opening the tent flap, he looks out cautiously.

In the cloud-veiled moonlight, the trunks of the pines make a stronger visual impression than the rain itself. Much of the sky is hidden from him by huge sheltering boughs, and he realizes that the rain must have become most intense for so much of the moisture to have seeped through the trees and to be spattering on the canvas top of his tent. He sees no lights in any of the tents nearby, nor anywhere else either. Rollins's tent is nearest to his own, he believes, and that one is very quiet. Lieutenant Colonel Sheridan's is next, and grouped close together Senator Vest's and Governor Crosby's. No sign of stirring anywhere.

He has brought the cheroot with him to the flap of the tent so that if anyone is watching him directly, it might seem natural for him to be standing there smoking. Now, since the coast seems clear, he tosses down the cheroot, stamps it out, and goes back to his tent in order to strap his sidearm, a pistol, to his waist. The tomahawk remains in his saddlebag; he realizes at once that he cannot take it to Robert Lincoln's tent, no matter how cunning its purpose.

With the pistol firm in its holster, he strides immediately from the tent out into the woods, hatless. He could be answering a call of nature if anyone has noticed him depart, and perhaps he arms himself even on such a venture.

He moves directly toward Lincoln's tent. The ground is soft underfoot, but not mushy. Even without the loud rhythm of the rain, it is unlikely that anyone would hear him traverse the twenty yards or so to Lincoln's tent. Nevertheless, there has been some show of posting pickets at night, a standard practice, he supposes, in an army bivouac, especially when important dignitaries are visiting. But Sheridan anticipates neither wild Indians nor wild beasts, and has discouraged excessive vigilance.

Booth stops outside the tent, hoping to be able to detect the sound of heavy breathing. If Lincoln be indeed ill—as he looked—it is possible that he will still be awake. Booth is not sure how Lincoln will respond to an intrusion if he is alert.

But there is no sound, except for the rain. Boldly, Booth pushes aside the flap. Inside, the darkness is complete. No candle or lantern is burning; there is only a sense of somewhat greater density in the blackness at one side of the tent. Booth waits, hoping to be able to make out the definition of Lincoln's body on the cot. Then he hears the sound of a gulped breath, something like a snore, which is surely the sound of a man sleeping.

Booth eases himself down until he is in a sitting position on the ground, very near to the sleeping man's head. He holds his right hand on his pistol, for if there is a ruse, he may expect instant reprisal. The more he looks, however, the more he feels certain that the face is Lincoln's, and now he croons in a soft voice, "Mr. Lincoln . . . Mr. Lincoln . . ."

He makes no effort to touch Lincoln's shoulder, or to rouse him in any further way.

At last there is a stirring of the figure on the bed, and an alarmed voice, clearly Lincoln's. "What is it? . . . Who's there?"

"I am here, Mr. Lincoln," Booth says in a sinister tone. "I have long wanted to talk to you where we have complete privacy."

"Arthur?" Lincoln says hoarsely. "Surely we can have this conversation in the morning."

"It would please me to have it now," Booth says, "when the army is not at your right hand." Booth takes the pistol from the holster at his side and pulls back the hammer in such a way that Lincoln cannot help but recognize what sound it is.

"Are you mad?" Lincoln asks.

"I have never had a satisfactory explanation from you," Booth says, "as to how my Fredericksburg File came to be stolen from your home. I have had no details."

"Details!" Lincoln exclaims. "You are insulting and—"

"Now, I warn you," Booth says, "to keep your voice down, Mr. Lincoln." Although the rain is loud, his heart is beating rapidly all of a sudden. He is surprised to find himself abnormally excited when he has only a moment before imagined himself perfectly cool. Indeed he is a little surprised at himself for having drawn the pistol so precipitously.

Lincoln has sat up in the bedroll. Booth can smell his breath without being able accurately to make out his face. But as Booth speaks the words, "Mr. Lincoln," a different form than the one belonging to Robert Lincoln comes into his mind's eye, and he finds himself struggling as he has often struggled in nightmares to resist firing the fatal shot. But in the nightmare the shot always goes off in spite of the struggle.

"The file was simply stolen," Lincoln says suddenly. "One day it was in my bedroom safe; the next day it was not. How am I to say how it was done?"

"Have you no speculation?" Booth asks.

"It was a total mystery to me," Lincoln replies, and starts to pull his feet out of the bedroll. "For you, it was a case worth calling in the Pinkertons—"

"What are you reaching for, Mr. Lincoln?" Booth asks in alarm.

"My robe, sir!" Lincoln exclaims. He is standing with his back to Booth, apparently in his underwear, groping endlessly at the far end of the cot.

"All right, sit down," Booth says sharply. Lincoln does so, pulling his arms into the sleeves of his robe. I must be careful not to do anything I will regret, he thinks.

"You have no wish to conceal the names of members of the conspiracy who killed your father, have you, Mr. Lincoln?" Booth now asks.

"No, why should I?" Lincoln says sullenly. "Most of them are dead anyway; it is ancient history." He sits like a figure made of ice.

"And have you no knowledge of the so-called Soho Gang?" Booth challenges him.

"Never heard of it. Is that a Pinkerton discovery?"

Booth rises to his feet, sighing dramatically. "Why do you continue to dissemble, sir? Don't you think I know by this time that those protected by the army and assisted by the Pinkertons must have much

to hide. You scheme to undermine the power of the Presidency itself.'"
When Lincoln offers no defense, Booth sharply asks, "Do you take no
responsibility for what happened to my aide?"

"What aide?"

"What aide!" Booth exclaims, hardly able to suffer the arrogance
of the man. "You were not born to the purple, Mr. Lincoln. The lad
killed or kidnapped at the Maine Avenue docks! Does that mean nothing to you?"

"Sir—"

"The lad duped at the Ebbitt House with gardenia and open
umbrella!"

"Sir?"

But there is a sudden noise at the tent flap. A lantern flashes in
Booth's eyes; he feels a sudden stabbing panic as he hears a voice:
"Stop right there!"

But he does not stop. In the same second that Sheridan speaks,
the fired pistol jumps in Booth's hand. The loud report and the blaze of
blue seem to streak directly toward Lincoln.

"Grab'm," General Sheridan's voice calls out.

As Lincoln's body is collapsing to the ground, simultaneously a
figure behind Sheridan, an enlisted man in oilskins, flings himself directly at Booth, who has started toward the light. Another enlisted
man—no more than a bulky shadow—adds his slippery weight, and
the two wrestle Booth roughly to the ground.

"Hold your fire! Hold fire!" Sheridan barks.

Under the growing number of torches being raised high, Booth,
prone, is at last able to turn so that he is facing upward and sees the
wet and astonished faces of the enlisted men who have pummeled
him to the ground. Stunned as they are, he rolls away from them,
saying nothing.

On the other side of the tent Lincoln stirs too. He rises vigilantly,
his eyes fixed on Booth, for he is obviously not wounded. The ball has
missed him.

"What in tarnation goes on?" Sheridan booms.

Booth says, as if in surprise, "It went off as I was looking at it! It
just went off. . . . My dear Mr. Lincoln, are you all right?"

Lincoln says nothing. He holds his ground, staring grimly at
Booth, who is still on the floor of the tent.

"It missed y', did it?" Sheridan asks him.

"Yes. It missed," Lincoln says unsteadily.

Several others have arrived at the tent flap. Quickly, Sheridan

intercepts them. "Fired by mistake," he declares loudly. Booth can see Rollins most immediately in the light; behind him he makes out Vest, bareheaded.

"Corporal," Sheridan now says, "would you mind lettin' 'em all know there's nothin' to panic about. And, Sergeant, you might set a picket at the perimeter here, eh? . . . I think we can take care of this not-so-big mishap among the brass here, don't y' think?"

The corporal and the sergeant seem satisfied to be out of it. Following them to the entrance flap, Sheridan bawls amiably into the rain, "Go back to your tents! All clear here!"

After a minute, when his own lantern is the only illumination remaining, he turns and hangs it on the centerpole in Lincoln's tent.

Booth begins again, "Mr. Lincoln, I can't tell you how grieved I am by this terrible carelessness on my part."

He gets to his feet. Lincoln meanwhile does not move.

Sheridan steps backward, forcing a laugh. "Well, now," he says. "I'll tell you, Mr. President, Mr. Lincoln and I had a kind of boy's telegraph system worked out between his tent and mine." Sheridan reaches down to the foot of Lincoln's cot to where Booth can now see a wire connected to a device that looks like some kind of circuit breaker. Clearly Lincoln used it to summon aid when he seemed to be reaching for his robe.

Sheridan says, "Y' see, Mr. President, before we left Chicago we got a letter from a man who said he was Mr. Lincoln's guardian angel. Didn't have any other signature. But the man claimed he once saved Mr. Lincoln's life on a railroad platform in New Jersey. Now, y' know, he said he had a vision that Mr. Lincoln was in danger of his life on our pack trip here. So what—what could we do but make some extra arrangements to protect the Secretary, and"—Sheridan forces another laugh, staring right at Booth—"and by Jeremy, the threat we run into is somethin' like—like this here."

Booth senses they suspected all along where the danger was going to come from. He sees his pistol lying on the ground next to Lincoln's cot. He can hear the sound of the rain and the sound of voices outside. He has been betrayed by Edwin, his brother, in whom he made the mistake of confiding. The ignominy is complete.

"And, Mr. President," Sheridan says suddenly, watching Booth eye the pistol on the ground, "a weapon with a hair trigger like that one ain't fit for human company. You just give it to me, and I'll get rid of it somewhere. If you would?"

"Don't let him pick it up," Lincoln says sharply to Sheridan.

As Booth reaches, Sheridan says, with his hand on his own weapon, "Oh, he'll hand it to me by the barrel, won't you, Mr. President?"

Booth does. His composure has returned, and he says nothing as he hands Sheridan the pistol.

"In some other country," Sheridan remarks lightly, "takin' a weapon from the head of state is what they call a military coup d'état. . . . But here we don't exaggerate such things. Accidents happen."

"I will never forgive myself," Booth says after a moment.

Having pocketed the pistol, Sheridan says that when he is appointed chief of staff next month—it being "common knowledge" that that will happen—he can keep an eye on the government the rest of the term. "Y' weren't planning on running for another four years anyway, were y'?" Sheridan asks.

"He won't do that if he knows what's good for him," Lincoln says crisply.

"Now, now," Sheridan interposes. "You two have got to get along with each other the rest of the way. Why don't y' just come forward here and shake each other's hand?"

Lincoln's eyes meet and engage Sheridan's. After a minute, Lincoln stands and extends his hand to Booth.

"I bear no grudges, Mr. President," Lincoln says.

They shake on it.

Presently, when Sheridan leaves them alone a moment later, Booth senses that, as in a French melodrama, a curtain speech remains yet to be given. Although he is the President, he senses that the curtain speech does not belong to him.

Lincoln says, "You are too single-minded, Mr. President. You think that your obsession must be everyone else's too. People may, you know, legitimately pursue their private interest. They have the right to do that in this country."

Facing him, Booth wonders what would happen if tomorrow he faced the whole assemblage, down to the lowest enlisted man, and said, "You got me, boys. I am John Wilkes Booth in disguise. But I will not be blackmailed by those who have nothing in their hearts but greed and ambition. I here give you the roll of conspirators."

"You complain about the kidnapping of your aide," Lincoln says, his robe hanging loosely. "Perhaps men who object to your single-mindedness are warning you that their privilege to pursue their private interest takes precedence over any one man's need for glory."

Booth smiles faintly. Hypocrite, his silent tongue pronounces. You know, or nearly know, as you stand there, that I am John Wilkes Booth, murderer of your father, and yet you do nothing.

"You talk of granting privileges," Booth says, pitying the man. "You and your kind grant every privilege but the privilege to secede."

He does not mind having stepped out of character. He does not mind having thrown down the gauntlet.

But Lincoln looks right past him.

"Secede, by all means," he says indifferently. "Beginning from my tent."

"My pleasure," says Booth, taking the last word after all. Turning on his heel, he makes the famous quick exit into the wings.

PART SEVEN
The
REST CURE

NEWS FROM THE DIAL PRESS

New address: Doubleday, 245 Park Avenue, New York, New York 10167 (212) 953-4661

THE CHESTER A. ARTHUR CONSPIRACY

William Wiegand

August 12, 1983 $16.95

A Novel

The wild premise of this novel is that John Wilkes Booth did not die but lived to fall in love with the wife of Chester A. Arthur and, upon the sudden death of the latter, assumed his identity and went on to become president of the United States!

The research that author Wiegand has done on the times and of how a president lived in those days is fascinating.

```
*************************
*
* N.B. This is a specially bound advance
*       reading copy sent to you in lieu
*       of bound galleys to help you prepare
*       your reviewing schedule.  Hardcover
*       copies of the book will be ready in
*       early July.
*
*************************
```

1

AN ESTATE IN SUSSEX
SOME YEARS AFTER

Under a pale sun that diffuses an unnatural glow over the vast green lawn that slopes down from the many-gabled manor house, a youthful peer of the realm—Lord Woodmere, by name—has taken it upon himself to cross to the lower level of the terrace, where a cluster of his uncle's guests have gathered. They seem to be waiting for the horn to be sounded before deciding where next to move. Not far from the tea table, Woodmere spots the Mortons, the American couple with the attractive ward, Nellie Arthur.

"Bit early for tea, isn't it?" he calls jovially to Major Morton. "Would've thought they'd wait for the hunt to return. Do you ride to the hounds, Major Morton?"

The major answers in the negative. He stands stiffly, a man of middle height with a dark moustache. The ward, Nellie, holding a parasol, is a short distance away, conversing with an older couple.

Woodmere addresses himself to the major's wife. "Delighted to see you again, Mrs. Morton," he cries. "We met in the foyer of the Lyceum. With Mr. Clarke."

Her hair is white. Woodmere recalls that she is hard of hearing, having been stricken with diphtheria shortly before the couple left New York.

"I do remembuh that, milord," she says in a somewhat toneless manner. She adjusts the faille collar of her wrap without smiling at him. Morton wears belted tweeds.

With the hunting party on the verge of returning, Woodmere decides to get to business. Nothing to be ashamed of.

"Y'know, Major," he says with a rueful smile, "I was able to get young Arthur to present me to his sister before he rode off with the others. But she seemed rather standoffish." Over the major's shoulder, Woodmere appraises Nellie's wasp-waisted form. "Is she still in mourning for the late President?"

Major Morton seems to size him up for a moment. But Woodmere is confident of the impression he makes. Blessed with golden ringlets and deep-set eyes, he is handsome as well as rich.

"Nellie was close to her father, of course," Morton says at last.

"And President Arthur's passing was sudden?"

"I believe it was . . . anticipated," Morton murmurs.

Guests are moving across the lawn. The grass is damp with dew, but the air is not chilly. Woodmere tries to recall what town it is that the Mortons have settled in. He thinks perhaps they've settled near the Clarkes, who are socially a bit shady, except of course in Bournemouth.

He takes a stab. "Now that you are settled in Bournemouth—"

"Actually we are settled in Poole," the Major says. "You may be confusing us with the Clarkes, who are in Bournemouth. Down the road."

"Now that you are settled in Poole," Woodmere continues boldly, "I wonder if I may call on Miss Arthur some time."

The three of them have begun moving, drawn along by the current of guests, toward the arbor where tea is being poured. A glance at Mrs. Morton informs Woodmere that she is hearing nothing of what has been said. Her marmoreal expression seems rather like those in the recent portraits of Her Majesty the Queen.

"I should like to assure you—" Woodmere begins.

"Excuse me, milord," says the major, his head cocked. "Is that the hunt I hear returning?"

Sure enough. Woodmere cups his hand behind one of his ears. "The hounds. About time," he murmurs. And then in a very loud voice to the lady: "The hounds, Mrs. Morton!"

"In time foah tea after all!" she replies agreeably.

The remark takes him so by surprise that he bursts into uncontrolled laughter. When Major Morton looks at him with asperity, he feels a fool and wishes he could think of an immediately sobering topic. But all he can think of is the American Civil war, which is perhaps *too* sobering. An aide of Morton's was lost in one of the chief battles of the conflict. Fredericksburg, Woodmere believes. They talked of it at the Lyceum. He hopes it was not Chickamauga, a word that makes him laugh beyond all help.

Fortunately, the sound of the hunting horn from beyond the hill supplies the distraction he needs. As the guests reverse themselves and begin descending toward the porte cochere in order to welcome the riders, Woodmere watches Nellie approach the Mortons and himself, carrying her parasol at a demure angle. She is wearing a becoming plaid wool dress with a wide sash and puffed sleeves. Her gaze in the direction of the baying hounds is natural and modest. Although she is taller than Mrs. Morton, and nearly as tall as the major, Woodmere considers her well proportioned. Her brown hair is caught up in back under a charming straw boater.

By the time the hunting party surges over the hill in a phalanx of red coats and top hats, their sturdy mounts pumping under them, Woodmere has drifted several steps to his left in order to place himself at Nellie's shoulder.

"They have the fox!" one of the young ladies who stands under the porte cochere exclaims.

And so they do. Alan Arthur himself has made the kill. Standing in the stirrups, he holds aloft the brush, quite the American show-off. He nods to the acclaim of the bystanders, laughing proudly at the remarks directed at him.

"Would be dreadfully boring to ride so far," he calls out over the din of the canines, "and have nothing to show for it!"

Everyone laughs, including Woodmere, although personally he regards riding to the hounds as a bit of a sell.

"Bravo, Alan!" Nellie and some of the others call.

"Bravo!" Mrs. Morton cries. The first animation of the afternoon lights her face.

Alan blows the lady a kiss.

Although Major Morton is well within earshot, Woodmere murmurs to Nellie, "May I call on you some time in Poole, Miss Arthur?"

He is stunned that she hardly looks at him while saying in a clear and distinct voice, "It would be useless, milord. I am sorry, but a total waste of time for both of us."

Hollowly, Woodmere laughs again. He sees the major gazing into the crystalline sky with a curiously preoccupied air.

2

SCOTLAND YARD

Is it that a comely woman knows how easy it is to win admiration for her outward form, and thus can never forget the man who saw through to her soul?

So Booth, in a philosophical mood these days, has begun to ponder.

One drizzling afternoon, while on business in London, he pays a visit to the police. He wishes more than ever to try to find out what has become of Raymond, and although he does not ask her, he sometimes believes that Nellie has that need too. Ushered into a musty side office with a single bleak window, he is told, "The sergeant will be with you in a moment, Major Morton."

Booth nods and sits down stiffly, by now used to his manners as a retired military officer. His new name, Morton, has been taken from a character in a novel written by his medical friend Weir Mitchell. Mitchell's Major Morton went to Europe after the war because he was disillusioned with American society.

The musty office is dark as a tomb. When the chalky-faced sergeant appears, Booth is precise. Might the Yard have a record of the so-called Soho Gang, he asks. (Or was it, alas, the hoax it seemed from the start?)

"Why, sir, they're all Soho gangs," the sergeant tells him in a perky voice. "If it comes to that, Soho's where the criminal class tends to be found."

Twisting his moustache, Booth asks if the sergeant can recall that any one of the Soho gangs—safecrackers, perhaps?—had gone on to America.

"Might have."

"Names like Palmer? Jenkins?"

"They don't ring a bell, sir."

"The Gent?"

"No, sir." The sergeant kneads his hands, as though washing them.

Booth oddly has the feeling that he has been appraised as one of the criminal class himself.

"Never mind, then. Thank you, sergeant," he says politely. He takes up his umbrella and goes back out into the rain.

On the walk to his brother-in-law John Clarke's club, where he is to meet that gentleman, he considers with regret that months and years have been lost in pursuing the inquiry about Raymond. Originally, Arthur's death was to have occurred about a month after the inauguration of Grover Cleveland. But Nell fell ill, and was slow recovering. Later there was difficulty obtaining a suitably Arthurian corpse.

A tedious time it was that final summer in New York when Booth had to put on the makeup every day and languish like Volpone in the master bedroom of the Lexington Avenue house, impatient for the day he could finally end the masquerade with its endless procession of bedside visitors. Then, with the date at last announced and the funeral arranged, Alan grew sulky (God knew why), and for a time threatened not to attend the final rites, unable, he said, to go through what he called a "mockery" a second time.

"The first time was no 'mockery,' " Booth undertook to remind him. "You were properly mourning the death of your father, even though the rest of the world mourned your mother's passing."

"And whom shall I suppose I'm mourning for this time?" Alan retorted. "We do not all have your talent for theater!"

It is in this fashion that the family has elected to bear itself toward him. Nell and her children refused, of course, to consider joining any circuses in Europe. Instead, it was decided to take a house on the Dorset coast, just across the river from where Booth's invalided sister Asia Clarke and her husband lived.

Not that the Arthurs show any regard for the Clarkes. Nell claims to be too hard of hearing to be able to pay social calls on Asia. In this and other ways Nell has been a disappointment to Booth. He believes sometimes that the only mission left is to locate the vanished Raymond, be it for Nellie or for his own troubled conscience.

With this in mind, as soon as he finds Clarke, he draws him aside into an alcove off the cluttered smoking room with an air of great confidentiality. The club is a bit seedy; it accepts actors, even music hall actors, if they are over sixty. Clarke is himself a producer of operettas, and is forever being buttonholed.

"We can talk in a corner of the butler's pantry if the matter is as private as all this," Clarke says to him uneasily. Booth has prodded Clarke toward the very edge of a cushioned seat while brandishing a thin, tabloid-sized journal, which he first came across in the club several weeks before.

"You are aware," he murmurs to Clarke, "that I have been searching for news of my aide, who vanished in Washington four years ago."

"And so?"

Without another word, Booth deposits the ill-printed publication into Clarke's lap. A privately-issued periodical, it contains erotic descriptions of bizarre sexual activity between members of opposite sexes, between members of the same sex, between people and domestic animals, and so forth. Much of it—including the "discipline"—appears to take place in upper-class sanctuaries of iniquity, for the participants are usually titled and the language elevated, if one could call any language "elevated" that deals with such foul subjects.

When Clarke looks up, with no particular expression on his face, Booth says, "There is a chance . . . a slight chance at best . . ." For some reason he cannot go on. What he wants to say is that Raymond, given his proclivities, might have been sold into service by the Soho Gang, and he could be somewhere in the purlieus of London ready to be rescued at that very moment.

"Only give me the address," Booth suddenly blurts, "of a single one of these fetid dens. And I will take it from there!"

Clarke says, "Dear man, there aren't any fetid dens. It's all in the fevered imagination of Oxford boys. Don't you know fiction when you see it?"

Booth gives Clarke a long, ambiguous glance and drops the subject at once.

Privately, he still believes in the existence of the dens. But what could one say? Clarke, who dressed like a riverboat gambler, would clearly never be invited to one.

The only other glimmer of hope for Raymond—and somehow even more like fiction than the other leads—has come in a letter Booth received from Chandler shortly after they arrived in England. An American naval captain reported seeing a youth who looked much like the President's aide while on government business in the port of Foochow, China. The captain had been riding in a rickshaw through the narrow streets of Foochow, heading back toward his ship in the harbor, when from the other direction came a large wagon containing a number of casks and barrels. On the bed of the wagon, in addition to several coolies, was a young man of less than medium height, who looked much like a Caucasian. Although his head was shaven, the youth on the wagon looked familiar to the captain. But it was not until the latter was back on the ship that he realized that the young man closely resembled one whom he had seen several times at the side of President Arthur.

Although Booth, on learning this, had at once cabled money to Chandler for the hiring of agents to go to Foochow—anyone but the Pinkertons!—not a word further has been received.

3

POOLE

One evening when Booth and Nell are playing cribbage before the fireplace in their modest two-story cottage, Nellie appears with the announcement that Charlie Pinkerton is to land in Southampton on Tuesday week, and she proposes that they meet the ship.

"Charlie Pinkerton?" Booth exclaims. "Young Charlie? Is his father accompanying him?"

"A male cousin, I think. On his mother's side."

"What can they want? I desire nothing to do with them." He catches Nell's eye as she is about to play a card. "Do you?"

But she does not answer him. She puts down the eight of spades and says "Fifteen two." Rarely does she reply to his questions anymore, and he cannot always attribute it to her deafness. She is alert in so many other ways. Her attention to a card game is unusual for a woman. But she does not often converse with him.

At times he wishes she realized that the most difficult thing he accomplished in his life was not to become President, or any of the other things he achieved, but to keep his romantic promise to her that he would take her away from the alien North and carry her to Europe, where they would be reborn in a society that would nurture her children as surely as it nurtured the two of them. As she looks up at him quizzically, waiting for him to play a card, he considers repeating his question. But he does not. Her hair is white; her face has gone plump and settled; sometimes she looks like a child in a painting, smug and devious at the same moment.

He, on the other hand, looks not much different from the way he looked in Paris when they pledged themselves. The recovery of himself took great effort. He had hoped, once he had reshaped his body, thrown away the lifts in his boots, and dispensed with all the cosmetics he had worn—first as President, then as the dying invalid for the benefit of the visitors in New York—that he and Nell would meet again on some natural plane of discourse. But it has not occurred.

Booth decides, prudently, to accompany Nellie and her mother to Southampton. Charlie Pinkerton's excuse for coming to England is

:that he intends to matriculate at St. Ambrose's College, Oxford, begin-
:ning in the Michaelmas term. That is the story.

While waiting for Charlie to clear customs, Booth notices that
Nellie's face seems to be growing more and more flushed. When
Charlie finally appears, Nellie has developed an unusual stammer.

"Charlie, this is my new guardian—uh, M-M-Major M-Morton."

Charlie extends his hand to Booth. He has become a strapping
young man, clear-eyed and healthy-looking with a flashing smile.
"Auntie Lew" returns the smile that Charlie offers her with surprising
warmth.

Later, in the carriage (a large one, which Booth has hired for the
day), Booth asks Charlie, "But what happened to your cousin, Mr.
Pinkerton? I heard you were traveling with your cousin."

Charlie smiles and says that he came ashore in the pilot boat last
night.

"Do I know your cousin?" Booth asks.

"Joe Leffingwell?"

They are always ready with names: the Soho Gang, Palmer, Jenkins, The Gent. "Does your cousin work in your father's agency too?"
Booth asks.

"He's in the brokerage business, sir."

"And knew someone in the pilot boat?"

"Oh, dear!" Nellie explodes with some dismay. Booth sees that
she does not like his questions. She is very flushed. He wonders if she
is attracted to Charlie Pinkerton.

Nell enters the conversation to remark that Charlie might enjoy
joining the hunt sometime. Has he thought about riding to the hounds?

"I don't know, ma'am," Charlie says. "I think grouse hunting
might be more in my line."

"Pheasant!" Nellie corrects him with spirit. "It's called pheasant
around here."

"Oh, is it?" Charlie returns, grinning.

Booth scowls. Letting his absent gaze rest on the gray, choppy
waters of the Channel—they are riding along the Channel road toward
Poole—he ponders the implications of what he sees. A sentimental
connection with Charlie would be debasing to Nellie. In her beauty and
innocence she is about to be seduced by the same secret police that
undermined the lad who worshipped her like a goddess. How can she
so soon forget the one who loved her soul?

＊

Much later, when they have reached their cottage, where Charlie has already been invited to stay as a house guest, Booth drops the three of them at the gate and continues on with the carriage and driver to the stables, planning to talk to one of the grooms about having his bay mare ready for an early morning visit he wishes to pay the following day to his sister Asia in Bournemouth.

However, when he learns from the driver that the groom is away, he gets out of the carriage when he is just round the corner of the house. With darkness falling and a faint odor of mustard in the air, he crosses along a wall to the rear entrance of the cottage. Just as he comes through the open gate, he hears the voices of Nellie and Charlie, who have lingered for a private conversation in a spot where they cannot see his approach. He stops.

"I cannot endure it when I have to lie to you!" Nellie exclaims in a hushed but anguished voice.

"Never mind it, Nellie," says Charlie.

Heaving a sigh, Nellie says, "Well, I never did mind . . . with anyone before this. But to you . . ."

Charlie says that if she should ever positively *need* to tell him the truth sometime to remember that he was brought up to have the highest respect for confidentiality.

"Oh, I have much to be grateful for here, Charlie," Nellie responds breathily. "I could never violate that trust. You must not ask too much of me . . . too soon."

Charlie replies that he certainly will not do so. "We'd better get inside now. Before he gets back."

"Nellie! Charlie!" Nell is calling from one of the windows.

"We're coming!" Charlie cries.

Until the door closes, Booth stands quietly, clenching and unclenching his fist. Then he swats once with his gold-knobbed cane at the hollyhocks growing along the wall. Now and then he wishes he still had the sword-cane of his youth so as to be able to cut a real swath. He wonders if he has any power at all anymore.

("Dearest Mamma," she writes, "I am as cared for and protected as a woman could possibly be.")

Her mother is in heaven, but Nell feels close to her. Not that she believes she is going to heaven soon herself. Walking about the garden under small, scudding clouds, she shapes messages to her mother, whom she feels closer to since her hearing has faded.

("Dear Mamma, Alan has been received by the Prince of Wales.")

It is interesting to be able to express her sentiments in such a way that her mother will be satisfied. Nell is pleased with her children, but the word "satisfied" is the right one to use to her mother, lest Nell seem vain about them.

("Dearest Mamma, Nellie has a beau, but it is kept a secret from my husband.")

Patiently she is tending to the primrose and the wallflowers in the dooryard when her husband returns from town.

And has Charlie Pinkerton left us? he asks. Where has he gone?

To Oxford, I presume, she replies.

Later her husband goes upstairs as though to check whether Charlie has really cleared out.

Nellie has fallen asleep in the window seat, he says when he comes back down. Nell looks at him with an air of incomprehension, and he shouts, "NELLIE HAS FALLEN ASLEEP IN THE WINDOW SEAT!"

("Dearest Mamma, When asked where the beau has gone, one simply says, 'To Oxford, I presume.' ")

Would you like to walk into town with me sometime before tea? her husband asks.

Have we not gone there twice this week already?

("Dear Mamma, My husband has business in town, which often keeps him occupied. . . . As for me . . .")

You show me very little feeling, Nell.

His words hardly penetrate to her. Their sound is heard as though through a featherbed.

("As for me, dear Mamma, I still practice my religion. . . . Sorry that Leander left you. Did he never return?")

In his walks around Poole, Booth keeps a sharp eye peeled for evidence that anyone is watching him. If he is on foot, he will come to a sudden halt just after he has gone around a corner and wait to see if he is being followed. It is Charlie's cousin Leffingwell whom he expects to be trailing him. Whenever he notices a strange young man in town, particularly if the young man looks American, he grows suspicious and sometimes makes inquiry of others to see if they are acquainted with the stranger.

Those whose surnames contain three or more syllables he has

developed a visceral antipathy toward: Pinkerton, Leffingwell, Coventry, Kappenhalter . . .

He began losing his power to these people about the time he became President. They lurked in the shadows. Instead of getting closer to the file while he was the President, he seemed to get farther away from it.

Puzzled at the way things have turned out, he finds himself going over almost every afternoon to see Asia, often doubling back on his trail to make sure he is not followed. Asia sometimes has news of the family, such as the death of their mother awhile back. His own failure to be dead has turned out less of a shock to Asia than it has been to others.

"We knew something was not right all along," Asia tells him one afternoon in her singsong voice that gives emphasis to every second word. Dressed in a purple poplin dress, she reclines on a couch in her sitting room with a coverlet draped over her large feet. "The letters that man wrote: we could tell. We could read between the lines." She has a mighty gesture with the right hand as though she is pointing a direction to someone who is lost. "We could tell by his tone that you had survived and escaped."

"Edwin? What was his tone?" he asks, aware that she has named a source of his powerlessness.

"Holier than thou!" Asia says, pointing again. "I never liked that man. Let the rest of the world love him, adore him. I never thought he had any fellow feeling." She remarks again on a letter that the Clarkes received from Edwin when he first learned his brother had taken residence in England. " 'You may shelter him if you like,' is what he wrote. 'But if Johnny ever sets foot on these shores of ours again, I will expose him at once.' That's what he said. I showed you the letter, didn't I?"

Booth nods. Sadly, he remembers Yellowstone, where Edwin took the side of a Lincoln against a Booth.

"You needn't doubt he means it," Asia says quickly. "That one has his tentacles out. He has always been like a sea beast—jealous, jealous."

Booth shifts his weight uneasily. Asia is of an age with Edwin, and so she should know what she is talking about.

"On his last tour over here," Asia continues, "do you think he paid any attention to us? I mean, are we mere provincials? His own brother-in-law is a producer, and helped make members of the touring -company comfortable when asked. But who is invited to the Duke of

Kent's with the great Edwin? Second- and third-rate actors and actresses, that is who! Even the *stage manager*! I do not lie."

Listening, Booth wonders if it is also possible that Edwin is the one who ordered done to Raymond whatever was done.

"I do not care myself about fetes at the Duke of Kent's," Asia declares. "Too ill to attend, am I not? But my husband—in the business of theater—shouldn't the advantage to him be seen of being invited to the duke's?"

"Along that line," Booth murmurs in a small voice, "Ted has never been fair to me."

"Of course he has not!" Asia cries, throwing up both hands this time for emphasis; perspiration beads her forehead. "He has presented you to the world as a madman! Does he ever speak of you as a patriot? Never. General Lee, and others who fought for the South, are by now accepted as national heroes, noble opponents. Why are you not noble?"

Booth cannot help but nod again. Abraham Lincoln would himself be ennobled by ennobling John Wilkes Booth. Would Hector of Troy have been remembered half so long if he had been struck down by some lunatic instead of the demigod Achilles, who was driven by a sense of honor comparable to Hector's own? The answer throbs in his soul.

"You must write a book about it," Asia tells him. "You must! Or the world will only have Edwin Booth's version of you!"

"I cannot," he says promptly. "Unless I procure the Fredericksburg File. It is the only proof of what I say."

"And is not your word as good as his?" Asia asks, heaving a deep breath.

Neither of them needs to answer that. Booth gives a shudder, and wishing his sister a swift adieu, promises to visit her very soon again.

Several days afterward, sitting up late after Nell has retired, he comes across an article in the *Fortnightly Review* concerning politics in America. Such articles are rare in British periodicals, and as he reads he is initially heartened by the fact that there is none of the usual reference to "corruption" in Washington. Instead, the author considers why the American system has "thrived" in spite of a paucity of "trained leaders."

But Booth's disappointment grows when the Presidents that came after Lincoln are referred to as "limited men," whom the author damns with faint praise. The Arthur administration is called "a triumph of mediocrity."

"Why not," Booth demands aloud, even though he is alone, "call it a frustration of genius!"

He tosses the review aside and prepares to write a letter to the editors, describing the achievements of the Arthur administration (before Sheridan!). He will represent himself as a student of American political history, who will enumerate the accomplishments. Thus, "(1) The reform of the Civil Service system," and "(2)"—after some thought—"the expansion of the Navy." For "(3)" he lists, "the revival of a two-party system in the South," conceding that the achievement might seem recherché in Britain. After pondering and staring into the fire, he adds "(4) The design of a Presidential flag" and "(5) The renovation of the Presidential Mansion." What else? Integrity of purpose?

Suddenly he leaps to his feet and throws down the pen. Angry at himself for contemplating writing about the Arthur administration when he has more eloquent things to utter—yea, write if it comes to that—he paces for ten minutes, then sends to have his horse saddled and rides it through the sleety rain directly to Asia's house.

When he arrives, a carriage is stopped there in the street.

At the door, the servant Osgood, a pimply oaf, says, "I am sorry, Major Morton, but the doctor is with Mrs. Clarke."

At this point the much-absent Clarke himself appears on the stairs. Just as Booth is about to call to him, he looks down at Booth and declares, "We can see no one tonight!"

With that, Clarke disappears, and Booth is left to find his way back to Poole through the Channel fog and rain. Clarke has always resented him for having himself been thrown into jail after the Lincoln assassination simply because he was the brother-in-law of the assassin.

Being without gloves, Booth grips the reins in his cold, wet hands and angrily spurs the horse back along the narrow road as though he were hoping the pace would throw the beast. A just way for Booth's life to end, some would hold, thinking it a proper fate for a reckless man. How few knew he was among the most prepared of individuals. Both in the theater and afterward. There was no costume he was not ready to fit himself into, no *tableau vivant,* however wearisome or unnatural, in which he was not ready to incorporate himself, once he had made up his mind.

Yet none saw him as a great planner and executor. Nay, only a sudden and violent end would suit him. "Killed by a maddened horse!" —it was the very demise that Dun and others had wished for him.

Let them be hanged! He steadies his boots in the stirrups, licks the rain off his lips. Perhaps, instead of writing letters to the *Fortnightly Review,* he will write something larger about his experiences. As Asia suggested, he will write his memoirs. Of course everyone will call it fiction, perhaps even call him a fiction. But even without the Fredericksburg File to document its truth, it can show the young how a great idealist may be a great organizer as well.

So resolved, over the next few weeks Booth occupies the daylight hours at his kneehole desk, penning what he can remember of his earliest days in Maryland. Smiling inwardly, he finds himself reliving his earliest performances. While yet a small child, for example, he undertook desperate measures to win the attention of his brothers and sisters. Once he rode Firebrand, the gambler's horse, so ferociously through the yard that two old hens were trampled under the hooves. But he achieved the notice of the others, even their tacit admiration; after all, they were actors, too, and had the same hungers as he.

What lesson can be drawn from this, he is just pondering when the postman rings. Nell, who is sitting across the room from him embroidering a sampler, has looked up; perhaps she heard it too. Since the servants are in the village and Nellie in London (supposedly with her McElroy cousins), Booth answers the ring himself.

He sees at once that the letter is from America, and addressed in Chandler's hand. Even before he opens it, he has the feeling that it will be exciting news.

Quickly his eyes jump past the first few words:

. . . gratifying report from San Francisco that Raymond has been rescued from China and has arrived in that Western city recently!

My informants say that Raymond's father, who I confess that I was unaware existed, himself discovered Raymond in Foochow and accomplished his escape. The father appears to be a seaman of some experience. From what we are able to adduce, Raymond was shanghaied aboard an American ship—we know not by whom—but somewhere off the Chinese coast the frigate he was on was boarded by Chinese pirates. One expects he may have undergone some unspeakable experiences afterwards. Certainly many of the Americans taken were tortured and killed. Somehow Raymond was able to persuade one of the brigands that he was ransomable. However, he fell into the hands of a Chinese merchant who postponed the ransom demands, possibly out of an unnatural attraction to the young man.

Some of this, my friend, may be inaccurate. But at least Raymond is alive. Do you want me to put him in touch with you or not? He and his father are expected to be returning to this part of the country eventually.

My personal regards to you, and to your family.

Faithfully,
Chandler

"Marvelous news!" Booth exclaims to Nell. "Raymond has been rescued from China. He has been found alive!"

But Nell's expression as she looks up from her sewing is frozen. Perhaps her eyes have narrowed slightly, and he is certain that she has heard him, for he has spoken very loudly. Does she still value the lad so little?

"Curse him!" Nell says suddenly, eyes staring straight ahead.

Booth is astonished that her dislike has not abated over the years. "Do you not remember how loyally he took you to St. Mary's—"

"Curse him, I say!" she repeats. "He is an angel of dahkness. Once banished, he shall remain banished!"

Although she has scarcely moved, her cheeks have colored and the expression in her eyes is fierce enough to penetrate him. He has the terrible feeling she is going to tell him things he does not want to hear.

"If I see him around us any moah," Nell declares, her voice rising, "if I see him around Nellie, this time *I* shall kill him!"

Booth stands over her. He means his tone to be firm. "This is nonsense!" he cries. "You have no reason to—"

But she pops up directly in front of him, her sewing still in her left hand. Her eyes appear glazed. Then, with her fist half closed, she swings her right arm up and forward as though casting grain. She strikes him full force across his left cheekbone.

"Alan banished your deah Raymond once! He can banish him again!"

In a daze, she sits down again, as though she hardly realizes she has hit him. Stunned, he shakes his head in disbelief. No, it was impossible. Not Alan. To have fashioned the separate encounters with Raymond, the letter from The Gent . . . it was beyond Alan.

"You are imagining things," he shouts at her. "Not Alan."

"I tell you what I know!"

"But he uttered nothing to you of this?"

"There ah things a brother does foah a sister that do not need to be uttered," she grandly affirms.

Booth presses his finger against the sting of his cheek. Of course she is out of her mind. The ravages of diphtheria would have contributed.

But he cannot think what to do. It is not "his dear Raymond" after all; it is Nellie's. He must confront Nellie as soon as she comes back from London.

Nellie, however, does not return from London. One morning in *The Times* he reads that Mrs. John E. McElroy of Albany, New York, has announced the betrothal of her niece, Ellen Herndon Arthur, Junior, to Mr. Charles Pinkerton of Washington.

Booth experiences a queer feeling of lassitude. So she is delivered at last to the whelp of the hireling cur. This, the flower of the South, promised to the son of a police agent.

And the girl's own mother has connived in the union. He knows, for she prowls about the cottage like a tigress. As though resuscitated by the word from London, she seems to hear less and less of what he says but rather throws herself into newfound tasks with restless energy. Twice she gives the servants two days off, and both times completes all their work by noon of the first day.

Booth longs for the period at the Soldiers' Home when Alan shared the responsibility for looking after Nell. With the hope in mind that Alan might be willing to resume the arrangement, he decides to write Alan at his *pied-à-terre* in London. While he is at it, why not invite the whole bunch—Nellie, Charlie, Alan, the McElroys—down for the weekend in Poole—as a way of indicating that he wishes the young couple well?

In the letter he will also mention that although Raymond has lately been found in China, it is now, of course, too late for him to be considered a suitor for Nellie's hand. No reference will be made to the circumstances of Raymond's abduction; why antagonize Alan with rash innuendo?

While Booth is walking about determining how each phrase may be struck off with a flexible firmness, it comes to him that the letter he really wants to write is to Raymond. Accordingly he makes his way to the pantry, where he knows the dairyman has left some milk for the cook's little boy. No one is around, so he pours and drinks three glasses of warm milk to compose himself for his task. Then he returns to his desk beside the fire and begins to write.

First, he says that he hopes and trusts that Raymond is strong enough to accept the fact that Nellie has been promised to another.

Five years and more is a long time to be away. . . . Booth forms the sentences quickly; the pen fairly flies over the page. Raymond must know how tirelessly his former mentor strove to preserve Nellie's hand as a proper reward for Raymond's courage and loyalty.

Dipping the pen in the inkwell, Booth is pleased to feel satisfaction at his own courage. With "President Arthur" decently interred, there would be no real need to resume contact with Raymond. But was loyalty to be repaid thus? Never. The young man would feel injured and bewildered at being abandoned by his promised bride. He would feel the added pain of the apparent loss of the man in whose service he had suffered the interruption of two periods of disagreeable incarceration (first in the Tombs in New York, then in Foochow, China) without ever knowing, for example, if the Fredericksburg File, for which he had given so much, had been secured or not.

"No, alas, the notorious file never came into my hands," Booth writes. He invites Raymond to guess at the terrible treacheries behind the letters from The Gent. A hoax they were: the perpetrators apparently had no intention of selling the precious file. They wished instead to strike fear into the President, to bully him into inertia by shanghaiing his favorite aide.

Although someone begins knocking at the back door of the cottage, Booth keeps on writing. Page after page is filled with his eager speculation about the political conspiracy that they all, Raymond included, have fallen afoul of. Did the Fredericksburg File still exist, he asks, the best hope for justice and purpose in the world? Or had honor disappeared forever?

The knocking finally stops. Perhaps the caller has gone away; Booth isn't interested. He feels instead as he writes that few will understand what he is talking about. Only Raymond and the boys of '65. And the boys of '65 are dead by the hangman's rope. Much moved by recollecting this, Booth writes that Raymond must reply to him directly. Initially he imagined that the letter, which he will ask Chandler to forward, would bear no return address. Now he finds himself imploring Raymond to answer. "I beg you to let me hear from you: Major Morton, Poole, Dorsetshire, England, Great Britain."

Booth advises that it is even possible that he and Raymond may meet again. Not on English soil, which is hostile to Raymond. But back in America, where some fine day the shadow of a rumor will perhaps arise that the Fredericksburg File has been seen, has been touched. And the quest will resume.

4

WASHINGTON

(from the *Washington Daily News*)

CONDITION OF MR. EDWIN BOOTH SOMEWHAT IMPROVED

NEW YORK—Mr. Edwin Booth has been resting more comfortably during the past week, his physician, Dr. Artemus Allen, reported in New York yesterday. Mr. Booth experienced a partially paralyzing stroke in April, and has been unable to leave his bed at The Players Club since that time. While he has not performed in the theater since his Hamlet two years ago, he attended the theater frequently until his stroke. His physician expects

Through an error in the printing the story breaks off at this point, and one looks in vain for a continuation. A certain middle-aged man, who has bought the issue of the *Daily News* containing this account from a street corner vendor at H and Capitol streets, starts up from his reading of it in the tree-flecked sunlight at the electric trolley stop. Onlookers, who take him to be a government clerk, note the distressful way he rolls up the paper, but then he takes his place with others at the curb, where the trolley can be seen to be approaching. When the trolley squeals to an eventual halt a minute later, its jostled windowpanes visibly shuddering, the man with the newspaper uses the stout cane he carries in his other hand to help him climb the step to the trolley platform.

Out of deference to the ladies, he removes his neatly blocked hat when he sits down inside. The weather is warm but not yet as humid as it will be in the city in another month or so. Breezes wafting through the open windows—here bringing the aroma of freshly baked bread —keep the short trip pleasurable. He is a clean-shaven man with a compact frame, although he is by no means slender. In deep meditation, he stares directly up the center aisle of the trolley car. Not the hum of voices, nor the rub of metal wheels on the rails, nor the high clatter of horses' hooves and carriage wheels in the cobblestone street distract him from his reverie.

For it is the illness of his older brother that has been described in the newspaper article. While he has read other accounts of Edwin's stroke, for some reason the incomplete account, which he has just read, has sent his mind racing to finish the story.

If not in today's story, then in tomorrow's, Edwin, in his bed, will raise himself up on one elbow, and, half-paralyzed, point his finger into the air and pronounce to the newspaper reporters gathered around him a final *j'accuse*. Can it be any other way?

"Gentlemen of the press," he will gasp, thin-voiced, but with the old sense of cadence, "the assassin of Abraham Lincoln still lives! No longer can I be my brother's keeper. God help me, but I believe him to be back in this country, and at large!"

What a Niagara of awe and amazement will proceed from that utterance! What actor was ever granted a finer deathbed scene?

In Washington on the trolley car, the fugitive can but strive to rely on his one God-given talent: staying in character. To escape Edwin's tentacles, as poor Asia called them, he has hidden himself, like the purloined letter in Poe's story, in "the most obvious place." If Poe is right, there is nothing to fear.

The trolley arrives at the Tenth Street stop. As Booth gets off, stepping down with his cane onto the curbing, he has a peculiar sense that life has come full circle. The trees are in spring bloom, the aroma of horse droppings is fresh and acrid, the people on their way to work are neatly and attractively dressed in spite of the depression in the economy. There is an air of *déjà vu*.

Having tossed his copy of the *Daily News* away in a trash receptacle, he takes a familiar route along Tenth past F. Some of the older buildings have been replaced or remodeled, and the street has been paved. Still, it is an old friend. He works in an annex of the War Department, one of the buildings that has been altered.

Once it was known as Ford's Theater.

He does not expect to see Raymond, or Raymond's father, until noon. Climbing up to the second floor of the converted theater, he goes to a job two stories higher than Raymond and his father go to theirs. Do fellow clerks think it odd that "Mr. Herbert Wood," a man of some culture, should spend his lunch hours so often with two of the manual laborers from the crew of the George Dent Company?

The company has been bringing electrical power to one after another of the government buildings in Washington, and even Ford's Theater must submit. Now, in its present function as the Tenth Street Annex, the theater appears on George Dent's list as a structure that needs its floors to be braced and reinforced before the wiring can be installed. But for Booth and Raymond and Raymond's father, Dent's project is not just a project, but is also a dimension of their strategy, for on the second floor of this building, locked away with other War Department records, rests the famous Fredericksburg File.

Or so Booth has been told. If the report is true, it takes one's breath away. At the moment, as Booth settles himself at his rolltop desk, where he will spend the day certifying drafts of payment for veterans of the Grand Army of the Republic, the file is said to be lodged no more than a few yards away from him in the large safe in Master Sergeant Allison's office.

"Good morning, Wood," the sergeant says, passing through.

"Good morning, Sergeant," Booth says. He has no unmonitored access to the safe as yet; indeed he does not know its combination, but that the file is there he has the word of Raymond and Raymond's father.

Their story is most curious. Feeling depressed in England after Asia's death, he had almost given up on ever hearing from Raymond when a strange letter at last arrived from Washington. Strange because the lad's letter made no mention of his beloved Nellie or her bridegroom. Nor did Raymond offer a single remark on the period of his long captivity in China. Instead, he spun an elaborate account of the surprising appearance of a metal box marked "Fredericksburg File" in the bed of a delivery wagon in which Raymond, his father, and some other workers were riding while transporting certain records of the War Department from the main building to the annex on Tenth Street, where veterans' pensions were computed.

Raymond's manner in the letter was most literate (perhaps he was trained by the Chinese as some kind of scribe). He inquired at the close if the "Fredericksburg File was still of interest to my correspondent." Then he assured Booth that he and his father were going to be working on the crew that would install the electric plant in the annex on Tenth Street. For "satisfactory remuneration," there might be a way for Raymond to get hold of the file "if the interest was there."

Of course the interest was there. But to quiet his initial suspicions of a trap, Booth tries to remain cautious. Coolly, he pens a letter: "If you in your work" should come across the material in question, "your correspondent might be interested in having a look at it." However, "I am changing my address shortly" and "I am not eager to retain my contacts with America." No need to take foolish risks.

But again, destiny intervenes. That afternoon, before mailing his letter, he comes across a headline in *The Times*: "Mr. Edwin Booth Dangerously Ill in New York." He finds himself shaken by the news. Could it be a further trick to make him believe that his brother's vigilance is broken at last? Surely *The Times* would not be a party to such a swindle.

Nay, his throbbing brain and his beating heart tell him that Edwin's illness is a fact. That it should happen just as he'd heard from Raymond is inevitably an omen: the tide of fortune has to be "taken at the flood, dear Brutus." He must himself book passage. If Raymond and his father take it upon themselves to act recklessly, the file could be lost forever.

Rather than sending the letter that he has written, he writes and sends a very different one.

That evening as Nell returns from Sunday vespers, he tells her of his decision.

"I'm leaving on a short trip," he says. "While I'm gone, you must stay with Nellie and Charlie in London. Or else summon Alan back from Scotland."

"Alan is with the Prince of Wales," she reminds him in reproach.

And bloody good company for him, too, Booth thinks. If anyone could find Alan's accent intelligible, it might be the royal family.

"I'll be in America awhile on business connected with the file," he informs her, resting his hand on the cold tiled stove that they installed in the cottage shortly after they moved in. "I'll be back soon."

She puts down her prayer book and walks apart with her back turned. "You'll nevah come back," she says. "I know you."

"You are my only love," Booth says, and because her back is turned, he repeats it in the voice he used to reach the back rows. "YOU ARE MY ONLY LOVE!"

She does not turn. Very well. She hardly cared for him much any longer anyway.

"I know you," she says once again in the toneless voice.

Later, on the morning before he leaves, he takes note that tears are standing in her eyes. But he does not see them shed. True to a vow taken long before in a carriage with its curtains drawn, she will not weep for him.

He lands in New York disguised as a commercial traveler, pomaded and with shaved sideburns. On the pier he half expects somebody's agents to lay hold of him, particularly since he has been compelled to travel with his Morton passport, trusting that the alterations in his appearance will go unnoticed.

However, no one bothers him. In rational moments he discounts the fear that Dun, or Lincoln, or any of the survivors of the assassination plot could have lured him back to America when they were so happy to see him leave. Nor is the new administration in Washington —Democrats again—apt to be sending Pinkertons for John Wilkes Booth when it has a Wall Street panic on its hands.

In optimism therefore, and faithful as ever to his character, he allows his leather-soled shoes to give echo in the colonnades of Grand Central Station when he reaches that edifice. In the first hour of dawn, there are few travelers in the great depot, and he swings his leather sample case jauntily at his side, studying the passing faces in the manner of a traveling salesman, all cheek and self-satisfaction.

A number of hours later, when he finally reaches the Baltimore station in Washington, where Raymond and his father are supposed to meet him, he feels unaccountably tired. He thinks he has not felt such weariness since '65, and this is surprising since the train connections he made in New York were excellent. The beautiful car he rode in was named "The Nellie Bly" after a New York newspaper reporter who has become world-famous, although a woman.

He puts a smile on his face; after all, a joyful reunion is about to take place. Scanning the faces of those around him, he anticipates that Raymond will be unable to recognize him as he looks now. It amuses him to plan to pass right in front of the lad, and when Raymond inevitably looks beyond him, he will clasp him in a fervent embrace.

But his eyes search in vain in the pools of dim electric illumination along the platform. At last, he signals for a porter to carry his luggage and follows the man to the interior of the station.

As he passes through the ladies' waiting room—very near to the spot where Garfield was shot down by Guiteau—he sees from a distance two short men gazing directly at him. The furtive way they stand against a black cast-iron paling and the uncomfortable way they wear their bulky working-class clothes make him think at first that they are Pinkertons. Each wears a narrow-striped railroadman's coat and a cap with a large bill, and each keeps his right hand in his right patch pocket.

Booth freezes. As they move directly toward him, he notices that they bear a close resemblance to each other; but it takes another few seconds before he is able to resist the impulse to flee. A painful flicker in the eye of the younger man stops him. It is Raymond, his skin chalky, his eyebrows somehow made lighter. The other man has sharper features, ruddy but with an aristocratic, epicene look. He is not what Booth would have expected; indeed, before Booth left England he had read *The Picture of Dorian Gray*, by Oscar Wilde, and this man could have sat for the illustrations of Dorian Gray.

But it is Raymond whom Booth goes to and clasps roughly in his arms. "My boy!" he exclaims, feeling much emotion. "My boy, you are home again!"

He is looking over the boy's shoulder at the father, whose eyes squint rivetingly at Booth. More upsetting is the sound that issues from Raymond's throat.

"Ah-ah-ah-ah-"

Booth glances with alarm, first at Raymond's anguished blue eyes, then at the other man, implacable, feet wide apart.

The man says, "Them heathens! They cut out his tongue, mister."

Shocked, Booth holds Raymond away from him. He groans.

"They did it sure enough," the man affirms. "Long afore I found him."

"Ah-ah-ah-ah," Raymond begins again.

"That ah-ah-ah does ye no good," Raymond's father directs, and Raymond closes his mouth. Booth, who has had a glimpse inside it, shudders and looks away.

Raymond's father, built low to the ground, has picked up the valise and sample case Booth has brought. "My mates call me Chief," the man says. "As designates my rank aboard ship—Chief."

"I see," Booth says, finding himself following the Chief and the luggage. He grasps Raymond by the arm.

"Ay, Chief. Chief only," says the Chief. The doors to the street stand open; Booth can see the horse cabs waiting.

But the way he has been snatched up by the man leaves him a little uneasy. Before they board the cab that has been summoned, Booth says, "My stick, please . . . Chief."

The Chief sets down the bags and hands Booth the article in question, glancing strangely at Raymond. The cabbie is already loading the bags. Raymond's face seems to pale for a moment as Booth cradles the gilded handle of the cane loosely in his hand, standing stiff, staring in the dim illumination at this poor shadow of a lad who was to have wed his Nellie, who was to have become his heir. So much for Horatio Alger, my dear Raymond! So much for the hope of the golden future!

*

The destination which the Chief has chosen is a tavern well out 15th Street in the workingman's neighborhood. The driver lets them out at the ladies' entrance. Inside, no one in the taproom is dressed anything like Booth, and the patrons give him a fair once-over.

The Chief stops for a bite of free lunch at the bar, then picks up the bags again and directs the party to a small table in a private alcove. Booth feels the weariness coming back.

"Lad," the Chief directs, "tell Murphy we are in private business 'ere and fetch each of us a pint." When Raymond seems to hesitate, the Chief says, "Need be, ye write it down for Murphy. Ye have a fine hand, no need to be ashamed on it."

Raymond moves off with a craven obedience that disturbs Booth. The Chief says, "Depend on it, sir, I have us meet not in the roomin' house where the pryin' landlady could say we was formin' a conspiracy —the three of us."

Sitting, the Chief assays a harsh laugh. Booth is uneasy again; it is as though the Chief means to allude to the conspirators who once met in Mrs. Surratt's boardinghouse nearby.

Booth says, "I am most distressed by what has happened to your son. It's unthinkable that human beings—"

"Ay, sir," the Chief promptly interrupts. "That's as may be. But the lad lacks a practical side, don't he?"

Booth frowns and starts to speak again.

The Chief says, with an expansive stretch of his arm, "Now who could get shanghaied to China cold sober? I vow, on the Maine Avenue dock after dark, and he don't even have hisself a weapon—"

"I daresay I was partly at fault, sir—"

"Not at all, sir," says the Chief. "If he be workin' for a man such as you with some authority—as you had at the time, sir, I understand —he must 'ave a practical side, look out for hisself a little. Now, did he not 'ave a like experience while workin' for you, sir, and how he wound up condemned to the Tombs for a time?"

Booth concedes the Chief's point.

The Chief goes on.

"The lad writes it down that he also did it for love of a girl. Your opinion, sir—is that practical, particular as she goes off and marries another, as I am given to unnerstand, while he is away? . . . What should he expect?"

Booth shrugs politely. The man retracts his thin lips from white, even teeth.

"On the ship they took him on," the Chief says, "they even showed 'im the money order they was paid for shanghaiing 'im." He puts his hands on the table. They are thin, with prominent veins. "I rescued him in China, you know. People on the shore think that we who sail the seas are all jolly tars. Not so. In return for the lad's tongue, I cut off one brigand's ear. I stabbed another in the gut."

"Good Lord," Booth gasps.

" 'Twas necessary. They made him their fancy man. He would go on in that way, waitin' for his friends in power to save him."

Raymond is on his way back to them, carrying three pints of beer. Booth says to the Chief, "Well, what good fortune that he survived and you found him."

"Ay," says the Chief. He now studies Raymond with great severity. Raymond sits down, expressionless. The blue eyes, under the bleached eyebrows, gaze at Booth. Raymond takes a sip of beer, leaving a smear of foam on his upper lip.

"Now," says the Chief to Booth, "to business. We propose that ye pay us one hundred dollars, U.S., each, advancin' it so as we help ye, sir, secure your file."

"All right," Booth says, "I'll pay you that advance tomorrow." He keeps to himself that he has that much and more in his valise lest the old pirate cut off his ear for it and stab him in the gut besides. With "Murphy" the pallbearer no doubt.

"In case of the success of our business," the Chief goes on, "practical experience tells me, sir, ye will be able to sell that file to your friends in power. How much ye earn I don't know. Bloody little difference it make to me, as my friend in Hong Kong used to say. Eh?" The Chief tries his harsh laugh again. He does not seem worried that any of his proposals are going to be turned down.

"I am not in it for the money," Booth says.

"Ye may not be," the Chief says, taking a short drink from the tankard before him. "But the lad and me is. The lad is concerned about practical motives now. He is. Eh, lad?"

Dutifully Raymond nods.

The Chief looks sour; perhaps Raymond has nodded too quickly. "Two hundred dollars more when we get ye the file. Each," he declares. "Cash on the barrelhead. Cash on the barrelhead tomorrow and cash on the barrelhead after ye get the file."

Booth says, "I agree to the terms. But before you try a direct assault on the government safe, I would like to try to get a position at the annex myself." He smiles. "You see, gentlemen, the nature of a conspiracy, if some will call it that, is that all must work together according to each man's talent."

Booth waits for the Chief's assent. A publicized theft of Stanton documents might yet draw unwanted attention, particularly if a safe has been forced in the bargain.

"We allow that!" the Chief declares heartily. "Now, would ye also like our assistance, sir, in securing you a room?"

This offer Booth declines and begins gathering up his possessions. "I am not unacquainted in Washington," he says. The Chief's personality does not inspire Booth's absolute confidence in any case. But before he departs, he asks the Chief where the annex in question is located.

"Formerly a theater," says the Chief.

"Ah-ah-ah-ah" Raymond begins suddenly, gazing at Booth with a look of pure effort.

"Formerly Ford's Theater," the Chief says with another harsh laugh. "A crime was committed there once. Do ye know?"

"I am not unacquainted in Washington," Booth repeats without raising an eyebrow. He shakes hands with the Chief, then with the lad. He wishes to hear no more vocalizing tonight from Raymond. He is bone-tired.

The room Booth takes is in one of the transient hotels where he lived briefly in the spring of '65. The practice here is that one must carry one's own bags up the stairs without assistance. As a young actor, however, he never took a room above the second floor. Now, although a former President, he must accept accommodations on the third. But some believe that the night air is less hazardous at that elevation.

That night he dreams he is making love with the redheaded Nellie Bly. But there is little time for it because her father, a seaman named Kappenhalter, is expected to return to the house at any moment. They are in the very act of coition when her father's footsteps are heard outside on the stairs. In panic he still determines to reach climax and does so even as the steps are outside the door. The father passes by, but as Booth looks down at the woman, she opens her mouth as if to scream. In horror he sees she has no tongue, and although no sound is issuing from her throat, he claps his hand roughly over her mouth so as not to have to see a mouth without a tongue. Her head is snapped back with such force that when he lifts her shoulders he sees her head is lolling backward like a doll's.

He wakes up in a perspiration, gets out of bed in his nightshirt, and pours himself a glass of tepid water from the china pitcher. Then he walks about for a while in his bare feet until he begins to feel cold. He wishes he still had the quilted robe he used to put on when he had bad dreams at night in the White House. And in Poole with his Nell.

Presently he crawls under the threadbare blanket and tries to fall back asleep.

The next afternoon Booth writes a letter from "Major Morton" to Senator Chandler, requesting a special character reference for himself under the name of Mr. Herbert S. Wood, the name he has chosen to register under at the transient hotel.

Later at the Senate building when he delivers the letter to a secretary, he is startled to run directly into Lucy Hale Chandler, who is ascending the steps as Booth is going down. Involuntarily, he lifts his hat, but does not speak; and she does not recognize him. He is dressed as a parsimonious clerk, his hair parted in the middle, his sideburns bare. She is dressed in brown wool and seems a great deal older than when she planned those lengthy banquets for him at the White House, to say nothing of the time when, incorrigibly romantic, she had stolen for him her father's credentials for the inauguration. How boldly a woman acts when she gives her heart!

A few days later, with his letter from Chandler, who is on the Military Affairs Committee, Booth is awarded an "automatic pass" on the Civil Service examination for bookkeepers, so that he can "get in the saddle" (the examiner says) as soon as possible. A pang of ironic regret touches him: the Civil Service Commission, fashioned with such heartfelt care during the Arthur administration, appears no less corruptible than the old spoils system, where you had to know Senator Conkling or one of his cronies in order to get a job. It is as though Garfield died in vain after all.

Booth means to make sure that at least Lincoln did not.

He studies bookkeeping. Once again, the discipline of his role requires that he be *au courant* with the technical terms of a profession. The Library of Congress supplies him with many volumes, and he is inclined to assume, with his gift for quick study, that he should soon be as adept a bookkeeper as he was a wine steward or a President. But it proves the most difficult of his parts.

Immediately, Master Sergeant Allison, of the snow-white hair, flings his work back into his face.

"Mr. Wood, you're failing to factor in the diminishing percentage quotient."

Booth partly comprehends that sliding scales of bonuses are to be paid from time to time to the ravishers of his beloved Confederacy. But he so persistently fails to compute the bonuses high enough that he is soon transferred to Death Benefits, where his main duty is to remit a flat sum to the survivors of deceased veterans. Here his conscience goes untroubled. Another Yankee bluecoat has expired, and he has no compunction about overpaying widow and children.

Sergeant Allison, with wattles under his ears like a turkey, seems leery of his new employee, no matter how ingratiating Mr. Wood tries to be.

"Go away now, Mr. Wood," he commands, while turning the dial on the second-floor safe. "Go away, I say!"

"Dear me, Sergeant," Booth says. "I do not mean to pry."

"Military secrets here, Mr. Wood," the sergeant says importantly. Whenever a field grade officer of the Grand Army of the Republic dies, the sergeant delivers the officer's dossier to the safe. Once the dirty secrets are sealed away, canonization can begin. The safe is an appropriate place for the Fredericksburg File.

"Are Secretary Stanton's records in the safe?" Booth risks asking.

"Who told you that? Go away, I say!"

Booth realizes he is becoming careless and impatient in his pursuit of the file, and he particularly resolves to be more cautious when one evening after coming home from work he notices that some of his papers have been moved. He begins to wish he had his old sword-cane with him. The harmless stick which he carries now—though Raymond and his father look at it with trepidation—offers cold comfort if the pair of them should turn on him.

More and more, he has been forced to speculate about the money order which Raymond is said to have seen aboard the ship. Since Alan for a time received an allowance in the form of "pay to bearer" money orders, Booth must wonder if his treacherous "son" gave one of these notes to the abductors with the deliberate purpose of implicating its signer, "Chester Arthur," in their scheme.

So transparent a ruse he cannot believe that even Alan would have attempted! Nor if he had, would Raymond feel such credulity as to be presently plotting Monte-Cristo revenge on his old mentor. Nay, Booth has had enough of being suspicious. To behave in such a fashion suggests the infirmity of a mind like Guiteau's. His own mind is ever young and faithful.

*

The Chief presses for action at the annex.

"Let us get to it, let us heave to, Mr. Wood!" he demands, chewing on bread and sausage during lunch hour. "The contract work is almost done. The foreman allows no more than another week."

Booth meets the Chief and Raymond behind the livery stable, the same one where he hired his mount the night of *Our American Cousin*.

"I am looking for a better method," Booth says.

The Chief scowls. The Chief's plan for getting to the file is to dynamite the safe open one evening and, as soon as they have what they want, to pull down the entire building behind them on the way out.

Booth dislikes the scheme. If, as the Chief says, the floors of the building are but precariously supported by special jacks while the electrical wiring is being installed, then why will not the initial explosion of the safe door likely bring the building down around their ears before they even have a chance at the file?

The planners hit upon a compromise. It is seen that by obstructing the installation of the electric plant as long as possible, they will extend the time Booth needs. Nor is a tactic to cause the obstruction difficult to come by.

Each night, and even late in the day when the foreman's back is turned, the new wires are secretly severed by Raymond and the Chief. But lest human sabotage be suspected, dead rats, which have been poisoned elsewhere by the conspirators, are brought in at night and left in the basement of the building.

The puzzled contractor must conclude that the strange breed of rat, peculiar to Ford's Theater, gnaws on electrical wiring and immediately perishes from the shock of it. Who knew but that the discovery might one day be turned to commercial advantage, and make Mr. Edison famous as an exterminator too? But in the meantime orders are given that baited traps be set in the annex for the purpose of catching the rats before they can gnaw on the wires.

This effort serves to facilitate the work of Raymond and the Chief, who are now able to bring in their dead rats in other traps, and to deploy them each night while removing the contractor's empty ones. In this way, the strain of Ford's Theater vermin is made to flourish in spite of the heavy toll taken by wire-poisoning and patented lethal devices.

The rats, however, are a tiresome business. Booth begins to shudder at the furry, bloody sight of them, clutched three and four at a time in the Chief's meaty paws. He prefers to pursue the acquaintance of some of his fellow clerks in order to learn if any of them has become privy to the combination of the safe in some bygone day.

With Melders, a senior clerk, Booth makes a little progress. Melders is a chip-on-the-shoulder Democrat, who has been in civil service since the first Cleveland administration. A tall man with a magisterial manner, Melders speaks in a reedy voice. "Take it for all in all," he says one day, "old Harrison was the only fair-minded Republican since Lincoln."

"But how about President Arthur?" Booth cannot resist asking. "He was the President who signed the Pendleton Act."

Melders looks to be in deep water over the Pendleton Act, but acknowledges that Arthur was not as bad as some. "Rather a fop though, wasn't he?" Melders asks.

"It was his style," Booth says.

"And if it was, I don't have to like it," Melders replies with heat, and turns away.

When in a more morbid mood, especially if it is a cloudy day and Sergeant Allison not around, Melders likes to talk in a low whisper about the ghost of John Wilkes Booth, which still haunts the premises.

"Booth never left Ford's Theater, not in his spirit," Melders whispers, his eyes wide as saucers. "On the nights in the springtime you can still hear his voice crying *'Sic semper tyrannis!'* downstairs back in the records section."

"Who says they hear it?" Booth asks, interested.

"Janney, the night watchman. Some nights it's the muffled report of the pistol shot first, then Booth's cry: *'Sic sem-per ty-ran-nis!'* " Melders draws out the words into a lingering moan. "Janney sometimes would hear the sound of a great thud. Booth landing on the stage, you know, after his jump from the box. He cries out again as he hits the boards, his spur having caught in the presidential flag—"

"I didn't know they had a night watchman here," Booth says.

"Not anymore," Melders says. "Janney passed beyond."

"Sic . . . semper . . . tyrannis," Booth echoes in a ghostly voice.

Melders gives a half-frightened laugh, then says, "These days it isn't Booth I worry about, Herbert, so much as it is the electric people. Ever since they been working down in the cellar, with their digging and their remodeling, the floor's been shaking—you know it has!—and with the shocks they could give us with their currents—"

"That's your century of progress for you," nods the older man.
"Give me Booth," says Melders.

In New York, the Great Actor's condition worsens again: all the newspapers carry the story. In Washington, the other Booth reads of his brother's illness in a conflict of anxiety and relief. If he does not wait until the last breath is drawn, he has the sure feeling that Edwin will yet rise up and strike him down: any explosion in the capital will bring a vindictive Edwin back to life. But if he bides his time, there will be a moment with no one to stop him.

"Never in the bargain, was it," the Chief says ominously one noon, "that we would spend a month trappin' rats for ye? What I would like to know, sir, is if ye have the two hundred dollars for each of us, ready cash, the night the deed is done."

"I am waiting for the right time," Booth says. "You've seen my money."

"A man what has two hundred dollars don't necessary have four hundred dollars on top of it," the Chief says with a snarl.

Using a pocketknife, Booth cuts from a roll of bologna that he has brought for his lunch.

"Huh-huh-huh," Raymond is laughing for some reason. He laughs while he eats.

Raymond's teeth are rotting, Booth sees. The tongue is bad enough without having to look at the terrible rotting teeth, as though Raymond were himself gnawing on the electric wires every night. His complexion seems grayer by day, his movements more ferretlike.

"Raymond," Booth suddenly cries. "Raymond, you believe, do you not, that I have the four hundred dollars for you when the work is finished?"

Booth thinks achingly of the bright-faced lad in crisp white, attending to the morgue with his copy of Horatio Alger near him on the freshly scrubbed slab. Beyond rescue now.

Raymond looks him squarely in the eye and goes, "Huh-huh-huh-huh—"

"It was not my doing, Raymond," Booth blurts, "to let her marry a Pinkerton."

The Chief gets to his feet, managing to stand between Raymond and Booth while pretending to be poking in his lunch bucket. He does not care for direct communication between Booth and the lad; he declares all that to be "water over the dam"; the four hundred dollars is "the practical matter."

"Ye blow open the safe," the Chief says, "and blow it soon."

"Ye'll blow it when I say," Booth snaps.

The next day, fortune turns.

"With your interest in the war, Joe," Booth says to Melders, the interest having earlier been established, "you must have lighted on some good things in that safe a time or two."

Sergeant Allison, whose desk is opposite the safe, has stepped out of the office for a few minutes, and Melders and Booth, like many of the other employees, are relaxing. Some of them take nips from bottles they have hidden among the shelves.

"Naw," Melders says. "The letters and such that politicians write, that's not my interest. Most o' that is just blabber anyway. I saw what went into that safe the first week it got here, or a lot of it. . . . I was in charge o' the safe at first."

In the next moment Booth learns that Melders knows the combination of the safe.

"Truly?" Booth exclaims, his heart thumping. He tries to look calm.

Melders spreads his fingers upside his mouth and says, "If you ever want to look at all them 'interesting documents,' the combination is the date o' Appomattox." He grins and winks. "Ninth day, fourth month. Six. Five."

"Astonishing," Booth says. He feels himself stroking his fingertips.

"Naw, only way the sergeant could remember it!" Melders laughs.

Booth does not confide in the Chief or in Raymond that he has learned the combination of the safe. He is waiting for news of his brother's death. Each morning and each evening he hurries to see the newspaper. Meanwhile, he contemplates how he will steal the file. The safest time to make the attempt would seem to be at night, except that on the second floor of the annex the light of a lantern will call attention to an intruder.

Whenever he does it, he will do it alone. Booth is feeling uneasy about the Chief. The Chief imagines the file to have an easily convertible market value. Booth cannot forget his talk of stabbing in the gut and slicing off the ear.

At last one morning, as Booth enters the dining room where the other boarders are eating breakfast, he notes a measure of animation in the conversation.

"—and what a cross he had to bear all those years, the poor and wretched man!" he hears Mrs. Sandifer, the landlady, exclaim.

Booth senses at once that the press has reported that Edwin Booth has breathed his last. He finds himself trembling in spite of himself.

"Oh, Mr. Wood," Mrs. Sandifer calls to him, "won't you sit down and join us? No one objects that you're late."

Booth murmurs an apology and hurries out, saying that he has urgent business. He reminds himself that what he truly feels is freedom at last from monstrous hypocrisy. Only Edwin Booth could come off a three-day drunk and still be ready to set his brother straight. Only Edwin Booth could be passionately involved with the most worthless of women, and still call his brother "unstable." Only Edwin Booth could count the receipts of an evening three times over, pinching each penny, and then call his brother the kind of actor interested only in the size of the audience.

A flood of tears comes to John Wilkes Booth's eyes. Well, he had seen the last of him, Edwin the Pious. Who would set the standards now?

It is already very warm. By the time that Booth, who walks all the way, reaches his place of employment, he has pulled himself together. Usually the contractor's men were milling about the sidewalks even before the War Department clerks arrived. Today, however, the street is strangely quiet. No raucous rat patrols thudding in and out of the basement; no covert smirking from Raymond and the Chief, who would have spent part of the night stocking the basement with the dead rats they are now helping to remove. None of that. Booth has a vagrant notion that in memory of Edwin Booth's death—confirmed in newspaper headlines—Ford's Theater has been shut for the day.

But Sergeant Allison soon appears with the more mundane cause. "Seems quiet, don't it, Mr. Wood?"

Allison explains that the electrical workers have been moved on to another job. Until the men in charge can find a way to get rid of the omnivorous rats in the cellar, the electrification of the annex has been indefinitely delayed.

"It's my opinion," Sergeant Allison adds, "that the years this building was used as a playhouse produced the rats we got." The sergeant believes that actors frequently ate in their dressing rooms and left rotting food behind that, when devoured by the rats, evolved a whole new species of vermin. "None of the other government offices has such rats."

Booth says, "You ought to go down to headquarters and tell them what you think." He is looking for a way to get rid of the sergeant for a time.

"Pah!" says the sergeant sourly. "We don't tell what we think in the cavalry, Wood."

All that morning Booth keeps a close watch on the sergeant. But, as usual, the sergeant is never far enough away from his desk for Booth to make any attempt on the safe. He knows, too, that the sergeant eats his lunch at the desk. By eleven o'clock the weather has grown so warm that everyone is working in his shirt-sleeves and Allison is waving a heavy cardboard fan in front of his face. Down in the streets, drayage carts roll by, some of them filled with fresh fish or crabs. The aroma of the sea rises to the second floor. Booth thinks longingly of a sea voyage back to England. His life, after all, is more comfortable there. One last effort in behalf of the old values, the true values, and he will go back forever to a well-earned retirement. Perhaps he will take his Nell to a good doctor in Harley Street to see if something can't be done to improve her hearing.

At noon Raymond and the Chief show up, carrying their lunch buckets. Booth is not surprised to see them. Under the boiling sun, the Chief's expression is fierce.

Before they eat, Booth puts on his hat and the three men walk a short way down Tenth Street from the annex. The Chief is vehement. "Tonight we should do it! Tonight we should blow the safe and make the haul!"

Booth says that it cannot be tonight; he watches the thin curl of the Chief's lip. "Meet me later," Booth says to them. "Near the fountain outside the Franklin School at seven. I promise you disposition of this affair."

Raymond and the Chief reach the assigned meeting place that evening about fifteen minutes early. It is still light. Booth, arriving on time, carries the hickory cane that has given them pause in the past, and with children playing in the park nearby, Booth feels secure. The place may even have a sentimental association for Raymond, who used to pick Nellie up there each day after school and drive her home.

Indeed, poor Raymond sits by himself on the stone bench under the Franklin statue with his hand on his stomach as though he had an ache there.

The Chief, attired in one of his long-sleeved, striped shirts, confronts Booth with his thumbs hooked in his trousers pockets. "Now, then—" he begins.

Immediately Booth hands the Chief a small packet, then walks over to Raymond and gives him one of the same kind. "I'm calling off the pursuit of the file," he says to them. "I believe it's hopeless, but in order to express my thanks, I'm paying you a large part of what we agreed on."

"Part?" the Chief mutters unpleasantly. He is already examining his packet.

"Almost all," Booth says. "Count it."

Raymond meanwhile keeps transferring his packet from one hand to the other, and without separating the bills, he seems to be forming a word: "Cuh-cuh—"

"Yes, count!" Booth says, remembering oddly that "Count" was the name Raymond was to call him by on the night he first brought Raymond up to his rooms; aspiration filled the lad's eyes on that occasion. Now there was nothing.

"My count, lad," the Chief declares, "Is one hundred eighty dollars. What's your count?"

"One hundred eighty dollars as well," Booth confirms. "That should be fair payment for your time and trouble. After all, none of the final risks that we anticipated have to be taken."

"You're yellow if ye call a halt to it now," the Chief sneers.

Booth tightens his fingers on his walking stick. "Maybe you'd like to know why I didn't give you each the full two hundred, why I—"

The Chief begins to laugh hoarsely, his eyes squinting. "Don't bother tellin' me, Mr. Herbert Wood."

Booth turns to Raymond then to bid him good-bye. But what use is it? A sly and pointless expression has descended over Raymond's features. Booth can hardly keep from shuddering. Perhaps that is why he has withheld from them the whole of the money that he promised. His nature is not parsimonious, but what other way does he have to show how deeply he resents the human wreckage before him? It is not a matter of a tongue. It is a matter of all the advantages the lad has had; even the bloodlines are good. Look at the father's thin lips, fine aristocratic nose. There are noblemen in their background, he feels sure. But they have become as coarse as the commonest moneygrubbers in the streets. No god have they but Mammon.

Their small grasping appetites could not be sated to the last dollar, even though it would have been easier for Booth that way. He cannot reward Raymond's father for the hideous example he has set.

Without saying another word, Booth turns on his heel and walks away.

When he is out of sight, the Chief smacks his lips. "Had a captain once, Raymond, who would have a man flogged at the mast one day, then pick a bone with 'im the next because the bloody shirt offended his decorum."

"Uh-uh-uh-uh—"

"No mercy, you say?" The Chief shrugs and looks thoughtful. "My life on it that he has the combination to that safe, and will try to open it tonight or tomorrow." The Chief tells Raymond they will spend the time between, preparing the basement of Ford's Theater. And not with rats.

"Revenge is always sweet!" the Chief declares.

The next morning Booth leaves his rooming house early, carrying a packed valise, having confided to Mrs. Sandifer that he is taking a better job in Richmond. In his salesman's sample case he has also packed his memoirs. He hopes that before the morning is over the case will hold the contents of the Fredericksburg File as well.

As he climbs into a carriage, hailed some distance away, he believes he catches sight of a figure, perhaps even two figures, lurking behind a fence at the corner of the street. Let them, he thinks. Let them chase him to the station for their last twenty dollars. All he is going to do right now is check his valise there and purchase his ticket to New York. A merry chase he will lead them if they wish it that way. Besides, he is carrying with him his walking stick. Magical, they think it. His special angels protect him.

After his business at the station is finished, Booth instructs the driver to go past the Capitol in order that he may find one of the uniformed messenger boys who work in the area. When he spots a likely lad, he first presents him with a handsome tip and then a sealed message that must be delivered to Master Sergeant Allison at the War Department Annex on Tenth Street at precisely nine A.M.

Does the young lad understand the urgency of the matter?

He does.

It is the same hour, although John Wilkes Booth does not know it, that the funeral for Edwin Booth is to begin at the Little Church Around the Corner in New York City.

*

"You are ill, Mr. Wood?" Sergeant Allison asks him. "You're not up to snuff?"

"On the contrary, Sergeant," Booth replies. "It is only that I have some work on my desk that I must complete before I can go downstairs and work with Melders on the '88 records."

The sergeant has assigned him for the day to a chore on the first floor, a location that will be inconvenient for his attempt on the safe. With forty-five minutes to go before nine o'clock, he must employ delaying tactics.

"Well, well," Sergeant Allison says. "My patience is not limitless."

You old nanny, Booth thinks. Quickly he turns back to his desk and begins to write furiously, feeling Allison's eyes on him. Because he has no work—he has done his last piece of work for the government of the Yankees—he pens another installment of his memoirs. Call it "diary" rather; he likes to write of events—this event!—at the very moment of experience.

The messenger boy appears well before nine. Booth keeps his head down so that the boy will not recognize him and give the show away in some manner.

Sergeant Allison's eyes pop open. Plainly he is taken aback by the official nature of the communication being handed to him.

"For me from the Secretary's office?" the sergeant asks.

It is even so. The letterhead is one that Booth has pilfered from the records section downstairs. Allison opens the missive with shaking fingers, and reads. "Sergeant Allison, You are requested to appear at 10 A.M. this date, Office of the Secretary, Department of War. Please be prompt." Booth has added the signature of the Secretary to the secretary.

The effect is all Booth could have hoped. For an instant he believes the sergeant will crawl under the desk, for he bends his forehead toward the surface of the walnut as though already practicing supplication. Immediately after that he throws up his hands, submitting his fate to the winds of power. Then he claps the arms of the chair with his two large hands as though he expects the winds will transport him to the War Department in that very chair if he holds on tight.

Booth has never seen such an expressive performance outside a theater. Eventually, however, the sergeant consults his pocket watch, and with a new flinging of his arms at the difficult task that he has ahead of him, he fairly leaps from the desk, scurries about for his uniform coat, and, tucking in his stomach, buttons his coat with much puffing. Then he is out of the office like a streak.

Some distance up the street, holding a horse they have hired at the stables, the Chief and Raymond watch the sergeant go rushing off in the opposite direction.

"You see, lad," the Chief says. "It's the sergeant. Our man's used his trickery to get the sergeant from the office. Now his highness'll sure go to the safe; that's why he took his bag to be checked at the railroad station. My life on it."

Raymond stares across the saddle of the large horse he is holding toward the building the sergeant has come out of. The foot traffic on Tenth Street is heavy, mostly men and boys. Further up, the children are playing tag, one or another of them running into the street now and then, barely avoiding the passing carriages and wagons.

On the second floor Booth waits tautly. Although Melders has been downstairs all morning working on the '88 records, two other clerks have stopped in the hallway to talk; talks when the sergeant is not around are always leisurely. But Booth reflects that he must be patient.

He feels suffused with energy, nevertheless. All the mistakes he has made, and yes, the mortal sins he has committed, may yet be redeemed by the success of this deed. Why it should be so is not at this moment clear in his head. But he knows there must always be a way to achieve one's redemption. By the Lord, he believes that there are judgment days when the sheep are separated from the goats, when all doubts are resolved. God resolves them.

Down in the street, the Chief gives Raymond fifteen cents.

"Remember," he tells the lad, "not till ye see the safe door is opened . . ."

Raymond takes the money and heads across Tenth Street to a residence directly opposite the annex. Next to the steps is a hand-printed sign, which reads: "See the Bedroom in Which Pres. Abraham Lincoln Died—15¢."

While Raymond disappears up the steps, the Chief leads the stable's black gelding around on the alley side of the annex where he hitches the beast; then, nodding to a familiar passerby, he descends to the cellar door and enters. He goes at once to a stout hempen line lying on the floor of the gloomy and deserted cellar; last night, after sunset, he and Raymond strung lines among the huge metal braces that were

installed to prop up the floors of the building while the electrical instal-
lations were in progress. The Chief and the lad weakened the bracing
as far as possible, then with various slip knots of the sort known to a
sailor, a web was woven connecting all the weak points under the
control of the single line which the Chief now passes through a grimy
cellar window, the sash of which he raises, and—since no one is about
—climbs out of. By degrees, but with businesslike briskness in case
anyone glances his way, he manages to cinch the end of the line to the
pommel of the saddle of the black gelding, who eyes the Chief idly.

To have to undertake all this in broad daylight is not what the
Chief planned. But the momentum of what was begun the night before
is irresistible. Had their fellow conspirator returned under cover of
darkness to open the safe, as the Chief expected, all the long frustration could have been relieved then. Judgment would have been more
precise.

But the Chief's experience of the world is that the innocent are
often punished along with the guilty, not that he believes any man is
truly innocent anyway. Judgment will have to occur in this rougher
fashion. Some would say he had a streak of cruelty in him. Well, well,
so God created him.

From his post at the entrance of the alley to the street, he can see
up to the window of the Lincoln bedroom where Raymond has already
arrived. At least he sees a shadow of Raymond, not much more than
that, in the glaring sunshine of the day.

Their horse is poised at a spot not far from where that other steed
leaped into full gallop, bearing its broken-legged rider, twenty-eight
years before.

Raymond is found to have a clear view of the activity across from
him on the second floor of the annex. When he sees the safe opened, he
will give the signal, the Chief will mount, strike the horse, and ride
down the alley away from notice.

The Chief squints and waits.

Booth, meanwhile, stands before the safe. He has turned the dial
left to nine, right to four, left to six, and right to five. Not the date of
the end of the war, Booth vows! The war has never ended.

The metal handle yields with a click. He pulls open the heavy
door and is faced with a network of compartments and cubbyholes.
Every niche seems to be crammed with papers and folders. The Great
War is here, not mere ink and paper to Booth, but the manifold pas-
sions of the conflict that the authorities have locked from sight.

Out! Out into the light! He sees a bundle of papers marked "Edwin Stanton—Private" and he has no doubt. The bundle is bound with twine. Booth reaches for the bundle and finds himself tearing at the twine. One strand is weak with age and pops open, rolling the bundle of documents onto the floor in front of the safe. In the heart of the great bundle is a cold metal box. Would it be marked "The Fredericksburg File"?

Hungrily Booth reaches.

A creaking sound makes him look upward. A feathery trickle of dust showers on his forehead and shoulders. In another second he senses an unsteadiness in the very ground on which he is standing. Some alarmed shouts are raised across the room, and as if in a dream an entire wall starts buckling away from the window frames it contains. Three men near those windows have flung themselves from their desks and started running for the stairway.

Now a great ripping sound—nails torn out of wood—cracks from the ceiling above. Immediately a large fissure forms in the ceiling. Booth has not moved. He feels riveted to the spot. He believes that perhaps it is safest where he is standing. The only other person who seems not to have moved is a tall, pale man with a dark beard, his shoulders flat against the wall behind him. He wears old-fashioned clothes, including a shawl, and stares directly at Booth. While he looks familiar, Booth cannot recall him as one of the clerks.

But now the floor beneath Booth begins giving way even as the ceiling starts to fall. The floor splits and begins sinking on a fissure line along the middle of the building, and as it does, the safe starts to spill all its records and documents out of the cubbyholes directly onto him. Then the safe itself starts to roll, and for the first time he realizes he is in mortal danger. With incredible swiftness the whole building seems to be collapsing in upon itself.

Booth clutches the prize he has sought—the metal box—and as the safe rolls deliberately toward him, he sees the growing fissure beneath his feet. The crack is so wide that for a split second he can see the ground floor, the desks there, some men looking up in alarm. Then the dust obscures the gap. The noise is thunderous.

I will jump, Booth thinks. I will jump from here. I will jump out of danger. There, I have always been able to jump.

And as he does, as he jumps or falls, his leg is given a sharp, final blow by the rolling safe. His heel catches in the disintegrating floor, and there are no final cries, no Latin, no last defiances. And once again the leap itself has missed being that ideal expression of a man not bound by earth.

Others scream. And he falls among them in the plaster and planks and rotting debris.

A block away, Sergeant Allison, who has been looking for a cab, hears the terrible noise and comes running back down Tenth Street. All the carts and drays in the street are suddenly headed in the same direction, and people in the street run with their mouths open. Women hold their skirts and run.

The sergeant can hardly believe his eyes—the entire building has collapsed. Through a miracle he has escaped death by minutes. The sight is appalling. Men crying in pain. A few are lying in the street, and one—could it be Perkins?—is walking around in a daze, plastered white with dust and holding his mangled left arm in his right hand.

"All right now! All right!" the sergeant cries. He has not heard such piteous moans since Gettysburg. "Bind up the wounds!" calls out the sergeant. "Don't let a man of them bleed to death!" He flings off his coat. Other men have already flung off theirs, and some have begun moving gingerly into the ruins. The center part of the building, in a cloud, has plunged right on through to the basement.

"The firemen are coming!" someone shouts. The sound of the fire truck is audible from a great way off, the sounding whistles and the relentless thunder of the horses' hooves.

Two of the men walking in the ruins the sergeant recognizes as members of the contractor's crew. Allison calls to them to ask if any of the contractor's crew has been trapped in the basement. But the two men work so fiercely throwing up planks and turning over furniture—searching out buried victims, no doubt—that they do not have time for an answer.

Sergeant Allison sees them ignore one groaning victim whom they are near. Perhaps they are looking for their friend, Herbert Wood, whom Allison has seen them with on lunch hours. The spot where Wood was working, Allison is shocked to see, must have gotten some of the worst of it. But Good Lord, the men on the first floor, they must have been buried at the bottom of the whole thing.

"Over here! Over here!" someone calls. "Help dig this man out! This man is alive!"

The sergeant hurries swiftly to the spot where people have partly uncovered a man who is moaning in terrible anguish.

"With a will, boys! With a will!" the sergeant cries, wrenching board after board away. The victim is a clerk who worked on the third floor, the sergeant soon sees.

By and by, in the horror of all that is to follow at Ford's Theater on that day, the sergeant forgets that he has noticed Wood's two friends behaving, he might almost have been able to admit, as though they were looting the ruins. He even forgets for a time about the order he received to appear at the War Department that fateful morning, and when he remembers it days later and inquires, nobody at headquarters can any longer remember what they wanted him for that day.

The other matter that surprises the sergeant in passing is a newspaper story printed late in the week, which says that the name of "H. S. Wood," who was originally listed among the twenty-two dead, did not belong there. An "unidentified source" has reported that no such man ever worked in the building. This astonishes Allison, since he has himself seen Wood's broken body; the man was quite dead. And furthermore someone claimed the remains rather soon after the accident.

Well, never trust the printed word, Allison says to himself.

Note: The Fredericksburg File is at present in the hands of a private collector, who also owns the holograph memoirs of J. W. Booth, covering the years 1865–1893.

Virtually all newspapers published on June 10, 1893, carried accounts of the disaster at Ford's Theater and of Edwin Booth's funeral. *The New York Times* displayed the former story on page one, the latter on page 12—without noting any connection.